SPITFIRE

"By the way," Jessie said, "how long are we staying with this wagon train? I have a homestead, and—"

"I know what a mess you're in because of me. But I'll get you out of everything—including this marriage—and safely back home as soon as I can."

"And, Josiah, how will you do that?" Jessie shot back.

"I planned on leaving you at Camp Nichols—"

"I know and that was fine but that was before I was corralled into this marriage. Do you think that you're just going to dump me off with no explanation about why I'm married to an outlaw?" Anger punctuated her every word. "Well, answer me! And you'd better, because the minute I tell my story, you'll be thrown in jail!"

"You'd like that, wouldn't you?" Josiah said. "I ought to shake the salt out of you, girl."

"Go ahead! Why don't you? Are you a coward, too, as well as a liar and murderer?"

Everything was deadly quiet as he grabbed her, then let her go. She fell in a heap on the bed and burst into tears. "Leave me alone! That's what you were going to do anyway. So just leave now! I hate you!"

CHERYL ANNE PORTER

LEISURE BOOKS NEW YORK CITY

*To Paul,
then, now, and forever love.*

A LEISURE BOOK®

December 1993

Published by

Dorchester Publishing Co., Inc.
276 Fifth Avenue
New York, NY 10001

Printed in the United States of America.

Chapter One

The thickening dusk hurried Jessie's feet as she approached the root cellar behind her cabin, her arms full of the late summer harvest from the garden. Only a matter of several steps, the distance seemed forbidding to her, a stark reminder of her aloneness. The rolling prairie around her stretched to the far hills. Giving in to the unsettling feeling that she was being watched, she glanced over her shoulder one last time before she put down her load. She needed both hands free to manage the heavy latch.

Jessie's breath caught in her chest when she realized the door was already unlatched. Thinking for a moment, she decided she was more tired than she thought. Of course she had to have opened the latch sometime earlier. After all, she was the only person on the homestead. Jessie told herself she was just being silly as she pushed the door inward. Still, she could not explain the feeling of foreboding which was raising the hairs on the back of her neck. Calling herself a fraidy-cat, she picked up her load and entered the cellar.

Just two steps inside the cool, dank darkness of the earthen cavern, Jessie's load was ripped from her arms when two hands shot out, one grabbing her by her shirtfront and the other covering her mouth. Hauled up tightly against a sweating, lean frame, her feet almost off the ground, she could only push feebly against her captor. Somehow, her terror-filled mind registered a moan escaping the mouth so close to hers; she also became aware of something warm and sticky flowing through her fingers. Breathing raggedly through the small airway left to her between the strong fingers over her mouth and nose, Jessie fought off the dizzying waves of unconsciousness which threatened to engulf her.

"Goddammit, kid, hold still. I'm not going to hurt you."

These words, forcible but barely above a whisper, instantly stilled Jessie. The hair on her neck rose again, whether from fear or his warm breath against the side of her face, Jessie could not have said. She heard the weariness and the pain in his voice, but her first thought was for herself. She had to get away.

Despite his promise not to hurt her, he showed no sign of loosening his grip. As Jessie tried frantically to swallow the panic in her throat, she suddenly felt herself sliding with the man down the earthen wall of the cellar. Oh, dear God, no, her mind screamed, not this! She was now pinned on the hard-earth floor with the man half on top of her. Sure he meant her harm, she struggled in earnest, determined she would not be taken like this. To her surprise, her struggling efforts easily dislodged the unresisting male body from on top of her. Not taking time to wonder why he didn't grab her again, Jessie jumped up and ran out of the cellar; never before had she locked the crude cellar door so quickly.

Using the locked door for support, she bent forward, rested her hands on her knees, and took in great gulps of the fresh evening air. Her heart, already threatening to jump out of her chest, gave another lurch when she opened her eyes to see blood all over her hand and arm.

"Evening, son. Trouble?"

Jessie jerked her head up to find herself facing several horsemen, who half ringed her in the near darkness. They numbered about eight or nine, she guessed. They were heavily armed and covered with the dust and grime of a long ride. She had a sudden, unsettling feeling that she'd seen these men before. And that she hadn't liked them then, either. Somehow, she knew she'd be safer in the cellar right now.

Seeing the way they were all speculatively gazing at her, Jessie was silently grateful she had on her father's shirt, pants, and hat, all too big for her, but all covering her female form and her long, dark hair. No wonder they mistook her for a boy. Intending that they would not find out otherwise, Jessie pulled her father's old, wide-brimmed hat down even lower over her face and cinched it tighter under her throat. She was amazed it had not come off in her struggle in the cellar.

"Who are you? What do you want?" she asked, standing up straight now and deepening her voice, willing the quaver out of it.

Cheryl Anne Porter

The men shifted in their saddles; Jessie's eyes traveled from one to the other of them as they exchanged glances she could not interpret. Finally, the one who had spoken earlier leaned over his pommel, his rifle resting loosely in his hand, and said, "This here's a posse, young'un. Your pa about?"

"That's my father over there," Jessie answered, pointing to the fresh grave off to the side of the cabin. "Next to my mother." A more worn grave rested beside the fresh one. As the men all turned their heads in the direction she pointed, Jessie quickly blinked back the hot tears in her eyes. She didn't want to appear weak to these men.

With their attention momentarily diverted, Jessie whipped her bandanna out of her shirt pocket and quickly wiped off the blood from her hand and arm. As she stuffed it back in her pocket, she was struck by what was bothering her about these men. They couldn't be lawmen at all. The only law out here on the Cimarron Cutoff was the soldiers at Camp Nichols who protected the wagon trains on the Santa Fe Trail. So who were they really? And why did they seem familiar?

As the men refocused their gazes on Jessie, her mind was racing with thoughts of who the man in her cellar could be—one of this band of men? Had they shot him? Why had they shot him? Should she turn him over to them or not?

"We're right sorry for your troubles, son. But I'm afraid we got to add to them. We got a wounded outlaw out here close by that we need to catch and take back to justice." His words were punctuated by snickers and snorts from the other men, quickly quelled by a sharp look from him.

10

A sharp thrill of danger raced through Jessie. In an instant she knew these men would kill the bleeding man in her cellar if she turned him over to them. They were lying to her and looked like a pack of wild dogs. Without even thinking why, Jessie decided to cast her lot with the wounded man. He'd said he wouldn't hurt her. Somehow, she knew she could believe him—just as she knew she could not believe these men in front of her.

Her mind made up, she determined to get rid of them—and fast—so she could see to the bleeding stranger in her root cellar.

"I haven't seen anybody about here but you," Jessie lied, trying to keep her voice low and steady. Sweat ran down her back and between her breasts as she watched them exchange glances all around again. Her palms itched as she tightened her hands into fists at her sides. She chanced a glance down at her hands; to her relief, most of the blood was gone from her hand and arm, and what remained was dry and brown. It could be mistaken for dirt or mud.

"Is that so?" the same man countered, pushing his hat back and raising one eyebrow. He didn't believe her, Jessie knew it and stiffened, fully expecting them to pounce on her, kill her, and then the man in the cellar. To her surprise, they didn't, but the leader's next words turned her surprise to a lurching feeling in her stomach. "Mind if we camp over by your barn for the night? It's too dark to push on now."

"What about your outlaw? Aren't you afraid he'll get away?" Jessie could hear the fear and desperation in her voice, so she knew they could, too.

"He ain't goin' nowhere. This here's his horse, and there's blood on the saddle. That's why I think

11

we better stay close by tonight—fer yer pertection, ya see."

Jessie hadn't noticed the riderless horse before, but it now had her full attention. The big roan's reins were tethered to the pommel of the man who was talking to her. Just then, the horse's ears pricked forward, his nostrils flared, and he gave a soft nicker. She was sure he smelled his master. She had to act quickly before the roan gave the wounded man away.

Not able to come up with a decent reason why they couldn't camp on her land, Jessie told them to go on over there and set up camp. At least they'd be a ways removed from the cellar.

As the men slowly rode the distance over to the barn, leaving Jessie standing there alone, she heard stirring noises and moans from behind her in the cellar. She was at once faint with relief that his sounds could not be heard by the men, but also tense with dread about how she was going to see to his wound, or wounds, without being discovered. She did not know why they hadn't simply killed her, looted the place, and searched out their prey, but she did know she wasn't about to provoke them into it.

Knowing she could not remain standing in front of the cellar or go inside it without attracting the curiosity of the riders, she forced herself to ignore the low moans behind her and to walk the few steps to the small split-wood cabin she called home. Once inside, she lit the stub of a tallow candle for some light. Next, she pulled the rough calico curtain across the small window opening which faced the barn. She needed light and privacy to gather all the things she needed to take out to the cellar just as soon as the

12

men by the barn were settled in. Every few minutes or so, she pulled a corner of the curtain aside to see if the men were sleeping.

The light from their campfire showed her that they were still awake and moving about, some eating, some smoking, and some seeing to their horses. Inside her cabin, Jessie felt just as much a prisoner as the man in her root cellar was. She slid down the wood and clay wall under the window to sit on the hard, bare floor and wait for the men to go to sleep. Her meager supplies rested beside her on the floor; she looked at them again to be sure she had everything—clean cloth strips for bandages, a small basin of water, and some salve her mother had used on all cuts and scrapes.

Jessie felt the tears come to her eyes again as she thought of her parents. She missed them so. They'd been so hopeful when they'd left Missouri five years ago in 1860 to join the wagon trains which regularly left Independence, Missouri and traveled the Santa Fe Trail to sell goods to the citizens of New Mexico, a new United States territory since the Mexican War ended in 1848. Her father had sold their dry goods store, bought a huge wagon to load the goods into, and a sturdy team of twelve oxen to pull it; meanwhile, her mother had closed up the house, packed what they could realistically bring along, and off they went with their only child, thirteen-year-old Jessie.

In less than a week they had given up their life in cash-poor Missouri to start over in a "new world," as her father called it. Those new citizens had wealth, but no supplies, while he had supplies and no wealth, he'd said. The decision seemed very reasonable when put that way. But nothing could have prepared them for the hardships they endured on the trail. Once out of Missouri, the wagon trains were on their own, for Missouri marked the boundary then of the United States. No law from there on out except for the soldiers in the scattered Army forts which had sprung up after the Mexican War to protect these huge trains, numbering sometimes as many as two hundred and fifty wagons.

Jessie felt as if every mile of that trail from Independence to where she lived now on the Cimarron Cutoff near Camp Nichols was etched into her memory. There'd been prairie fires, disease, Indians, tornadoes, and long stretches with no water and no trees—just prairie, out of which could suddenly come the thundering herds of buffalo stampeding through the train. She could still see in her mind all the graves along the trail they'd had to stop to dig. Her parents had counted themselves lucky that they'd survived all that intact.

Jessie interrupted her memories for a moment to peek out the curtain. After quickly swiping at the tears in her eyes so she could see better, she saw the men still moving around. With a sudden scared thought, she crept over to the back door to see if any of the men were nosing about the root cellar. To her relief, they were not. Jessie eased back to her spot under the window. To her mind, if the men did not see a lot of movement from inside her cabin, they might settle in more quickly for the night; also, she did not want to draw any undue attention her way from those scruffy men. She still had on her father's clothes and hat, which she intended to wear until they left; she knew enough to know that a lone woman out here was easy prey to all manner of men. Her father had taught her about those things and had also warned her to be cautious.

Thinking again of her father, Jessie saw him in her mind's eye standing practically on this very spot when it had still been part of the prairie, but a part with a large stand of trees surrounding a natural spring set in rolling hills behind it. His businessman's eye knew this was where the money was. Weary travelers, tired of their scurvy-prone diet and the daily grind of the trail, would welcome the fresh vegetables, meats, and dairy products a place like this could grow. So here they'd stayed and prospered.

Within a few years, the Stuart Homestead, as it was known, became a regular stop for most trains risking the Cimarron Cutoff, a shortcut which took ten days off the long trip to Santa Fe. Even the sutler from Camp Nichols made regular trips here to buy produce for the soldiers. The sight of the Army supply wagon with its protective column of soldiers approaching their property was always a welcome sight to Jessie and her parents. Other than the wagon trains, the soldiers were the only other people they saw. With a pang, Jessie realized the Camp's supply wagon had been here only last week. She could look for no help from there.

Jessie silently prayed that a huge wagon train would show up. In all the confusion they caused, she just might be able to sneak herself and the wounded man in her root cellar out. More times than she could count someone on one of the countless trains coming back from Santa Fe said this was an ideal spot to locate and, rich with money from selling all their goods, had offered to buy the place from her father. She just might be able to quickly sell it to someone like that and make a clean escape. If nothing else, the arrival of a huge train of people, mostly teamsters who knew her and her family, just might serve to scare off those dangerous-looking men outside.

With a sigh, Jessie realized there was as much hope of that happening as there was of the Army riding in. No, she would have to rely on her own wits to solve this mess, just as she'd been doing since her father died two months ago of a rattlesnake bite. Dysentery had taken her mother three years ago. As much as Jessie loved this place, she knew she could never keep it up by herself. She hated the thought, but she knew she'd have to leave the homestead sooner or later. Well, maybe it was for the best, she reasoned with her protesting self. After all, she was a woman now, a woman who needed—what? Jessie had no idea exactly what, but she knew it was something. All her restlessness lately, despite the backbreaking work, had to mean something.

Jessie did not know how long the feeble knocking on her back door had been going on before she heard it, so absorbed was she in her thoughts. But now every part of her was attuned to the sound at the door. Her first terror-filled thought was of the men out by the barn. She quickly looked around the room for something she could use to defend herself; finally she decided on a large knife and held it at her side in her left hand, partially concealed by the loose folds of her father's pants. No one would think to look in her left hand, she reasoned, since almost everyone was right-handed. Jessie had never killed a man before, and hoped she did not have to now. Besides, she couldn't kill all of them once they discovered one of their own dead. She prayed it would not come to that.

Just before she opened the back door, she remembered the bandages and things on the floor under the window just behind her and to her left. With a swipe of her foot, she pushed them under the china cabinet her mother had insisted on bringing in the wagon. With trembling fingers, Jessie unlatched the door and opened it just a crack to see who was outside. Intending to discourage whoever was there, she was not prepared for the sudden crashing inward of the door which sent her tumbling headlong back into the room. She fell over the table and chairs in the middle of the room and landed in a heap by the fireplace.

Until her breath came back, all she could do was lie there gasping and groaning. She could see that the door was wide open, but her stunned mind could not figure out why there was no one standing in the doorway or in the room. Jessie appeared to be the only one in the cabin. Crazily, she thought of a tornado, but that could not be; there was no wind blowing.

And where was her knife? Surely she would need it now. Despite the blinding pain which stabbed behind her eyes when she turned her head, she did her best to look around her. No knife. She'd have to move if she wanted to find her weapon. Jessie felt like crying and giving in, but she knew she would not do that. Her Stuart blood was too strong and too stubborn. Besides, she needed to be strong for the wounded man; she had more than herself to worry about now. She was not alone in this. He needed her.

Very carefully she began to move her limbs to see if anything was broken. Nothing seemed to be. Gingerly she sat up, feeling all her sore spots, and forced her eyes to focus in the darkness of the cabin interior, lit dimly by moonlight shining through the open door. The tallow candle had gone out when she rolled over it on the table.

Jessie still had to solve the mystery of what—or who—had blown the door open. Gathering her courage and her bruised body, she crawled very slowly around overturned chairs, stopping when dizziness overtook her. Hitting her head on the hardwood wall had certainly not done her any good. Resuming her crawling search, she stopped cold when her hand came into contact with another hand—a large, rough hand. Jessie pulled back as quickly as her injuries would allow and stifled a scream in the back of her throat.

Sitting back on her haunches, she kept her hands over her mouth until the urge to scream passed. Only when she realized that the hand and its owner had not moved at her touch did her breathing begin to return to normal. Looking more closely at who was lying facedown in front of her, only half in the cabin, Jessie began to perceive that this was the man she'd locked in her root cellar—the wounded man; it had to be—no one in the so-called posse had been hurt. But how did he get out? She distinctly remembered bolting the door closed when she'd run out earlier. There was no way to unlock that door from the inside.

Deciding the answer to this question would have to wait, since the man was unconscious, Jessie turned him over as gently as she could, thinking of his wound. Then she set about pulling him the rest of the way into the cabin. She did this with a great struggling and grunting effort, for the man was easily twice her size, and she was all bruised from when he'd obviously fallen against the door when she opened it. Finally, she had all of him in her cabin; she quickly closed and latched the door again. He still had not moved on his own. Jessie sat with her back against the cabin door, arms and head resting on her bent knees; she had to recoup her strength before she began the task of getting him up onto a bed.

When Jessie raised her head again, she took in the whole man—or as much as she possibly could in the near darkness of the cabin. He was tall, muscular-looking, dark, covered in the same dust and grime as the men outside, and just as heavily armed. A large gun rested in its holster on a gunbelt which rode low on his right hip. The fact that he wore a gun did not bother Jessie—almost every man, including her father, wore a gun. But what did bother her was the way he wore it—not like most of the men she'd seen on the trail or even the soldiers at Camp Nichols. Theirs were worn more in a position of self-defense—higher up and securely holstered. But not this man's—he wore it like a gunslinger, low and ready, almost out of the holster, like a dare. Like he had something in common with those bad men outside.

Those men! Better make sure that they hadn't heard anything and weren't at this very minute on their way to her cabin. Well, if they were, at least now she had a gun, she thought. She very achingly and slowly got up, sidled along the wall to avoid stepping over the man on her floor, and pulled back the calico curtain. To her immense relief, the camp was quiet with no signs of stirring around. Letting her breath out at this one piece of luck, Jessie let go of the curtain and turned to look for the candle;

she stood the overturned table and chairs back up while she searched. When she found the candle she replaced it in its pan and set it on the table. Getting a match from by the fireplace, she lit the candle. Now she could focus her attention on the man on the floor.

He was so still that Jessie feared he was dead. With a sinking heart, and praying she did not have to dig yet another grave, she went to him and knelt beside him. He lay on his back with his face turned away from her. Jessie did not realize she was holding her breath until she let it out when she saw the even rising and falling of his chest. He was alive! Jessie did not know whether to laugh or cry, or both. He was alive! And he needed her. After a quick check of his left shoulder to be sure the wound had stopped bleeding—and to her immense relief, it had—she gently placed his head in her lap and turned his face towards hers.

Jessie was instantly struck by the youthful appearance of this man. Certainly, he was not as young as her, but neither was he as old as her father. But it wasn't his youthfulness which caused her woman's heart to beat faster.

Jessie found herself looking into the tanned face of the most beautiful man she'd ever seen. He looked almost innocent and childlike in his unconsciousness, she decided, as she tenderly pushed back a lock of jet-black hair from his forehead. Almost reverently she let her fingers trail over his high cheekbones and down the determined angle of his jaw. His slight growth of beard felt rough to her fingers, but his lips, slightly parted, were soft and firm at the same time. Jessie then held her fingers just above his open mouth to feel his warm breath run over them. She found herself wishing he would open his eyes so she could see what color they were. Almost without thinking, she let her fingers touch his long, dark eyelashes. His eyes squeezed more tightly shut and his nose twitched as his body instinctively reacted to her touch.

Jessie jerked her fingers away almost convulsively. What was she doing? Shocked at her own behavior and her reaction to this man, she got up after gently placing his head on the floor. She felt the need to put some distance between herself and his mesmerizing presence. She busied herself with retrieving the bandages, salve, and basin from under the china cabinet. Of course, the water from the basin was spilled all over the floor; Jessie made a face. What next?

Almost reluctantly and with the heat rising in her cheeks, Jessie approached her patient again. Why had she acted like that just a few minutes ago— rubbing her fingers over his face, all dreamy-like? Jessie knew she would not like to be pawed while she was unconscious. If she could forgive herself, she decided, it would be because she'd never been around any man except her father. Oh, the soldiers and the young men on the wagon trains all wanted to be friendly with her, but one stern glance from her father had put an end to all that.

Jessie refilled the basin from the water barrel kept indoors for cooking and washing. Then, kneeling beside the man, she began to unbutton his shirt so she could get to his wound. She tried her best not to notice his muscled chest with the dark, curling hair forming a fine mat across its expanse. The dried blood on his shirt caused it to cling to his shoulder, so Jessie wet down his shirt and gently peeled it from his wound. That done, she quickly tore away the remainder of the shirt, baring his torso to her wondering eyes. She shocked herself with the realization that she'd really enjoyed doing that.

With her cheeks burning from these unfamiliar thoughts, she cleaned his wound and assessed the damage. The wound was high in his shoulder; lucky for him—no vital organs there. Then, scooting around behind him, Jessie lifted him just enough to see that the wound went clear through. Another piece of luck. She wouldn't have to dig around in his shoulder for a bullet. Looking more closely at both wounds, Jessie realized he'd been shot from behind—the wound in the back of his shoulder was smaller than the one in front. She shook her head and pursed her lips in disgust at the men outside. "Back-shooting dogs," she said aloud.

After applying a liberal amount of the salve, with a silent prayer that it would keep infection away, to both wounds and bandaging his shoulder area as best she could, Jessie stood back to try to figure out just how she was going to get him up on her bed, the closest one to him. He was a lot bigger than her father, and she'd barely been able to move him when he got sick after the snakebite. Jessie was afraid that if she jerked and pulled on this man now, the bleeding would start again. Seeing no other choice, she decided to just make him as comfortable as possible right there on the floor.

Her mind made up, she swung his legs around, away from the cabin door, and scooted him even closer to her bed. That way, if she had to open the door to those men, they could not readily see him behind it. Next she decided that just in case he himself was dangerous, she'd better remove his gunbelt. Kneeling at his side, she saw the buckle rested at an angle on top of the closure to his pants. She paused for a fraction of a second; then, cheeks burning again, she very carefully unbuckled the belt with her fingertips. She lifted first one side of him and then the other until she got the belt and gun out from under him. She tossed it onto her bed and jumped back away from him as if he'd tried to bite her. She stared hard at him for several seconds as if he could tell her why she turned red and had clumsy fingers every time she touched him.

Getting no answers, she then put a pillow from her parents' bed under his head and covered him with a quilt her mother had worked on when they were on the trail. Satisfied with her efforts, but tired from them and still feeling the pain from her bruises, she stepped over her patient, moved the gunbelt over closer to the wall, and lay down on her bed, tugging her hat off. Probably she should have left it on, but all she wanted to do was rest. She put an arm over her closed eyes and gave in to her weariness.

Sometime later, Jessie awoke with a start and sat bolt upright, her heart racing; she hadn't meant to fall asleep! The cabin was dark; the candle must have burned out. She did not move as she allowed her eyes to adjust. Dim moonlight filtered through the calico curtains on the two windows in the cabin—the one over her bed and the one across the cabin from her—her peephole at the men outside. Thinking to check on the activities of those men, Jessie swung her legs over the side of the bed; she felt her feet thump against something not as hard as the floor.

"Ouch! What the hell—!" came the grunted words from the floor beside her bed.

Jessie jerked her feet back up onto her bed and sat there in shock. Who? Oh, no—oh, yes. The wounded man from the root cellar. He's awake, Jessie thought stupidly, not completely awake yet herself. Steeling herself to check on him, she leaned over the side of her bed. But as soon as her hand came into contact with the bandages she'd placed on his shoulder, her wrist was grabbed in a viselike grip and she was snatched completely off the bed. She landed full-length on top of the man with her breath knocked out of her.

"Who are you, and where the hell am I?" came the words almost growled into her ear.

Chapter Two

Jessie's shock to find herself lying on top of this man turned to anger at his continued rough treatment of her. This was the third time in one night he had either grabbed her hurtfully or thrown her down, or both.

"You let go of me right now, or I'll shoot you—and not in the shoulder, either," Jessie hissed.

She waited a brief but intense second, pinioned as she was to him by his grip on her wrist and his other arm thrown forcefully around her. What was she going to do if he didn't release her? If he did release her? And where had her courage come from? Had she really said she was going to shoot him?

Just as suddenly as she had been grabbed, she was released. Actually, it was more like she was rolled off him and onto the floor next to him; she felt his crushing weight on top of her now, sitting

25

astride her. All she could manage was a startled squawk before those same rough hands gathered up her shirtfront and placed a knife at her throat. Jessie felt her eyes bulge and her heart pound. Her breathing was very shallow and ragged.

"I asked you a question, kid. Who are you and where am I? And where's my gun? Is that what you were going to shoot me with—my own gun?" His voice was low and rough, but not weak like she would have expected, given everything he'd been through and the blood he'd lost.

Jessie swallowed hard, trying to wet her dry mouth so she could talk—before he slit her throat. "I—I'm Jessie," she stammered, deciding to start at the beginning of his questions. "You're in my home, and your gun is on my bed there."

Just as instantly the weight was lifted off her. With it, the threatening knife also went. Jessie immediately rolled onto her side and drew her knees up. She was sure she was going to be sick. She swallowed convulsively several times and put her hands over her face. Finally, her breathing and her stomach began to return to normal. She had no idea what the man was doing, and she didn't care. He was as bad as the men outside. She hated herself for having placed tender hands on his face earlier. She should have slapped it hard several times instead— and she would have too if she'd known he was this ungrateful and callous.

But Jessie sat up quickly when she heard booted steps coming toward her. They brushed by her without pausing and stopped at the door. Next she heard a sound she could not place for a moment, but then she realized it was the sound of bullets being loaded into a gun. Somehow, she knew those bullets weren't for her. After all, he thought she was just a kid. And no matter what else he might be, he probably wasn't a kid-killer. At least she hoped he wasn't.

Able to just barely make out his form in the dark, Jessie watched him to see what he intended to do. When he reached for the bolt on the door, she knew she could not let him go out there, despite the way he had treated her. To open that door was certain death—for her as well as for him. And, besides, she had some questions of her own she wanted answered—he owed her that much, she felt, because if not for him, she would not be in this predicament.

"If you open that door, we're both dead," Jessie said evenly.

Her words stayed his hand at the bolt. He turned towards her and stared hard at her for a second or two. Jessie stared right back unflinchingly.

"Then they're still out there." It wasn't a question, but Jessie felt the need to answer.

"Yes, they're out there. And they're pretty sure you're here somewhere, too."

"Damn!" He then looked around the dim cabin interior, taking in her parents' bed. "Where're your folks?"

"Dead."

"Did they—?" He pointed outside to indicate the men.

"No. My parents have been dead awhile."

"Then you're all alone here?"

"I was—until you came. Now I've got more company than I care to have."

"Yeah, I suppose you do," he answered, running his hand slowly through his hair.

Jessie watched him closely now as he took the few steps over to where she was still sitting on the floor. She noticed he walked a little slowly and unsteadily. So he was still pretty weak. When he got to where Jessie was, he sat down, crumpled really, on the floor with his back resting against her bed; he kept his left arm at his side, but rested his right arm on his bent knee. Jessie could see the fine patina of sweat on his face and heard his labored breathing. He put his head back and closed his eyes.

"Would you like some water?" she asked hesitantly.

With that, his head came forward, and he opened his eyes. Jessie felt very uncomfortable under his penetrating gaze; he seemed to really be seeing her for the first time. She could see that his eyes were large and dark, and glittering. She hoped the glitter wasn't from fever.

"You're not a boy at all, are you?" he finally said.

Too late Jessie remembered she had not put her father's hat back on. Her dark and curling hair fell past her shoulders to her waist. She quickly got up and went to the water barrel. "No, I'm not. You want that water?"

"That'd be nice, ma'am."

His emphasis on ma'am was not lost on Jessie. Her hands shook as she filled a tin cup and brought it to him, sloshing some of it on the floor.

As she offered the cup to him, he closed his fingers over her hand and guided the cup to his lips. Jessie's own lips parted, but no sound came out. She helplessly watched her hand go along with his to his mouth. When he finished, he let go of her hand.

"Thank you," was all he said. He leaned his head back again and closed his eyes.

Jessie slowly stood up, acutely aware of the effect he was having on her. She still felt the warmth of his touch on her hand—all the way up her arm. She felt a warmth of her own in her cheeks. Quickly she crossed to the water barrel and drew herself a cool drink. She gulped it back greedily.

Not knowing what else to do with herself, she went to the window and pulled the calico curtain back. All she could see were the red glowing embers of the campfire. One or two men with rifles walked around; probably posted guards, Jessie thought. She noted that the moon still rode high in the night sky; she decided it must be about midnight or right after.

"What's your name?" said a soft voice behind her.

Jessie jumped and whirled around when he spoke; she'd thought he was asleep. How long had he been watching her?

"What's your name?" he repeated a little louder.

"Jessie. Jessie Stuart."

"Jessie? Sounds like a boy's name."

"Well, it's not. It's short for Jessica," Jessie answered, somewhat tersely. She was determined not to be nice to him. Except for thanking her for the water, he hadn't been anything approaching civil to her yet.

"Jessica. That sounds pretty formal. It doesn't fit you—especially in that get-up."

Jessie looked down at her men's clothing and then back at him. She didn't have to answer that. Her chin went up in a stubborn tilt. Was he actually grinning at her?

"Did you do all this, Jessie?" he asked her, pointing to his shoulder and the bandages.

Jessie, relenting some in her determination not to be nice to him, nodded that she had and said,

29

"You're lucky. The bullet went right on through. All I had to do was clean up the wounds some." After a moment's hesitation, she got up the courage to ask, "Why would those men out there want to shoot you?"

"What did they tell you?" he asked her. His gaze was just as level as his voice; no trace of a grin remained on his face. Jessie knew she was on dangerous ground here. What if he really was an outlaw? But she decided to stick to the truth.

"Well, they didn't tell me much, really. Just that they're a posse and you're an outlaw."

"And do you believe them?"

"No."

"Why?"

"Well, for one thing, there's no sheriff out here to deputize a posse. There's only the soldiers at the camp." Jessie rubbed her sweating palms on the front of her pants. She remained over by the window.

"Smart girl. Anything else?"

"In the root cellar—you said you wouldn't hurt me."

"I said that? I don't remember . . . Wait! You're the kid who came in there earlier! I don't think I was any too gentle with you."

Jessie figured that was as close as she would get to an apology, so she decided to ask her other questions. "About the root cellar—how did you get out? I locked that myself after you tried to—I mean, after I got away."

"You mean you didn't let me out? Then I have no idea. I was barely conscious, but I remember someone coming in when it was dark and dragging me up here. I thought you did it, but now that I see how little you are, there's no way you could've." His eyes ran over her small figure.

Even though Jessie felt herself coloring under his gaze, she kept up her end of the conversation. "You don't suppose that one of those men out there let you out and brought you up here, do you?"

"Well, it wouldn't really make much sense—first they shoot me and then they save me. But if it's just you, me, and them here, I suppose it had to be one of them. Now that's interesting." He ran his hand over his stubbled chin and jaw as he spoke. Jessie felt a flush of guilt as she watched him tracing the same pathway her wandering fingers had followed earlier.

Jessie watched him a moment, as he was obviously deep in thought with his gaze directed at a point just to the left of her. Then, clearing her throat to get his attention, she said, "You still haven't answered any of my questions."

His eyes immediately focused on her over by the window. "Like what?" he said evenly.

Jessie could hear the cautious note in his voice, but she also heard the tiredness and the pain. She decided to hold her questions until he was more rested. She was exhausted herself and wanted to lie down.

Walking to him, she bent over and offered him her hands. "Here, why don't you let me help you to get up onto the bed. You'll be more comfortable there."

He looked up at her speculatively. Jessie waited, arms outstretched to him. When he hesitated, Jessie admonished, "If I was going to turn you over to those men, I would have done it already. They're getting plenty of rest right now. You'd better do the same thing. When morning comes—"

"Can you use a gun, Jessie?"

31

She pulled her hands back in surprise. "A gun?"

"Yes, you'll probably need one in the morning."

She hadn't thought about that. She'd used her father's old rifle on occasion, because he thought she should be able to use it what with the Indian threat and wild animals and such, but a pistol or to kill a man, no. "No, not like you mean, I haven't," she answered.

"You were certainly quick to threaten me earlier with my own gun, so I assume that if your life depended on it, you could kill a man?"

"If my life depended on it, yes."

"Good. Are there any other guns we can use besides mine?"

"My father's old rifle. I can shoot that. But his handgun—"

"Get them both, Jessie."

"I will if you'll get up on the bed. You need your rest."

He looked at her a long moment; Jessie set her mouth in a firm line to show him she would take no arguments. With a chuckle, he held his right hand out to her. With his weakened left side, he was a very cumbersome load for Jessie to handle. She took hold of his right arm and hand as best she could; powerful muscles bulged under her fingers.

Distracted as she was by this new sensation, she was not ready when he pushed himself up from the floor. She went up with him, her feet completely off the ground; being so unbalanced, she fell onto the bed with him. His grunt of pain was matched by her surprised yelp. She lay there with him on the bed in momentary shock, her limbs entangled with his.

Shock was instantly replaced by a flurry of activity as Jessie freed herself and quickly got off the bed.

Facing him now from the safety of the bedside, she saw he was too tall and too broad for her bed—his feet hung off the end and his shoulders touched both edges of the sides of her mattress. When her gaze traveled up to his face, she saw that his eyes were squeezed shut in pain.

Instantly remorseful for having increased his pain in her frantic efforts to get off the bed, she leaned close to him to be able to see his face. "Are you alright? I'm sorry if I hurt you. You'd better let me check that wound again."

Not getting any answer, Jessie started to lean over him to reach his wound, but his words stopped her.

"I'm fine. Now get the guns."

"I will," Jessie answered, straightening up and looking at him. "But first let me check your wound."

She reached over him again. To her chagrin, she practically had to lie on his bare chest to reach his wounded shoulder. She was very self-conscious about her unbound breasts brushing against his chest, but there was no other way to do this. Still, when her nipples hardened from the contact, she caught her breath and hurried her hands. All at once she felt a large, warm hand brush from her waist, up her back, to her shoulderblades. She pulled back in shock. "What are you—?"

"Your hair. It was in my face. I was just brushing it away. Settle down. I'm too weak to take advantage of you now. You'll have to wait."

Jessie was stung by his words and by the insolent grin on his face. Anger, shock, guilt over her attraction to him, feminine outrage—all these emotions vied to be uppermost in her mind. Finally, a mix of them all rushed out of her in a torrent of words.

"How dare you! You better not even try it! We could both be dead come sunup and all you can think about is—! Why, you ungrateful—!"

The sudden and insistent knocking on the cabin door cut Jessie off in mid-sentence. She whirled around to face the door; at the same time, she felt her wrist caught in a strong grip. She turned terror-widened eyes on the man in her bed. "What are we going to do?" she whispered. "What if they heard me? What if they—?"

"Hush! Get me up, and then answer the door."

As Jessie struggled to help him sit up, she called out to the door, "Hold on, I'm coming." When he sat up, he took his gun out of its holster and indicated to Jessie to help him get over by the door. "I'll be right there," Jessie called out again, afraid they would knock the door down if she didn't respond. When she had him behind the door, gun in hand and back supported by the wall, she reached for the bolt to unlock the door.

"Jessie, wait. Your hair—get your hat!"

Jessie's hand flew to her uncovered head. Where was the hat? In her panic, she couldn't think what had become of it. Her darting eyes took in the small room in a glance. It was too dim to see anything clearly. She then started a groping search of the room to find it. Just as the knocking resumed and she heard voices outside demanding she open the door, she spied the crumpled hat on her bed. With a small cry of victory, she seized it, bent forward to capture all her hair, twisted it up, and stuffed the hat down on her head, keeping it low over her face.

As she went to the door and unbolted the lock, her patient cocked his gun and raised his arm, ready for anything. Jessie, heart pounding and mouth dry, looked at him as she opened the door. He gave her a reassuring nod—and was that a wink?

Jessie had no time to think about it because all her attention was riveted on the two men on her doorstep. They both carried rifles. One of them was the man who had done all the talking earlier. Jessie noted that he was short and heavy, barrel-chested, and smoked a stinky cigar.

"What do you want?" Jessie asked, with a bravado she did not feel. She remembered, though, to keep her voice as low in pitch as she could.

"We don't want nothin', son. We're just checkin' to see if everythin' is okay up here. Skinner here thought he heard voices comin' out of yer cabin." He indicated the other man with him, a tall, gaunt-looking man with stringy hair.

Jessie's heart sank. So they were nosing about her property, maybe they'd even been right outside the cabin all this time. Acutely conscious of the man behind her door with the cocked gun, Jessie answered, "There's nobody here but me. I told you that already. Skinner must be hearing ghosts talk."

Skinner took a threatening step forward and growled, "Why, you little snot-nosed brat, I ought ta—"

His partner put a restraining arm out to block him. Jessie took a defensive step backward, which brought her gunman behind the door more plainly into her view. Out of the corner of her eye, but without turning her head even the slightest bit to give him away, she could see that he no longer rested against the wall, but was standing erect and alert, just inches from being seen by the two men outside.

"Forget it, Skinner. He's just a young'un. We got no quarrel with him." Even though he addressed

Skinner, he kept his ferret eyes on Jessie. She didn't dare even blink and breathing was difficult. Sweat born of fear ran down her spine. Finally, the barrel-chested, heavy man spoke again, but his words did nothing to reassure Jessie. "We'd best get on back to the camp. Jist wanted ya ta know we're about—if ya need us, that is."

The implied threat, the reminder that they were still out there and still watching, was not lost on Jessie. She did not have to answer them, however, because they turned to go back to the barn. Jessie quickly closed the cabin door and locked it firmly.

She bent forward convulsively and placed her hands on her knees. She willed herself not to be ill. Only after several moments of gulping in air for her starved lungs could she find the strength to speak. Looking around she saw her tall gunman sitting on the floor. His gun was lying on the floor at his side. He had his head back against the wall and his eyes closed.

Jessie could take no more of this suspense and danger. She had to have answers. Without even straightening up, she kept her eyes on him. "Just who are you?" she asked, a hard edge to her voice.

He lifted his head and opened his eyes slowly. "Josiah Tucker." He volunteered nothing else.

Josiah—somehow it didn't fit him, Jessie thought. But she had other questions. "They know you're here and hurt. Why don't they just rush the cabin and kill us both?"

"They're cowards, Jessie . . . and gunrunners. I've been riding with them. And they don't know just how bad I'm hurt. They're afraid I'd shoot some of them before they got me."

Jessie moved now to sit down beside him so she could hear him better. They had to keep their voices low, not knowing how close to the cabin someone might be. She was careful not to touch him in any way; his bare, muscled torso was very hard for her to ignore, especially the matting of dark, curling hair on his chest. She tried to pretend that he was not shirtless. Carefully keeping her eyes on his face, she asked "Would you?—Shoot them, I mean."

She heard a low chuckle to her side. "I already have . . . two or three of them anyway."

"Why? You don't look like those others, like you enjoy killing, like it's fun. If you're one of them, why are they after you? Why'd they shoot you?"

"Because I took something of theirs, Jessie, something they didn't want me to have." A hard edge came into his voice. "And I am just like them—I'm one of them. Don't make any mistake about that. I can kill just as easily as they can."

Jessie froze. Josiah Tucker was a killer. And she was sitting close enough to him to feel the warmth of his body. She had so many questions going around in her mind that she hardly knew which one to ask first. Finally, she settled on one that seemed the most important to her personally. "Are you going to kill me?"

When he looked over and down at her by his side, Jessie saw glittering eyes and a wide grin. "Now that's not usually the way I pay back someone who saves my life."

Jessie had to look down. One stare from him and she felt naked—or small—or vulnerable. She didn't know which. Shouldn't she be afraid of him, she thought? Why wasn't she? After all, the man was a confessed killer.

Deep in thought, Jessie was not aware that he'd reached out to her until she felt her hat being lifted off her head. Her hair fell in a cascade over her shoulder closest to him. This brought her back to instant awareness. She looked up at him, questioning eyes wide and mouth slightly open. In her innocence, she had no idea of the invitation she was offering.

His hand reached out to cup her chin and bring her mouth up to his. Jessie felt weak all over when she realized what was happening. She knew she should not allow this, but she was powerless to resist. She could not deny her attraction to him and what his touch did to her; she wanted to know how it felt to be kissed by this man.

When his lips touched hers very gently, Jessie suspended all thought and emotion to concentrate on this, her first kiss. She'd never known her lips were so sensitive; she could not give a name to the thrill of emotion that rippled through her when his tongue met her lips and swirled around them. She knew only that his touching her lips had also somehow touched every part of her body, even the part below her belly. The low throbbing there seemed to demand that Jessie move forward and deepen the kiss.

But before she could, the kiss ended. Jessie opened her eyes slowly to see his face just inches from hers; he was watching her, she knew, but she didn't care if he saw how he affected her. "Josiah," she breathed out, saying his name for the first time. His hand still cupped her chin.

"Shhh, little Jessie. That was my way of saying thanks for saving my life." He took his hand away from her chin.

Jessie nearly fell over; she hadn't realized she'd been almost solely supported by his hand on her chin. To steady herself she instinctively reached out; her hands came into contact with the bare flesh of his arm and chest. He, just as instinctively, reached out and took hold of her arm to steady her.

"They're blue!" Jessie blurted out.

"What's blue?" Josiah asked, amusement lacing his voice.

"Your eyes. They're blue. I couldn't see them before when you were passed out, but now with the moonlight shining right on you, I can see them. And they're blue!" She said all this with the laughing voice of an excited child.

She didn't know what to think when he suddenly pulled away from her, a frown lowering his eyebrows. Reholstering his gun, he slowly, and without waiting for help, pulled himself up to stand. He seemed to be looking for something.

Jessie, still on the floor, picked herself up and brushed the dirt off her rump. What had she said to change his mood? Why did he look angry?

"Where's my shirt?" he asked abruptly.

"It's over there by the bed, but you can't wear it now," she answered. His raised eyebrows and questioning look made Jessie confess everything, "I had to tear it off. I couldn't help it. It was all bloody and stuck to your wound."

He just stood there staring at her. Jessie wished she could read his mind so she could find out why he was so angry all of a sudden. His even stare made her fidget; she began to twist her father's shirt in her fingers. Then it hit her. "You can wear one of my father's. I have them right here in his trunk still." Then in a softer voice, "I couldn't bring myself to throw them out yet. It didn't seem right." The little catch she always got in her voice when she talked about her parents came back. She got quiet and looked away from the sympathy she saw in his eyes.

After a moment, she sniffed and moved over to a much worn travel trunk by her parents' bed. She opened it and rummaged around a bit before she came up with a shirt she deemed suitable. Holding it up to the moonlight to see it better, she remarked, "Yes, this is the one. It was always too big for my father, so maybe it will fit you." She held it out to him, but then remembering his wound, she got up and took it to him.

Despite his insistence that he could get it on himself, Jessie helped him, or tried to. He was so tall she didn't even come to his shoulder. Very carefully she pulled the shirtsleeve up over his injured left arm and then walked around behind him to let him slip his right arm through. She could barely get the shirt up around his shoulders properly; she had to stand on tiptoes. When she stood in front of him and prepared to button the shirt, he waved her hands away. He was frowning again, Jessie noted, when she looked up at him.

"Thank you—again," he said, a little more softly but not with the heat of his first thank-you, the one that came with the kiss. "Don't worry with the buttons. Get your father's guns and all the ammo. Put them on the table and then get some rest. I'll sit up while you sleep."

"But you're hurt!" Jessie protested. "I'll stay up while you rest."

"No, Jessie; now do as I say. I was passed out long

enough to consider it a rest. You sleep. I'm going to need you fresh in the morning."

Jake sat in a chair at the table in the center of the small cabin. The dim interior of the cabin was growing lighter by the minute. He knew he didn't have long to check and load these old guns Jessie had given him. Every few minutes he got up to look out the window; so far the camp was still not stirring. Jake knew that band of thieving murderers were in no hurry—they knew he was wounded and cornered. They'd do well to remember that a wounded and cornered animal was the most dangerous sort, Jake thought.

Still, he wasn't half as concerned about the men outside as he was about the girl inside. Jake looked over at her sleeping figure. He smiled and shook his head; no, she wasn't sleepy at all, maybe she'd just lie down for a minute. She'd been sound asleep within two minutes of putting her head on the pillow. Jake's smile faded. What in the hell was he going to do with her? He couldn't take her with him, but neither could he leave her here to be killed. And that was exactly what the pack of jackals outside would do, too, if they discovered him gone and her here.

Jake knew he could have slipped out at any time during the night and made his escape alone. Slipping around the careless guards to get Blaze, his big roan which he'd seen when he'd peeked out the window a minute ago, and lead him away a safe distance before he mounted him and rode off would have taken him about five minutes, he figured, even in his wounded condition.

Thinking of his shoulder wound, Jake tried his left

41

arm. He grimaced in pain as he raised his arm, but was relieved to see that he still could use it some. At least it wasn't his right shoulder, his shooting arm. Jake thought back to yesterday. A lot of things remained unclear to him. Like how had Hayes, the short, fat, cigar-smoking leader, and his henchman Skinner found out who he really was? Jake could think of no slip-up of his which would have told them he was a U. S. Marshal. They'd been going to kill him in his sleep, the cowards, but Jake had been warned by a note he found in his bedroll—he'd been just as surprised about getting the note as he had been about discovering that someone in the gang could read and write. Who among Hayes' confederates had warned him—and why?

Even with the warning, Jake had barely escaped alive; he'd had to kill three of them to get away. He'd been shot as he rode off on his big roan. With Hayes and his men right on his tail, he'd headed in the direction of Camp Nichols, but blood loss had weakened him too much, so he'd made it only as far as this homestead. The last thing he remembered was getting into the root cellar after he shooed his horse away. Then Jessie had come in.

Jessie. Jake looked over at her again. She'd saved his life. Damned if he'd let her lose her life for saving his. He got up and went to stand next to the bed. He looked down at her; she was so small. Or maybe he was just so big. Jake smoothed her hair back from her tanned face. How old could she be? Fourteen? Fifteen? And she'd been working this place alone? She might be small in body, but not in spirit. Jake had to laugh softly—she'd sure been ready to kill him in a heartbeat earlier. And she was bossy, telling him when to lie down or stand up, when to drink and what to wear. He let his gaze travel over her. She was lying on her side in a ball. As best he could tell, what with her being in oversized pants and shirt, she was slender, but he also knew her to be firm and womanly—hadn't he had her in his arms twice already?

Jake felt a protective surge in his heart toward this young girl, but he knew it was more than that, too. Hadn't the feel of her when she was checking his bandages or helping him with his shirt aroused him? There had certainly been nothing protective about that feeling! He decided that his reaction to her had more to do with the length of time he'd been away from women than it did with any true attraction to her. He berated himself for kissing her. He felt somehow as if he'd taken advantage of her.

Well, not that she hadn't enjoyed it, too. Her face had shown that much, and her outburst about his eyes, which had embarrassed him, told him she was curious about him. Just what he needed now—a child infatuated with him. He knew this could go no further—not in his line of work. Being a U. S. Marshal working undercover as a gunrunner meant he traveled alone and kept to himself. It was safer that way—for him and for everyone else he came into contact with. Including this girl. She'd just have to go on thinking he was Josiah Tucker, killer and gunrunner—and a thief who'd steal from other thieves. He couldn't tell her that it was evidence he had stolen. Letting her know he was Jake Coltrane, U. S. Marshal, could get her killed. He decided his duty to her would end when he safely deposited her at Camp Nichols. But for now, she needed him, and he would take care of her.

Jake knew he would have to awaken her pretty

quickly, but for now he let her sleep. With one last look at her sleeping face and one last touch to her hair, he turned back to his task at the table. He'd no more than seated himself when a shotgun blast outside sent a bullet through the window behind the table. As pieces of calico curtain and shards of glass pelted the room, Jake instinctively hit the floor, only to look up to see Jessie come suddenly and violently wide awake. She sat up, clutched her stomach, and screamed. Jake saw a red stain widening underneath her fingers.

Chapter Three

"Tucker! We know yer in there. You better come on out right peaceful-like. We know yer shot! There's nine of us, and we got yer horse. You cain't get away. Come on out now an' we won't hurt the boy none. You hear me, polecat?"

While Hayes was talking, Jake reached up from the floor to the table to retrieve the guns and crawled the few feet to Jessie. He hoped they hadn't heard her scream, but he couldn't risk her feminine voice being heard. He roughly pulled her off the bed and onto the floor. He shielded her body with his, and put one hand over her mouth. He looked down into brown, uncomprehending eyes. Had the bullet—? Quickly, Jake ripped her shirt open to see if she'd been shot. Her terror-filled eyes looked wildly into his, but this was no time for niceties or explanations.

"This here's yer last chance. If 'n ya don't come out now, we're comin' in after ya. And the boy!"

Jake heard Hayes' yelled threats, but he had his mind and eyes full of Jessie, trying to see where she was bleeding. He was finally able to swallow his fear when he saw that she hadn't been hit by the bullet, but had been cut just below her breast by a flying piece of glass.

A part of his mind registered that Jessie was indeed a full-grown woman with firm, ripe breasts capped by rosy-brown nipples. That impression was made on his mind almost without him knowing it. Right now he was concerned for her life.

The gash was not deep or gaping, but it was bleeding quite a bit. Jake applied pressure to the wound with one hand and began speaking in soothing tones to Jessie, telling her she was okay and not to scream. When the convulsive rising and falling of her chest and the wild look in her eyes began to subside, Jake took his hand off her mouth, eased his weight off her, and closed her shirtfront as best he could. He stroked her hair to help ease her fears. He desperately needed her to calm down so he could deal with Hayes before he stormed the cabin.

Finally Jessie nodded to Jake, which told him she was now calmer and more in control of herself. Jake knew she was truly all right when, a few seconds later, she rolled to her side and reached for the rifle, checked to see that her wound had stopped bleeding, and stuffed her shirt down the front of her pants. "Tell me what to do," she whispered. She assumed a crouching position, ready to move in any direction.

Jake gave her a quick squeeze on her arm and a brief smile. Then, in quick, short sentences, in a voice just above a whisper, Jake instructed, "Cover the other window and the front door. But keep your head down. I'll get the window Hayes shot out. I'm going to try to stall him a little. Follow my lead." Jake started to move to his position, but was stopped by Jessie's voice.

"Josiah!"

He turned back to her. "What?"

"Be careful."

"Yeah. You too, kid."

"Josiah! . . . Thanks."

"Just returning a favor. Now go on."

He dismissed any further discussion with a wave of his hand toward the window over her bed. He knew she'd be safer there because there weren't as many hiding places for Hayes' men on that side of the cabin as there were on the side he was covering. He knew Hayes would have most of his men ranged out by the barn and horse corral, both of which were on his side. The only hiding place big enough for a man on Jessie's side was the root cellar, but it was nothing more than a mound of dirt since most of it was underground. She could easily see any movement from there.

When he saw she was in position, kneeling on her bed and looking out the window through a slit in the curtain, he stood beside his window and called out, "What do you want, Hayes?"

"Don't stall me, ya varmint! You know full well what I want. I want you and what ya took from me."

Jake curled up the corners of his mouth, but no one would have called it a smile. So Hayes hadn't moved in any; his voice was just as far away as it was when he shot the window out. The coward.

47

Jake called back, "What do you want me for?" He chanced a quick peek out the window to locate Hayes' men.

"Why, I want you to come on out so I can kill you off. Now why won't you oblige me?"

Jake heard the men laughing at Hayes' lame attempt at humor. That's just fine, he thought, your laughter helps me locate you. He'd found seven of them. "Should I come out back-first since that's the only way you shoot a man?"

There was dead silence outside for a split second before Jake heard a strangled "Why, you—" and then a hail of gunfire. He'd already jumped over to the side of the window after his last comment, knowing what would come. He held up two fingers to a wide-eyed Jessie to indicate she had two men on her side. She nodded her comprehension, raised her rifle, and broke out the window with the barrel. She began firing in the direction of the root cellar, hoping to pin the two men there. Sure enough, two gun barrels poked up from the other side of the earthen mound and began firing back.

Bullets struck both sides of the cabin, but very few came inside. The two small windows were the well-constructed cabin's only vulnerable areas. The pattern of hits against the outside of the cabin told Jake he'd been right. The men were mostly out by the barn and too far away to do any real damage. But he also knew that wouldn't last long. They'd move in after a while, knowing they had more men, more guns, and more ammunition. He needed a plan—and quick.

Jake yelled for Jessie to hold her fire for now and let them shoot out their anger and ammunition.

She obeyed and lay on her bed for cover. Jake sat on the floor under his window across the cabin from her. When he did, he saw a trapdoor under Jessie's bed.

Very quickly he scrambled over to her and took her arm. He startled her since she had her face to the wall. She tried to jerk away from him until she saw who it was.

"You scared me!"

"I know. I'm sorry. Listen, Jessie, the shooting is letting up. We don't have much time. We have to get out of here. Quick now—what's this trapdoor to under your bed?"

Under any other circumstances Jessie would have looked comical with her head and long hair hanging off the bed as she looked under it. When she raised her face to Jake, it was red from blood rushing to her head. "Oh my God! I forgot about it. It's an escape tunnel Daddy dug when we first got here. He was afraid of being trapped in here by the Indians. We never had to use it, so I forgot about it. It goes out to the barn."

Jake could have kissed her, and would have, too, if he could have found her under all her hair which had fallen forward. "Quick now, Jessie, help me move your bed."

Staying low to avoid any stray bullets, Jessie tumbled headfirst off her bed, a relic of her life in Missouri, and like Jake, grabbed onto the iron framework under the tick mattress. Weakened as they both were from their wounds, it took both of them to scoot the bed out of the way. When the tunnel trapdoor, stuck by five years of disuse and dirt accumulation, would not give to Jake's straining efforts to open it, he produced a long knife from his boot to cut quickly around the outer edges of the square door's frame.

Jake looked up when he heard Jessie's quick intake of breath. He followed her eyes to his knife, which had been at her throat earlier. She'd just have to trust him for now.

Just then, the trapdoor gave with Jake's renewed efforts and opened with a rush of dirt, cobwebs, and stale air. Jake and Jessie looked down into the black maw of the tunnel and then up at each other. Jake read the fear on Jessie's face. "It's either the tunnel or them, Jessie."

"I know, but I feel like I'm going down to hell."

Jake grinned at this and put a reassuring hand on her arm. "I'll go first and then help you down. Just exactly where in the barn does this tunnel come up? I'd hate to pop up right in the middle of Hayes and his men."

Jessie thought for a moment. Jake knew it was hard to concentrate with the bullets pinging off things inside the cabin, but the gang was moving in on them and his patience with her was running out.

"Quick, Jessie—think! We don't have long!"

"I know! I'm trying!" she wailed. Then it came to her. "Wait! I've got it—the back of the barn in a horse stall. Daddy never used that stall—he just put hay in it to cover the trapdoor. He didn't want to escape Indians only to be trapped by a horse standing on the door."

"Smart man. Are you ready now? Okay, let's go!" With that he lowered himself into the tunnel.

Jessie almost turned away—she couldn't shake the image that he was slowly being swallowed up by the open mouth of a giant goblin. Then it was her turn. She handed down her rifle to Jake. After he laid it down next to his feet, he stretched his hands out to her.

"Come on, Jessie. It's alright. There's a ladder here you can use. I'm right here. I won't let anything hurt you." He spoke like he would to a frightened child, which was just how Jessie felt. With a loud gulp, she gathered her courage and started to climb down. As soon as her feet were on the ladder, she felt Jake's reassuring hands holding her and steadying her. In a matter of seconds, she was standing on the tunnel floor, bathed in the light which filtered down from the cabin. She let her breath out slowly, but quickly sucked it back in with a cry of fright and grabbed Jake around his midriff when he reached up and pulled the trapdoor shut.

The total and abysmal blackness and quiet of the tunnel was almost too much for her. Only Jake's arms around her and his quiet voice kept her from panicking totally.

"Jessie, it's okay. I'm right here—just like I promised," Jake soothed her. He then gently held her away from him and reached down to retrieve her rifle; he thrust it into her hands. "Here. Carry this and follow me. This tunnel is only wide enough for one person and not high enough for me to stand up. I'm going to have to feel my way along, so hold on to my belt."

As he turned around and guided her hand to his belt, Jessie felt her courage returning. After all, she'd faced down that gang earlier and then she'd helped pin them down with gunfire—surely if she'd been prepared to kill a man, she could do something as simple as walk through a tunnel. Even a pitch-black, narrow, smelly tunnel. Jessie gripped Jake's belt more tightly and caught her lip between her teeth.

Jake moved forward at an agonizingly slow pace, crouching and feeling his way. Every so often his groping hands would loosen earth from the tunnel walls, and it would fall to the ground and make Jessie stumble. Even so, she did not loosen her grip on Jake's belt; in fact, she wasn't sure she would ever loosen her grip on his belt.

After what seemed like hours, but in reality was only several minutes, Jake's hands came to the ladder at the other end of the tunnel. Jessie bumped into Jake from behind when he stopped abruptly. She heard a strangled "Ouch!" from in front of her.

"What is it?" she whispered, almost afraid to hear his answer.

"Jessie, we're here—the end of the tunnel."

"Oh, thank God," she breathed, almost slumping against him. She'd thought before now that she had overcome her childhood fear of dark, enclosed places, but now she knew better. Had it not been for his nearness and reassurances, she knew she would never have been able to walk the length of the tunnel. Alone, she would have sat down in the dark, covered her face with her arms, and screamed until she died.

"Jessie! Let go of my belt."

With a start, Jessie realized that he was trying to pry her fingers loose. She released his belt, but grabbed onto his shirt. She had to maintain contact with his body, because she certainly could not see him in the dank darkness all around her. She noticed that he too kept his hands on her as he turned around to face her. She wished she could see him; it was so eerie to hear his voice, but not to see him.

"Okay, Jessie, now here's what we've got to do. Are you listening?" he whispered quickly and fiercely.

"Yes. Keep talking. Please." She could feel his warm breath on her face as he talked; it helped to settle her nerves, knowing he was that close to her.

"Good girl. There's probably no one left in the barn. But just to be sure, you wait in the tunnel until I have a look around. If everything is okay, I'll come back for you, get my horse, and then turn theirs loose. That'll slow them down for a while and give us a chance to get away. You got all that?"

Jessie was nodding as he talked, but then remembering that he couldn't see her, she said, "I've got it. Just don't leave me here in this tunnel for too long."

A chuckle from him was all she got by way of an answer. He let go of her and turned to climb up the ladder. Jessie heard irregular breathing and low cursing from him as he went up the few rungs; she knew his shoulder wound must be hurting him and slowing him down. She hoped he didn't start to bleed again. Next she heard bumping noises, accompanied by grunting and heavy breathing; she assumed he was pushing against the trapdoor. Jessie held her breath, praying it would open.

Just when she'd about given up, she saw a tiny sliver of light break through the stale darkness. She almost cried out in relief, but quickly clamped her hand over her mouth. The sliver slowly turned to a slice of light and then to the most beautiful ray of daylight Jessie had ever seen. She realized she actually had tears in her eyes. She wiped them away and chastised herself for being such a baby about the darkness.

She watched him climbing up the ladder while holding onto the trapdoor until it was completely up and he was out, so he could set it down quietly in the hay of the stall. The last thing they needed right now was the loud thump of the door to alert Hayes to their presence in the barn. Once he was out of the tunnel and out of Jessie's sight, she could do nothing but wait while he checked to see if the way to the horses was clear.

She found she didn't mind so much still being in the tunnel since there was daylight and air coming down to her. But when she heard her dairy cows mooing outside, her shoulders slumped in dejection. She knew they would be at the pasture gate waiting to be let in and milked. Poor things. Their bags would be full and painful. And the chickens—they needed to be fed. Who would do that now? She was thankful that at least the big work horses and the cattle were in the open pasture and had water, too. She wanted very badly to see to her animals, but knew that would be more than foolish. They'd just have to wait until she could get back home. Jessie wondered when that would be.

She stayed pressed against the earthen wall and out of sight. She never took her eyes off the opening, praying that the only face that would appear there would be Josiah's. Jessie frowned. There it was again—that name. It just did not fit him.

But what if it did fit him; and he was who he said he was? Where'd that leave her? Oh, God, here alone. That thought sent a jolt through her. But, no. He'd have killed her outright already if he was like them. Jessie slowly shook her head. He wasn't like them—

he just wasn't! He was too nice, too caring . . . too handsome. Jessie caught her breath—and he rode with those horrible men and said he was a killer and admitted he'd stolen something from them, something important enough for them to want him dead. Why couldn't she just accept him at his word? Why did that damned kiss of his keep getting in her way?

Jessie angrily wiped at her mouth. Fool! He said he was a killer. There was no law that said you couldn't be a killer if you were handsome and had some manners, some concern for others, some conscience. Just because she liked the way he looked, the way he felt, it didn't change who he was, silly name or not. She'd definitely been alone out on this prairie for too long if she was willing to throw in with an outlaw just because he kissed her. Suddenly Jessie felt very stupid, very young.

And the quiet above her suddenly seemed very ominous. She was alone. He was gone. The weight of her rifle in her hand reassured her somewhat, but she knew she didn't have a chance against nine men. Looking back through the darkness of the tunnel and then up at the light above her, Jessie made up her mind.

She climbed very slowly and awkwardly because of the rifle in her hand and the cut on her midriff. As she very cautiously approached the opening in the stall, she heard guns firing. She stopped to listen. After a moment or two she realized the sounds were close to the cabin. Good. That meant the men weren't close to her and she could safely climb out. She didn't know where Josiah was or what he was doing, but she hoped he was safe. She felt he should be since the horses were nowhere near the cabin, but were tethered right outside.

Just as Jessie pulled her weight up onto the rung which would bring her head above the opening, she felt herself being hauled up roughly by the back of her shirt. The shocking suddenness of this attack left her voiceless. In one split second, the front of her shirt gathered around her neck to choke her; she dropped her rifle in the hay and could do nothing but dangle there helplessly over the tunnel's maw, her arms and legs jerking like those of a marionette.

In the next split second, she was grabbed roughly around the waist and sent tumbling backwards into the hay; she landed on top of her captor, who gave a whoosh as if all the air in his lungs had been forced out. Jessie struggled in vain to get away, but the grip was too strong. Tears stung her eyes from frustration and fear, but also from pain because her wound was bleeding again from where her shirt had been torn away from the caked blood. If she was going to die right here, then she was going out fighting. She made no sounds or cries, because she didn't want to attract the other men. Maybe no one but this one man had seen her. If only she could get to her rifle . . .

After a few seconds of futile struggle, she was thrown off her captor and plopped squarely on her bottom in the hay. She sat down so hard it rattled her teeth. But, in an instant she was on her feet in a crouching position, looking all around her for her rifle. She instinctively put one hand over her bleeding wound. She didn't stop to think why she was not grabbed again, or shot, or stabbed, or . . .

"Are you looking for this?" came the fiercely whispered question.

For the first time, Jessie looked up. There sat Josiah; he was holding her rifle out to her. "You!" was all she could get out. She instantly straightened up, only to have him trip her with his booted foot into the hay again. She landed on her back with her arms near her head.

"Get down! Are you trying to get yourself killed?" he hissed into her ear. He was beside her on the ground in the hay, but was leaning his weight into her, holding her hands above her head, and pressing her to the ground. "Didn't I tell you to stay there in the tunnel until I came back?"

"Yes, but I couldn't figure out why you would," Jessie hissed. With his face only inches from hers and his angry breathing mixed with her panting breath, she looked into his dark blue eyes and watched his expression change from fierce anger to surprise. She didn't know what to make of this. She could do nothing but lie there and stare back at him until he decided to let her go. Sweat, dirt, and lines of pain and exhaustion marred the face so close to hers. She couldn't help herself; despite everything, she still thought he was the most beautiful man she'd ever seen. Abruptly he let go of her. He sat up somewhat slowly and then offered his hand to her. After a second's hesitation, she took his hand and allowed him to pull her up to a sitting position. She kept her other hand over her wound.

Hay now mixed with the dirt, blood, and sweat on Jessie. She sat passively as he clumsily plucked strands of hay out of her hair. Then he pulled her shirt up to a modest level to check on her wound. Grimacing at what he saw, he tore away the hem of her shirt and pressed it against her wound. Jessie still sat like a helpless child and watched him tend

57

to her. He then surprised her with an apology.

"Jessie, I'm sorry if I hurt you. When I saw you coming up out of that hole, I knew I had to get you out of there fast. Some of Hayes' men could already be in that tunnel. Once they realized we weren't firing back, they moved in. I watched them for a minute to be sure none of them came this way. You've got to start trusting me—I told you I would come back. Just now I grabbed you because I was afraid you would fall back into the tunnel if I surprised you by saying something. I didn't know I was latching onto a hellcat!"

By now he had packed her wound and torn off part of his own shirt to wrap around her to hold the bandages in place. He stood up slowly to peer over the top of the stall. Satisfied that no one was coming, he pulled Jessie up and handed her the rifle. He silently pointed to the open barn door just outside the stall and indicated she should follow him. Jessie swallowed hard and nodded. This was it.

She shook her head to clear away her stupor. She would need her wits about her now. She pulled her hand out of his and brought her rifle up to the ready position. He gave her a wink; this time, she winked back. She watched as he flattened himself against the barn wall and looked outside to make sure their way to the horses was clear. Jessie's heart was warmed by his earlier show of concern for her; it also made her feel guilty for thinking he'd left her and for thinking of him as a killer like those other men. But if he wasn't one of them, that left even more questions unanswered. Why had he been with them if he wasn't one of them? Jessie frowned, her mind working. She had no time to reflect further, though, because right then she saw him signal for her to leave the stall and come to him.

Taking a deep breath to steady herself, Jessie quickly moved out of the stall and over to the open barn door. She pressed herself closely to his back. Still looking outside, he reached back, putting his hand on her arm to keep her safely behind him. As she looked at his back, so broad and strong, Jessie knew in her heart that once she stepped out of this barn with this man, her destiny was clearly in his hands—outlaw or no outlaw.

Chapter Four

Jessie did not know which one was stinging her face more—the glaring sun, the relentless wind, or the flying strands of the big roan's mane. She was crouched low over his muscled neck; her hands were tangled in his long mane in a desperate effort to stay on his bare back as he covered the open prairie at a staggering pace. Jessie felt both exhilaration and fright. She was more used to her plodding farm horses; she'd never been on a horse with this much spirit and speed. She silently prayed she could keep her seat on his sweating and straining back.

She knew, though, that there was no way she would be allowed to fall off, for Josiah was pressed to her back, his arms under hers and extended to handle the reins as they rode double. Jessie felt she could have remained like this forever, but she knew better. He was taking her to Camp Nichols, leaving her there. And then he was leaving, too. That's what he'd told her once they'd gotten away from her ranch. And she knew she should be glad to be left at the safe, familiar camp, glad that this man behind her, this outlaw, was getting out of her life. But she wasn't. And she didn't know why; she just knew that it hurt to try to think about it.

She also couldn't figure out why she cared what happened to him either. She had asked him if he was worried about being recognized by the soldiers, but he had shrugged off her question, seemingly unconcerned for his own safety. Well, if he didn't care why should she?

Her mind, so overworked in the past twelve hours or so, was almost numb. She found she couldn't maintain a single train of thought for long. Instead she gave herself up to purely physical sensations and impressions without allowing her mind to make any judgments. She just wanted to feel for once. Freeing her mind, she found she was most aware of the body which was molded to her back.

He almost completely covered her small frame as he bent low over her; his muscled arms against her sides wedged her in his embrace; his chest was flat against her back and, if Jessie looked up and slightly over, her nose would barely touch his chin. The warmth of him against her buttocks and the feel of his long legs, so hard and muscular, against her shorter, softer legs were totally new sensations for Jessie. She liked it—a lot.

When her shocked young girl's conscience registered reproofs at her own newly awakened woman's emotions, she pushed aside the girl in favor of the woman. She knew that the answer to all her recent restlessness rode behind her—she could feel his heart beat against her back and she could hear his breathing in her ear. With this thought, a woman's smile briefly rode on the girl's lips.

Jake's mind was working overtime. Years of training and experience as a U. S. Marshal sustained his sleep-starved and pain-racked body to keep him alert and functioning. He would collapse later when they were safe at Camp Nichols and after he had checked in with the colonel.

Still uppermost in Jake's mind was the girl in his arms. A smile came unbidden to his lips. How could he not think about her? Her hair was blowing in his face and her body was molded to every inch of his. He was very aware of just how feminine she felt. It had been so long since he . . . No, he shook his head, she's just a kid, despite her woman's body. As if needing proof of that, his mind offered him a vision of her breasts exposed to his eyes when he'd ripped her shirt off her earlier to see if she was shot. Forcing that picture away, Jake fought to convince himself that he should think of her as only one more detail he had to attend to before he got back onto the trail of the gunrunners. He'd see her safely to the Camp, and then she'd be the Colonel's problem. But, as soon as he had her itemized and prioritized in his mind, she wiggled against him, adjusting her balance on Blaze's back. Jake rolled his eyes and took a firmer grip on the reins. That damn Camp better pop up soon!

But Jake knew they would have to stop long before they reached the Camp. Blaze had tremendous stamina, but even he could not sustain this pace for long without rest, water, and food. Jake also knew that he and Jessie needed all those things, too. So, danger or not, they would have to stop at the small natural spring, about ten to fifteen minutes ahead, which was surrounded by a stand of scrub oak trees; it represented the halfway point between the Stuart Homestead and Camp Nichols, still another four or five hours away, even after the two or so hours of hard riding they'd already done. Well, Jake sighed inwardly, at least the grazing there for Blaze would fill his belly and renew his strength. As for him and Jessie, they'd have to wait to eat.

Jake was glad now that his present undercover assignment had put him in this area often in the past few months. His initial briefing at Camp Nichols had familiarized him with the area, including the Stuart Homestead, but until yesterday he'd had no reason to go there. He was concerned, though, about why Hayes, a link in the gunrunning chain, was going to the Stuart place. Who was he meeting there?

The thought of Hayes brought a snarl of contempt to Jake's lips. He knew Hayes and his cutthroats were somewhere behind him and determined to catch him before he reached the Army outpost. And he knew they were in none too charitable a mood—his last sight of them over his shoulder as he sped away with Jessie on Blaze had been of them racing around trying to catch their horses he had untied and shooed. Skinner had been shooting at their retreating figures while Hayes was stomping on the hat that he'd thrown onto the ground. Knowing Hayes' murderous rages like he did, Jake decided that any stop he allowed himself had better be brief. If Hayes caught up with them, it would be their last stop.

Jake's mind came sharply back to the present when Blaze stumbled on one of the uneven swells in the prairie. Jake felt Jessie stiffen in response, even as he did. Immediately he began reining Blaze to a walk. His mount's sides and neck were flecked with foam; his deep red coat was even a darker bronze where rivulets of sweat ran down his belly and flanks. Jake let the reins out even more to allow Blaze to walk with his head lowered. He hated having to ride Blaze this hard; he knew that the great stallion would run until his heart burst if Jake asked it of him. But Jake would not do that. His respect for and reliance on his horse was too great; he would never abuse him.

As Blaze walked on, Jake wordlessly slid off his back and then handed Jessie down. He answered her questioning look. "There's water and shade ahead. We'll rest there."

She nodded in response and fell into step alongside him and Blaze. Jake looked over at her as she stared straight ahead. In all his twenty-seven years, he'd never met a woman—girl—like her. Even with everything she'd gone through because of him in the past twelve to fifteen hours, not once had she complained or hesitated to do what he told her. Poor little thing, he thought, seeing her streaked with dirt and sweat, her shirtfront stained with blood. She surely was one of a kind; his experience with women told him that much. She had a lot of spirit and stamina, just like Blaze; Jake admired those qualities in a person—and a horse.

Suddenly, despite his tiredness, his injuries, and the danger, he broke out into loud laughter. Comparing Jessie to Blaze was just too much for him. Somehow he didn't think either one of them would think the comparison a favorable one. He had to stop and put his hands on his knees to keep from falling over laughing when he looked from Blaze to Jessie. They both had the same look on their faces: brown eyes widened and head turned slightly askance. Jake was sure Jessie's ears would have pricked forward like Blaze's if she'd been able to pull it off!

Jessie didn't know what to think. Had he suddenly gone mad? He'd seemed perfectly reasonable a few moments ago. Jessie looked all around her. Nothing but unbroken prairie, her, a huge horse, and a crazy man.

"Josiah, are you all right?" she finally ventured, thinking he'd been hit with some sort of fit, like her father had been after the snakebite. He'd acted really crazy, too, and saw things that weren't there. Jessie felt like crying. There was no way she could manage him and the horse and get them to Camp Nichols.

She wasn't sure he'd heard her and started to repeat her question when, to her relief, he finally stopped laughing and straightened up. "Yeah, I'm fine," he said, wiping the tears from his eyes. Then he added, with a chuckle in his voice, "Come on. Let's go get that water."

And that was it. No explanation. He just started walking toward the small stand of trees ahead, holding his horse's reins like before, as if nothing had happened. Jessie stood rooted to the spot and watched his retreating figure. She was immensely relieved that he was rational—that ruled out fever. But she had no idea what to expect from him next. He was so full of surprises. Jessie took out after him, shaking her head. He sure kept a girl on her toes.

Later, Jessie allowed a contented sigh to escape through her lips. Hands behind her head, her eyes closed, she was lying in the shade of the trees after drinking deeply from the spring. She'd even been able to clean her wound and then wash some of the dirt and sweat off her face, neck, and arms. She felt like she'd been here for hours, but it was really only minutes. She didn't even realize she was smiling until Josiah's voice interrupted her peace.

"What are you smiling about?"

Jessie opened her eyes to see him still lying close to her, but raised on one elbow now so he could watch her. He was chewing on a piece of prairie grass. The sunlight filtering through the tree branches overhead was glinting off waterdrops still in his jet-black hair. That, combined with his sparkling blue eyes, relaxed posture, and wide grin made Jessie feel anything but relaxed. Especially since he still had his shirt off, which he'd removed for her to check his wound.

Now his tanned, muscular torso drew all her attention, despite her best intentions not to notice. Jessie found she had to look away; her own thoughts embarrassed her. And she certainly did not want him to read them on her face. So, she looked just beyond him to where the big roan grazed. Once the horse was rested, they would resume their hard ride to the Camp.

"Oh, I don't know why I'm smiling," she finally said, closing her eyes again. "What were you laughing about a few minutes ago?"

A deep chuckle was his first answer. "I can't tell you that. You wouldn't like it."

Now what did that mean? Jessie opened her eyes and turned her head to look squarely at him. She pulled herself up on an elbow, mimicking his pose, and asked pointedly, "Were you laughing at me?"

"Well, no, not really. More like at you and Blaze."

"Blaze?"

He used his thumb to indicate his horse behind him. A wide grin split his face, showing even, white teeth; Jessie sat up abruptly and narrowed her eyes at him.

"Hey," he said, sitting up too, and holding his hands out defensively, "I said you wouldn't like it."

Too late. He was pelted with a handful of dirt and grass. "Don't you dare laugh at me! Especially when a horse—!" she fussed, looking around her for something more substantial to throw, something like a rock.

But she never got a chance to find one, for the next thing she knew, she was lying on her back in the grass with the big lug half on top of her, holding her hands over her head. Her shock registered in her widened eyes, but they quickly narrowed when she saw he was again laughing at her.

"Get off me, you ape. You're hurting my cut. Ow, ouch!" Jessie cried in mock pain, but it worked.

Instantly he pulled his weight off her, his gaze going swiftly to her midriff. But any apologetic feelings he might have been about to express instantly disappeared when Jessie shoved him backwards and started for him.

"Oh no you don't," he challenged. He rolled to one side as swiftly as his shoulder would allow; he was barely quick enough to grab her wrist and stop the jab she meant for his stomach. Before she knew what was happening, she found herself quickly pulled sideways onto his lap; if he thought he was going to hold onto her until the fight went out of her, then he—!

The fight went very suddenly out of Jessie when she found herself face-to-face with him. She looked into his eyes only to see him studying her just as intently. After only a moment of this, Jessie could stand it no longer and lowered her eyes. Despite all her earlier womanly thoughts and feelings, she was still just a girl in most ways. His sapphire-blue eyes told her exactly what he was thinking, and she found she was somewhat frightened about what could happen next.

"Jessie."

When he said her name like that, so soft and warm, Jessie was reminded of a warm summer breeze. That same breeze floated gently over her senses, making every nerve ending tingle wherever her body was touching his. And that was almost everywhere. She watched as his hand came up from her thigh to cup her chin and lift her face to his. Despite the warmth surrounding her, she felt the hair on her arms rise. Her heart beat against her ribs. She reached up to put a small, trembling hand on his rock-hard arm. Her lips parted to receive his kiss as his head slanted toward hers.

But she never got that kiss. A loud warning neigh from Blaze brought Josiah to his feet in a flash. He pulled Jessie up with him and held onto her, but Jessie felt he really wasn't aware of her now. Her gaze followed his to Blaze, who stood intensely still, ears pricked forward, nostrils flared, looking toward a small rise some distance from the spring. Jessie's mouth went dry and her legs felt like water when she saw, coming from that same rise, a great cloud of dust and the sounds of hooves—a lot of them moving fast in their direction.

"Damn!" Josiah said through gritted teeth. Jessie was sure he was not aware that he had tightened his grip on her almost to the point of pain. He whistled to the big roan, who cantered toward them, reins looped loosely over his back.

"Is it Hayes?"

He looked down at her when she spoke. His expression told her he had forgotten he was holding onto her. "Could be. It's the wrong direction, but he could have circled around without us seeing him. I have to assume it is, though. Come on—let's move."

With his strong grip on her elbow, Jessie walked as fast as she could to keep up with his long-legged stride. She was glad she was still in pants—a cumbersome skirt would have seen her facedown more than once at this pace. Jessie hit the stallion's back with a thump as Josiah none too gently handed her up. He then retrieved his shirt from the ground and put it on, grimacing from having to move his shoulder so much. Agitation was set in every line of his face as he nimbly, despite his bandaged shoulder, mounted Blaze behind Jessie and caught up the reins.

"There's no place at all to hide out here," he said aloud, but not particularly to Jessie. He turned Blaze in a quick circle as his eyes scanned every rise and fall around them on the prairie. The roan pranced and pivoted, nearly rearing in his excitement; he'd caught the tension in his master. Josiah had his hands full keeping the spirited animal still. "Hold, Blaze. Easy!" he commanded.

Jessie dug her fingers into the horse's mane; she didn't dare speak and distract Josiah even more. She had the distinct, guilty feeling that he, had he been alone, would not have been caught like this.

He definitely would have been more alert and single-minded. So the last thing she wanted to do now was remind him of her presence.

Jessie almost fell off when Blaze bolted forward at Josiah's command. If she'd thought her heart was in her throat before, she was now sure it was lying on the ground somewhere by the spring they'd just left behind. She had no idea how Josiah had decided on this direction because she could see no place low enough to hide them and Blaze; she couldn't even see a scrubby bush of any kind to mask their presence. But, pressed against the horse's neck by Josiah's weight behind her, all she could do was trust his instincts. He'd gotten them this far relatively unharmed.

Just as suddenly as Josiah had ordered Blaze forward, he just as abruptly pulled him to a body-lurching stop about fifty yards from the spring. The roan's great neck arched and he stiffened all four legs. Jessie had both arms around his neck when he finally shuddered to a standstill. Instantly Josiah's hands were around her waist, pulling her off with him, much as he would have a saddle.

As soon as they were clear, Josiah pulled down on the reins; at this command, Blaze lay down on his side on the ground. Josiah then quickly pulled an astonished Jessie down to the ground with him and wriggled them into a position between Blaze's legs where they could watch the approaching riders over the top of the horse's heaving belly.

They were lying on the far side of a small rise in the ground, but its cap of high prairie grass made an effective barrier between them and whoever was just now topping the hill by the spring. Jessie looked over to see that Josiah had his gun out; he rested his hand on Blaze's side to steady his aim. His face was grim; small rivulets of sweat told of his tension and the heat.

Jessie lowered her head and pressed her face to Blaze's side; she was amazed that such a large animal could be this still and quiet. She stroked him with one hand, realizing that in this position, Blaze would take most of the bullets in a gun battle. She closed her eyes to whisper a small prayer that that did not happen.

Her prayer was interrupted by Josiah's relieved voice saying "Oh thank God." She opened her eyes to look first at Josiah, who'd slumped against his horse's flank, and then in the direction of the spring. As she stared openmouthed, Josiah pulled her to her feet with him.

The first thing that caught her eye was the flag of the United States, and then she realized that all the men in blue dismounting at the spring were U.S. Army troops. They were saved! Jessie's knees sagged and her eyes began to roll back in her head; Josiah quickly caught her up and cried, "Oh no, you don't! Not now! Come on, Jessie, wake up!"

To this end, he repeatedly but gently smacked her cheek with his fingers. Jessie came to and instinctively grabbed for him to keep from falling; she got two handfuls of shirt, but he pulled her to him and leaned over to look into her eyes. "Are you okay?"

Jessie found her voice. "Yes, but you won't be if you slap me again!"

Jake allowed himself a laugh and hugged her to him. "Yeah, you're fine!" Jessie tried to pull away from this indignity, but gave up. He was too strong, and she was too weak.

Josiah held her with one hand and, with his other hand tugged on the reins and gave an "Up!" command to the still-prone Blaze. With a great shuddering effort, the horse regained his feet, tossing his neck and stamping the ground. Jessie broke away from Josiah to hug the roan's head to her. "Good boy," she very lovingly told him. For her efforts, he nudged her, almost knocking her down.

Of course, all their activity had at once attracted the attention of the cavalry troop. Several of the soldiers were ranged around the spring, long rifles at the ready. A small contingent of them was slowly riding toward them, guns also out. Alarmed, she turned and spoke in a low, urgent voice. "Josiah, wait! Maybe these soldiers might recognize you? Maybe they know about Hayes and his gang and that you ride with him!"

She kept forgetting he was an outlaw. Why had she thought they were saved? If they knew he rode with Hayes, they might arrest him—or worse!

Josiah never took his eyes off the soldiers, but he did reholster his gun and begin to wave to them. "That's a chance I'll have to take. Just wave and act happy to see them. I'll think of something to tell them. Please, Jessie, just trust me and believe me, you won't regret it. Just play along with me." Then, turning briefly to her, he favored her with one of his rare smiles. "And thanks for being concerned about me."

That stopped Jessie cold. Was that what she was doing, showing concern for him? Yes, she reflected, she definitely was. And now he knew it. Well, she should be concerned, she reasoned, she hadn't saved his life back at the cabin only to have him lose it now. Feeling very superior with that thought, she turned her face slightly away from him, raised her chin, and crossed her arms under her breasts.

The deep chuckle she heard next to her did nothing to assuage her pride. "Okay then, you're not concerned about me—just your own skin. Remember, if they know I ride with Hayes, they'll think you do, too, since you're with me."

Great day in the morning! Jessie hadn't thought about that. She abandoned her stoic pose for the shocked one she couldn't help. Her next outburst was instantly quelled by Josiah when he put his arm around her and kept a very firm grip on her shoulder. Jessie had no choice but to submit and face the soldiers who were just then reining their horses to a stop right in front of them. She could barely breathe or swallow. What would they do to a woman outlaw? She shuddered to think! Her only hope was that some of these men might recognize her from their frequent supply trips to her homestead. But, looking into their faces, she didn't recognize any of them. Her heart sank even further. What had this impossible man gotten her into?

"Morning, Sergeant. Are we ever glad to see you! Ain't that right, honey?"

Honey? Jessie turned disbelieving eyes on him. He had the most idiotic smile on his face that she'd ever seen, and that accent! But the glare in his eyes when he turned to her warned her. That, and the digging of his fingers into her upper arm.

"Uh, oh yes, right. Boy, are we glad to see you," Jessie played along, trying to match his accent and tone. A sharp kick to her calf told her she was overdoing it. She pursed her lips and looked up sharply at Josiah, but he never took his eyes off the soldiers.

The sergeant looked from one to the other. Jessie swallowed hard; even she could read the skepticism in his large, ruddy face. He still had his rifle out and pointing at them. Then, taking in their wild, dirty, and disheveled appearances, and the horse behind them with no saddle, he asked, "You folks got troubles?"

"Yes, we do, sir. We're lost," Jake answered.

We're lost? That's the best he could come up with? We're lost? More like we're sunk, Jessie thought. She barely stopped herself in time from snorting out loud.

"You're lost?" the sergeant repeated; he started to say something else, but stopped, looked hard at Jake, then turned to his men, and shrugged his shoulders. They worked their lips as if trying not to laugh. Then, turning back to Jessie and Jake, he said, "Well, young'uns, out here with no food, no wagon, no saddle even for your horse, I guess you are lost. Or on the run from someone."

Jessie had heard this tone before; her father used to use it on her when he caught her lying. She sucked her bottom lip into her mouth, and waited.

After an eternity, or so it seemed to Jessie, the sergeant put his rifle back in its loop on his saddle, and told his men to do the same thing. A wave from him to the men at the spring put them at ease, too. He turned flinty eyes on Josiah, who still stood with his arm tightly around Jessie's shoulders. "I'm thinking you better come up with a better story than that to tell her pa. Even I can see through it—and I don't believe it."

Josiah grinned widely. "Yes, sir."

Jessie had no grin though. Her pa? What did he mean?

"Come on, you two. You can ride with us to rejoin your wagon train." With that, he turned his horse around and headed for the spring, apparently confident that they were no threat and that they would follow him as instructed.

And follow him they did, with Josiah keeping a tight grip on Jessie and hushing her every attempt to protest or to question him. Frustrated and yanked along, Jessie fumed inwardly. If anyone would have told her that Josiah Tucker would act meek and silly, she would have laughed. But here he was doing both. By golly, she needed some answers. She stopped so suddenly that neither Josiah nor Blaze was prepared. Blaze bumped into Josiah, sending him stumbling forward; he nearly lost his footing. "Damn it, Jessie," he said through gritted teeth.

His grip on her arm tightened as he shook her, not violently but enough so that she got the idea that the simpleton he'd been posing as was gone and the man she knew was back. "Just what the hell is the matter with you?" he continued.

"*Me?* Me?" Jessie cried aloud, but then instantly lowered her voice when the sergeant looked back over his shoulder at them; he shook his head and rode on for the spring, leaving the two kids behind to fight it out.

"What is going on? Why were you acting like some kind of idiot to that sergeant? And what's this about my pa, and calling me honey, and a wagon train, and—"

"Think about it, Jessie. The less said, the better. I let him draw his own conclusions and, in doing so, he told us what our story was. All I said was we were lost; I didn't say from what or who. He decided we're two kids who sneaked off from their wagon train to

75

be alone for a while and then got lost. Right now I'll bet he even thinks we're arguing over what to tell your father."

If Jessie had not already been stopped in her tracks, this would have done it. Her mouth dropped open and she stared wide-eyed at Josiah and then, turning her head slowly, at all the men by the pool of water. They all thought . . . ? That she and . . . ? Were . . . ? The explosion of red in her face went right down her neck to disappear into her shirt. Instantly her hands covered her embarrassed face. To have them all think that—how could she face them? But then she had another thought, one which made her angry. Down came her hands to form fists by her sides. She was as close to Josiah as she could be without touching him. She strained her neck to get as close to his face as she could. "And you let them think that we were—that we were—"

"Yes, I did. What'd you want me to tell them? The truth?"

Jessie slumped with this reminder of their predicament, one that was growing more and more precarious by the moment. "No, I don't guess you could," she sighed. Josiah took her arm again, this time more gently, and they began walking slowly back to the spring.

"What are we going to tell them when they find out there's no wagon train?" Jessie asked, almost whispering.

Josiah kept his eyes forward as he answered her. "I'm betting there is one, because the soldiers ride out to meet the trains, remember?"

"Oh no, that's right," Jessie's words came out with a lot of air. This was worse. "Then they'll find out we're not really with that or any other train."

"Exactly."

Jessie walked along silently for a moment or two. Then another, even worse thought came to her. "Where do you suppose Hayes and his men are? Why haven't we seen them yet?"

"Exactly," came the grim answer.

Chapter Five

Fortunately, the arrival of the contingent of soldiers at the wagon train was fraught with much confusion and activity as the wagons stopped and people got out to greet them. Everyone milled about, taking this rare opportunity to stop at midday and visit, and even prepare a quick meal. Now that the wagon train had protection through hostile Indian territory, the atmosphere was one of relief which quickly led to a celebration.

No one, not even the sergeant, noticed the great, red horse with two riders slip off and quietly wander in amongst the heavily laden wagons. Jake was betting that even if the sergeant did notice, he wouldn't say or do anything, feeling his duty to get them safely here was done; they could face their frantic parents by themselves.

Jake kept Blaze pointed toward the rear of this

mighty train, numbering in the neighborhood of two hundred wagons. This was good—safety in numbers, a chance to remain anonymous, and even get away without being missed, if the need arose. To the few men and women who did give them curious looks as they rode by, Jake nodded his head in greeting, acting for all the world like they were simply heading back to their wagon. He only wished that Jessie, riding behind him now, did not have her arms so tightly about his waist and her cheek pressed to his back; she looked every bit as scared as he knew she was. Still, he was grateful for her uncharacteristic quietness and lack of questions. He had to keep reminding himself that she did not have his maturity and most importantly, training in hiding her feelings and acting a role to save her life.

Even though Jake looked casual and relaxed to the bystander, in reality his sharp eyes were taking in everything and everyone around him. If he blended in so easily, so could Hayes. The high-wheeled wagons, four abreast in long columns, offered a thousand places to hide. Thinking along those lines, Jake had his right hand resting lightly on his thigh, only a few inches from his holstered gun. His fingers itched from tension.

Jake was betting that just because these people had been traveling together for over half of the nine hundred miles it was from Missouri to Santa Fe, it didn't mean they knew everyone on the train. That was not likely, if for no other reason than that most of the drivers were teamsters and not families looking to relocate. This trail was a supply line and driving the wagons was a business, a dangerous business, not one conducive to friendships and a lot of chitchat. So, if they knew anyone, it was usually the people in the few wagons around them.

Also, wagons joined up at different points on the trail; the new ones were assigned to the rear of the train. The churned-up dust they ate was their punishment for not being in at the beginning. Thus, Jake knew that by heading to the rear, everyone would assume they were new to the train and that's why they didn't look familiar.

About halfway through the train, Jake felt Jessie sit up and pull away from him slightly. Alert to this change in her, but without even changing his expression or slowing Blaze, Jake questioned her, keeping his voice intentionally low. No one looking at him would have even noticed that his right hand had moved closer to his holster. "What's wrong? What do you see?"

"Food," came the plaintive answer.

A thin smile twitched at Jake's lips. He should have known. His own stomach had started acting up. He didn't know when she'd last eaten, but it had been over thirty-six hours for him. He supposed that next to keeping their hides alive, feeding their hides was definitely number two on his list. Had he been alone, he would have merely slipped behind a wagon and watched for a chance at an untended pot. He'd done this often enough when undercover, but that would be hard to explain to Jessie. No, not a good idea. Okay, food. For about the hundredth time since this morning, Jake wished for his saddle. There was a good supply of beef jerky and hardtack biscuits in his saddlebags—not wonderful food, but it kept you alive.

"Hey, mister, come here. You don't look so busy.

Come here and give me a hand. You on the horse, there!"

It took a moment for Jake to realize he was being summoned. He brought Blaze to a standstill and looked around him. He could feel Jessie moving behind him. She was probably looking all around, too, for the voice.

"Right here next to ya, ya danged fool!"

Finally getting a fix on the voice, Jake looked over to his left at the back of a wagon. No one. As he leaned forward slightly, a round, suntanned, wrinkled face popped out at him through the opening in the canvas top. Startled, Jake pulled back on the reins; Blaze pranced and Jessie grabbed onto Jake tightly.

For the second time in two days Jake found himself confronted by a woman in men's clothing who was insulting him. The giggle he heard coming from the woman perched behind him on his horse was not lost on him. The woman in the wagon was heavyset, gray-haired, and short; her too-big plaid shirt, worn pants, and boots reminded him of someone he knew and was close to—literally. An old wide-brimmed straw hat attempted to cover thick gray hair, short wisps of which kept escaping and falling into her straining, red face.

Gray eyes snapped at Jake as he sat, dumbfounded, on his horse. "Well, what in tarnation are you a-waitin' for? Help me get this dang pot unstuck! Can't you see I'm a lady who needs help?" With that, she gave up her fight with the pot, stood, hands on her ample hips, and glared at Jake.

"Yes, ma'am, I'm coming right now!" Never let it be said that Jake Coltrane did not know when he was bested. He dismounted, leaving the reins with Jessie. She was making no effort to hide her enjoyment of his being ordered about and called names.

"That's more like it, Sonny. Now get in here and pull up on that trunk while I pull this old pot out. I'll never get no food into me like this. How in the world it got stuck under there, I'll never know."

Jake, hands on the back of the wagon gate, one foot on the wagon bracing and one still on the ground, turned a comical face to Jessie and mouthed "Food!" before he hauled himself into the wagon. Jessie's stifled giggles overflowed at this. She leaned forward to hide her face in Blaze's thick mane.

But she instantly sat up straight when she heard the strangled cry from Jake. He'd forgotten about his shoulder. He was holding his arm and leaning against the back of the wagon; his face was contorted in pain and covered with sweat. The old woman was even now climbing out of the wagon, her face puckered in concern. She kept looking from Jake to Jessie. Jessie was already off Blaze and trying to run to Jake. But her wound kept her from moving too fast.

"Get over here and help me with him, child. What's wrong with him anyhow? He looks big and strong enough. And great Lord, look at you—why are you a-holdin' yourself like that? Get over here. Let me take a look at the both of you."

By now, Jake had regained his control. The last thing they needed was her loud voice drawing attention their way. A quick look around, though, told him that no one was looking their way. Apparently most everyone had taken their pots of food to the big cook fires started at intervals throughout the train. Still, Jake intercepted Jessie by a hand on her arm;

explanations would not be easy. They just needed to get away on some pretext.

"Well," the woman repeated, "I'm a-waitin'. What happened to you two?"

Jake looked over at a wide-eyed Jessie, trying to think what to say. But Jessie beat him to it. "We were running away from some outlaws who were trying to kill us, and we ran into the soldiers!" There, the bald-faced truth—and all out in one big breath and one big sentence.

For a moment the old woman was stunned into silence, just as Jake was. He was glad his teeth were his own, for otherwise they would have fallen onto the ground at his feet. Jessie was staring at him, wild-eyed, hand over her mouth. What had she done? Jake calculated that one, maybe two, steps would bring her within his reach; he could then pinch her head off.

"Why, child, how you do go on! Outlaws, indeed. A-tryin' to kill you. I never heard the like. You must be raving from a fever. Come over here."

Jessie was now in the protective embrace of the older woman who was ushering her around to the side of the wagon to the water barrel. Jake, completely forgotten, followed them. Now Jessie's face was being wiped with a wet cloth, and she was drinking from the dipper. The old woman was feeling Jessie's forehead with one hand and trying to raise her shirt with the other one to see her injury. "Well, there's no fever. Let Bertha have a look, child. Now, don't be modest with me. There's nothing I've ain't seen. I've doctored every living thing there is for more'n forty years."

She now looked up at Jake; her look told him he might have to go for his gun. "You do this to her,

young man?" she asked, pointing to the angry, red
weal on Jessie's midriff. She held Jessie's bunched
and upraised shirt in her other hand.

"No, ma'am, I most certainly did not. I'm the one
who saved her from the outlaws. They did that,"
Jake replied, slipping back into his simpleton role.
For whatever strange reason, Jessie's outburst with
the truth was working. He'd stick with it for now.
He quickly winked at her to let her know it was
okay. Her thin, little answering grin told him she
understood.

"Oh, fie on the outlaws!" Narrowed gray eyes and
hands back on the hips told the story. "Now I don't
know what trouble you two got, but don't let me
hear no more wild tales about outlaws and such."

"Yes, ma'am," Jake assured her. That was fine
with him. He hadn't wanted to mention them to
begin with.

"Good, now that's settled." She then busied herself with getting out a large leather bag from the
crowded interior of her wagon. From this bag she
produced all sorts of medical-looking instruments,
bottles, and bandages. She first turned her attention
to Jessie's cut; tsk-tsking and head shaking seemed
to help her get the job done more quickly. Jessie
done, she turned on Jake. "Come here, boy, and
let me see to you, too. I swear. What young people
don't get themselves into these days." Shaking her
head and pursing her lips told Jake very eloquently
what she thought of him.

Jake hesitated for a moment. He wasn't really sure
he could explain the gunshot wound, but he really
didn't have much choice right now. He realized that
they were committed to this course of action, and
to bolt at this point would really arouse her curi-

osity, making her more likely to repeat her story to someone in charge. What they needed now was less attention, not more.

Misreading Jake's hesitation, Bertha chided, "I ain't a-goin' to bite you, son."

The woman made Jake sit down and open his shirt. To her credit, she barely registered surprise when she saw the obvious nature of the wound after she'd unwound Jessie's clumsy bandages. Only a slightly raised eyebrow and a direct look into Jake's eyes gave her away. She said not a word and made quick work of cleaning up the wound and rebandaging it.

Any hope Jake and Jessie might have had to get away at that point was dashed when Bertha stepped back, brushed her hands together in a very business-like manner, and asked, "Now, where's your wagon? You both need to get those dirty clothes off those wounds before you infect 'em."

The silence was deafening. Jake and Jessie exchanged glances. Bertha stopped in the middle of putting away her doctoring things to see why no one answered her. She looked from one to the other of them and let out a heavy sigh. "Just as I thought," she fussed, an airy wave of her hand punctuating her words. "You two ain't got nothin' but yourselves and that horse. Danged if you ain't even a part of this here wagon train. What you got to say to that?"

"You're right," Jake replied, sticking to the truth. It had worked for Jessie; just maybe it would work again.

"Well, danged if I don't know what's really a-goin' on here. You two can't fool me with your wild story about outlaws and such! You done stole this little girl here from her family and run off with her to marry her, didn't you? I'm a-bettin' her daddy gave you that bullet to your shoulder and she cut herself gettin' over a barbed fence! Now that's just what happened, ain't it?" Bertha thoroughly loved this story—at least her loud laughter and knee-slapping seemed to say so.

Surprised as he was by her conclusions, Jake latched onto this story. In fact, the more his mind quickly went through the details, the more perfect the story was. It even fit with what the sergeant thought. And now that he thought about it, eloping lovers was exactly what they appeared to be. He liked it—it was a great cover story. And besides, what harm could it do? He just hoped Jessie remembered what he'd said about the sergeant—let him draw his own conclusions and then tell you what your story was—and played along.

Just to be sure, he quickly went over to Jessie and put his arm around her shoulder, giving her a very affectionate kiss on her temple—this was for Bertha's benefit, too. Jessie turned a red face and shock-widened eyes on him. Jake answered her with his mouth set in a straight line and a quick nod of his head in Bertha's direction. Jessie quickly looked over at Bertha, who now had her hands folded in front of her and was beaming at the happy couple, and managed a smile—sickly, in Jake's opinion, but a smile nonetheless.

"Well, if this don't beat all!" Bertha gushed. "Now we've got to get some food into you. I'll bet you two think you can survive on love, but old Bertha here knows different. Come on, child, help me get out some vittles we can eat cold. We done wasted too much time now to worry with a cook fire. We'll be headin' out again any minute now, I suppose. Young man, you make yourself useful by getting your horse and tying him up over here to my wagon. Out here in the middle of nowhere with just a horse. I swear. Never saw the likes. You two just better stay with me. No telling what sort of trouble you two could find out there on your own. Maybe even some of them outlaws you were telling me about." This sent her into another gale of laughter.

As she talked and laughed she busied herself and Jessie with preparing a cold meal of biscuits, beans, and bacon. Plain fare, but Jake's mouth watered nonetheless. It was all he could do not to dive right into the middle of the cook pot and make a pig of himself. When Jessie held a plate out to him, he noticed how she kept her eyes lowered and how pink her cheeks were. He was sure the food was much easier for her to swallow than was this notion of her having a lover.

As Jake ate—or more accurately, gulped the food down—sitting cross-legged on the ground across from Jessie, he kept his eyes on her. It wouldn't be hard to pretend he was her lover. He couldn't deny the attraction he felt or the memory of her body against his, the way it had been several times already for different reasons—none of them having anything to do with love, though.

He just wished she weren't so young and so obviously inexperienced. Well, that was probably okay, too; that could be explained away as young bride jitters. No one had to know they weren't really married, and he really had no intentions of actually sleeping with her. This was a cover, nothing more. In fact, with her so secure here, Jake figured he could probably get away on his own pretty soon and get back to his assignment. Now, dammit, why did he feel so guilty about even thinking of leaving her?

Later, with the wagon train on the move again, Jessie found herself perched on the buckboard seat by Bertha. She was amazed at how expertly the older woman handled the team of mules. Missouri mules—they made Jessie homesick for the life she'd known before coming here to the Cutoff. But, she sighed, there was no family back there for her anymore, just like she had no one at the homestead waiting for her. No, Jessie thought, shaking off the melancholy that was creeping up on her. She could only go forward, like this wagon train, and see what adventures lay ahead.

This instantly lifted her spirits. She let herself get caught up in the excitement of all the noise and activity around her. She had always been a little envious of the people on the countless trains which had stopped at her parents' homestead. They were going places and seeing things, and all she could do was stand there and watch them arrive and then leave. She'd always wondered what lay at the other end of the Santa Fe Trail; her parents had stopped at Camp Nichols and settled. Jessie had never been further than that.

Well, she inhaled deeply and smiled, here she was on a real adventure. Just her and Josiah. She stole a look at him riding alongside the wagon on Blaze. As always, her heart beat a little faster when he was close to her. Since he wasn't looking at her, but straight ahead, Jessie let her gaze stay fixed on him.

"That's a right handsome young man you picked for yourself, child."

Jessie quickly turned her head to look at Bertha.

Did she miss nothing? Still, Jessie felt her face coloring some. "Yes, he is," she answered briefly, remembering Josiah's warning not to give anything away by talking too much and volunteering too much information. Still, she hated being evasive with this kind and helpful woman. After all, wasn't she sitting here in Bertha's wagon, wearing Bertha's clean shirt, just as Josiah was, and with her belly full of Bertha's food?

"Ya know, child, I never did ask ya'll yer names. I'm Bertha Jacobson from Lexington, Missouri." She freed one hand from the many reins she held and vigorously shook Jessie's hand. She looked expectantly at Jessie.

"Uh, well," Jessie stalled, her mind racing. She and Josiah hadn't discussed this. "Uh, I'm Jessie and he's Josiah."

"Yer last name, child. Yer new last name. Yer Mrs. who now?" A friendly smile lit Bertha's face.

Jessie wasn't quick enough for this question. Her new last name—as in married? Jessie felt her chin begin to quiver, despite her best efforts to hide it. She bit her lip to keep from crying. What should she say?

The smile fled Bertha's face. "Why that low-down snake in the grass! Yer young man ain't got aroun' to making you his wife yet, has he?"

"Uh, no. But it's not his fault!" Jessie rushed on. "We just ran away this morning, you see, from over by Camp Nichols, and there was no one to—to—"

"Well, don't fret none, child. I'm sure it will happen soon enough. You'll see." With that, Bertha turned her attention back to her mules.

Jessie breathed a sigh of relief. This business of lying by telling the truth was hard on a person.

Still, she felt proud that she had handled that one on her own. Josiah would be proud of her quick thinking, too, she was sure. With a small smile of self-satisfaction, Jessie put the whole incident from her mind. She thought no more of it that afternoon. The swaying of the wagon over the uneven ground, the swaying of the prairie tallgrass in the gentle wind, and the bright afternoon sun all combined to lull Jessie to sleep where she sat.

That evening, Jessie sat cross-legged on the ground with her back against one of the wagon wheels. Jake sat facing her. They were silent as they finished their supper, the same food as at noon, but this time it was warm from the cook fire. The only sound was the scraping of forks against tin plates. Bertha had eaten quickly and excused herself. Blaze was tethered close by, behind Josiah; the setting sun cast an even redder hue on the stallion's blazing coat. Just as Jessie looked up at him, the horse raised his head, looking alertly at something—or someone—behind Jessie.

Jessie stopped her fork in midair. She knew what this meant. Even enveloped as they were in the camping noises of this many people, noises which had not phased Blaze at all, he had just caught a strange scent or sound.

"Josiah," Jessie warned. His head snapped up, eyes as alert as Blaze's. Jessie nodded at the roan, "Look at Blaze."

It took Josiah no more than an instant to turn toward his horse and then back to Jessie, putting his hand on his holster as if to reassure himself of his gun's presence. Tensely cautious, he put his plate on the ground and stood up swiftly. Jessie did the same when she heard the rising volume of human voices coming their way. Josiah signaled for her to come stand by him; if they had to make a run for it for any reason, he wanted her handy.

Right then, a large group of wagoneers, teamsters and some families, headed by Bertha, came around to the far side of the wagon where Josiah and Jessie were and confronted them. Several of the soldiers were in the crowd. Jessie moved closer to Josiah, who put a reassuring hand on her arm. To save her life, Jessie could not have said why all those people were grinning at them. Some even poked each other in the ribs and exchanged knowing glances. She looked up to see Josiah's frowning face. But, her head snapped back to Bertha's face when she began talking.

"Look what I found, child," she said, directing her attention to Jessie. She pushed forward a tall, thin man with a kindly face, wispy hair, and wire-rimmed glasses. He ducked his head briefly as a greeting. He had a black book in his hands. "When you told me this afternoon that you two weren't hitched yet and you bein' near to tears over it, I took it upon myself to ask around for a preacher. And I found one! Say hello to the Reverend Wilkins. He's going to marry you up right legal-like tonight!"

Chapter Six

Jake couldn't imagine what could go wrong next. Maybe a thundering herd of buffalo? Indian attack? Rattlesnake bite? What? He was sitting on the ground, arms resting on bent knees, with his back against a tree stump. Jake absently stroked the tethered roan's velvet nose as he thought, and watched the goings-on in Bertha's wagon. The lit lantern inside it threw distinct shadows on the canvas covering.

Poor Jessie. Jake felt really bad for her. There she was in the back of a wagon being trussed up in a borrowed dress to be married to a man whose real name she didn't even know. Jake pulled a piece of tallgrass out of the ground and absently played with it. Blaze moved off to continue feeding. Jake wasn't worried about this wedding; after all, Josiah Tucker, someone who didn't really exist, and not

Jake Coltrane, was getting married. Jake was almost positive that the ceremony would not be binding on either one of them under those circumstances. Even if it was, Jake could later tell her the truth, and they could have the marriage annulled.

But that wasn't what really bothered him. Jessie was what really bothered him. There she was, an innocent kid, until Jake had involved her, however unwittingly he might have done it, in this convoluted mess. She had no idea in hell what was really going on. No idea that she was a pawn in a deadly game. Jake had to marry her to preserve his true identity; to do anything else would raise too many questions, not to mention eyebrows. Of course, he could just mount Blaze and ride off for Camp Nichols, check in with the colonel, and move on from there. He couldn't tell the sergeant here who he really was because he suspected that someone in the Army was involved. Therefore, only Colonel Carson at the Camp knew who he really was. Riding away was definitely what he would have done before—before yesterday, before Jessie. He surprised himself with these feelings.

For the first time in his life, he felt responsible for someone else. Truly responsible if he married her, Jake grunted, laughing at his own lame joke. Well, damn it all to hell, she'd saved his life. He owed her something in return, didn't he? Yes he did. He couldn't see himself, as Josiah Tucker, just riding out and leaving Jessie here in a wedding dress and among strangers, far from home, with no way to get her real life back. He couldn't do that to the kid.

He still thought of her as a kid. Jake's brows almost came together over his eyes as he thought about her age and frowned. He had never asked her. It had never come up. Jake realized he hadn't wanted it to come up. As long as he was able to think of her as a young girl, a really young girl, the easier it was for him to keep his distance. He felt bad enough for kissing her once already and for trying to a second time. If the soldiers hadn't come along right then, there was no telling what would have happened.

Well, one thing was certain. He knew exactly what could not happen tonight after they were married. Not under any circumstances. With that, Jake thought he had himself under control. But then he recalled the feel of Jessie in his arms, her soft kiss, her hair blowing in his face, the feel of her in front of him on Blaze, her doe-brown eyes and parted lips, her full breasts pressed to him . . .

Jessie stood among the many stacked boxes and crates in the back of Bertha's wagon. She looked at herself in the long mirror Bertha had produced. The lantern suspended above her head cast shadows in the corners, adding to the sense of unreality that Jessie felt. The girl who stared back at her from the mirror looked pale and scared. Her dark, curling hair was pinned up on her head, but long tendrils of curls fell over one shoulder. The cream-colored, high-necked dress she wore was covered in the same color lace; a wide ice-blue sash tied into a trailing bow in back. In her hands the girl held her veil.

"Now don't you fret none, child. You're supposed to be scared and nervous on your wedding night," Bertha chatted on, straightening here and tugging there on Jessie's dress until she was satisfied that everything was perfect. "Yessiree, if over two hundred wagons loaded with fancy goods can't come up with everything for a decent wedding, then nobody can." She now took the veil from Jessie and, standing behind Jessie so she could see the result in the mirror, placed it on the young, dark head in front of her. She met Jessie's eyes—wide and unblinking—in the mirror. "Child, you look beautiful." She shook her head and made little clucking noises with her tongue.

"Now you wait here," she instructed an unmoving Jessie. "I'm going to go see to the rest of the preparations. I do believe that everyone is going to show up. Good news travels fast, they always say. After all the problems and deaths these people have been through on this trip, a good wedding is just what they need to cheer them up!"

With that she was gone. Jessie finally let her breath out and plopped down in a heap on the nearest box. She could certainly use some cheering up herself. She rubbed her temples and then looked around her. How could she be getting married? This was all too unbelievable. Much like Josiah's reaction. Jessie cringed now, just like she had then, when she recalled his face—his unshaven jaw had clenched and his eyes had blazed into hers, but for the benefit of the crowd confronting them, he stayed in his role of eloping young lover by smiling broadly and proclaiming, "Now if this don't beat all!"

Jessie had to agree with him there—this definitely beat all. Letting that sergeant and then Bertha believe they were running away to marry had certainly seemed the safest story at the time. My, how things do turn upon themselves, Jessie thought, shaking her head. Her mind railed against this forced marriage—that was just what it was, really—a forced marriage. Their own lie was forcing them into it. In all her daydreams about the man she would marry and what her wedding would be like, she'd never come up with this one! Marrying an outlaw out on the open prairie—an outlaw she'd known only one day. An outlaw who didn't want to marry her any more than she wanted to marry him.

Jessie wished she'd been able to speak alone with Josiah before she'd been whisked away by Bertha. No telling what he was thinking! But surely he knew that the last thing she'd been doing was trying to trick him into marriage. What earthly reason would she have for doing that? She didn't love him, she knew that. She was very attracted to him, but that wasn't enough to . . . Josiah's bare, muscled chest with its fine matting of dark hair, his blue eyes which could sparkle or bore right through her, his strong arms pulling her close for one more kiss . . . No! Jessie tried to blank these images from her over-active mind. Attracted, yes. Love, no.

But maybe there was some way out of this! If she could find Josiah, if he was close by, maybe they could escape again on Blaze. No one would chase them—sure, they'd wonder what had happened, but they were too busy with their own problems to worry about what two young lovers did! Jessie jumped up with that thought and made her way to the rear of the wagon. This was so simple, she wondered that Josiah hadn't come up with it himself.

Jessie drew back the canvas curtain and looked to where Blaze had been tethered earlier. Josiah's name had been on her lips, but the words died, along with something inside her, when she saw that the horse was gone. She stood there numbly holding back the cover and staring out at the spot where she'd left them, as if by sheer force of will she could make them reappear. But they didn't. *He left me, he left me . . .* the refrain kept repeating in her head. *How could he leave me?*

For that was just how Jessie felt. She'd been so close to him for the past twenty-four hours and shared so many dangers with him that he did not seem like a stranger, like an outlaw to her. How could he care so little for everything she'd done for him that he could just ride out of here the first chance he got and leave her behind to explain? Jessie's mouth straightened in an angry line. She'd accepted the fact that he was an outlaw, but she'd never figured him for a coward.

And another thing—none of this was her fault. This whole stinking mess was his doing. She hadn't been the one who'd crawled, shot and bleeding, into his root cellar. Well, better to learn his character flaws before she married him—wait a minute, Jessie warned herself. That sounded like she'd been jilted by someone she loved, someone she'd been serious about marrying. Jessie gave what could only be called a snort. These people might think it was a real wedding, but the bride and groom knew better. With a sense of finality, Jessie lowered the canvas curtain and crossed her arms angrily. She was glad he had left. She was. Really. The hot tears spilled out of her eyes and ran down her cheeks.

The sudden throwing back of the canvas curtain brought Jessie around in a whirl. Her hands went instantly to her eyes; she didn't want Bertha to see her crying. She wasn't ready yet to answer questions.

"Jessie, what's wrong?"

Jessie's hands parted instantly. It was Josiah! And he was all cleaned up, shaved, and just like her, in borrowed finery. Since he was standing outside on the ground, she could see him only from the chest up. In one hand he had Blaze's reins, which he was tying to the back of the wagon. She barely refrained from throwing herself into his arms. He hadn't left her! Through the watery cascade still in her eyes, she saw the concern on his face. "What's wrong?" he repeated.

"Nothing. Nerves, I guess. Bertha says all brides are like this," she said through little hiccups of emotion.

"Even when they know it's not a real marriage and not to a man they love?" His words would have been cruel except for the softened tone of his voice and the half-smile on his lips.

Jessie felt the hot tears come to her eyes again. "Oh, Josiah, look at me. Look at this dress and this veil." Her hands went from one to the other as she spoke. "This is ridiculous."

"Well, maybe the circumstances are, but you truly look beautiful, little Jessie. You are indeed a grown-up woman after all." His eyes warmed to a dark blue as he took in every outlined curve of her, every soft detail, every dark curl on her head.

Jessie's tears dried instantly under this scrutiny. It embarrassed and warmed her otherwise, but still she needed to say some things to him. She knelt down on her side of the raised gate and put her hands on the top of it. This put her almost level with Josiah. "Josiah, you have to know that I never cried to Bertha about us not being married yet. She was questioning me and misunderstood what—"

"I know, little Jessie," he said tenderly, brushing back a curl from her eye. "I don't blame you for any of this."

His hands on her face made it hard for Jessie to swallow. She hurried on with her words. "We don't have to get married, Josiah. I was thinking that we could get away—right now—on Blaze, just like this morning, and—"

The hand came away from her face. Why did he look angry, or was it insulted, or disappointed? Jessie couldn't tell. "And go where, Jessie? Camp Nichols is now further away than when we started. And we still don't know where out there in the darkness Hayes is." He swept his arm out behind him to indicate the vast prairie. "And we can't run Blaze in this darkness. He could break a leg in a prairie dog hole."

She hadn't thought of that. "So we're stuck? We have to get married?" she asked plaintively.

"Afraid so. Look, Jessie, I know you must hate this whole thing. Just try to remember that it's not a real marriage—just a real wedding. You and I know the truth. We're not runaway lovers at all. I can't get you out of this tonight, but if you hate the idea so much, there is a way for you to get yourself out of it. What I mean is, *we* don't have to get married. I have to get married. *You* have another option. You can tell the sergeant the truth, the real truth, and be done with me." With that, he started to pull away from her and the wagon.

At that moment, the sounds of approaching voices filtered down the long rows of wagons. They grew steadily louder. The wedding was coming to them. Jessie's head turned automatically in the direction of the voices and then right back to Josiah. He raised

99

an eyebrow, as if to say, well, Jessie, what will it be?

"Well, here we are, child. Everything is ready. Are you?" Bertha beamed, her broad apple-cheeks dimpling with her smile. She looked expectantly from Jessie to Jake and back again.

Jessie saw the Army sergeant right behind Bertha, along with the preacher and about a hundred other people. Some of them had even put on Sunday clothes in honor of the occasion. She slowly stood up and held her hand out to the man she knew as Josiah Tucker. For better or worse, she couldn't desert this man now and she was willing to play along until she found out what and who he really was.

"I'm ready," she said.

A great cheer went up from the crowd. Jessie allowed Josiah to take her hand and help her step gingerly over the wagon gate. She held her long skirt up with her other hand. Once she was on the ground, Josiah looped her arm through his and, escorted by a gaily chattering crowd, they walked to the large cookfire where the ceremony was to take place.

Nestled alone in the dark in her hastily arranged marriage bed in the back of Bertha's wagon, Jessie could still hear the fiddles and the laughter of the celebrants. Just because the happy couple left after a few dances, amidst much good-natured ribbing, didn't mean the party was over. Bertha told her before they left the cookfire that she would sleep with some folks she knew and that the wagon had been readied for them by some other folks during the wedding. Jessie hadn't known what to say to that; she'd blushed a deep maidenly red, much to the delight of the assembled "guests."

And poor Josiah—if one more man had given him a congratulatory pounding on the back, every now and then hitting his wound, she was sure he would pass out or shoot someone. As it was, all he did was grin and bear it.

The wedding clothes and the wedding bed hadn't been the end of the surprises, either. Jessie twirled the narrow gold band around on her ring finger; Josiah had on one just like it. He was as surprised as she was when a complete stranger offered them the rings right before the wedding. He had a supply of rings he was taking to New Mexico and would be honored if they would accept them. Jessie figured they'd have to wear the rings at least until they separated from the wagon train and went on to Camp Nichols.

That brought a frown to Jessie's face. Josiah had it all planned. He'd leave her under the cover of night so the soldiers wouldn't see him and after he left her, the soldiers would see her safely back home, and her life would go on as before. Jessie shook her head; she just could not see herself going back to her old life. Even though it was only yesterday, it seemed to her like her solitary existence on the ranch was a thing of the distant past. In fact, she had trouble thinking about what it was she used to do before Josiah had come into her life. So much had happened. So much had changed. For one thing, she was married. At least in the eyes of the law.

Right then, at that point in her thoughts, the canvas flap opened and in climbed Josiah, backlit by the moonlight. His grimace told Jessie that he was still feeling all the backslapping. He didn't retie the canvas flaps, so some moonlight filtered in. Just like last night at her cabin, Jessie thought. As she watched, he worked his shoulder around in a slow arc. He then turned to her. It was all she could do not to duck under the covers she had pulled up to her chin. No man, except her father, had ever seen her in bed. And now here was this man who had every legal right to . . .

"Relax, Jessie. I'm not going to do anything," came his tired voice out of the semidarkness. Jessie watched as he searched around for some place to sit. Giving up, he sat on the edge of the bed. The covers crept up a little further.

He reached over to pull them down so he could see her face. Jessie tried to look unconcerned, but she knew she was probably failing miserably. Her white knuckles on the blanket told their own story. He just looked at her and began loosening his collar. That done he took off his coat and gunbelt; he then leaned over to remove his boots. This was done with much straining. "Damn this shoulder," he suddenly spat out into the heavy silence.

Jessie jumped involuntarily. This brought his eyes back to her. Jessie felt her own widen in response. He turned his whole body toward her now, one arm resting on either side of her, his bent knee next to her covered thigh. Jessie suddenly felt very warm and wished she could throw her covers back. But that would have been worse, for then he would know that all she had on was the clean shirt Bertha had given her this morning. No one had thought to provide her with a nightgown. Or maybe they didn't think she would need one.

Oh, this was awful. All those people thinking they were . . . she couldn't complete the thought. But her body got the message. A warm tightness formed in the pit of her belly, like when he kissed her. She found she couldn't look at him right now and turned her head toward the canvas-covered wagon side.

"Look at me, little Jessie."

Jessie knew what he was thinking when he called her "little Jessie," so she didn't want to look at him. That look would be on his face, the one that said he wanted her, and it made her want to kiss him and do things to him like touch him and hold him—and more.

But she responded to his fingers on her chin and turned to face him. Yes, there was that look, only this time it was a little bit different, a little more tender. She waited for him to speak.

"Look, I told you I'm not going to do anything. You can relax. I wouldn't force myself on any woman, much less a child like you."

"Child? I'll have you know I'm eighteen and every bit a woman—" Jessie shot back, dropping her hold on the covers and sitting up so fast she smacked her forehead into his mouth.

Instinctively they both cried out and grabbed their injured areas. When Josiah's hand came away from his mouth, Jessie saw a little bit of blood. She'd busted his lip with her hard head. Taking her hands off her forehead, she reached out to touch his mouth, but he caught her hands in one of his and wiped his bloodied hand on the bedsheet.

"There," he said. "The deed is done. I was wondering how I was going to accomplish that. And I probably deserved a hit in the mouth for everything I've put you through."

Jessie lost his half-apology in her wondering what he meant. "What deed? What are you talking about?"

103

Josiah looked like he hadn't heard her right. "You mean you don't know? Great. Didn't your mother tell you anything?"

"Tell me what?" Jessie demanded. It was hard to act authoritative dressed in a man's shirt and sitting in bed.

"About . . . uh . . . you know, what happens when a woman—for the first time—she bleeds—" Josiah gave up and jumped up, running his fingers through his hair and pacing the narrow confines of the wagon interior. He looked almost angry when he turned back to her. "How in the hell did you get to be eighteen and not know anything? Most women have two to three babies by your age."

"And just who was I supposed to marry and learn all this stuff from? You've seen where I live." Jessie had her arms crossed under her breasts and her head cocked to one side.

"Forget it. I don't even know why we're having this conversation. I'll tell you this much. The blood needed to be there by tomorrow. It'll stop any curious questions Bertha would have had otherwise when you two are alone in the wagon."

"And that's another thing," Jessie said, pointing a finger at him. "Just how long are we staying with this wagon train? I have a homestead full of animals to care for, and a garden coming in, and wagon trains, and—"

"Please, don't remind me. I know what a mess you're in because of me. Believe me, I do. Just trust me for now, Jessie. I'll get you out of everything— including this marriage—and safely back home as soon as I can."

"And how can you do that?" Jessie shot back. She pulled herself up onto her knees on the bed and put her hands on her waist. "Maybe you haven't thought about this, but I have. What's to stop Hayes and his men from coming back to my place and torturing me or killing me because I rode with you and might know where you are?"

"Jessie, you're not going back home until this thing is over with. I planned on leaving you at Camp Nichols—"

"I know what your plan was. And that was fine when I was just an inconvenience for you, when you were just saving me. That I could have explained to the people there. But that was before I was corraled into this marriage. Do you mean to tell me that you're just going to slow Blaze down long enough to dump me off at the feet of people I have to see every month? With no explanation about why I'm married to an outlaw? Or hadn't you thought that maybe they might wonder about that? So what am I supposed to say—how am I supposed to explain this?" Anger punctuating her every word, her every move, Jessie held up her left hand and pointed to her wedding band.

Josiah just stared at her and didn't answer for a minute. "Cover yourself, Jessie," was all he said, and he said it very evenly through gritted teeth.

It took Jessie a second to comprehend what he'd said. He pointed to her chest area. She instantly looked down to see that, in her twistings and turnings in the bed, her shirt had come unbuttoned all the way to her waist. It now gaped open to reveal most of her breasts and her bandage-covered midriff. She quickly closed the shirt, tugging one side over the other and holding them together with her crossed arms. She was so angry she was sweating, causing her loose hair to stick to her face. But, she

105

didn't dare let go of the shirt to brush it away. "And just how long has my shirt been open like that? You could have told me!"

"Jessie, think about it. I did tell you—and I really didn't have to, you know. It just fell open when you raised your hand to show me your wedding band."

That silenced her for a moment. No matter what else he might be, he was also now her husband. It suddenly occurred to her that he had every right to see her breasts—and more. Not wanting to give him time to come to that realization himself, Jessie very hurriedly, and with more heat than necessary, picked up the argument where they'd left off.

"And don't you change the subject, Josiah Tucker. My open shirt won't get you off that easily! As usual you haven't answered me—and you'd better, because the minute I tell my story, those men will throw you in jail!"

"No, they won't; but you'd like that, wouldn't you?" Josiah shot back.

"Yes—no! And why wouldn't they arrest you? Were you going to lie to them, too?"

This brought him to the bed in one long stride. He towered over her, but Jessie refused to back down, even when he grabbed her up by her shoulders, pulling her halfway off the bed. She defiantly raised her chin and stuck her bottom lip out at him. His deeply blue eyes blazed fire into hers.

"I ought to shake the salt out you, girl!"

"Go ahead! Why don't you? Are you a coward, too, as well as a liar and a murderer?"

His lips pulled back into a snarl to reveal gritted teeth; too late, Jessie realized she'd gone too far. She was sure she would be his next victim. She had the eeriest feeling, as if she were suspended in time. She wasn't even sure her heart was beating, and she didn't dare breathe. Everything was quiet—deadly quiet as he glared at her, more than glared; he looked like a kill-crazed animal to Jessie.

Just as suddenly as he had grabbed her, he let her go. She fell in a crumpled heap on the bed and burst into tears. Great racking sobs shook her body as she cried into the pillow. She didn't know what he was doing until she felt his hands on her shoulders again, but this time they were gentle and were trying to turn her over.

"No!" she sobbed. "Leave me alone—that's what you were going to do anyway. So just leave now! I hate you!"

But he was not to be brushed away. She felt his weight press down the bedding next to her, and then she was being lifted onto his lap. With one hand, he held her head to his chest; his other hand was around her waist. Jessie realized she was actually being rocked and patted. He was soothing her like he would a small child. But she didn't care—not right now anyway. Everything was just too much for her and she needed to be held.

Jake shook with the force of his own emotions. With his chin resting on the top of Jessie's head and his arms about her, all he could think of was that he could have killed her—very easily. He could have snapped her in two. He cursed his nasty temper and the effect this small girl—woman—had on him. He'd never before given up the iron control necessary for his line of work, so why now?

He stroked her silky hair and rocked her. She had two handfuls of his shirt clutched to her. Jake thought back to her last outburst. Was that the third

107

or fourth time in one day she'd been afraid he would leave her or had already left her? Well, add a fear of being alone to her fear of dark, enclosed places like tunnels; Jake shook his head. A smile played with his lips.

When he thought more about it, he felt he could understand her fear of being left alone. After all, her parents were dead—they'd left her. And people didn't just spring up here in the middle of the prairie—she had to have left from some place, been uprooted at some time.

And now here he was. He had to leave her. But, like it or not, he was, at least for the time being, her anchor. And he didn't like it—not one bit. There was no room for a wife and a family . . . That stopped Jake cold; he even stopped rocking and looked down at her. No room for a wife? Well, here she was in his lap. Finally he had to admit it to himself—his anger this evening had to do with the way he was drawn to her despite his head sending up warning bells, and with the very fact that she was now his wife, and with the fact that there wasn't a damn thing he could do about it. No way could he consummate this marriage. That would make it real—for her, if not for him.

He realized Jessie was getting quiet and still. He looked down and tilted her chin up. She was asleep. He planted a very small kiss on her lips and gently put her in the bed to one side. He put on his boots and left the wagon to go tether Blaze out by the tree stump where he'd been earlier. Coming back into the wagon, he took his boots off and lay down beside Jessie, drawing her into his arms.

He told himself this bed was so narrow he had to hold her or fall off. Her warm, barely clad body did nothing for his resolve or his control, though. It was only by gritting his teeth and forcing himself to think of other things that he could finally ignore the scent of her and the feel of her very womanly curves in his arms, and drop off to sleep.

Damn this was torture! was one of his last waking thoughts. His other thoughts included coming up with a plan to separate him and Jessie from this wagon train. One thing was for sure—leaving this wagon train together would be a hell of a lot simpler than leaving her alone at Camp Nichols was going to be—for her, of course, not him. She was getting too attached to him, he rationalized; it would hurt her, but she'd live. Just then, his hand went to his chest; he was sure the heaviness there was from his shoulder wound.

Chapter Seven

Jake stood with Blaze while he drank deeply from the small stream near the wagon train. The sun was just now peeking over the low hills on the horizon; the deep-night blue lost ground to the hazy pinks and reds of dawn. Only a slight breeze whispered around Jake and tickled the leaves on the surrounding trees. He inhaled deeply. The late-summer, early-morning air already held the hint of the pounding heat of the afternoon sun.

Jake laughed at himself—this morning was the quickest he'd ever gotten out of bed. No way could he trust himself to lie there next to Jessie, especially with her head on his shoulder, her arm on his chest, and a bare leg thrown over him. And her long, black-brown hair fanned all over him. And of course there was his hand on her bottom.

Then he found himself responding to all this femininity and even heard the little voice in his head saying, go ahead, she is your wife, after all. It didn't help to know that, given her past responses to him, she would have allowed, even welcomed, his advances. But that was as far as it got before he firmly extricated himself from her hold and slipped out of the wagon. He was glad then that he had slept with his pants on.

There was nothing like the cold bath he'd just taken in the stream and the scraping off of his beard with his knife to cool him down. Bertha had left out soap and towels for them in the wagon last night. Just like a honeymoon suite, Jake thought. Wrong thought. Here came thoughts of Jessie and here came the effect she always had on him. Damn! The sooner he deposited Jessie at the camp, out of his reach as well as Hayes', the better off they'd both be.

By the time Blaze was through drinking, Jake was once again in control of himself. He was glad of that because other people from the wagon train were starting to show up at the stream to let their animals drink and to refill barrels. Jake spoke to a few of them in passing and recognized some of them from the wedding last night. He was only tepidly friendly—years of undercover work had taught him to avoid getting to know people too well. You never knew which ones you'd have to face with a gun in your hand. Jake even now wore his gun and took note of everything going on around him, without seeming to. That damn Hayes could be anywhere, and anyone on this train could be involved in the gunrunning. Until he knew better, he trusted no one.

111

As he walked back to the wagon where Jessie was, he fervently hoped she was up and dressed. She was too much for him in his bed, so close and yet so far away. She might as well be on the moon for all he could touch her.

Jake was shaken out of these thoughts by the sounds of galloping hooves. He stopped where he was, almost to the wagon, and listened. His trained ear told him the noise wasn't buffalo—not enough hooves and the ground wasn't trembling with their weight. So it was probably horses. Stepping from between the huge wagons, Jake saw the dust of several horsemen as they rode away at a gallop. Jake was instantly alert. The horses were heading back the way the wagon train had traveled yesterday. Something was wrong. The sudden dryness in his mouth and the tightness in the pit of his stomach told him something was very wrong.

He dropped Blaze's reins, knowing the stallion would follow him, and took off at a run for Bertha's wagon. Even though it was only a distance of yards, Jake felt like his heart would burst before he got there. No, no, no, was all he was thinking with each heartbeat and each running step. His first sight of the wagon heightened his sense of dread. The back flaps were not down as he had left them, but were drawn sharply back and over the sides of the wagon, and the gate was down. Maybe Bertha had come back; it was his only hope.

Jake ignored the sharp bursts of pain in his shoulder as he jumped up onto the gate and burst into the wagon. Jessie's name died on his lips when he saw the mess. Signs of a struggle were everywhere; crates were knocked over, their contents spilled onto the floor. The covers on the bed were thrown to the other side of the big wagon's interior. But Jake was not concerned with these; his trained mind merely took in these details. The object of his concern lay unmoving on what was left of the bed. Jake immediately went to her, kicked a small crate out of the way, and knelt beside her.

"Damn you to hell, Hayes!" Jake cried out in anger and anguish, looking at her still form. He also cursed himself because his moment of inattention, his moment of non-vigilance, had caused injury to another innocent person. Jake quickly looked her over. No obvious signs of injury; no blood at least. Jake put two fingers to her neck trying to feel a pulse. There was one, a strong one. He dropped his head in relief and let his breath out. His head snapped back up when she started to moan and come awake. Jake put his hands on her shoulders; not knowing who was attacking her now, she began to fight him and hit out blindly.

"No, Bertha, it's okay. You're all right now. No one is going to hurt you. Bertha, wake up. Where's Jessie? Where's Jessie, Bertha? You've got to wake up and help me. Come on now."

Finally his insistent words penetrated her fog and Bertha opened her eyes. Seeing Jake there, she tried to sit up, tried to speak, but fell instantly back onto the bed, holding her head and moaning.

"I know it hurts, Bertha, but you've got to try. You've got to help me, if we're going to get Jessie back." Jake gently brushed her hands away from her head and felt around there. He found a huge lump.

Those bastards—she was an old woman. Jake figured he knew why they hadn't just killed her and Jessie outright. Hayes wanted him, and him

113

alone. Too many murders would draw too many lawmen after Hayes, and that would endanger his gunrunning business. No, to kill one undercover lawman, whose death would go unpublicized to protect the operation, was Hayes' aim. Jake knew Hayes had figured out his identity and was gutless enough, and devious enough, to try to draw him out by using Jessie. Jake vowed he would kill Hayes if he harmed her in any way.

"Oh, my head, son. My head," Bertha moaned aloud. Then she grabbed up a handful of Jake's shirt as he bent over her. "Those men—they took Jessie. I tried to stop 'em, but they was too many. You got to go after 'em!"

"I know you did, Bertha. And I will go after her. I promise you that. But you've got to help me. Tell me exactly what happened and everything that was said."

"That child has some mean kinfolk. No wonder you had to run away to marry her. What've they got against you? The fact that you're decent and law-abidin'?"

Jake almost smiled. He knew she was feeling better now. She was getting feisty. As much as he hated to push her just now, he felt he had no choice. With every passing second, Jessie was being carried further away. "Bertha, are you completely awake now? Good. Here let me help you sit up. Do you want some water? No? Do you feel like you can answer some questions now?"

With her head in her hands, she nodded yes. Jake had to admire this woman—she was strong, and not given to hysterics. Had she been otherwise, Jake knew he would have lost valuable time calming her down.

"Those men who took Jessie, did they say anything or do anything that would tell you where they're headed?"

She looked askance at Jake, as if he were a little simple. "Well, son, if they're her kinfolk, I imagine they'll just ride on home with her and wait for you."

"They're not her kinfolk, Bertha. I know this all sounds crazy, but I don't have time to explain. You'll just have to trust me. Now, what can you tell me to help me get her back?"

After giving Jake a sideways, narrow-eyed stare, Bertha thought for a moment before she began to speak. "Now, let me see. They was some of the same men I seen talking last night to the Army sergeant who brought you two here. They busted into my wagon right after I got here this morning. Jessie was still asleep, poor child. They kept a-yellin' where was Coltrane, where was Coltrane. I told 'em I didn't know no Coltrane. That made 'em real nasty-like. Just then, Jessie woke up. They spied her and grabbed her up, and her a-kickin' and a-fightin' every inch of the way! Just before they conked me on the head, they said Coltrane would know where to find her. And that's it. Who's this Coltrane fella, anyway?"

Jake saw no way out. After only a second's hesitation, he said, "That's me."

"That's you?" she came right back. Jake was once again favored with her sideways, evaluating look. "Well, I didn't get this old by asking questions that was none of my business. Look here, Tucker or Coltrane, or whoever you are, do you know where they're a-takin' her?"

115

"Yes, I do. The Stuart Homestead," Jake answered her very abstractedly. He stood up and began adjusting his gunbelt and checking his ammunition; his mind was racing with everything Bertha had told him. She had unwittingly confirmed two of his suspicions—that the Army was involved on some level in the gunrunning, and that Hayes had indeed been hiding in the wagon train.

"You can't go alone, son. There's too many of 'em. I can help you. I know where the Stuart place is. A train I was with a few years back stopped there."

Jake went to her and put a hand on her shoulder. "I thank you for that, but I can't let you endanger yourself any more than you already have." When she started to protest, Jake cut back in. "No, Bertha. Your leaving the wagon train would draw too much attention. I have to ask you not to tell anyone what really happened—especially the soldiers. My life and Jessie's depend on your silence. You can make up some story about us deciding to go on home now that we are married, or some such thing. Other than that—nothing. Now I have to go." He turned to leave, but was stopped by Bertha's restraining hand on his arm. He gave her a questioning look.

"At least let me fix you up some food and a canteen of water. You'll be a-needin' 'em. And take my saddle—no, I want you to have it. It'll make the ride easier for you. And here, take this, too. For the sun and all." She handed him a Stetson hat she'd pulled out of a nearby box.

"Bertha, I can't take these things. Jessie and I won't be returning to the wagon train. I couldn't get them back to you."

"Then you just consider them wedding gifts," she insisted, pressing the hat into his hands. "Now, time's a-wastin' while you stand here and argue with me. Get that saddle on your horse and I'll fix your provisions. Go on—scat!"

Giving her a quick grin and an affectionate squeeze on her arm, Jake turned to go. Once more her voice stopped him.

"Coltrane, just one thing."

"Yes?"

"You and Jessie. You weren't really a-runnin' from kinfolk what didn't want you to get married, were you?"

Jake grinned again. "No. No, we weren't." With that, he jumped to the ground, untied the saddle from the side of the wagon, and went to saddle Blaze.

He was too far away then to hear Bertha talking out loud to herself, "Well, I'll be! And here my darn-fool meddling got them married. It might get me killed, but I've got to know what's a-goin' on that got me conked on the head. Santa Fe can wait; right now I'm a-headin' for the Stuart Homestead."

Jessie didn't know which hurt the most—her jaw from where Skinner had hit her to stop her struggling, her wrists from the ropes which bound them to the pommel of the horse she was riding, her cut midriff, or her bottom from the jarring, bouncing ride through the wagon ruts made only yesterday. She was humiliated to be among these low-down sorts with only a shirt on. How she wished she'd left those borrowed bloomers on!

But it was too late for bloomers or wishes. The wind and sun were once again burning her face and legs, and her hair was blowing wildly out behind her. Jessie's mind was just now shaking off the numb terror of her abduction. All she could think about was Skinner and a Mexican man bursting into the wagon, grabbing her, and hitting Bertha hard on the head. She prayed that Bertha's kindness had not gotten her killed. Jessie knew that all her tears were not just from the wind and sun.

And Josiah. Jessie tried her best to turn herself so she could see behind her, see some sign that he was riding out after them. But, try as she might, she could not turn around far enough. And since her horse's reins were held by Hayes himself, she had no way of suddenly breaking away from these outlaws. Outlaws. Jessie took in the slouching, grim-faced men riding all around her. Josiah was one of these outlaws. Jessie's tears fell even harder.

She tried to think about where they were taking her and why. She knew why—to draw Josiah out and then kill them both. That thought sobered her some. The tears quit falling. She forced herself to pay attention to where she was headed. With the sun about even with her right shoulder, she knew it had to be about mid-morning, so they had been running for more than a few hours. With only the wagon ruts to guide her as to where they were headed, Jessie knew that they would pass very close to her home-stead if they stayed on this northerly course. Unless they had a secret hideout somewhere, the only other place they could go, besides her homestead, was to Camp Nichols. Somehow she just did not see them riding into the arms of the law.

Just then Jessie thought she dimly remembered Skinner telling Bertha to tell—who? Colter or Coltrane, something like that—that he would know where to find them. This thought made Jessie a little more hopeful that Bertha was

alive. Maybe Skinner had only knocked poor
Bertha out, just like he'd stunned her with his
fist, so she wouldn't raise a fuss but could wake
up to give a message to that Colter or Coltrane.
Jessie only hoped that Bertha had more of an
idea than she did about who Coltrane—yes that
was it!—was. The only person Jessie could come
up with would be the Army sergeant. But that
didn't make any sense either. Why would outlaws
tell the Army where they were? After all, it was
the military's shipment of guns they stole.

None of this made sense to Jessie's spinning head.
She tried to put it from her mind and to concentrate on keeping herself alive. She felt relatively safe
as long as they kept on the move. But once they
stopped for water and rest, or once they arrived
at their destination, Jessie knew that her chances
of keeping herself intact and alive were cut in half.
Especially seeing how close Skinner rode to her
and the way he kept looking at her. She sincerely
hoped that he did not recognize her as the "boy"
at the homestead who had ridiculed him in front
of Hayes when they had come asking about voices
that Skinner said he heard coming from the cabin.

Jessie was brought back to the present by the
commotion at her side. Skinner reached over to
her horse's bridle to help slow him down. Looking
wildly about, she realized that they were all coming
to a stop. The men, except Skinner and Hayes, got
off their horses to rest them; some of them drank
from their canteens, but no one offered Jessie any
relief. Not able to watch the men drinking while
she was so parched, Jessie turned her attention to
the two leaders. When Hayes and Skinner made no
effort to lower their voices, it was with a sinking

heart that Jessie realized the reason—they didn't expect her to live long enough to repeat what she heard.

"What the hell we stopping here for, Hayes? There ain't no water hereabouts."

"Ain't water I'm lookin' fer. I'm sendin' two men back to ride around that last hill we just come over to see if Coltrane is follerin' us yet."

Skinner gave a little snort. "Why, of course he is. We got her." He jerked his thumb back, indicating Jessie. She sat up a little taller in her saddle; she'd be darned before she let these rattlesnakes know she was afraid.

"Well, I just want to be sure he ain't bringin' no one else with him."

"Like who—that sergeant and his soldiers?"

At this they both broke into loud guffaws of laughter. Jessie's brows dipped in a frown; why weren't they afraid of the soldiers? There must have been about twenty or more of them at the wagon train, certainly more than Hayes' nine. And who was this Coltrane to care what happened to her and why would he want her?

When they finished laughing at their private joke, Skinner added, "You better let me go with 'em, Boss. Some of these boys ain't too bright and might not find their way back." This was followed by another burst of laughter.

Jessie was disgusted; they weren't even loyal to their own, and didn't even care if the other men overheard them. With Hayes still laughing, Skinner called out, "Sanchez, Romero, come on. We got some scoutin' to do."

The two men got up with grunts and muttered oaths, mounted their tired horses, and followed

Skinner. Jessie recognized the one called Sanchez as the one who had participated in her abduction. He had been very free with his hands, letting them wander over her near-naked body until Skinner put a stop to it—angrily and quickly, too, now that Jessie thought about it. She turned some in her saddle to watch the three men ride off.

"Thinkin' 'bout tryin' to git away, missy?"

Jessie jerked back around at the sound of Hayes' voice so close to her. He'd brought his horse around to her other side and was even now putting a dirty hand on Jessie's bare thigh. The skin on her leg crawled, showing Jessie's disgust as clearly as her expression did. Without a word, she spit in his face.

There was instant silence among the five remaining outlaws. They stopped whatever they'd been doing and stared like statues at their boss and the girl. Jessie caught them out of the corner of her eye, but all her hatred was reserved for Hayes. She never even looked away. She'd acted without thinking, but even though she knew she'd gone too far and she could lose her life right here, she was still glad she'd done it.

Hayes slowly took his hand off her thigh, untied his dirty bandanna from his neck, and wiped his face off. His beady, ferret eyes remained locked with hers. He threw his cigar to the ground. He then turned to the five men and said, "Hey, boys, now won't this little hellcat be fun tonight? Wonder if ole Coltrane will still want her so bad after we're all through with her. I'll just bet that Skinner and them Mexicans will want in on the action, too."

The men hooted and laughed, calling out obscene things they were going to do to her. Hayes laughed right in her face and moved his horse away from her. He still held tight to her mount's reins. Jessie's blood ran cold. Had she not been tied to the horse, she would have fallen off him in a dead faint. What Hayes had planned for her was much worse than death, much worse. Even though Jessie trembled, she managed to still keep her chin high and her expression clear. She promised herself that she would take her first chance to escape, or denied that, she would grab any unwatched weapon she could and do away with as many of them as she could before they could kill her.

Hayes ordered the other men to mount up, telling them they would have their chance tonight, but he was first. With that, they rode off at a canter, putting distance between them and the wagon train, but also going slow enough to allow Skinner and the other two scouts time to catch up.

Jessie fervently prayed that Josiah would find her before nightfall. If not, she would just have to see how quickly she, too, could become a murderer. She remembered Josiah's question to her at the cabin—could she kill a man if her life depended on it? She'd answered yes then without understanding the accompanying emotion that went with those words. Now she knew how it felt firsthand. Maybe she'd judged Josiah too quickly and too harshly when she branded him a murderer. After all, here she was contemplating the same thing. To keep up her courage, she clung to the murderous rage; it was more comforting than fear.

Before they had ridden too far, loud reports of gunfire in the hills behind them brought Hayes and his men up short. They had their guns in their hands and the horses turned toward the sound almost before Jessie realized what she was hearing. She waited as tensely as they did to see or hear what would happen next. They didn't have long to wait, for over the rise came a lone rider, his horse stretched flat out, covering the ground at an alarming pace and heading right for them. Jessie's hopes for rescue rose briefly, but were dashed instantly when Hayes spoke.

"Don't shoot yet, boys. It's Skinner. But he ain't got Romero and Sanchez with him. Keep a lookout—someone's got him on the run."

No one spoke again until Skinner caught up with them. The closer he got, Jessie could see that he kept looking behind him as if he was being followed, but try as she might, she could not make out anybody else in the distance. No raised dust behind Skinner told of other riders. She slumped dejectedly in her saddle.

Skinner reined up hard when he got to Hayes. His sweat-soaked stringy hair and foam-flecked mount told of fear and flight. He reported to Hayes in a gulping voice, stopping between short sentences to catch his breath; his large Adam's apple bobbed up and down with each swallow. "It was that damned Coltrane . . . he ambushed us . . . got Romero and Sanchez cold before I could even get off a shot . . . I might have hit him . . . couldn't tell . . . he took off for some trees back there . . . probably still there, thinking we aim to come back and git 'im."

"Damn his hide!" Hayes spat out. "I should-a killed him the minute I knowed who he was. Vasquez ain't gonna like this."

"What ya want ta do now, Boss? Want ta go back and git 'im?" Skinner asked. He opened his canteen and drank down several quick gulps. He kept his eyes on his boss.

"Now, hush up and let me think a minute. Ain't so sign of 'im comin' this way yet. Maybe ya did git him, Skinner. But maybe ya didn't. I don't want to lose no more men by ridin' back inta his ambush. An' as long as we got the girl here, Coltrane will keep followin' us and won't be reportin' in to anyone and messin' up our plans. We better ride on; we got ta get that shipment right quick-like. We can do that and git Coltrane at the same place and time."

"Yeah, that's good thinkin', Boss. Coltrane will have ta go slow, thinkin' we ambushin' him somewhere. And we can git our business done afore he even gits ta the Stuart Homestead. Then, we'll have the guns, the girl, and Coltrane. Yep, I like it!" Skinner recapped his canteen and hung it from his saddle; he swiped a dirty arm across his mouth to dry it. "Let's go git them guns!"

The men spurred their horses forward, hooting in laughter at their own smartness. Jessie was stunned. Her mind reeled, not so much now from the heat and the lack of water, but more from everything she'd just heard. Her head had snapped up at Skinner's mention of her home—the Stuart Homestead. From what she could make of it, everything would happen once they got there. She calculated that would be sometime tomorrow morning.

As her bone-jarring ride continued, Jessie tortured herself with questions she could not answer. She had learned enough from listening to Hayes and Skinner to know that the only reason she'd been taken and kept alive was because of Coltrane wanting her badly enough to risk his life to get her back. What was she to him? She wondered again. And what was Coltrane to these outlaws?

124

And where was Josiah? Was he coming after her? And the soldiers—wouldn't they come, too? She thought she knew Bertha well enough to know that she would raise an alarm once she woke up from being hit on the head. If she woke up. That thought made Jessie shudder. Poor Bertha. She was so kind—and so innocent in all this. It just wasn't fair. Please let Bertha be alive, Jessie prayed, closing her eyes. And please let Josiah come for me. Please. Jessie squeezed her eyes shut even more tightly, trying to force an image of Josiah to come to her. And it did—but not one she'd bargained for.

Devilishly blue eyes, a firm mouth slanting over hers, and a muscled, tanned torso popped into Jessie's mind. She almost choked on the image, and forced it and the sudden warm tension in her belly to go away. After all, why should she want him? He obviously didn't want her. If he did, he would be chasing Hayes down like the animal he was, like this Coltrane was doing. Jessie continued to torture herself with images of Josiah finding her gone, of being glad she was, of taking off and throwing away his gold wedding band, and then of riding off, not caring a fig what happened to her.

What more could she expect from an outlaw? She knew that the gold band on his finger would not make him feel like he owed her anything. He hadn't wanted to marry her, much less even to touch her last night; and that was all well and good with her—she didn't want him to touch her, either. If he tried, he'd get what he deserved. Just like these low-down outlaws would if they tried anything. Jessie was now back to where she'd started. She was angry again, murderously angry.

*   *   *

The riderless horse coming toward him confirmed for Jake that he had indeed heard gunshots just a few minutes ago. He reined Blaze to a halt and sat tensely in the borrowed saddle, waiting and listening. Jake's mouth was set in grim lines—if they'd so much as harmed a hair on her head . . . But, before he could spur Blaze forward, he heard another horse approaching him from over the hill in front of him. Jake nudged Blaze toward a stand of three or four trees to his right. No sense being a clear target. But he stopped Blaze before he ever reached the trees. This second horse was also riderless. What was going on? Before this horse spooked at Jake's presence and ran off, Jake took in the ornate saddle work, the kind with a lot of silver and tooled designs, the kind done in Mexico.

Jake turned Blaze back onto the trail. He wouldn't find any answers sitting here. He moved forward cautiously, attuned to every noise and every movement around him, knowing how Hayes worked best in cowardly ways like ambushes and back-shooting. But, Blaze's sudden high-prancing, neck-arching sidestep as they came around a small bend in the trail would have gotten a less experienced rider thrown to the ground. "What the—?" was all Jake could manage as he fought to keep Blaze from rearing. Then he saw them, too—two bodies. They were lying face down on the trail about twenty yards ahead.

"Whoa, easy there, boy. Easy," Jake crooned and petted the high-spirited animal, all the while keeping his eyes on the bodies and then sweeping the surrounding area with a quick glance. Whoever had done this was long gone. Jake dismounted; keeping a firm grip on Blaze's reins, he approached the bodies. When he was a little closer, he was struck by the unsettling feeling that these dead men were not strangers to him. The sight of the ornate silverwork on the dead men's chaps and spurs and the wide-brimmed sombreros they wore instantly brought the Mexican saddles on the riderless horses to Jake's mind. Romero and Sanchez. Jake knew it even before he nudged the bodies over with his toe to get a look at their faces.

This didn't make any sense. Jake knew for a fact that he was the only one following Hayes. So who could have done it? Hayes wouldn't kill these two—they were Vasquez's men, the Mexican link in the gunrunning operation. Jake could just see Hayes trying to explain this to Vasquez; Vasquez had them ride with Hayes to "protect his interests," a nice way of saying he didn't trust Hayes.

Vasquez was a very rich, aristocratic Mexican rancher—or so he appeared to be. A cutthroat revolutionary with a need for Colt revolvers was more like it. So many shipments had been diverted to Vasquez that there was an actual shortage of Colts for the Army's use. No one had to remind Jake of just how important his success in this mission was. It gave a sense of urgency to everything he did.

But he had to admit his urgent need to find Jessie and get her to safety was much stronger in him than was the mission. She had saved his life, and now he had to do the same thing for her. Her, he could help, unlike these two who were lying dead on the ground. Jake remounted Blaze and moved around the bodies, giving them one last look. He didn't feel sorry for them at all—they were in the same category as Hayes, as far as Jake was concerned.

But, the question of just who did kill them and why kept nagging at Jake. The only logical conclusion was someone in Hayes' gang. Jake felt this was as much a mystery as who had dragged him out of the root cellar and up to Jessie's door two nights ago. That had to have been someone in the gang, too, and most likely the same person.

No, none of this made sense, Jake reflected as he rode off after Hayes and Jessie. Then, catching sight of the gold band on his left hand, Jake laughed to himself—now that made the least sense of all! He couldn't believe he'd met Jessie one day, married her the next, had only shared a fairly chaste kiss or two with her, despite sleeping with her for two nights, and now, on the third day, had lost her. *No*—he hadn't lost her. She'd been taken away from him. And Jake didn't like that, not at all. She was just an innocent kid, despite being a married woman of eighteen.

Big, dark-fringed brown eyes; silky waves of black-brown hair; a small, scared figure in a dark tunnel; full, rosy-tipped breasts. These varied images turned slowly through Jake's mind. He felt the tension in him grow, angry tension and, yes dammit, sexual tension. But that was too bad, he told himself. He'd just have to get over wanting her. She deserved better—better than what she was going through now and in the past few days, better even than what he could ever offer her. Not that she would want him.

Jake knew what his more immediate mission was. He had to get Jessie free—free from Hayes and free from himself—and back to her own life, where she had a chance of finding a loving husband who'd give her everything she wanted. Someone she could count on, someone she deserved. No, that ring on his finger didn't mean anything. The marriage was a sham, a cover, something they'd both had to do, not wanted to do. She deserved better than this, better than him.

With a nudge of his knees, Jake urged Blaze forward. Hell wouldn't be able to hide Hayes and his gang if any one of them touched her in any way. Even though Jake knew in his mind that he had to stay calm and think clearly if he hoped to get both of them out of this alive, he couldn't deny or suppress the murderous rage that gripped his heart.

Chapter Eight

"Come on, ya flop-eared galoot! Gitty up, ya danged sack of bones and long ears! I'd have me better luck a-ridin' a buffalo! Ain't nothin' more stubborn on God's green earth than a Missouri mule! I'll eat you for dinner if'n you don't git to movin'!"

The mule's long ears pricked back and forth, but nothing else happened to prove he heard Bertha's threats or felt the switch on his rump as she prodded him onward. Bertha's red face and wild hair told of her frustration with her mount. Honest to Pete, she didn't know why she'd hung on to him for the past eight years. She'd never even named him—didn't deserve one. "Mule" was good enough for him.

Bertha looked back over her shoulder at the departing wagon train moving in the opposite direction from her. She waved one last time to the people she knew in one of the rear wagons.

She knew they'd get her an honest price in Santa Fe for her goods. Their teen-aged son had been thrilled with the chance to drive a big wagon all by himself. These were home folks from Lexington; she could trust them with the money until she met up with them again in Missouri.

Bertha smiled smugly to herself; she was pretty proud of the little story she'd made up to tell them. She'd said that she was a-headin' for the Stuart Homestead, that the missus there was distant kin of hers and was sick and needed her help. She'd gone on to say that Jessie knew of the Stuarts and had just mentioned to Bertha about her cousin's illness. No, she let on, this was surely not what she planned when she left Lexington, but you know how it is, family is family. And maybe she could do some good with the newlyweds' families, maybe smooth things over some, and tell them for sure the two was married and not a-makin' it up.

Yes, Bertha thought to herself now, that was a pretty good story, even if she had to say so herself. And just a lone rider a-leavin' the wagon train wasn't bound to cause so much of a stir—not like a wagon a-pullin' out would. So she hadn't done nothing to hurt the kids any—no one but the people she'd turned her wagon over to even knew she'd left. And it'd be nightfall before they had a chance to even tell anyone who might ask about her. By then, anybody in the train who concerned Coltrane would be too far away to do them any harm.

So here she was now, headed for the Stuart place with just herself, the danged mule, and some provisions. She was glad now that this wagon train had not stopped at the Stuarts'; if they had, she couldn't have used her story about being related and all. The

Stuart Homestead had been a planned stop, sure enough, but the message had been passed down the line from the lead wagons that the sergeant said it wasn't safe to go there just now—something about hostile Indians in the area. Bertha wasn't worried about Indians bothering her; she knew they thought it was bad medicine to mess with crazy people. And what could be crazier than an old woman on a mule out here by herself?

And maybe she was crazy for poking her nose into whatever trouble the two kids was in. But, dang it, she felt like she'd added to their troubles by a-causin' them to have to get married. And here they'd had no intention of doin' so! None of this made sense to Bertha. What was these kids a-runnin' to or from? Couldn't even tell the soldiers what was a-goin' on. Must be something to do with the law. Now, Jessie was too sweet an' innocent a child to have done anything wrong. But now that Coltrane fella—he looked like he knew how the cow ate the cabbage, as they said back home. Yes sir, Coltrane had that savvy look about him, like he'd seen a lot and done a lot in this world. If they was in real trouble, it was likely because of his doin's.

Well, one thing was for sure, whatever the problem was with those kids and those bad men, the kids could use another gun on their side. She wasn't known as the best shot in Lexington for nothin'. She had her third and last husband Henry, God rest his soul, to thank for that; he'd taught her the finer points of shooting a gun before they signed on with the wagon trains. Yes sir, this was her fifth trip to Santa Fe, her third one by herself. Ole Henry only made the trip twice before he died. That'd left her alone—never did have no kids. Maybe that was why she took so quick-like to Jessie. The child seemed to need motherin'.

For the life of her, Bertha could not figure out how Jessie got hooked up with Tuck—Coltrane. Now, there was the devil of it! Why in the world would he lie to Jessie and even marry her under the name of Tucker when his real name was Coltrane? What was he a-hidin'? Well, she harrumphed, whatever it was, she sure as shootin' knew Jessie wasn't no part of it. Might have to protect the child from Coltrane, too. Wouldn't let no man use a girl like that. She decided that Coltrane had a lot to prove before he got by her with Jessie. She knew for a fact that he'd already taken advantage of her twice—married her under a false name and then he'd bedded her on their weddin' night—she'd seen the sheets. But, on his side, he'd been a wild man when he'd seen she was gone and he'd took right out after her alone. Maybe he wasn't all bad.

"Now, git on up, there, mule! Git on! You think I didn't know you'd slowed down some more? You ain't as smart as you think! Now come on! Git!" With much prodding, switching, and cussing of her mule, Bertha inched ever closer to the Stuart Homestead.

"Suit yerself. You ain't hurtin' me none if ya don't eat," Skinner said; with a shrug of his bony shoulders, he put Jessie's food on the ground by her and sat down nearby. He kept his eyes on her while he ate.

Jessie looked at him and then at the hard biscuit, jerky, and the tin cup of water beside her. She wasn't being stubborn; she would have loved to eat, but her hands were still too numb to grip anything. She rubbed her wrists as best she could to get the feeling back in them. Even this was painful because the rope had rubbed them raw. She shook her hands vigorously, hoping that would help. After a few minutes of rubbing and shaking, she was able to grip the tin cup with both hands and get her first drink of water since that morning. Nothing had ever tasted so good. She wished she had enough to pour some on her sunburned thighs, but she was afraid to draw attention to her state of undress by asking for more water for that purpose.

When she had drunk all her water, she reached for her food and began chewing it slowly. A sound from Skinner made her look over at him. His smug look as he watched her eat irritated Jessie. But she was too near exhaustion from the hours in the saddle, hours under the baking sun with no relief, to care if he thought he'd won a victory of some sort. Jessie turned away from him with a disdainful air she did not feel.

In fact, she was sure she would be crying right now if she'd had enough water in her to make tears. She refused to acknowledge to herself that she was near defeat, but it was true. Right now she didn't even care what happened to her. She ate her rough meal almost mechanically, suspending thought willingly. It was enough right now to just sit in the grass in the late-day shade and chew. The tree she was sitting against was rough to her shirt-covered back, but she didn't mind. She'd inched as far away as she could from where Hayes and his men were laughing and eating. She was relieved when Skinner finally got up and moved away from her. He made her very nervous by staying so close to her all the time.

Alone now, Jessie took the time to look around her. Open prairie with only a few hills and trees dotting the landscape. The tall grass waved hypnotically in the breezy wind that blew her hair continually into her face. Jessie didn't even bother to brush it away. What was the use? She felt her eyelids begin to droop. The warmth, the shade, and the food combined to make her drowsy.

"Here, put these on. And drink up. We got to go now."

Skinner's rough voice and something landing in her lap brought Jessie to instant wide-eyed alertness. She jumped visibly and had to sit blinking for a second or two before she could register what was going on. She looked in her lap—a pair of pants. Shading her eyes, she looked up at Skinner, but the sun blocked his face from her. She did, however, see the tin cup he held out to her. He'd refilled her water. Jessie was not about to ask questions— she quickly took the cup and greedily drank down the water. Handing the cup back to him she said, "Thanks, Skinner." Those were the first words she'd spoken to anyone in this gang since this morning.

"Don't make nothin' out of it. That'd be a mistake on yer part." He then turned away stiffly and crossed his arms, obviously waiting for her to put the pants on. Jessie still sat for an instant, puzzled by his reply, but even more so by his show of concern for her. Then, shrugging her shoulders, she got up as quickly as she could move her sore muscles and, bracing herself by leaning her bottom against the tree, pulled on the pants. They were obviously an extra pair of Skinner's because they were so long that she could have fit into them twice, and they weren't the cleanest. But she was not complaining.

135

She rolled up the bottom of the pants as best she could, but left them long enough to cover the tops of her burned feet when she was in the saddle. Since he'd not given her anything with which to hold the pants up, Jessie just held them with her hands.

She cleared her throat to let Skinner know she was done. When he turned around, Jessie saw a muscle twitch in his jaw as he looked at her, and some emotion flickered across his face. It wasn't humor, even though she knew she looked funny enough. No, it was something else, something that troubled him. But whatever it was, it was gone in an instant. "Come on," was all he said before turning away and walking toward the horses.

As she walked toward her horse, Jessie wished she had three hands as she struggled to keep the pants up around her waist and at the same time hold up the bottoms of the pants so she didn't trip. So intent was she on her task that it was a few moments before the men's catcalls and jeering broke into her consciousness. With a shock, she realized they were taunting Skinner, and not her.

"Why, Mother Skinner, ain't you the sweetest one!"

"Lookee here. He done covered her up right prim and proper-like. She won't need them pants tonight!"

"Yeah, maybe Skinner thinks if he's all nice to her, he won't have to fight her tonight to get what he wants!"

"Hey, Skinner, I heard of giving someone the shirt off yer back, but not the pants off yer—"

Skinner's fist in his mouth cut off whatever else the man had been going to say. He landed on his back on the ground; blood spurted from his mouth.

He put his hand to his mouth, wiped at the blood, and jumped up. "Why, you—"

"Knock it off, the both of yaz!" Hayes yelled, getting between the two men. "We ain't got time fer this. All of ya mount up. I mean it, Skinner, cut it out."

After a tense second in which the two men stayed squared off with fists raised, the other man gave first. "She ain't worth it nohow," he grumbled, lowering his fists and bending over to pick up his hat. He kept wiping away the blood from his split lip as he mounted his horse. The other men had been bunched around the two fighters, urging them on, but now they too dispersed and went to their horses.

Skinner wiped the blood from his knuckles onto his shirt, pulled out a knife from his saddlebag, and came toward Jessie with it and a length of rope, the rope which had tied her hands to the pommel. He was glaring at her, as if she'd caused all this fighting. But Jessie's eyes were on the rope. She felt her chin begin to quiver; she didn't want to whimper, but she really didn't think she could stand having her wrists bound again. They were already raw and bloody, like Skinner's knuckles.

But once again, Skinner surprised her. He used the knife to cut the rope and handed the shorter length to Jessie. She took it, but raised questioning eyes to him. "Fer yer pants. Tie 'em up so's they stay on," was all he said.

He turned and walked back to his horse. Jessie could only look at his retreating back again and wonder about him. She then quickly threaded the rope through the beltloops and knotted it in front. That done, she mounted her horse and waited. She wasn't tied now, and she held her own reins. No one was paying any attention to her just now. Jessie looked quickly around her. Maybe she could get away!

Then she met Skinner's eyes. She realized he'd been watching her to see what she would do. His point was made. If she didn't want to be left tied, undressed, and unfed, then she'd have to cooperate. His kindness had a price. His black eyes, even darker than Jessie's, looking at her over his hawk nose and wide, grim mouth, told her that if she tried it, there would be no more considerations. Jessie looked down and slumped the slightest bit. She couldn't risk losing whatever slight protection he was giving her, for some reason known only to him, from the rest of the men. And, besides, where would she go that they couldn't find her out here?

When Skinner reached over and held his hand out, Jessie very reluctantly handed over the reins. She took hold of the pommel as the gang started out again. They were moving closer and closer to her homestead. There, on familiar ground, she would make her stand or her escape. That is, if she survived tonight. Revived by the rest, the food, the water, and the clothes, Jessie felt her fighting spirit coming back. She still hadn't given up hope, either, that Josiah was indeed somewhere out there, waiting and watching for a chance to rescue her.

The man she knew as Josiah was at that very moment concealed from her sight in a small, dry rill between two low hills. He was lying on his belly watching them move off. Even though he was too far away to make out specific people and specific actions, he'd seen enough to know Jessie was okay. She had to be the little, short one in the baggy

clothes. He almost grinned at this. That was practically the only way he knew her. And he'd seen
the fight. Couldn't tell, though, who was involved.
And he could only wonder what they were fighting
about.

When they saddled up and moved out, Jake did
the same. He'd pretty much been forced to match
all his actions to theirs. He stopped when they did,
ate when they did, and rode when they did. Jake
always hated this part of his job, because it required
patience, something he did not have an abundance
of. Waiting and watching grated on his more natural
instinct to direct action. But he knew that a rash act
on his part right now could get both him and Jessie
killed. And that certainly was not part of his plan.

But, hell, nothing that had happened in the past
few days had been part of his plan! Being found
out by Hayes, shot, chased, running off with Jessie,
meeting up with the cavalry, joining a wagon train,
getting married—no, none of those could be called
a plan. Thinking how one small girl had upset this
entire mission, his and Hayes', causing both of them
delays and headaches, Jake laughed out loud. The
sudden noise in the otherwise quiet prairie startled
Blaze. He broke from his loping gait to sidestep and
fight the bit in his mouth. Jake quickly brought him
under control and reassured him with a pat on his
neck that his master was indeed not suffering from
sunstroke. A flick of Blaze's sensitive ears let Jake
know that Blaze was not entirely convinced.

As the afternoon and the long ride wore on, Jake
maintained his distance behind Hayes and his men,
who were setting a swift pace. There were no more
stops for food or rest. Jake knew the reason for their
hurry—they were late meeting the next shipment of

139

Colt revolvers meant for the Army. Their chasing Jake and Jessie to the wagon train and now having to backtrack had cost them a day. Jake reflected that if they harmed Jessie it would cost them more than a day; it would cost them their lives.

A grimness settled over Jake once more. He knew, as sure as the sun was beginning to set, that his time for waiting and watching would be over this very evening. Jake welcomed the chance to do something decisive for once, the chance to make things happen. He was tired of all the running away he'd been forced to do lately. He usually met trouble head-on, but not this time. He had more than his own life to consider. He now had Jessie—his wife. He allowed the word to slowly seep into his mind. Wife. Sham marrige or not, that was what she was. And that made him responsible. He now understood why the higher-ups preferred agents like himself not to be married. It slowed a man down, made him more cautious, less willing to take a risk. Jake promised himself that as soon as this assignment was complete his first task would be to have this marriage annulled, if indeed it was legal at all. Jake did not like the sudden pang this thought caused him in his stomach—or was that his heart?

He pushed all thoughts and pangs about Jessie from his mind in order to concentrate on being ready for action when the time came. Exactly what he did depended to a large extent on when and where Hayes made camp. He didn't worry about being detected by them; he knew they were aware of his following them. After all, wasn't that their objective in taking Jessie? Lead Jake, like a lamb, to the slaughter? Still, Jake was not keen on confronting them in daylight out in the open. He stood a better chance of success with night covering him and giving him the element of surprise. Yes, they knew he was coming, but they didn't know when or from where. And that was as good as having another gun or two on his side.

As the blazing late-summer sun set low over the horizon, Jessie felt her hopes sinking with it. How could she survive what Hayes had planned for her? Even more, would she want to survive it? She only hoped that she was so numbed and tired that maybe she would pass out and die before she had to experience much. But she knew better, even as she thought it. She'd never be too bone-weary tired or numb or burned or raw not to fight them every step of the way. Jessie gritted her teeth together in determination. She'd make them pay for what they got.

But when Jessie saw where they were going to camp for the night, she sat stiffly upright and tensed every muscle. Hayes had reined up at the same spot where she and Josiah had bathed and rested only yesterday morning, the same little stream with its stand of scrub oaks where Josiah had almost kissed her, the same spot where the soldiers had found them. The irony of this was too much for Jessie. No, not here. They couldn't ruin this place for her, too, not like they'd ruined her home with violent memories.

At this point in her thoughts, Jessie was brought back to the present by her horse stopping. She looked at Skinner. He was dismounting and indicated to Jessie to do the same. He'd ridden them over to the tree furthest away from the stream where camp was being set up. He tied both horses to a low limb and began unsaddling his mount. Jessie did likewise, keeping her horse between herself and the remaining men. She drew the heavy saddle off. It hit the ground with a thud. She stood there and stared dumbly at it. She wasn't sure she had the strength to lift it to put it against the tree trunk. Finally she managed to half-drag it the few feet to where she wanted it. She slumped down in a heap, resting her back against the saddle. She was hugging her knees to her chest and had her forehead resting on her knees when Skinner spoke to her.

"I'm taking the horses to water. You stay here. Do I need to tie you up?"

Jessie merely shook her head without looking up.

"I didn't think so." With that, Jessie heard him move away, taking the horses with him. After a moment or two, she raised her head slowly to see what was going on in camp. No one was paying her the least bit of attention as they worked at getting a campfire going. She saw that all the horses were unsaddled, hobbled, and were grazing close by. Some of the men, Hayes included, were at the stream washing off the dirt of the trail. Jessie was glad then that Skinner had left her here; she'd rather be thirsty and dirty than draw any attention to herself at the stream.

With no prying male eyes watching her, Jessie slipped around to the far side of the tree trunk to a small area of scrubby bushes to relieve herself. She was glad of the privacy for the first time today. When she stepped back out of the bushes, still tying her rope belt, and came around to the side of the tree trunk where her saddle was, she saw Skinner running towards her. She caught the look of relief on his face when he caught sight of her; he slowed to a walk and had his usual passive expression on his face when he reached her. "Here," was all he said, thrusting a canteen full of cool water and a bandanna at her. He turned away and walked to the campfire.

Jessie knew it was useless to thank him, so she didn't even try. And, besides that, thank him for what? Keeping the prisoner alive until they killed Josiah? Or until they could ravage her like Hayes had said? Thank him for hitting her in the jaw this morning and for shooting at her yesterday? No, she didn't owe him any thanks. Jessie took a long drink of the water and then wet the bandanna so she could clean herself up a little bit. That done, she ran her fingers through her hair, trying to get some of the thousands of tangles out of it. She told herself the tears spilling down her cheeks were from pulling at the tangles.

"Here, eat this," Skinner said, thrusting a tin plate of food into her hands. If he noticed her tears at all, he didn't comment on them. He sat down by her and began eating his supper.

Jessie looked at the coarse food through blurry vision. Wearily she swiped at her eyes, sniffed, and inhaled a shaky breath. She stopped in the motion of picking up the spoon on her plate and turned to Skinner when he suddenly spoke. For his part, he kept eating and never looked at her as he talked. "Don't worry none about them. They ain't goin' ta do nothin' to ya."

Jessie looked at his thin profile for a long moment before she spoke. "How do you know? You weren't there when Hayes said—about tonight. You didn't see the look on his face."

"Didn't have ta. I know 'im."

"What made him change his mind?"

"Didn't. Oh, he's goin' ta try, sure enough. But won't nothin' happen." He kept his eyes on his plate as he scraped at the remaining beans. He indicated to Jessie to eat, but her stomach was already full—of dread.

"Skinner, what are you saying? If he's still going to try, and the rest of the men too, just who's going to stop them? Me?"

Now he looked at her, a piercing stare full of a very strong emotion. His mouth turned down in a frown—or was it a snarl? Jessie held her breath and her silence. Was it starting now? Did he mean they wouldn't do anything because he was going to attack her first? Had he bargained for her and won? Fear, a cold trickle down her back, kept her rooted to the ground and staring back at Skinner.

He turned his eyes back to his plate, taking his last bite of biscuit. After he swallowed and took a swig of water, he said, "You'll see soon enough." He nodded his head in the direction of the stream, put his plate down, and stood up.

Jessie jerked her head in the direction he'd indicated. Her heart lurched and bile rose in her throat when she saw Hayes, flanked by the other men, approaching her and Skinner. They were all leering at her, some rubbing their hands together, some poking at others and saying crude things, and some were just laughing. Jessie immediately jumped up to face them. Her heart pounded so hard she had to keep blinking back the stars behind her eyes which threatened to make her pass out.

"Hey, Skinner," Hayes good-naturedly called out as he approached, "me and the boys think you've

had this little lady to yerself far too long. We promised her a little bit of fun this evening, and we aim
ta have it right now."

His men behind him nodded and laughed. One of
them called out, "Yeah, we even bathed some so's
we don't smell lak skunks. Weren't that consider-
ate?" He got the laughs and pats on the back he
wanted.

Jessie's eyes darted from one man to another,
and she sank her teeth into her bottom lip. She
tried to ready herself for the attack when it came.
She didn't have long to wait, for just then Hayes
grabbed her arm to pull her toward him. She reflexively pulled back and away from him, but his grip
was too strong; she found herself thrown up against
him and held there by her arm being twisted behind
her back. The only air she could get was filled with
Hayes' filthy scent.

An involuntary cry escaped her lips when he jerked
her head back by her hair and forced a slobbering
kiss on her mouth. Jessie kicked out and scratched
at him, but made no more of an impression than
an enraged kitten would. Over her own gagging and
choking, she could hear the taunts and hoots of the
men who ringed her. When he finally released her
mouth, Hayes held her a few inches from him and
began tearing at her shirtfront. "Let's see whut's
been bouncin' around inside this here shirt all day,
missy."

Jessie took in several hazy, time-slowed impressions at once as she tried, with her free hand, to stop
his groping efforts. The taunts and hoots continued;
Hayes grabbed her other hand and held it behind
her with his one hand; her mind screamed for help;
she weakened at the sight of Hayes' blood-engorged,

sweating face; and she heard the tearing of fabric.

If events moved slowly up until then, they now moved at a lightning pace. A hurtling fist, seemingly disconnected and from out of nowhere, smashed into Hayes' bulbous nose. Blood spurted onto Jessie, and she cried out as she hit the ground. Not fully comprehending yet exactly what had happened, Jessie remained where she was, numbly staring as Hayes and Skinner rolled over and over in the tall grass. Forgetting her, the rest of the men, no more than a pack of jackals, now ringed and taunted the two battling men. Before she could fully register this, a shot rang out from outside the campsite. One of the taunting men fell backwards, blood spurting from his shirtfront right over his heart.

All was sudden stillness as the men stared at their fallen comrade. Even the agitated horses froze for a suspended second, as did Hayes and Skinner. Then, as one, all heads turned in the direction of the gunblast. No one was visible outside their camp. Then, frozen, suspended time erupted into a flurry of new frenzy as every man scattered, heading for cover and reaching for his gun. Another shot rang out, pinging in the ground just at Hayes' feet. He quickly, for a such a stout man, rolled to his feet and took off in a crouching run for the stream.

Skinner was at Jessie's side before she'd even thought to move herself to cover. He grabbed her elbow and ran with her to the safety of the trees, and away from the remaining men. She crouched behind the tree where her saddle was and watched Skinner as he rolled on the ground to a position several feet from her. Scrubby bushes and tall grass afforded him a little cover as he pulled his gun out of its holster and cocked it. Jessie was too frightened to do more than just note the fact that Skinner had his gun trained on Hayes and his four remaining men, and not on the unseen gunman.

Bullets now flew through the air from Hayes' position by the stream. They were firing blindly in the direction of the two earlier shots, somewhere several yards to Skinner's right and at a small rise in the ground there. There were no answering shots coming from that direction now. Jessie noted that Skinner had not fired a single shot yet; he seemed content to wait and watch for now. He kept his eyes on the men at the stream, apparently unworried about whoever was behind the hill and had already killed one of them.

Jessie inched around the tree until she had a better vantage point for seeing the action. The rough bark against her cheek and hands felt reassuring to her—much better than Hayes' meaty paws had. Jessie shuddered and squeezed her eyes shut as she tried to block Hayes' attack on her from her mind. Then she saw the fist connecting with Hayes' nose and then the two men struggling on the ground. Realization dawned and she opened her eyes with a start. Skinner! She turned her head to stare at him there on the ground. He'd been defending her! He was the one who'd hit Hayes! But why? It just didn't make any sense; after all, he was Hayes' right-hand man? Wasn't he?

Jessie had no more time to think this through, for at that minute a bullet scudded into the dirt between her and Skinner. Jessie jumped back behind the tree at the same time that Skinner rolled over once to his right; their eyes met briefly across the distance, hers full of fear and his questioning. Jessie raised her hand in a small wave to let him know she was okay. He nodded and inched forward to a large rock, training his gun once again on Hayes's men.

As he kept peering from side to side over the rock, Jessie realized he couldn't get a clean shot off because the campfire was between him and the men ranged along the downward slant of the stream bank. If he was going to help, he was going to have to move. Jessie held her breath when he pulled himself up to a crouch and zigzagged through the trees and underbrush, further and further away from her, but nearer to whoever else was shooting at Hayes. Jessie let out a relieved sigh when he made it safely to a small hill out of the line of the campfire. With deadly aim he began firing towards the stream. One luckless outlaw raised up too much and was instantly picked off by Skinner. Jessie had to stop herself from cheering. She didn't usually condone killing, but she felt nothing for these men—if they could be called men. To her, they were getting no more than they deserved. No more than they were going to do to her and Josiah.

Josiah! Of course! That was who was over there behind that other hill! It had to be! Jessie couldn't believe she hadn't thought of it sooner. He had come for her! He had! She felt a thrill that had nothing to do with fear run through her. She craned her neck and strained away from the protection of the tree as much as she dared, hoping and praying for just a glimpse of Josiah, anything to let her know he was okay.

"Gotcha, you little hellcat!"

Jessie's scream was muffled as Hayes' hand clamped over her mouth and nose. His other hand held her tightly about her midriff, digging into her cut. She tried to fight, kick, bite and

148

scratch, but she couldn't get away. Her mind was reeling from panic, fear, and lack of oxygen; but Hayes' words rang loudly in her ears.

"Stop firing! Stop firing!" His men quit on cue and the noise suddenly ceased. Hayes stepped out into the open, using Jessie as a shield, and continued. "Coltrane, you better listen to me! I got the girl right here. I got 'er, and I'll kill 'er if ya don't come out right now and throw yer gun down."

There was a tense moment when nothing happened. The gun barrel pressed to her temple quieted Jessie's struggles. But at least now she could breathe. Her eyes wildly searched the two hills for some sign of movement. Nothing. Even the prairie seemed to be holding its breath. Only the crackling of the dying campfire broke the tense silence.

"Dammit," Hayes muttered under his breath. Then he yelled out to the low hill, "Don't play no games with me, Coltrane. Ya ain't cum this far to have me kill 'er now right in front of ya. Git out here now, or she's dead."

For emphasis, he cocked the gun at Jessie's temple and grabbed onto her more tightly. Only a fleeting second or two passed before a tall man stood up from behind the farther hill. Jessie sucked in a quick breath as the man threw down his gun and began walking slowly toward them, hands raised above his head. The smug chuckle in her ear and the low "Gotcha, you son of a bitch" nearly put Jessie over the edge when she realized that the man coming toward them was not Coltrane, was not Skinner, but was Josiah!

"No!" was all she cried out when the gun at her head moved to point at her husband's heart.

Chapter Nine

Jessie's cry wrung at Jake's heart as he slowly advanced on Hayes. He had to keep his fists balled at his sides to keep from rushing the bastard and freeing Jessie. He hated the sight of her trapped helplessly in Hayes' hold. The only thing that restrained him was knowing that such a rash act would surely get them both killed. On his right he saw Hayes' remaining men coming up from the stream bed to stand behind their boss; all of them had their guns aimed at Jake.

And to his left, just out of the corner of his eye, Jake could see the glint of Skinner's gun trained on Hayes. Jake did not know why Skinner had turned against Hayes and was helping him and Jessie, but he wasn't one to question aid from any quarter when the odds were so obviously stacked against him. Jake hoped that Hayes was so intent on having him at long last in his grips that he'd forgotten about Skinner. If so, Skinner, whom Jake knew to be a deadeye shot, would be even more effective when the shooting began.

And begin, it would. Jake was certain of that. He felt very naked right now without his own gun. His knife in his boot would be of no help against the several Colts aimed at him. Jake loved the irony of that; it seemed he'd found some of the stolen shipment of Colt revolvers—they were staring at him. Jake knew that keeping Hayes talking and distracted for as long as possible was his only hope for causing something to happen which would give him a chance to get Jessie and himself out of the line of fire. He would just have to be alert for his best chance.

The only evidence of Jake's racing thoughts were his eyes darting to every man and every detail of the landscape in his line of vision. Timing now would be crucial; every dusty step he took toward Hayes in the changing colors of evening brought him closer and closer to either death or escape.

"Stop right there, Coltrane," Hayes ordered.

Jake did just that. He looked directly at Jessie for the first time. Several emotions played across her face, but chief among them was the confusion and disbelief she must be feeling upon hearing the man she knew as Josiah Tucker answering to the name of Coltrane. Jake had to look away from her brown eyes and back to Hayes. A muscle twitched in his jaw; another reason to hate the man. This was not the way he had intended for her to find out his true identity. But it couldn't be helped now. He'd just have to explain later. If there was a later.

151

Cheryl Anne Porter

"Seems we done this before, huh, Marshal?" Hayes sneered. The men behind him chuckled softly.

Jake couldn't stop himself. "Yeah, but I seem to remember that my back was turned the first time."

Hayes straightened and narrowed his eyes. "You sure got a smart mouth fer someone in yer position, Coltrane."

"What have I got to lose, Hayes? You're going to kill us both anyways. Why shouldn't I say what I think? I'd like my last words to at least be memorable."

Jake saw the effect his words about dying had on Jessie. But he couldn't help it. He had to cater to Hayes' ego.

"If ya got any last words to say, Coltrane, now'd be as good a time as any to say 'em."

Hayes' words got his men's attention. They straightened up and cocked their guns. Their narrowed eyes told Jake that the time was near. He had to talk fast or die.

"I guess what I have are last questions, Hayes. Since it doesn't matter anymore, since you really outsmarted me, there's a few things I'd like to know."

"Like what?" There was no mistaking the cockiness, or the wariness, in Hayes' voice.

Jake kept his relief off his face. It was working. Telling Hayes how smart he was was keeping the bullets from flying. Now to see if he could make something happen. "Well, first off, how'd you find out I'm a Federal Marshal? No one else, on any other case I've been on, has found me out. I guess you're smarter than I thought." To himself Jake thought, you'd have to be or you couldn't pull on your boots.

It galled Jake to say these flattering things to Hayes, but he knew he did not intend to die and he just might get some important information from the vain little rooster. Of course he already knew quite a bit about how the operation ran since he'd ridden with Hayes for the last couple months, but there were other details he needed filled in.

Sure enough. Hayes drew himself up and even preened some. Jake noted that his hold on Jessie was loosening.

"Shoot, I knowed who ya was before ya even joined up with me. Gave me quite a hoot to pretend I didn't and to let ya ride with us. Ya see, I seen ya checkin' in with Colonel Carson at Camp Nichols."

"But how—?"

"How'd that tell me ya was a Fed? It didn't, but MacKenzie did. He hung around the Colonel's aide and asked a few questions—of course, the liquor he gave that clerk helped loosen his tongue up some. No reason for the clerk not to trust MacKenzie."

"MacKenzie?"

"Yeah, the sergeant what brought ya to the wagon train—and right back ta me." Hayes allowed himself a superior, crowing laugh at Jake's expense.

Jake didn't mind Hayes' laughing. It gave him time to think. Sergeant MacKenzie, huh? That was how they always knew when the shipments were coming in. It made Jake sick to think that U. S. Army soldiers were involved, but it proved Kit's, Colonel Carson's, suspicions were correct. Jake filed this bit of information away. It also rankled Jake to realize that the sergeant too knew all along who he was and had not believed the runaway lovers story. Jake decided that the sergeant's day would come, too. Now he concentrated on finding out more.

"So why didn't you kill me as soon as I showed up at your camp?"

Hayes shifted Jessie's weight on his arm before he answered. Jake's eyes went straight to hers; he tried to convey the message of courage to her. He saw she was staring blindly at him. Like she doesn't know me, he thought.

"As much as I'd've liked to right then, me and MacKenzie decided we'd draw too much attention by killin' ya right off. I didn't need no soldiers hot on my trail just when I was runnin' the guns to Santa Fe. And see, you wuz goin' to be a present from me to Vasquez. That'd be one meetin' ya really would have enjoyed, Marshal. Vasquez' boys have a real way with words."

While Hayes enjoyed a laugh with his men again, Jake sorted through what Hayes had just told him. Vasquez. Of course. The rich plantation owner in Mexico who harbored dreams of ruling all of Mexico and not just his little corner of it. A revolution required a lot of guns, guns a Mexican citizen could not come across the border to get and take back with him unnoticed. So there had to be someone, a contact or an accomplice in Santa Fe, Hayes' destination, an American citizen, helping Vasquez. This tightened Jake's jaw further. Filthy traitor. He'd get whoever it was, and he'd pay just like Romero and Sanchez had. With his life. Just like Hayes was going to, if Jake could help it.

Jake had to struggle to keep the triumphant expression from his face. Now all the puzzle pieces fit. He decided to use Hayes' own words on him. "Are you sure you want to kill me now, Hayes? You better think about this. What's Vasquez going to say when you show up without Sanchez and Romero?

Who's he going to take his anger out on?"

That got him—good. Jake watched as Hayes' face turned white under his usual ruddiness. His mouth worked a little before he answered. It was plain he'd forgotten about the two Mexicans. "Why, I'll—I'll tell him the truth. That you killed 'em, and I killed you for him."

"Now, Hayes, you know that's not the truth. I didn't kill them. They were already dead when I found them." Jake was genuinely puzzled. Who did kill them?

"You're lyin', Coltrane! Anyhow, Vasquez won't know the difference once you're dead."

The talking was over. Hayes' men reassumed their alert postures, ready now for action, for killing. Jake threw up a hand to stop them. His delays hadn't worked. They still had their guns on him, he was still unarmed, and Jessie was still in Hayes' clutches. Maybe he could save her. "Wait," he cried out. Seeing he had their attention, at least for the moment, he continued, "Let her go, Hayes. She didn't do anything. She's just a kid."

Hayes snorted and laughed. "Ya married a kid? That's not what I been feelin' over here. This ain't no kid. And I can't let her go. She done heard too much, just lak you. But I do think I can do somethin' nice for her. Give her somethin' worth dyin' for, if ya know what I mean, Fed. Now don't fret none, I'll let you watch and then I'll kill her. You can watch that too. That's the kind of man I am." An evil, leering grin covered Hayes' face as he congratulated himself on the effect his words had on Jake.

Jake's teeth and mouth clenched into a snarl, but he kept his head. This was the "something" he'd been waiting for. The bastard wouldn't get far with his little bit of fun. He'd have to let go of Jessie at some point—and when he did . . . ! Jake hoped Skinner was thinking like him and was ready. This was it.

Jake didn't have long to wait. Feeling safe with his men's guns on Jake, Hayes holstered his own gun and flung Jessie to the ground; an involuntary cry was wrung from her when she landed hard on her outstretched arms. Hayes stood at her feet with his legs spread apart as he began to undo his gunbelt.

Hayes' gloating, bloated expression turned to one of sheer shock when a gun sounded and he looked down at himself to see a spreading red stain on his crotch. For one suspended second, he didn't even appear to realize he'd been shot, and neither did his men behind him. They were turning in all directions looking for the gunman. The numbness gone, Hayes dropped to his knees with his hands over his crotch; he opened his mouth to scream, but could make no noise. He then fell face-first onto the ground and rolled onto his side, his back to Jessie, howling and vomiting.

Jake, like Hayes' men, was not totally aware of what was happening to Hayes. For at the first sound of the gunfire, Jake had dropped and rolled and crawled his way to Jessie. She did not even seem to be aware of what was happening. Her shock-widened eyes were on Hayes. Jake grabbed her up in his arms on the run and headed for the nearest cover, the large rock behind which he'd first seen Skinner. He'd fully expected to feel a bullet in his back at any minute, but luck was with him, and he made it safely to cover.

From behind the rock, with Jessie sitting with her back to it and his arm protectively across her chest, Jake raised up some to see what was happening and to see if he stood a chance of getting to a gun so he could help Skinner. Still, he hated to leave Jessie just now. He was sure she was in shock, because she was almost completely unresponsive. But he couldn't leave Skinner out there alone. Jake felt he owed him more than that.

Jake did not have to feel torn for too long, because he saw, to his surprise, that Skinner had already picked off two of the men, Cooper and Davis. The third one, Dawson, was dragging himself along the ground and holding onto his bleeding, outstretched leg. He never made it to cover. The next bullet from Skinner caught him right in the chest. Jake did a quick inventory—who was left? Simmons. Jake looked around the campsite, but couldn't see him anywhere. Probably gone to ground like the snake he is, Jake thought.

For the moment, no more bullets flew through the air. All was quiet now, except for Hayes' groaning, agonizing yells. And they caught Jake's full attention for the first time. Jake saw Hayes writhing around on the ground in his own blood and vomit. "Son of a bitch," Jake breathed, his own eyes widened now. Just then, Hayes pitched over for the last time as a bullet caught him in the head. Jake jumped in surprise and turned his head toward the low hill where Skinner was slowly standing up.

At the same second that Jake remembered Simmons, a gun fired from the direction of the stream. Jake's head turned to the sound of the gun and immediately back to Skinner,

Cheryl Anne Porter

who pitched backwards from the impact of the
bullet that hit him in the chest. He grabbed at
his wound and fell to the ground.

Jake ducked down behind the rock, hit it with his
fist, and cried softly, "No, dammit." He looked at
Jessie, who stared blankly back at him. Her dirty
little face broke his heart. He had no way of knowing if she'd ever be the same again. Too much vio-
lence might have killed her inside. Jake caressed
her cheek and pushed back a wisp of hair which
clung to her dirt-streaked face. He hated to do it,
but he had to leave her to check on Skinner. He
didn't think she'd go anywhere, so he kissed her
forehead, and then took off at a scramble for Skinner's hill.

Bullets scudding into the ground just behind him
told him that Simmons had indeed seen him. Jake
dove the last few feet to make it behind the hill.
Jake found Skinner lying very still, but he wasn't
dead. He watched Jake through pain-riddled black
eyes. Jake put a hand on his arm and said, "Hang
on, man, hang on." He then picked up Skinner's
revolver and started to turn away.

But Skinner stopped him by putting a restraining
hand on his arm. Jake turned in his crouching position to look at the wounded man, who was working
so hard to tell him something. "Don't try to talk,
Skinner."

But Skinner would not be denied; urgency tinged
his face and his words. "I got him, Jake. I got him
good. He won't do that no more." The effort cost
him; he dropped his head back onto the ground,
too weak to say anything else.

Jake pressed his lips together and placed a reassuring hand on Skinner's arm. He then turned his

158

attention to finding Simmons. Just as he positioned himself on the hill to be able to see over it, he heard a cacophony of sounds.

A mule hee-hawed, a gravelly voice yee-hawed, a man yelled "What the hell!", and then a tremendous blast was heard. It took Jake a few seconds to soak all this up. What the hell, indeed, he thought. He looked over at Jessie. She was on her knees peering over the top of the rock; she turned to Jake and shrugged her shoulders. Jake could have sunk down to the ground in relief. She was okay.

The quiet was broken again by the same gravelly voice calling, "You 'uns can start a-comin' on out now. I got the bastard—with a buffalo rifle, no less." Cackling laughter filled the air.

"Bertha!" Jessie cried out joyfully. She jumped up and ran to the stream, weaving her way through the dead men as if they'd been nothing but rocks or fallen branches.

Bertha came into view, ample bottom first, as she tried, with threats and curses, to get her mule up the incline from the stream. "You lop-eared polecat! I ought to feed you to the wildcats. That'd fix your ornery old hide!"

She got only that far before Jessie was in her arms and sobbing. "Now, there, there, child. It's all over. Ain't nobody a-goin' to hurt you now." She stroked and patted Jessie's hair and shushed her tears. She freed one arm from Jessie's embrace to wave to Jake.

Jake put his forehead to the dirt of the hill in relief. He said a silent prayer and then turned to Skinner. He expected to find him dead already, but he wasn't. Jake coddled Skinner's head in his lap and brushed away the stringy, lank hair from his sweating, contorted face. "Why, Skinner, why?" Jake asked softly.

Black eyes opened to him. Breathing was difficult; Skinner swallowed convulsively. "For the girl" was all he could manage before closing his eyes again. For the girl? This made no sense to Jake. For Jessie?

He looked up to see Jessie and Bertha standing close by on the other side of Skinner. Jake hadn't even heard them approach. He watched as Jessie's tears started anew and she dropped to her knees beside the fallen man. She then surprised Jake by leaning over to plant a kiss on Skinner's forehead. When had he come to mean so much to her? Jessie turned stricken eyes on Jake and explained, "He was kind to me today. He brought me food, these pants. He protected me from the other men. We just can't let him die."

Jake didn't have the heart to tell her that Skinner was already close to death. He'd seen too many wounds like this; Skinner was through. It was just a matter of time. He put a reassuring hand on Jessie's heaving shoulder, but had no words for her.

Just then, Skinner opened his eyes, but they were unfocused. Jake gently said, "Jessie, you better tell him right now what you have to say to him. It won't be long."

Jessie looked at him through tear-soaked eyes. She swiped at her eyes and dried her hands on Skinner's pants that she was wearing. She turned his face very gently toward her and told him, "It's me, Skinner. Jessie."

With great effort, Skinner feebly raised a hand, as if searching for some contact with her. She quickly took it in hers and held it close to her. When he spoke, his voice was almost a whisper.

160

"Jessie." It seemed to comfort him to say her name. "Couldn't . . . let him hurt you."

"No, Skinner, he didn't hurt me. Thanks to you. You're a good man," Jessie told him, her voice barely above a whisper. Her throat was too thick with tears to speak any louder.

"No," he said, almost adamantly. "I'm . . . not a good man. I . . . done some bad things. Killed people. Robbed people. But Hayes . . . killed my . . . sister. He hurt her . . . like he tried to . . . with you. Couldn't let him . . . couldn't. I . . . promised myself I'd . . . kill him . . . if he tried to . . . hurt another girl."

Jake and Jessie exchanged looks as Skinner's voice trailed off for the moment. His labored breathing filled the space between them. Jake looked at Bertha, who was making little sympathetic clucking sounds and shaking her head.

Jessie once again spoke softly to Skinner. "Is that why you rode with him? For a chance to kill him?"

"Yes," came his answer, barely a hissing whisper of a word. "He . . . never knew . . . it was my sister he . . . I found him and . . . joined him . . . and played up to him . . . until I . . . killed him . . . and everyone in his gang who . . . my sister . . . even those Mexicans. Jessie . . . not a good man. Not good."

"Skinner!" Jessie cried when his last breath escaped him. It took both Jake and Bertha to pull her away from Skinner's limp body. Jake held her in his lap until her great, racking sobs began to subside and she fell into exhausted sleep. The night closed around them.

When Jessie awoke the next morning, it was to the sound of dirt being shoveled. She opened her eyes to see rosy dawn light filtering through the tree branches directly above her. She lay very still. She didn't want to move, or to think. She just wanted to lie there, to be left alone.

She took in the sounds around her without really hearing them. A mule brayed, Bertha cussed, pots rattled, a horse stamped and snorted, birds chirped in the trees, but above all these sounds was the steady chunk-chunk of a shovel in dirt. Jessie closed her eyes again. Two salty tears squeezed out from under her lids.

When she awoke next, the shoveling had stopped. She was glad for that. Bright sunlight now filtered through the branches over her head, and she found she was hot under the blanket which had been thrown over her. Tossing back the cover, she sat up and looked around her. The bodies were gone. She was glad for that, too. She spotted Blaze, the huge roan stallion, grazing by the stream. The other horses, and Bertha's mule, were tethered between two trees. She next saw a fresh grave with a crude wooden cross at its head. She quickly looked away; it was still too painful. She did not want to dwell on the horrors of yesterday.

The turn of her head brought Bertha and Josiah— no, what was his name? oh yes—Coltrane into her sight. They were sitting by the campfire which now was just glowing, red embers. They were drinking coffee and talking. Josi . . . Coltrane was shirtless. Behind him a shirt was stretched out on a bush to dry. The bandages which covered his shoulder and wound around his chest were starkly white against his tanned, muscular torso. Bertha must have changed them. As Jessie watched, he laughed at something Bertha said and ran a hand through the thick, black waves of his hair.

Jessie found she couldn't look away from . . . Coltrane. She frowned. The name still did not come easily to her mind. Some things hadn't changed at all, she thought. He was still the most beautiful man she'd ever seen, still the first man she'd ever kissed, still the first man to awaken in her the longings of a woman. And, looking down at her left hand, she remembered he was still her husband. But she didn't know him—not at all. That was what had changed. Oh, she knew his smile, his heart-stopping blue eyes, his laughter . . . she knew so much about him. But she didn't know him. What was he? A Federal Marshal?

She'd fought with him side by side and slept with him side by side, and risked her life for him, even married him, but he still hadn't trusted her enough to tell her who he really was. This angered Jessie. Just who was she married to? Josiah Tucker, gunrunner, or Whatever-his-first-name-was Coltrane, Federal Marshal? Or was she married at all since Josiah Tucker wasn't really a person? Was she Mrs. Tucker, Mrs. Coltrane, or still Miss Stuart?

Deciding she would get no answers sitting here under a tree by herself, Jessie arose, very stiffly and very carefully, and went behind the trees to relieve herself. That done, she walked over to the campfire. Her approaching footsteps gained her the attention of two pairs of eyes: gray, anxious ones; and blue, frowning ones. To the gray eyes, she smiled and accepted the offered tin cup of steaming, black coffee and the plate of food. After she sat down cross-legged on the ground, she turned to the blue eyes, and asked, "Just what is your first name?"

Cheryl Anne Porter

Over the rim of the tin cup she raised to her lips, she saw the look that passed between Bertha and . . . Coltrane. With a loud show of getting up and dusting herself off, Bertha excused herself on the pretext of seeing to that ornery mule of hers and all her newly acquired horses.

Both Jessie and Jake watched her walk off. Jessie turned back to Jake and repeated her question. "What's your first name? I can't keep calling you Coltrane or Marshal."

"It's Jake. Jake Coltrane."

Yes, this name fit him a lot better than Josiah Tucker. "Jake Coltrane," she repeated out loud, as if weighing the name for some important reason.

"Look, Jessie, I never intended for you to find out—"

"I know that."

"Let me finish. Please. For you to find out the way you did. I couldn't risk telling you who I really was. That knowledge could have gotten you killed."

"Well, not knowing certainly kept me safe, didn't it?"

In the silence that followed her last statement, she began eating her breakfast as if nothing at all were wrong. She didn't even feel bad about being sarcastic, about being unfair and not giving him a chance. She was hurt and angry, and he should know just how she felt.

"I guess I deserved that," he said evenly.

Jessie looked up from her plate and chewed silently while she stared at him. She was not in a forgiving mood. She was still numb from yesterday. As yesterday's events crowded in on her, she put her plate down and pushed it away from her. A gulping sob escaped her when she turned to look at the grave. Without looking at Jake, she asked, "Is that Skinner?"

"Yes," came the quiet reply.

"Where're the other . . . bodies?"

"Don't worry about them. Bertha and I took care of them."

She now turned her tear-streaked face to Jake. "I can't help but think about Skinner."

"I know. Me too."

"He was a good man, you know. I mean, deep down inside."

"I think he was better even than we knew."

"What do you mean?" Jessie asked, wiping the tears from her eyes. She no longer felt so angry with him, seeing his obvious pain, this shared pain of theirs.

"I mean I think he's the one who warned me with a note that Hayes planned to kill me." Seeing Jessie's questioning expression, he added, "Right before Hayes shot me, I found a note warning me. It's probably the only reason I'm alive now."

Jessie thought about this, and then so many things suddenly became clear. Almost eagerly, she moved closer to Jake and said, "Do you think he's the one who took you out of the root cellar?"

"He had to be, didn't he? He probably even came to the cabin door with Hayes to let us know they were listening outside, so we wouldn't be loud."

"And when he hit me and Bertha in the wagon, it was probably to keep the other one—what was his name? Sanchez?—from hurting us worse, maybe even killing us."

"You're probably right. And remember when we rode out of your barn on Blaze? Skinner was shooting at us. Now that I think about it, I never saw him miss anything he shot at. He was missing on purpose."

Jessie was even able to share a small laugh with Jake over Skinner's efforts to thwart Hayes in every possible way he could. Until the time came to kill him.

Jessie got quiet and looked down. She drew aimless designs in the dirt until Jake's voice caught her attention.

"Jessie, you never got to say good-bye to Skinner. Come on," he said softly, stretching his hand out to her.

Jessie took his hand and allowed him to pull her to her feet. Arm in arm they walked slowly over to Skinner's grave. This was no time for recriminations and anger. Right now Jessie needed Jake's strength; she needed to lean on him.

When they stopped in front of the fresh mound of dirt, dirt which smelled so . . . so earthy and alive . . . Jessie knelt down and put a hand on the grave. Jake's warm hand on her shoulder comforted her. She breathed, "Good-bye, Skinner. You won't be forgotten."

She raised watery eyes to the crude cross at the head of the grave, and read what Jake had carved on it: "Skinner, A Good Man."

Chapter Ten

Jessie floated dreamlessly in the cool, sun-dappled water of the stream. She fanned her arms to keep from floating downstream; a beatific smile lit her face. This was pure heaven. The sun seemed to be playing peek-a-boo with her and the tree branches which overhung the stream. In fact, Jessie played a game of moving first one way and then another in the water until she was either in the sun or out of it. She smiled at her own childishness. The gurgling stream seemed to laugh with her. She was relieved to know that she could still enjoy innocent fun.

The piece of soap provided by Bertha—what would she pull out of her saddlebags next?—helped Jessie to wash away the grime and mostly awful memories of the last two days. Hayes and his men were gone, as gone as were the suds which the cleansing stream rinsed from her hair. The gently swirling water even soothed her sunburned legs and feet. Jessie wished she could just stay here like this forever.

"If you don't get out of there soon, you're going to look like a prune."

Jessie gasped and sat down on the bottom of the shallow stream, crossing her arms over her breasts. She didn't dare move her hands to swipe the cascading water from her face. She couldn't really see anything of him except a watery image, but she knew he'd be grinning and enjoying his peep show, the brute. "Just how long have you been there?" she sputtered indignantly.

"Long enough. Why?"

"You brute! Have you no decency?"

"If I didn't have any decency, you wouldn't be alone in that water!"

That did it. Jessie made a vicious cutting motion with her hand through the water and sent a small wave splashing in Jake's direction.

"Missed me!" he called out tauntingly.

More angry than modest now, she wiped at her eyes with her hands and blinked several times. Yes, there he stood. Completely dry. Grinning. Thumb hooked in the front of his pants, one knee bent. No shirt on. So superior. In his other hand he held out to her the dry shirt Bertha intended for her to use as a towel.

"Jake Coltrane, you drop that shirt and get out of here this instant!"

"Make me," he dared.

Jessie could think of nothing else to do. *"Bertha!"* she screamed. *"Bertha!"*

Poor Bertha came at a dead run—for her—down the embankment to the stream. In her hands she carried her buffalo gun. Her straw hat flew off; both Jessie and Jake, wide-eyed, followed its skittering course and watched helplessly as it stopped under the feet of Bertha's mule. He promptly trounced it until it was dead. He then picked it up and began munching on it. Jessie turned laugh-filled eyes on Jake, who was biting his bottom lip—hard.

"Hang on, child! I'm a-comin'! What is it—a rattle-snake? A wildcat?" She looked around wildly.

"No, it's a polecat. A poisonous one," Jessie said, eyeing Jake, who was beginning to look a little sheepish about now. Teach him, Jessie thought.

"A poisonous polecat?" Disbelief made her voice higher. Still, she looked around from Jessie to Jake and the surrounding area. "Danged if I ever heard of a poisonous polecat. But if he pokes his nose around here again, I'm a-ready."

She swung her buffalo gun around wildly, sending Jake to the ground and Jessie under water. When Jessie surfaced, laughing hysterically and wiping the water out of her eyes, she saw Jake lying in the wet sand of the shore, convulsed with laughter himself.

Bertha, head turned slightly sideways, looked from one to the other. "Did you kids get into some loco weed?"

Jessie was helpless with laughter. Jake was in no better condition. All Jessie could do to answer Bertha was point toward the tethered mule and horses. Bertha, eyebrows almost meeting over her eyes in consternation, turned back to where Jessie pointed.

She did a double take when she saw her mule's breakfast and then instinctively put a hand to her head. No hat. She took out at a run, wildly waving her huge rifle. Even her steam-engine-out-of-control angry body, wildly flapping arms and yelled threats of dire harm did not cause the mule to blink. As placidly as a cow with its cud, he stood his ground, eyeing his mistress as if she'd been no more than an annoying insect. Even the mad plunging of the terrified horses who were tethered with him did not phase him.

Jessie and Jake, their own squabble forgotten, watched with huge grins and joy-widened eyes the duel between Bertha and the mule. The mule won by a decision—he decided to drop the hat quite nonchalantly to the ground at the last possible second before Bertha reached him and thwacked him between the eyes with a good-sized branch she'd picked up on the run.

"You better drop it, you fleabag, you poisonous polecat you." Bertha triumphantly bent over to pick up the very chewed-on hat. When she did, Jessie put her hands to her mouth and strangled a delighted "oh no!" Oh yes. The mule gave a solid nudge with his nose to Bertha's bottom, which sent her sprawling into the dirt. His loud braying could only be described as laughter.

Jessie was absolutely paralyzed with laughter. She was weak and choking for air. She laughingly called for help before she drowned. Jake finally was able to pull himself upright, deep chuckles still erupting, and hold out to Jessie the dry shirt in his hand. For her to reach it without completely exposing her naked body to him, he very gallantly came one step into the water and turned his head. Jessie gratefully donned the shirt while still in the water and buttoned it modestly.

Still laughing and shaking her head at all this hilarity, she stood up and waded out of the stream. She saw the laughter die on Jake's face as he watched her emerge from the water. She stopped just where the water met the rocky shore and looked down at herself. She might as well have been naked. The wet shirt clinging to every curve somehow made her seem more than naked, for it emphasized her breasts, chilled nipples erect, defined her small waist, and outlined her rounded hips much as a frame set off a picture. She instinctively crossed her arms over her breasts and looked up at Jake.

His blue eyes, usually clear and cool, were now almost midnight dark and somewhat hooded by his dark-fringed eyelids. His mouth, so passionate, so sensitive, was set in a straight, warm line. A muscle twitched in his jaw as he stared right into Jessie's soul. No words passed between them; none were needed. As Jake extended his left hand to help her up the embankment, and she placed her left hand in his, the sun sparked off the two gold wedding bands which bound them as surely as the passion that raged between them.

Had he felt it, too, she wondered—that spark. The one that made her feel like liquid fire coursed through her and formed a swirling whirlpool . . . down there. She felt it only when he was near, or when he touched her, or when he merely looked at her like he just had. Did he feel it? She wished she had the kind of power over him that he surely had over her. She was glad she did not have to look into his eyes right now as he preceded her up the embankment. She was sure that her feelings were once again written all over her face, which felt warm to her touch despite the chills on her body from the wet shirt. At least that was what she thought the chills were from.

171

After only a few steps they were standing at the top of the incline. Jake, with Jessie still in tow, walked toward Bertha and her mule. "So, Bertha, did you salvage any of your hat, or did your friend there finish it off?"

"The only thing around here that's likely to get finished off is that mule, and he certainly ain't no friend of mine," Bertha huffed indignantly. Her face was reddened from the effort of trying to saddle the sidestepping animal. On her head was now perched the mule's erstwhile breakfast. A few bites were missing from here and there on the brim, but overall, it was still intact.

Jessie had to clamp her free hand over her mouth to keep from shouting with laughter again. Little choking sounds came to her from Jake, who was standing beside her now. She didn't dare look over at him!

"Well, what are you two a-gawkin' at? Ain't you never seen a woman saddle a good-as-dead mule before? Let's break this camp and get a move on!" She stood facing them with her hands on her hips; vexation and heat combined to make her look like an angry elf. As she talked, her mule shook himself vigorously, sending the uncinched saddle thumping to the ground. Bertha's eyes almost popped out of her head when she heard the thump right behind her. She turned back to the mule, hands curved like claws and teeth bared.

Jessie would never know what happened next because she and Jake had taken that opportunity to scatter like flushed quail. Any cover, please, just any cover, Jessie prayed! She made it to the big rock, squatted down behind it and literally rocked the rock with her howling laughter. She looked over and saw Jake behind a tree, bent over and holding his sides. Tears poured from his eyes. When they both chanced a look back in Bertha's direction, all they could see was a wind devil of raised dirt and dust, flying arms and kicking feet; all they could hear was cussing and braying.

When the mirthful storm passed, Jessie literally had to drag herself up the side of the rock. Little hiccuping giggles kept her too weak to stand without help just now. Jake had recovered before her and was seeing to the saddling of both their horses. She saw Blaze standing stock-still, his attention held entirely by the mule-and-woman scene he'd just witnessed. A slow flick of one ear and a loud snort dismissed them as beneath his dignity.

Jessie, sides aching, lungs squeezed, slowly made her way over to the bush where she'd laid her clothes to dry after she'd scrubbed them as best she could in the stream before her bath. Her clothes, she thought, as she picked them off the bush and donned them, were not her clothes at all, but were Bertha's shirt and Skinner's pants. She once again rolled up the pants and tied them with the rope. Maybe Bertha could produce a pair of shoes or boots or moccasins or something from her magic saddlebags, as Jessie had come to think of them. After all, she'd already produced everything from camp supplies, food, clothes, soap, a brush for Jessie's long hair, medicines, and bandages so far—like a merchant on a mule, Jessie laughed.

Once she'd worked at drying her hair some by tossing it forward over her head as she bent over; and brushing it vigorously in direct sunlight, she, thinking along the lines of footwear and maybe even something with which to tie her long hair back,

173

approached Bertha and Jake. They were over by the string of horses tethered with Bertha's mule. When she got closer, Jessie slowed her steps when she realized they were in a heated discussion about something.

To get their attention and maybe stop their fussing, Jessie called out gaily, "Hey, you two, can't I leave you alone for thirty minutes without you arguing?"

Both heads turned simultaneously towards her. Bertha, lips compressed in a stubborn line, looked down at the ground, but Jake's angry blue eyes bored into Jessie's. She stopped instantly and drew in her breath, much as if she'd received a physical blow. They were fighting about her! What in the world . . . ?

Looking from one to the other, she asked, "What's going on, Bertha? Jake?" Without realizing it, she had assumed Bertha's stance, her legs spread apart and her hands on her hips.

Jake opened his mouth to speak, but before he could say anything Bertha cut in. "Now don't you fret none, child. We was just a-figurin' where to go and what to do from here."

Somehow Jessie knew she would not like the answer to the question she had to ask. "And just what did you two decide—without including me, I might add?"

Now it was Jake's turn to look at the ground. Bertha turned to him. "You might as well tell her. It's your plan."

Jake gave Bertha a quick, sharp look, and then turned his level gaze on Jessie. After a deep breath, he told her, "With Hayes and all his men dead, you'll be safe now at your homestead. Bertha can escort you home and wait there with you for the wagon train to come back. That way, she can get her wagon and mules back."

Jessie felt the ice in her veins. He was leaving her. "And what about you?" she asked in a very small voice.

"Jessie, you know who I am and what I do. I have to get to Camp Nichols as fast as possible, check in, and get on with my assignment. You two would just slow me down."

Jessie looked to Bertha. "He told me everything, child, while you slept this morning. He's got to get them guns for the Army." She now came over and put an arm around Jessie's shoulders. "I've been a-fussin' with him about leavin' you now when everything's so unsettled for you two kids. That crazy weddin' and all. But it seems them guns is more important right now, and you'll just have to wait." The longer she'd talked, the louder and angrier her voice had become. She'd nailed Jake to the ground with her eyes as she'd talked to Jessie.

Angry, white lines appeared in each corner of Jake's mouth. His eyes snapped black fire at Bertha. He appeared about to say something, but then must have thought better of it because he clamped his lips together. He turned on his heel and stalked away, his long stride carrying him to Blaze in only a few steps. His back to Jessie and Bertha, he rechecked every cinch and knot on the big stallion's bridle, reins, and saddle.

Jessie took all this in as if she'd been at the far end of a tunnel. She would never see him again after this day. He was just going to ride off and leave her standing here, as if she meant nothing to him, as if she weren't married to him, as if they had not been

175

through anything together. Now it was her turn to compress her lips and send angry sparks from her eyes. She loosened herself from Bertha's grip, balled her fists up at her sides, and strode angrily over to Jake.

Grabbing one of his arms from behind him, she turned him toward her. Raising her left hand, she pointed with her right hand to the wedding band she wore, the one just like his. She'd just remind him of his commitment to her, by gosh. "And just what about this, mister? Have you forgotten about this?"

"No, Jessie, I haven't," he answered very evenly. "I know how much you didn't want to marry me. Don't worry. I'll start the paperwork for an annulment as soon as I get to Camp Nichols. Now mount up."

With that, he turned from her and mounted a prancing Blaze. From the height of his horse's back, Jake looked down at Jessie. He then removed the gold band from his finger and handed it to her. "Here. A souvenir for you." He spurred Blaze forward and rode out of her life at a dead run.

Damn it all to hell, Jake raged, as he leaned low over Blaze's muscled, straining neck. He'd done the right thing, he knew that. Break it off clean. Don't hurt her anymore. He knew that she could now turn that hurt into hate. He'd purposely been so callous and distant. There was no other way he could have done what he did. He knew himself well enough to know that he was dangerously close to . . . caring too much. Couldn't afford that. No, this way was best. Hating him would get her through this a lot quicker.

Then she could go on with her life, find some young man more worthy of her to love and marry her. Someone who didn't have to look over his shoulder all the time; someone young enough not to be scarred by a war, or distrustful of everyone. Someone who would always be there for her and who would build his life around her. She deserved no less. Jake could tell just by looking at her very expressive face that she fancied herself in love with him. But Jake knew better. She just thought that because he was the only man, besides her father, she'd ever been around. It was that damned kiss in her cabin, he berated himself. Her first one. Yes, Jake decided, he'd done the right thing to clear out now, clear out before he did any more damage.

But, he knew that as long as he lived he'd carry in his heart the picture of little Jessie standing there looking down at the circle of gold he'd placed in her palm.

Bertha's nonstop stream of cheerful chatter made no more of an impression on Jessie than a bee buzzing around her head would have. She appreciated what Bertha was doing and why, but all she could honestly manage was an occasional nod, smile, or one-word response. Mounted on the horse that Hayes had placed her on yesterday—was it really only yesterday?, she rode very heavily in the saddle, exhausted from the crying she'd done after Jake rode out.

She now berated herself for that childish behavior. Was she such a scared little girl that she couldn't face life on her own without leaning on a man who wanted no ties, a man who made it very clear that he did not need or want her? Never again would she allow herself to be that vulnerable—or that stupid. She must be a woman now, a woman with her eyes open and her heart closed, instead of the other way around. She had responsibilities, after all.

Struggling with these thoughts, she was only able to give Bertha a weak little smile in response to some story she was telling in an effort to cheer her up. But a few minutes later, she looked over at Bertha and gave her a genuine smile of affection. What would she have done without Bertha? She was mounted on her flop-eared galoot, and was leading the string of horses that Hayes and his men would no longer need; she'd claimed them as her own. The extra horses made their pace slow and plodding, but that was fine with Jessie; the pace matched her heartbeat.

But even as slow as they were going, Jessie knew that they would reach her home this evening before sundown. Home. A bullet-riddled cabin with broken windowpanes. A neglected garden. Neglected animals. The Lord only knew what condition those poor animals would be in after being alone for three days. Especially the milk cows. Jessie looked forward to all the hard work that, even with Bertha's help, it would take to rebuild her homestead. It was truly hers now with her parents gone. And she would see that it prospered. She wouldn't let her father's dream die. She'd been a fool to think she'd wanted to get away from the solitary quiet of her prairie home. Well, she'd gotten away—and look at what it had cost her. Darn near her life. And her heart.

No! She refused to think of . . . him. The man-sized ring weighed heavily in her shirt pocket. She should have thrown it away, was what she should have done. Should have thrown it on the ground, hers along with it, and stomped them both into the dirt. Would have, too, she told herself, chin lifted proudly, except for being barefoot; stomping the rings, even though it would have made her heart feel better, would have only hurt her already sunburned and tender feet. She glanced down at the soft leather moccasins which now covered her feet. Bertha had pulled them out of her magic saddlebags, saying they were ones she wore in the evenings when her feet were hot and pinched from her boots.

Thinking of all Bertha had done for her and had come to mean to her, Jessie resolved to be a better companion. Bertha did not deserve this sullenness. After all, she wasn't the one who had used her and left her. And that was just what he'd done, too. Used her for a cover, just as surely as Hayes as used her as a pawn and then a shield. She decided that he, Mr. Jake Coltrane, U. S. Marshal, His All High and Mightiness, really was not much better than Hayes. He did what he had to, and took what he could, to get whatever he needed for his own ends.

And he didn't care who he hurt in the process. And not only Jessie. Hadn't he been yelling at Bertha this morning, and here she'd as good as saved his life yesterday when she shot that last badman? And not to mention all her kindnesses to them at the wagon train. Bertha's only mistake was in getting Jessie married to Jake. But still that too she'd done with the best of intentions. Yes, Bertha'd been used by him, too. Well, if he didn't care, then neither did she. She gave an emphatic nod of her head as if to punctuate this final thought on the subject.

"Child, you're a-goin' to fry your brain if'n you don't stop a-broodin' and a-frettin' this way."

179

Jessie looked over at Bertha's kind and concerned face. "You're right, Bertha. I was just thinking. You and I could be partners now. I mean, I need help at my homestead, and you're all alone—oh Bertha, I'm sorry. I . . . I didn't mean—"

Bertha cackled gleefully. "You don't have to be sorry, child. I know I'm alone. It ain't no shock. Now go on with your plan. I'm a-listenin'."

"Well, I was thinking that maybe you could just stay on with me and not go back to Missouri when the wagons come back through. The homestead makes good money. I could pay you—"

"Now stop right there, Jessie-child. Let me see if'n I have this straight. You want me to live with you and work for you at your place?"

Her tone of voice made Jessie afraid that she'd insulted this independent woman in some way. She quickly rushed in with "No, Bertha, not really work for me. But be my partner—you know, a business partner. It's a lot of hard work, I know. And it's not as glamorous or as exciting as the trail drive, but—"

Another cackling burst of laughter from Bertha. "Child, child, child. I accept!"

"—we could be together. And neither one of us has any family now—"

"Jessie! Look at me!" Bertha commanded, gray eyes alive with humor.

Jessie stopped in mid-sentence and did as she was told. "Yes, Bertha?"

"I already said I accept."

"You did? You do? Oh, Bertha, that's wonderful! But are you sure you won't miss your life on the trail, seeing exciting things, going places, meeting people, stuff like that?"

"Those things are your dream, child, a young person's dreams. You're the one who better be sure of this before we get to shaking hands on the deal."

"Why? What would I have to be sure about? I don't understand."

Bertha looked down briefly and fiddled with the lead rope tied to her pommel. When she looked up, Jessie swore she saw tears in Bertha's eyes. "Think, child. I ain't a-gettin' any younger. I ain't old by no means, so don't you get to thinkin' that. And I can sure enough carry my share of the heavy work still. But I ain't young. And it won't be many years before I'm the one, and not you, who'll need someone to take care of her."

"Bertha, you stop that danged, ornery mule of yours this minute. Don't look at me like that! I mean it," Jessie said emphatically, pulling up hard on her horse's reins and then nudging him closer to Bertha's mule.

For once, Mule decided to do as he was told and stop without an all-out brawl. When Jessie could reach Bertha, she put her arms around her in a great big hug, placed a wet, smacking kiss on her plump, age-lined cheek, and said, "There, it's done. We're partners. Forget the handshake! I prefer a hug anyway. Bertha, if I started taking care of you today and kept on doing so until the day you died years from now, I couldn't begin to pay you back for all the wonderful things you've done for me in the past few days. And, Bertha, I love you."

A big, fat, wet tear escaped Bertha's usually cheerful gray eyes. In the softest voice Jessie had ever heard her use, she said, "I love you too, child."

After that they rode on without talking. Only once in the next few hours did they break the comfortable silence between them. And it was Bertha who broke it, taking up the conversation of a couple hours ago as if no miles had passed and as if the sun had not sunk a little lower since she last spoke.

"And what about getting you married to the Marshal? Was that a wonderful thing I did?" Her voice rang with merry teasing.

Jessie took up the teasing vein, glad to find that she could already laugh about that and at herself, "Well, maybe that wasn't so wonderful!"

Chapter Eleven

Colonel Kit Carson paced back and forth in his command tent at Camp Nichols. A frown marred his high forehead; his deep-set eyes, under heavy brows, were troubled. Every now and then he ran a hand over his slicked-back, longish hair or pulled at his moustache in agitation. Finally, he stopped pacing and turned to the young man seated in front of his desk. "The packing slips you brought me from that last stolen shipment of guns are important evidence in this case, Coltrane. I'm sorry you had to take a bullet to do it. But the rest of your story sounds like a tall tale for sure."

"I lived it, Colonel, and I'm still not sure it's all real."

"And you had to marry the Stuart girl to keep your cover?" For the first time since Jake had been ushered into his tent, the colonel was able to smile.

"Yes, Sir, I did. That's another thing I'll have to straighten out later on." Jake really wished he didn't have to talk about that right now. He shifted uncomfortably in the wooden chair.

"I just hope you can. Of course, with Hayes dead we may never get some of the answers we need. Now that's not a criticism, son; I know you didn't pull the trigger, and you would have had to kill him yourself, under the circumstances, if that Skinner fellow hadn't beat you to it. Still, we don't know the extent of Mr. Stuart's involvement, if any, in this whole operation. He could have been totally innocent, and his place could just have been a convenient meeting point for MacKenzie and Hayes. Or Stuart could have been in on the operation; you know, like taking money to keep his mouth shut, or for just looking the other way when the guns changed hands."

The colonel ran a hand over his face tiredly. Jake watched him and became decidedly uncomfortable. If Jessie's father was involved with Hayes, then the government would take her land. Carson spoke again. "With Stuart dead too, this is all speculation, I suppose. A rattlesnake got him a couple months ago. This shipment due in would have been the first one since his death to come through. Would have been interesting to see if Hayes' way of doing things changed any once he found out Stuart was dead." The colonel shook his head, and then banged his hands on his desk in a businesslike manner. "Well, you're the only one who knows this operation inside and out, so you'll have to tell me what we can do from here." The famed explorer and scout waited expectantly for Jake to respond. He sat down and folded his hands in front of him on his desk.

"Well," Jake began, "I think I ought to deliver the

184

guns myself to Vasquez. He's a man who can appreciate a takeover; after all, he's planning one himself. I can tell him the truth—Hayes and his men are dead, and now he has to deal with me. He won't care as long as he gets his guns. And also I might be able to get him to talk about the whole operation—get him to name names, I mean. There could be more people involved whom we don't even know about."

"That's true, that's true," Colonel Carson said, obviously thinking ahead. "I have to say this, Coltrane. You might not like it, but I'm sure you know the law. If Vasquez implicates Stuart in any way, and we get proof of that, then we will have to seize the Stuart Homestead and everything on it. It would have to be sold to help make up for what we've lost in property. Just wish we had some way of bringing back the men who died protecting those shipments."

Jake felt a coldness in the pit of his stomach. The homestead was the only thing Jessie had now. If it was taken away from her, it would be because he, Jake, had done his job well. And, if finding out her father was involved with Hayes didn't kill her, losing her home would for sure. Jake mentally kicked himself for getting so personally involved. All his training had warned against it. Now he knew why. With a sick heart, he knew why. Even the innocent could be hurt, could be used, could be killed.

The colonel's voice brought Jake out of his dour thoughts. "MacKenzie knows about the Stuart girl and the other woman being involved somehow with you, so I'll post some men there for their protection. Maybe we can get MacKenzie to talk. He might know some other names, too, and if Stuart was involved."

"Yes, Sir," was all Jake could manage.

"Well, MacKenzie will soon enough be in custody—just like my drunken aide with the loose tongue. And MacKenzie doesn't know that Hayes is dead, does he?"

"No, Sir."

"Do you think you can trust the two women not to talk?"

"Yes, Sir."

"Good. Now we're getting somewhere. You can't ride into Vasquez's stronghold alone. He'd never believe that you killed Hayes and all his men by yourself. We'll have to provide you with a 'gang' of your own. And I believe I know just the ones for the job." With that, he arose and went to the tent's opening to talk to the guard outside. "Get me Lieutenant Patterson."

Jake stood up when the colonel did, and he now remained standing as the colonel returned to his side of the desk and sat back down. "At ease, Coltrane. Sit down. Old habits die hard, don't they?"

Jake smiled back at Colonel Carson. "Yes, Sir. All those years in the uniform during the Civil War, I guess."

"Glad that one's over," Colonel Carson said, shaking his head and looking down at his hands. Then he looked back up at Jake. "You're too young to remember the Mexican War back in forty-six, aren't you?"

"I remember it very well, Sir. I was just a kid, but my father was killed in it fighting with General Zachary Taylor at the Rio Grande in Texas."

"I'm sorry, Son, I didn't know." After a moment of silence, the colonel continued. "We're risking a war just like that one again with Mexico if we can't disarm Vasquez and inform the Mexican government of his plans to overthrow them. If Vasquez fights his government with American guns, they're going to think we supplied them and backed him. President Johnson does not want that to happen."

Jake sat up in his chair. "I am well aware of the importance of this mission to our government, Colonel. It is my intention to provide the President with the proof he needs to present to Mexico of Vasquez's activities—no matter who is implicated."

"Good. I'm glad to know you still stand firm on this. After what you've just been through, I had to be sure."

"I see," Jake replied. But he did sit back in his chair. Jake knew that he could not spare Jessie if her father was indeed involved. The law was the law. For the first time, though, he hated his job, hated the things it caused him to have to do, and the people he had to hurt.

From just outside the tent, the guard called, "Colonel Carson, Lieutenant Patterson is here as requested."

"Send him in, Corporal."

Jake stood up with the colonel and turned toward the tent opening. In stepped a tall, lanky, young man, immaculate in his blue and gold uniform. He snapped immediately to attention, and barked. "Sir! Lieutenant Coy Patterson reporting as ordered, Sir!"

"At ease, Lieutenant. I'd like you to meet Mr. Jake Coltrane, U. S. Marshal."

The Lieutenant performed a smart turn to his right and presented himself stiffly, but with extended hand, to Jake. Just as loudly as he had greeted the colonel in this small tent, he said, "Pleased to meet you, Marshal Coltrane. Lieutenant Coy Patterson."

187

Jake smiled as he shook the younger man's hand. "So I heard, Lieutenant. The pleasure is mine." Jake was thinking that this boy couldn't have been shaving for more than a couple years. He was blond, blue-eyed, freckled, and eager. This kid was to be in his 'gang'?

When they were all seated, Colonel Carson wasted little time in telling the young lieutenant why he'd sent for him. The longer the colonel talked, with Jake interjecting when asked a question, the more eager and delighted Lieutenant Patterson looked. Great, Jake thought, he thinks we're playing a game. Jake figured he'd straighten the pup out when they were alone on the trail.

After the lieutenant was dismissed with his orders to brief the ten enlisted men whose names Colonel Carson had given him, men whom the colonel trusted implicitly, and was told to be ready to ride tomorrow morning, the colonel turned his attention back to Jake. "I know he's young, Jake, but give him a chance. He's intelligent and very eager to serve."

"I could tell that, Sir. But if you trust him, then I do too. I also trust that the rest of my 'gang' don't look like freckle-faced kids? Vasquez won't believe they're outlaws. We'll look more like a nursery school outing." Jake tried to keep the groan out of his voice, but he failed.

"Jake, I think you've been at this game for too long! Patterson's not much younger than you are—and you look like a pup to me! See what I mean? But no, rest easy, the remainder of your men are all veterans—of the Army and of the war. Now, I'll have the corporal take you to your tent. I'm sure you can use the sleep."

"Thank you, Sir. Uh, just one more question has occurred to me, though, Sir. Just where are the guns we'll be taking to Vasquez?"

"Oh, didn't I tell you that? What with so many shipments being stolen and men being killed for them, we decided to have soldiers in plain clothes bring them in a wagon by a different route. See, they're kind of undercover too, like you; they're posing as teamsters on the Santa Fe Trail. They'll be waiting for you at the Stuart Homestead. Just think, Coltrane, you'll get to see your wife again!"

Jessie was already weary and she'd only been up a few hours. She wished now that she could have slept later this morning, but she didn't dare. She thought back to yesterday evening when they had finally arrived home. Home. Jessie liked the sound of that. Bertha had exclaimed and clucked, just like the chickens who'd made themselves at home in the cabin, over the mess: broken glass, bullet holes everywhere, blood, torn clothing, furniture knocked over, dishes broken. She'd tsk-tsked, shook her head, and then went to work cleaning house and shooing chickens.

While Bertha did that, Jessie had unsaddled the worn-out horse she rode and Bertha's mule, and then turned them loose in the corral with the other horses they'd brought along. She'd had to climb to the loft and knock a bale of hay out for them. That had nearly brought her to tears, it was so heavy. Luckily, there was still water in the trough.

And her poor cows. She was afraid they would be sick or dead from not being milked for so long. She'd immediately milked them, the poor mooing dears, and left them in the barn where she could

189

Cheryl Anne Porter

keep an eye on them. Fortunately, three or four of the cows had calves to relieve their bags somewhat. Jessie had to laugh. The calves were fine—and round as butterballs. She'd had the thought then that a wagon train might come through soon to buy up some of this milk. She'd have to churn some of it for butter, too.

Before she'd gone back to the cabin last night, she'd checked on the cattle and draft horses. As near as she could tell in the dark, since they'd been close by the barn as was their custom at night, they were all okay. The ample grass in the pasture had provided their food, and they drank water from the spring. Her animals tended to, she had dragged herself back to the cabin, and thrown herself, dirty, sweaty clothes and all, onto her bed and gone immediately to sleep, just like Bertha had done, too.

Now, as she hoed the garden, ridding it of weeds and choking vines, she paused to wipe her sweating brow with her shirtsleeve. She straightened up, put her hand to the small of her back and arched it and twisted from side to side to ease the cricks and kinks. Then, leaning on her hoe, she looked around the homestead. With Bertha's help it was already looking like new. Jessie sighed. There would be no replacing the precious windows that had been broken; she remembered her parents fussing about bringing them. Mother had won, of course. Oh well, she and Bertha would think of something to close them with long before it got cold, which wouldn't happen for another couple of months.

Deciding that this daydreaming about the future was not getting anything done in the present, Jessie went back to her hoeing. Of all the farm chores, she

190

hated this one the most—no, she hated the plowing the most. Or at least she thought she did. She'd not had to do any yet, but she knew how it had challenged and wearied her father. And he was a lot bigger than her. And, oh, even worse than the plowing was the harvesting. This was August now—harvesttime. She straightened up once again and groaned when she looked at the fields behind the barn. Row after row of the tall corn plants her father had so carefully planted and tended. When was she supposed to do that?

Jessie fought the sense of defeat which threatened to bring tears to her eyes. How could just she and Bertha manage? Jessie felt like a fool for her thoughts yesterday about keeping her father's dream alive—he wouldn't expect her to die trying. And all her noble thoughts of a solitary life, just her and Bertha, big landowners, rich and full of wisdom, greeting wagon trains and maybe even having a settlement spring up here one day. How silly!

With her thoughts directed so inwardly, Jessie didn't even realize for a second or two that she'd finished one row and was ready for the next. Surprised, she started laughing. Yes, she could do it, too—just like this, one row at a time, one chore at a time. Why, look at all she and Bertha had accomplished only yesterday evening and this morning! Who needed a man or extra hands? She laughed aloud now. Who needed Jake Coltrane?

Instantly, her spirits tumbled. She realized what she was doing. She was working herself to death in an effort not to think about . . . him. Absently now she reached inside her shirt and pulled out the piece of ribbon she'd tied around her neck last night. The two gold bands were looped through the ribbon;

Cheryl Anne Porter

Jessie fingered the rings and fought the lump in her throat. Who needed Jake Coltrane?

Jessie thrust the rings back under her shirt when she heard Bertha calling excitedly to her from the cabin porch. Jessie could see her waving her arms and practically jumping up and down. She looked around to where Bertha was pointing up the trail as it disappeared around a big hill, the direction from which the trains came. Sure enough, a cloud of dust preceded the wagons coming into view.

Thankful for any diversion from this hated hoeing and her dismal thoughts, Jessie dropped the hoe and ran for the cabin. When she got to the porch, she stopped beside Bertha, who gave her a big hug and chimed, "Our first customers!"

Jessie laughed. She was right! Their first customers. Instantly she was as excited as Bertha as they waited for the wagons to round the bend. The first wagon came into view; Bertha grabbed onto Jessie's arm. She covered Bertha's hand with hers. They kept grinning at each other, as Bertha said, like jackasses eating briars.

But wait. Jessie tensed. Bertha felt it and looked anxiously over at her. "What is it, child?"

"Bertha, this is strange. There's only one wagon and a few men. There should be more." Jessie craned her neck this way and that, but no, no more wagons.

"Should I get my buffalo gun, do you think?" Bertha was craning her neck, too.

Jessie laughed at that. That cannon could surely keep the peace! "No, Bertha, I don't think so. They could just be ahead of everyone else. We certainly don't want to seem unfriendly by waving guns at them."

"Well," Bertha said, not really convinced, "if'n you say so."

They moved off the wood porch to greet the lone wagoneers. As she walked toward them, she saw they were staring at her and Bertha just as hard as they were being stared at. Jessie laughed to herself; it must be the men's clothing she and Bertha were wearing. Nearly to the wagon, Jessie began taking in specific details. There were two men climbing off the wagon's buckboard seat. Two horsemen rode on each side of the wagon. They looked friendly enough; no guns out, no rifles out. And they were smiling. Jessie relaxed, telling herself she was jittery from her last encounter with horsemen in this very yard only three days ago.

All six men doffed their hats when they realized these were indeed women standing in front of them. "Howdy, ma'am, and . . . ma'am," they said all around.

"Good morning, and welcome to the Stuart Homestead." Jessie knew she sounded a little pompous, but what the heck. She figured that was the reason they exchanged glances when she told them where they were. "This your first time on the trail?"

"Uh, yes ma'am," a rather big, redheaded man answered her. "You could say that."

"Well, Bertha and I—I'm Jessie Stuart—are glad you decided to stop here."

"Yes, ma'am, everyone knows about the Stuart place. You could say we were practically ordered to come here," a young, gangly, brown-haired man answered, a huge smile on his face as he looked at Jessie. A sharp jab in his ribs from the big, red-headed man silenced him.

Jessie bit back a smile. Obviously the young man

was smitten with her. "Well, help yourselves and your animals to the water over there." All eyes followed to wherever she pointed as she talked. "And over there is a permanent place for a campfire—it's ringed with rocks; you can't miss it. You can tie up your horses over there by the corral. Were you wanting to buy any milk, eggs, greens, anything like that for your long trip ahead?"

This seemed to catch the men off-guard. They looked at each other and shrugged their shoulders.

Jessie tried another question. "How long do you plan on staying here?"

The same eager young man spoke right up, "Only until our contacts come. We're not with a train." He got another poke and another sharp look. He got quiet and looked down at his boots.

Jessie bit her lip to keep from laughing at the talkative young man. She attributed the other men's annoyance with him to the usual reticence teamsters displayed; they didn't talk too much or give too much away about themselves or their cargoes.

"Oh, I see," Jessie offered, trying to come to the young man's rescue. "You're waiting to join one. Well, one should be through anytime now—maybe even today. Look, I'll tell you what. We have so many extra eggs and so much milk that we couldn't possibly use them all before they go bad. Will you accept my gift of them to you for your noon meal?"

This got an instant, cheerful response from the six men. They were only too happy to get the eggs and milk themselves from out of the barn and the cool root cellar. Jessie'd had Bertha help her last night to set the large pails of milk in the cellar to keep it from going bad right off. As they set about their tasks, Jessie watched them for a few minutes. She

194

felt very magnanimous giving them the food; she knew that sometimes the people on the trains had no extra money. She couldn't sit here on all that fresh produce and not feed hungry men! She now laughed at herself. Between her tender heart and Bertha's, they'd be broke in six months for sure.

Jessie had just finished her lunch and was going back outside when she heard the sounds of approaching riders. As Bertha was still eating, Jessie told her to stay and finish; she'd take care of these people. Her first thought was of a wagon train, but she immediately dismissed this when she rounded the cabin to see a dozen or so more men on horses congregating around the lone wagon that had arrived earlier that morning.

As she approached the throng of dismounting men and milling horses, she began to realize that she'd seen some of these men before. They were from Camp Nichols. Indeed, some of them even greeted her as she passed among them, making her way to the center knot of men. As proprietor of the homestead, she felt it was her duty to welcome each new group and try to be of help. But this was definitely strange—the men were not in uniform. She did notice that they were heavily armed, though, and heavily supplied as evidenced by the pack animals they had along.

Her curiosity piqued, she shouldered her way to the small group of men standing with their backs to her. These men appeared to be the leaders, as they were deep in conversation with the large, redheaded man who'd come with the wagon, and were showing maps and papers all around. But Jessie's footsteps slowed and a knot formed in her throat as she came to stand just behind these men.

If that wasn't Jake Coltrane's back to her and if that wasn't his voice giving orders, then she was going crazy. Before she could do an about-face and get away, the large, red-haired man saw her, cleared his throat and nodded at her, more as a signal to the other men that they had company than as a greeting to her.

Sure enough. Jake Coltrane turned around to face her. His fiercely blue eyes rooted her to the ground. She didn't know she was going to do it until she did it, but with all her strength, she reached up and slapped the fire out of him.

Even though the blow jerked his head sideways, he calmly turned his face back to Jessie. A muscle twitched in his reddened jaw as her hand print became more and more clear on his cheek. All conversations ceased throughout the crowded yard as the slap rang through the company of men. Tears stung Jessie's eyes, just as her palm stung from the force of her blow, but she never looked away from him.

In the next second, all the men suddenly found reasons to disperse to other parts of the homestead. Talking too loudly and almost running, they made their escape, leaving Jake and Jessie virtually alone.

Jake brought a hand up to rub his cheek. "I guess I deserve that."

When Jessie brought her hand up again and drew her arm back, Jake caught it in a viselike grip. "Hold it, Jessie! That's enough! Do you hear me?"

"Enough?!" Jessie cried. "Enough? It will never be enough! You had no right—"

Her words were cut off when Jake grabbed her elbow firmly and began marching with her toward the gate to the meadow. She practically had to run to keep up with his long-legged stride. Pulling and jerking as she was against his hold on her, she stumbled and nearly fell. But Jake's strong grip on her forced her to keep her feet.

"Open that gate," Jake barked to the few men who had been unfortunate enough to be standing in front of it. They quickly did as they were told and got out of the way. "Don't let anyone else through here. I'll be right back," he told them grimly. Several answers of "Yessir" followed Jake and Jessie through the long grass of the meadow.

Jessie saw where he was headed. There was a large stand of scrubby blackjack trees surrounding the spring of water in the meadow. Jake waved his free hand wildly and made loud shooing noises to scatter the cattle under the trees. When they were on the other side of the trees, out of view of the yard, he swung Jessie around to face him.

"Let go of me, damn you, or I'll claw your eyes out," Jessie hissed, looking for all the world like a spitting wildcat readying for the kill.

She felt great satisfaction to see the startled look on Jake's face. He instantly let go of her. "Jessie, I—"

"Don't you Jessie me, mister. You have no right to—"

"I have every right, Jessie," he cut in, anger like a steel knife edging his voice. "In case you've forgotten, you're still my wife."

"Your wife?" Jessie squawked, choking on the words. How dare he! All she could do was stare openmouthed at him. He dared to bring that sham of a ceremony up, knowing it meant less than nothing to him? Did he really expect her to honor what was done simply to preserve his secret identity from her? "Well, you've certainly been one hell of a husband!"

"Dammit, Jessie, quit cussing. I don't like it when you do. It's . . . it's not ladylike." He finished lamely, looking unsure for once, even hesitant, as if he didn't know what to do with this spitting feline in front of him.

But that made no difference to Jessie. She was not about to feel sorry for him. No, sir. In fact, his last comment, a slur on her femininity, was the last straw. "When did I ever say I was a lady? And how would you ever know if I was one, Jake Coltrane? All you've ever done is drag me around this countryside and nearly get me killed—or worse!"

"Jessie, will you please keep your voice down," he said, looking through the trees toward the yard. "I'd rather settle this privately, if you don't mind."

"You can't come onto my land and tell me to be quiet! I'll yell all I want to, you son of a—!"

The word never got out. Jessie found herself in Jake's firm embrace, being kissed soundly. She knew in her wild struggles that he was doing it only to hush her, and not because of anything he felt for her. She pommeled his back ineffectually with her small fists. But, as his kiss deepened, her blows lessened in intensity and, before she could stop herself, she wound her arms around his neck. Even while she surrendered to his kiss, she hated herself for giving in to him. One kiss from him was all it took for her to forsake her pride and all her convictions? She didn't know if the small whimper which escaped her was because of his kiss or because of her weakness.

When he finally released her, Jessie sagged against him. Her heart was beating so wildly, she was dizzy. Her hat had come off in her struggles, and Jake was now stroking her long hair and whispering, "Jessie, Jessie." Still enfolded in his arms, she felt his wildly beating heart against her ear. She turned her liquid, brown eyes up to his face and gently fingered the angry red weals on his cheek.

"You did deserve that, you know," she said, the words not fitting the low, caressing tone of her voice.

Jake caught her fingers in his and put them to his lips, kissing each tip individually. "That and more," he admitted in a voice husky with desire.

Each of his nibbling kisses to her fingertips sent little shocking shivers through Jessie. She couldn't take her eyes off his mouth, but the rest of her body was concentrating on the growing, tight little bud that was the center of her desire. Jessie's mouth went dry and her eyelids drooped. She had to have more.

This time she took the initiative and brought his head down to meet her mouth. The swirling, enchanting dance of their darting tongues licked Jessie's desire into flames. There were no conflicts, no anger, no insults, no violent past between them now. Just this all-consuming passion of a man and a woman who could not deny what was so obvious between them.

Before she knew it, she was on the ground with Jake beside her. She watched herself practically tear Jake's shirt from him in her haste to run her hands over his muscled, tanned chest. She wanted to kiss him there and run her fingers through the dark fine, curly hair she'd seen so many times. She would not be denied any longer. In her passion-induced state which suspended rational thought and judgment, she even helped Jake remove her shirt. She saw his

199

eyes widen at the two rings on the ribbon she wore around her neck. He gave her a slow smile. Jessie responded by brazenly arching her back up to him, wanting . . . wanting . . . what? Oh, yes, that was it, she moaned when his mouth captured a rosy peak and his tongue brought the nipple to a stiff peak of desire. She had two handfuls of his hair as her hands directed his mouth to the other breast. She heard small, gasping sounds; they had to be coming from her. She didn't care. She needed more, more of him. With wild abandon, urging him onward, she raked her fingernails across his back and heard herself say, "Please, Jake, please."

He raised his head. Blue eyes almost black with passion bored into hers. "Are you sure, Jessie?" His words sounded raspy and breathless.

"Oh, God, yes. Please!" she begged, raising her head until she could place small, biting kisses on his unbandaged shoulder and up to his neck. Jessie felt the first stirring of her power as a woman when she saw his eyes close and she felt the great shudder which shook him with each of her kisses.

Somehow he pulled himself away from her and knelt beside her. Urging her to raise her hips, he undid the belt which fastened her pants and slid them off her, taking her bloomers too in the same motion. His strong hands on the bare flesh of her thighs and then calves sent ripples of pleasure from Jessie's center. He then took each boot off and slipped her clothes over her feet, baring her naked body to his eyes for the first time. The complete look of awe, desire, and wonder Jessie saw on his face made her very proud of her woman's body. It was her gift to him.

Beyond control of any sort now, Jake stood to

remove his boots and pants. He never took his eyes off Jessie for a second as she lay before him in the sweet, clovered grass of the meadow. She squirmed almost uncontrollably as she watched him unbuckle his belt and unfasten his pants. She watched the tantalizing dark line of hair which ran from his chest, down the center of his rigidly muscled torso, and disappeared into his pants.

Before he pulled his pants off, he sat by her, his eyes still holding hers, and yanked his boots off. He stopped undressing himself briefly to bend over her and kiss her ribs below her breasts, to kiss her belly and swirl his tongue around her navel. A little lower and he felt the quivering convulsions just above the thick, black patch of hair between her thighs. Jessie clutched at him, her eyes wide, her mouth open. Quickly now he divested himself of his pants.

Jessie caught her breath at the sight of him standing over her. She'd seen pictures of the Greek gods in the many, many books her mother had given her to read, but they were no match for the man in front of her. Even the white bandages over his wound added to his beauty. The stark whiteness against his deep tan only accentuated his lean, muscled frame. And he wanted her. There could be no mistaking that.

Jessie'd never seen . . . this . . . before on a man, but it's largeness or rigidness did not frighten her. After all, it was a part of him, and she loved him. She was proud that she could do that to him, that he wanted her so much. Crazily she wished she had some sort of . . . something . . . to show him so obviously how much she wanted him. She looked into his eyes and raised her arms to him, beckoning him to join her. And he did.

Cheryl Anne Porter

Very gently he used his knee to separate her knees. He lay on top of her now, supporting his weight with his elbows. Despite her raging desire and the marvel of his chest against hers, Jessie began to tense. She had no idea what to expect. Jake must have sensed this for he raised his head from kissing the column of her neck and her jawline to whisper to her, "I'll try not to hurt you, little Jessie. But there will be some pain—but only this time. Never again will I hurt you. I love you."

With that, he positioned himself between her legs. Jessie felt the first thrust of his manhood and she instinctively bent her knees, but she also tensed and dug her fingernails into his back. Jake stopped and spoke soft words of love to her, calling her name over and over until she was returning his kisses and moaning. Jessie felt herself getting moist around the shaft seeking entrance into her. Jake must have been waiting for that sign, because he once again mounted his assault.

One sharp, almost savage thrust tore through the last shred of Jessie's resistance. As she opened her mouth to cry out, Jake gave her a lingering kiss and began the gentle thrusts that Jessie knew beyond a doubt were what the nameless something she'd been longing for was all about. Not just this act, but this man. This man. No other.

She heard Jake's voice in her ear, she heard herself whispering back, and she even felt herself answering his thrusts with equal passion and force. Her nails raked his back; he grabbed her hair in his hands and kissed the dark, tangled tresses. Jessie felt her breathing and her desire swirling upward, upward, like a coil being pulled tighter and tighter at both ends as Jake's thrusts became more rapid and more rhythmical. Her body was made of nerve endings, raw nerve endings. She wanted, she wanted . . .

. . . this explosion of her inner bud, this opening of the tiny flower to full bloom, this dry feeling in the back of her mouth, this rhythmic convulsing in her belly, this weakness and warmth in her thighs, this full flowering of her womanhood which pulled Jake into her, demanding he give his all to her. And he did.

With one last, powerful thrust, she heard his great shuddering cry and opened her eyes to see him hang suspended over her for the briefest, longest second. She felt the flowing of his body into hers, the liquid giving of his power to her, the release of his juices which brought life to her swirling, eddying flower bud.

And then he lowered himself onto her. Jessie loved the slippery feel of him now, the thin patina of sweat which covered both their bodies. And the feel of his weight on her. It just felt . . . right. Even though he still supported his weight with his elbows to keep from crushing her, she pulled him to her and smiled. Somehow she knew this smile was like no other she'd ever given. How could it be? She'd never felt like this before, had never done this before. Of course she was different. She looked into blue eyes that sparkled now. Then she reached up and brushed away a stray, damp lock of hair from his forehead. He brought his head down and planted a little kiss on the tip of her nose. "My little Jessie," he said aloud, almost in a normal voice.

When he pulled himself up slightly and withdrew from her, Jessie felt so very alone. She knew now she would be complete only with what he could give her—not just his lovemaking, even though it was certainly wonderful enough, but with his body and soul. That's what love was. Love. Then it struck Jessie, and she turned to face him. He was lying on his side beside her, up on one elbow, one knee bent; he had been gently smoothing his hands over her belly and breasts. But now with her up on her side, he let his hand stray to the rise of her hip. He had a most wondering look on his face, Jessie decided.

"You said you love me!" Jessie cried. "You did, didn't you?"

He became instantly still, screwed his face up, and looked toward the sky. He drummed his fingers on Jessie's hip as if in great thought. She sat up and smacked at his upper arm playfully. "You did! Admit it!" Her hands went to her waist.

With a great chuckle and a warm look on his face, he said, "Now how could I deny it with you sitting there like that—with all your womanly charms exposed?"

"Jake Coltrane!" she scolded and launched herself at him.

He caught her in his arms and rolled onto his back, laughter rumbling through his chest. He placed her hands behind his neck and wrapped her in his embrace. "Okay, I said it. Now you say it."

"No," she teased, "I won't." She raised her head as much as was possible in his strong grip and whistled nonchalantly, looking everywhere but at him.

"Say it!" he growled, poking her sides with his fingers.

Squirming in laughter, she cried, "Stop it, Jake! Stop it! Okay, okay, you brute, I love you!"

With that, he released her and sat up himself. They faced each other, naked and in a meadow, very much like Adam and Eve, Jessie thought. From around her neck, he took the long piece of ribbon with the two rings on it. He broke the knot in the ribbon, let the rings slide into his palm, and placed Jessie's ring on her finger. He then gave her his ring. She placed it on his finger.

Jessie could barely breathe. "We are really married, aren't we?" she asked very hesitatingly.

Chapter Twelve

When Jake didn't answer right away, Jessie frowned. "We aren't, are we?"

Jake put a hand out tentatively and stroked her bare arm. "Jessie, to be honest, I'm not sure. I meant to check on that when I was at Camp Nichols, but there was no time. I do believe that since I married you using my alias, we are not legally married."

Jessie looked down at the trampled grass in front of her as she thought. When she saw the small bloodstain in the clover, her stomach lurched painfully and her eyes widened. Instantly she remembered what Jake had told her in Bertha's wagon on the night they were married—or not married—about blood the first time. And here it was. There was no way to undo this mistake.

If they weren't married, then what they'd just done was a mistake. If their marriage was a sham, then so was this act. She hated Jake for sullying this, too. Only married people were supposed to make love— her mother had said so, and she'd said Jessie was to save herself for her husband. Now she was ruined. Her throat constricted. How could she be ruined by something so beautiful and so good? She'd given herself so freely to him just now because she knew as his wife that it was right. But now . . .

When Jessie looked up, it was to give Jake a hard stare. She abruptly stood up, tore the ring from her finger and threw it on the ground. Jake's reaction was swift; he stood up in one fluid motion and grabbed her arm as she, with very jerky motions, retrieved her clothes.

"Jessie, what's wrong? What did you do that for?" he asked, pointing to her ring on the ground.

Jessie pulled her arm free, refusing to answer him or to look at him. If he couldn't figure it out for himself, then he was a big dolt. Her mouth set in an angry, firm line, she hastily dressed herself. The choking sobs threatened to spill out of her if she opened her mouth. She kept her eyes averted from Jake; she knew he was standing there watching her. She could feel his nearness.

"Jessie, will you please talk to me?" he pleaded. Out of the corner of her eye, she saw him bend over and pick up her ring. But she wouldn't take it when he tried to give it back to her. With a heavy sigh, he put it on his little finger; it would go only past the first knuckle.

Jessie stood under the large scrub oak tree, her arms crossed beneath her breasts, one knee bent. She knew without looking that he was getting dressed. She hoped the gentle wind blowing through her hair would help dry the tears spilling down her cheeks. He'd known they weren't married, and yet he still . . .

She was spun around before she could stop him. She was almost swayed by the anguished look on his face. But not quite. She tried to pull herself free, but his grip was too strong on her arms. "Jessie, you're going to listen to me. Even if we're not married according to the law, we're married by the love in our hearts. I do love you, Jessie. I do. You are really scaring me, because I don't know what crazy notion you've got going around in your head. You've got to talk to me now, because I'm leaving in a few short hours, and I don't know when I'll be back. You can't send me away like this, Jessie."

That struck her. She hadn't even asked what he was doing here with all those men. Despite her earnest intention not to talk to him, she asked, "So now you're going to leave me again—just like before? Every time I get around a stand of trees and water with you, I get loved and left. Do you do this to all your women?"

"All my women? What the hell—? There's only you, Jessie. See? I knew something crazy was rattling around in that pretty little head of yours." Jake smiled at her warmly and gently shook her, trying to cajole her out of this mood.

"Stop that right now, Jake Coltrane!" Jessie bolted, freeing herself. "You're treating me like a child. And I'm not one, you know. Thanks to you, I'm a woman . . . a fallen woman . . . but a woman." She couldn't stop the tears from falling in torrents from her eyes.

"What the—?" Jake cried out, laughter behind his words. "A fallen woman? Oh, for crying out loud, Jessie—"

That was the last straw. Fists balled up angrily, she got right in his face—or chest, more accurately. She had to strain her neck upward to look into his eyes. She knew that the heat in her face was not from the hot August sun high overhead. Her tears dried instantly. "Well, just what do you call women who do . . . that when they're not married?" As she spoke, she pointed to the ground where they'd just lain together.

Jake turned slightly away from her, hands on hips, head shaking. Then he rubbed a hand over his eyes, which were squeezed shut. Jessie waited. Just let him answer that one, she dared in her thoughts. So intent was she on nurturing her anger that she jumped when he finally spoke.

"You're so young," Jake breathed out, shaking his head. "Look, when two people love each other— truly love each other—acting on that love is never wrong. It's a very natural thing, Jessie—it's how people show they love each other. That's why it's called making love. Got that? Okay. Next thing. You're not a fallen woman by any means. You're not bad, either. Bad women, fallen women, don't make love like you just did. Men have a cruder term for what it is they do with women like that. Don't you ever think you're one of those women, Jessie. Are you ashamed or sorry for making love to me?"

"No," came her quiet answer. How could she deny it or lie about it? After all, she'd even begged him to . . . make love to her. Her cheeks burned anew with the pictures flashing through her mind, pictures of her and him there in the grass. How could she be so wanton?

Another thought struck her—and then another. He'd never said he was going to marry her for real.

He'd never said where he was going and why. Just that he didn't know when he'd be back. This was love?

"Then if you really love me, Jake, stay here now. Don't go away. Marry me and stay here."

Jessie did not feel as confident as her words sounded, especially when she saw him blink in surprise and take a step back from her. "Jessie, I can't do that. You saw all the men there and the wagon. I have to go. It's my job."

Jessie turned away abruptly, putting a steadying hand on the rough bark of the oak tree. His job. It would always come first. Just look at everything he'd already done in the name of his job. U. S. Marshal. A job that could very easily get him killed. This thought brought bile to Jessie's throat. What would she do then? She did really love him.

And now that she was no longer a . . . virgin, she could even be carrying his baby. Jessie's legs turned to water. She didn't know a whole lot about this man-woman thing, but she did know that. Her mother had always laughed about getting pregnant with Jessie on her wedding night, the first time her mother had made love. Jessie put her other hand to her throat, willing herself not to cry.

Jessie was not aware that Jake had come around the tree to stand in front of her until she, still looking at the ground, saw his boots. She slowly raised her eyes to his face, hoping her face was not as pale as she suspected it was.

He put a hand out as if to touch her cheek, but then dropped it back to his side. "I have to go. You know that. We can straighten all this out when I get back." Then, thinking of her father's possible involvement in the gunrunning, Jake added, "I'll have more answers then. Jessie, I shouldn't be telling you this, but it's also very important to your future that I go."

Jessie brought her brows together. Confusion and curiosity tinged her words. "My future? What does that mean?"

When Jake began making little gestures that told her he really had something disturbing to tell her, but didn't know how, Jessie felt her throat constrict, and her limbs grow heavy. Something was very wrong. The longer he waited to speak, the more she died inside.

"Your father may have been involved in the gunrunning, Jessie. I'm not sure yet. Most likely he wasn't, but I just don't know. But what you should know is that if I find out he was helping Hayes, then the government will confiscate your home—all of it and everything on it. Every animal, every stalk of corn. I'm so sorry, Jessie."

Jessie felt like she'd been turned to stone. Her father—involved with Hayes? *No!* her mind screamed. Take away her homestead—the only thing in her life she could count on? *No!* And the man she loved would be the one to ruin her father's name and his precious memory? *No!*

Suddenly she knew what she had to do. If Jake expected an outburst, he would be disappointed, she determined. All the anger, all the fear, all the hatred she felt at this moment centered on Jake and radiated at him through her dark eyes. "You're lying," she said in a low, raspy voice, and walked away.

Leaning his forearm against the oak, one knee bent, his other hand on his hip, Jake watched her go. What the hell had possessed him to tell her of his suspicions about her father? Did he think she would understand? Jake mentally kicked himself. He'd probably just cost himself the only woman he'd ever loved. Jake wasn't sure he could get her to forgive him even if he cleared her father's name. Jeez, he knew better than to get involved with the people in his assignments. No, that was too cold. Jessie wasn't "people." She was the woman he loved.

With those thoughts, he jammed his hat down on his head more tightly and walked back to the yard. None of the men were eager to look him in the eyes, and none of them said anything or made any reference to him being in the meadow for over an hour. Jake noticed that, in his absence, they'd readied everything for the trip to Santa Fe. But the second wagon of guns still wasn't there. Jake grunted impatiently. Great. Now they had to wait, something he was definitely not in the mood to do. But it couldn't be helped.

To pass the time more quickly, Jake once again briefed his men on their mission. Then, he personally checked the wagonload of guns again. He smiled at this. Just in case the deal went sour and none of them made it out alive, the firing pins had been removed from the guns. That way, they would be worthless to Vasquez. To cover that, Jake would tell Vasquez that he would get the firing pins when he gave Jake the money for the guns. Call it insurance.

Leaning against the back of the wagon, Jake looked around the yard at the men entrusted to him for this assignment. Good men, all of them. Some of them were married, had children. Some of them were very young and green—Lieutenant

Patterson, for example. Jake felt the weight of his responsibility to them fall on his shoulders. They did not deserve anything but his best, his undivided attention, during the next few months. But, for the first time in his career, he wasn't sure he could put aside his personal feelings—namely, Jessie.

He removed her ring from his little finger and then the one he still wore. He put them both in his shirt pocket and buttoned it. Then, crossing his arms over his broad chest, he called one of the men over and gave him an order to ride up the trail to see if he could spot the other wagon. The shadows in the yard were beginning to get long. He did not relish the thought of spending a night here with Jessie so close, yet so far away and troubled.

Jake took the few steps to the corral where Blaze was tied. The stallion nickered and pushed his nose against Jake's chest. Jake stroked the warm, velvety nose. He spoke softly to his mount. "Boy, this is no time for me to start having doubts about what I do. You know I have to turn in anything I find out about her father, don't you? I can't let tears and big, brown eyes stop me from doing what's right. You know that, don't you, boy? You also know I love her, don't you? And you know that love and this job don't go together, do they?"

The roan gave a mighty shake of his head, as if in answer. Jake chuckled grimly. He had only himself to blame for what happened this afternoon. He'd only meant to quiet Jessie when he'd kissed her. He hadn't been ready for the explosion of passion he'd felt. Never before had he lost control so quickly with a woman. What had happened to that iron control he was so proud of, and to keeping his emotions so detached? What the hell, he grunted, feeling his

blood rush to his crotch. Just thinking about her—
he took a quick spin around the wagon, pretending
to check every cinch and knot on it. Down, boy,
he kept repeating to himself. Making love to Jessie
had been the best thing he'd ever done in his life—
and possibly the worst. What had possessed him to
make love to her?

Jake further surprised himself by hitting his fist
against the wagon, startling the horses harnessed
in the traces. As he came to their heads and calmed
them, he looked over again at the cabin. Yes, she
was the one, but what was he going to do about it?
Hell, what could he do about it? Jake knew what
his problem was—he was too used to being the one
in control, the one saying how things would go.
And now he wasn't. A small, dark-haired, dark-eyed,
fiery-spirited girl had complete control over him.
Jake shook his head sadly, denying the tears that
stood in his eyes. He loved her, dammit. But could
they ever be together?

Jake forced the tears from his eyes. Couldn't let
the men see him like this. Had to get a grip. This
mission was too vital. With a hoarse cough and a
determined stride, Jake went to meet the rider he'd
sent out to look for the other wagon. He hoped
it was good news. But the way things were going
lately, he doubted it.

"Now, child, you just get this crazy notion out
of your head! You're not a-goin' anywhere, do you
hear me?"

Jessie looked at Bertha, who was standing by the
fireplace and pointing a wooden spoon at her. Bertha's face was damp from the heat of the cookfire;
gray wisps of hair clung to her forehead and plump

cheeks. Her brows were drawn together in the anger Jessie knew she was causing. But she couldn't help it. She continued stuffing things she thought she would need into the bedroll laid out on her bed.

With her back to the older woman, she said, "Bertha, please don't call me a child. I'm . . . a woman now . . . just like you. And please don't try to stop me. I'm going—somehow. But I'm going."

Bertha's next words told Jessie she was trying another tack since anger and threats hadn't worked. Jessie let her talk, but she knew this would not work, either. "Now, you listen here to me, chil—woman. Jessie. What about this here place of yours? Am I, a poor old woman, supposed to run it myself? That wasn't the deal, now was it? Why, all this work will probably kill me! Now how would you feel about that?"

Jessie rushed to Bertha and hugged her neck fiercely. Then, releasing her, but keeping a hand on her plump arm, Jessie told her, "Bertha, you old fake! This is the lightest work you've done in years—you said so yourself! And this is your place, too. Not just mine, remember. We're partners. This is your home, too. And believe me, I feel bad about leaving you here alone like this. But you're not really alone. Camp Nichols is close and the wagon trains come through all the time. Why, your train will be through before you know it!"

Bertha harrumphed her opinion of all this. Jessie tried again. "Please, Bertha, try to understand. I have to do this. I have to. I can't tell you everything, but you have to know that I wouldn't run off like a jackrabbit if it wasn't important. I'll be back before you know it."

Jessie walked back to her bed and began rolling

her things up. How could she tell Bertha that they could lose everything they had? She just couldn't find the words to say her father might have been involved with Hayes. All she knew was she had to find a way to clear her father's name. Or she had to hear him being accused with her own ears to believe it.

She'd seen the boxes of guns in the wagon—after all, they were labeled Property of U.S. Army. And those men with Jake. They were soldiers. She shook her head. It didn't take a genius to figure out that Jake and those soldiers were delivering the guns themselves. And they were pretending to be the gunrunners. Why else would they not be in uniform?

Jessie knew from recent experience just how much danger she was placing herself in. But somehow, someway, she was going, too. She would clear her father's name and memory herself. And, quickly slipping her father's handgun in among her things with a quick look over her shoulder at Bertha, if it became necessary, she would be able to defend herself. Never again would she be at the mercy of the likes of Hayes.

Jessie shuddered at that thought. A sniffle escaped her when she thought about Skinner dying to protect her. Never again would she let a good man die because she was so helpless. That thought brought her chin up and her lips firmly together. No, she was a woman now—in every sense. And for all she knew, she could even be a mother in nine months. No sitting, no waiting, no wringing her hanky and wondering what was true. Those bad men now had Jessie Stuart to contend with. And they better watch out.

Jessie looked up and out the window over her bed. Evening was almost here. The darker it got, the better her chances of hiding herself in the wagon. There were a lot of men out there, not all of them huge men. There were some slender, young ones. In the dark, with her father's clothes on, they'd never suspect a thing. She didn't know exactly what they were waiting for before they left, but she hoped they didn't wait until morning. Well, it couldn't be helped. She'd just have to sleep in the wagon to make sure she didn't miss leaving tomorrow morning. She prayed she wasn't found out until it was too late to send her home.

Now that she was packed, she could help Bertha with supper. Feeding all those men was no small chore. But at least she and Bertha were being paid. Jessie, reaching for an apron hung on a nail by the fireplace, looked again at Bertha. Bertha was confused and scared for her, Jessie knew that. If she felt bad at all about what she was doing, it was on Bertha's account. And the way Bertha was slamming lids on pots and slamming dishes down on the table, Jessie knew she still had some talking to do.

Letting her breath out heavily through her parted lips, Jessie tied the apron on over the blue checked gingham dress she'd put on after washing when she came in from the meadow. Bertha had known something was wrong. How could she not, Jessie thought. Her tear-streaked face, her grass-streaked hair, and disheveled clothes spoke volumes. Yet, Bertha hadn't said a word. She'd raised her eyebrows and that was all. Jessie wanted to tell her, but she was too ashamed. She'd lain with the man who could take everything she loved away from her. He'd said it was his job. Well, her job was to stop him.

Jessie didn't want to hear Bertha tell her that she'd been a fool to give herself to Jake. She already knew that. Even if Bertha's reaction would be one of sympathy and understanding, Jessie wasn't sure she could take that, either. But, she knew Bertha well enough to know that she'd probably grab up her buffalo gun and force Jake to marry her right here and now. Jessie could not stand the thought of that humiliation—or the look on Jake's face when he was forced for the second time to marry her.

Bertha's slamming things around and Jessie's deep thoughts were both interrupted by an abrupt knock at the cabin door. Since she was closer to it than Bertha, Jessie turned and opened the door. Her heart went to her throat. It was Jake! Maybe he'd come back to tell her . . .

"Evening," he said, rather formally. Since Jessie did not move from the open doorway or invite him in, he was forced to speak from where he was. He kept his eyes on Bertha. "I came to tell you that we're not leaving you alone here. I have orders to leave six men for your protection until Sergeant MacKenzie is arrested. He knows both of you are involved somehow with me, so it could be dangerous for you if he came here before Colonel Carson can arrest him. When our other wagon of Colts arrives, we'll be leaving for Mexico. Probably tomorrow morning."

Jessie felt her heart sink lower and lower as Jake spoke. He'd come here now on official business. No word of promise for her, not even a private look or gesture. It was as if this afternoon had never happened. Bertha was beside her now, wiping her hands on her apron as Jake spoke. Jessie was very afraid that Bertha would say something to Jake about Jessie's intentions.

"Well, at least I won't be alone. That's something," Bertha huffed, and turned back to her cooking.

Jessie's eyes flew to Jake's. If he'd caught Bertha's exact words, he gave no indication. Instead his eyes turned a very warm blue, and he smiled down at her. Jessie felt her mouth go dry and her breathing quicken. She hated that just one look from him could do this to her.

"You know, this is only the second time I've seen you in a dress," he said in a low voice. "You ought to wear one more often." His eyes raked her appreciatively.

Jessie's heart beat rapidly. She was helpless before him. She kept a firm grip on the open door to keep from reaching out to touch him. She almost sank to the floor when he reached out and caressed her cheek with the back of his hand. Then he turned and walked away. Jessie's gaze and her heart followed him until he turned a corner by the barn and was out of sight. As she closed the door, she comforted herself with the knowledge that she would see him again—very soon.

Chapter Thirteen

Jessie did not know if she was grateful for the heavy tarp covering her and the cases of guns in the back of the wagon, or if she hated it for blocking out the daylight and any fresh breeze that might waft through the wagon to cool her. Wedged as she was between the side of the wagon and the wood crates, she felt every bump and rattle of the wagon as it coursed along the Santa Fe Trail. Her hastily packed blanket roll lay under her, providing her only cushioning.

All the things she hadn't thought about in her determination to come on this trip now assailed her. She was hungry. Luckily, Bertha had relented and had packed her some biscuits, bacon, dried fruit, cookies, and a canteen of water. But Jessie couldn't get to them in her roll. The food was probably smashed to crumbs by her weight on it; and she was sure that the hard thing jabbing her full bladder with each jarring roll of the wagon wheels was the canteen lid.

And that was another thing. She needed to relieve herself—now. And the heat under this tarp was unbearable. Her father's long-sleeved shirt, even though she'd rolled up the sleeves, and his denim pants were anything but light and airy. She was hot under here—and itchy, sticky and irritable. She swore to herself that she'd never boil another vegetable now that she knew how it felt. She impatiently brushed long, damp wisps of her hair out of her face and tried her best to hold the masses of dark curls up off her neck. But that didn't help. There was no fresh breeze under this damnable tarp to cool her.

Jessie fought back tears of frustration and anger. To be undone by her own physical needs was too much. With her father's name and reputation at stake, she couldn't very well give in to the overwhelming desire to throw the blasted tarp off her, stand straight up, and yell "I'm hot; I need to relieve myself; I'm hungry; I'm thirsty; I hate this wagon; and how long before we're there?"

The picture she conjured up in her mind of the ruckus she'd cause if she did that dried the tears, but brought giggles dangerously close to the surface. To keep from actually shouting in laughter, Jessie clamped both hands firmly over her traitorous mouth. But stopping the laughter convulsions reminded her that her bladder needed relieving. She instinctively placed a hand down there. No, please, don't let me wet my pants, she prayed. That picture in her mind made the giggles start again.

Jessie was afraid she was becoming demented from the lack of air. Even that thought made her want to laugh more—imagine the mens' faces if this wild-haired, crazy woman with wet pants suddenly stood up amongst their precious guns and began yelling at them. Oh, no, don't make me laugh, she prayed. Don't make me laugh!

The sudden stopping of the wagon sobered her instantly. All physical needs forgotten, she tensed and listened. Her heart leapt into her throat when the male voices spoke so close to her ear. They were beside the wagon; the only thing that separated them from Jessie was the tarp over her and the canvas side of the big prairie schooner. She tensed even more when she recognized that one of the men speaking was Jake. And he sounded angry.

"This is all the hell we need—a broken wagon wheel. Damn! What next?" Then, after a moment of tense silence, "All right, men, we have no choice. Patterson, pull this wagon over under those trees. We'll have to camp here for the night. The rest of you men come with me and help unload the wagon." As he walked off with the men, Jessie heard his fading voice still barking orders. "Unhitch those horses! Put the guns under those trees! Cockburn, see what you can do with that wheel!"

Jessie breathed out her relief that it was the other wagon with the broken wheel. As the wagon she was in started moving again in a lurching circle with the driver—Patterson, wasn't it?—urging the big draft horses to turn toward the trees, she chanced a peek out from under the tarp. Looking towards the front of the wagon, she saw the back of the driver. She couldn't tell much about him, but his voice sounded young. Somehow that made her feel better.

Looking past his shoulder, she saw the sun riding low in the sky. She must have dozed more than she thought! It was late afternoon. Good, Jessie thought.

As soon as it was dark, she would sneak out of the wagon, stretch her muscles, relieve her stressed bladder, and eat. She very reluctantly pulled the tarp back over her head, taking one last breath of sweet, fresh air. For now, all she could do was listen to the sounds of the men unhitching the horses and setting up camp. Grunting and straining sounds and hammering assailed her ears; fixing a broken wagon wheel was no easy matter out on the prairie.

Later, when Jessie peeked out from under the tarp, it was just as dark as it was under her cover. Noises had died down in the camp; men were talking in low voices; an occasional stamping or snorting came from the tethered horses; and no one seemed to be doing much walking about. Jessie'd had only one tense moment earlier when someone checking the load in her wagon had pulled on the tarp, straightening it over the wood crates.

She'd hoped to be able to wait until even later to venture outside, but she really could hold her bladder no longer. It was now or never. So, very slowly she pulled the canvas tarp back and lay there blinking, letting her eyes adjust to the darkness. Then, breathing shallowly and moving slowly on her belly, she scooted to the back opening of the wagon and peered out cautiously. She put her forehead to the gate, thanking her lucky stars that the only thing she saw was the trunk of a large tree to her left and then open prairie all to her right. The men and the campfire had to be somewhere toward the front of this wagon, judging by the dancing shadows she saw over her shoulder when she looked toward the buckboard driver's seat.

So far, so good, she breathed, as she eased herself over the back gate of the wagon. In her hand she had the cotton cloth which held her food. Once out of here, she wasn't getting back inside until she absolutely had to. Being jounced around all day had even made her wound from the flying glass of a few days ago hurt again. With both feet now on the ground, Jessie paused to listen to the sounds around her. No footsteps approaching her. Good. She figured that two or three steps would gain her the dense undergrowth in this stand of trees. That and night was all she needed to do her business! One step . . . two steps . . . three . . .

"Ufhh! Sorry, pal. It's all yours now."

As the man who'd bumped into her as he came out of the trees moved around her and walked on without a second glance, Jessie stifled the scream that was in her throat. Her sudden sweat belied the evening cool. She swallowed the scream in her throat and hustled herself into the protection of the scrubby bushes and long prairie grass. If she'd thought she had to go before . . . ! She threw her food down, and with dancing steps quickly undid her belt and pants, squatted, and relieved herself. This was heaven.

That done, she retrieved her food and moved to another part of the wooded area to stretch her cramping muscles and to eat. Using the moonlight as a guide, she found a suitable tree in a tiny clearing to rest her back against, and sat cross-legged. She unwrapped her dinner; pretty smashed and crumbled, as she'd expected, but it still looked wonderful to her ravenous eyes. With her whole being concentrated on eating, she didn't even consciously think about anything until she began to feel at least partially full. Then, with her physical needs taken care of, her mind wandered to Bertha. As usual, thinking of Bertha brought a smile to Jessie's face.

Just as Jake had told them last night, six soldiers were left behind to provide Bertha, and presumably herself, protection from MacKenzie. Jessie wondered who would protect the soldiers from Bertha! She knew in her heart that the poor men had by this time put in a full day's work around the homestead and were now snoring away, exhausted from their labors. Their presence there eased Jessie's conscience some about leaving Bertha.

But she knew she didn't have to feel badly. Bertha had hugged her before she'd sneaked out of the cabin and into the wagon, and told her that sometimes a woman just had to do what she had to do. There was no accountin' for it. But she'd also said she was glad she wouldn't be there when Mr. Jake Coltrane, U. S. Marshal, found out he had a stowaway!

Jessie shuddered. What would he do? What wouldn't he do was more like it, she snorted, taking another bite of her cookie and chewing thoughtfully. A little late to worry about that, she told herself as she swallowed and reached for her canteen. Her hand froze in mid-reach as the sound of footsteps moving ever closer to her assailed her ears. She listened intently. Only one set of footsteps. Whoever it was, he was alone. The footfalls were coming from her right, which meant her visitor had walked all the way around the perimeter of the trees to reach this point. Probably the soldier on guard duty. Jessie remained perfectly still, her hand still out to reach for the canteen.

She gulped hard when the footsteps stopped not more than a few feet from her. He was on the other side of the tree she was leaning against. Holding her breath, her heart thumping in her ears, her eyes as wide as an owl's, Jessie sat tensed for anything. Several minutes passed. Nothing. Why didn't the dolt go on, Jessie thought irritably. If he was on guard duty, then he should . . . go guard something!

Jessie couldn't stand the tension any longer. Her mother had told her a hundred times that her curiosity would get her killed one day. This just might be the day, Jessie thought, as she eased herself ever so slowly into a crawling position and quite stealthily worked her way on all fours around the tree trunk. Luckily this was summer, so the ground was soft and the grass was tender, even under the trees. No dry leaves to crunch and give her away.

Snap! Jessie froze. The sound echoed like a cannon in the otherwise quiet darkness. The man had his gun in his hand almost before he spun towards her. Too late, Jessie could now feel the dry little twig she'd placed her knee on and then all her weight as she'd been inching forward; she quickly shrunk back in a squatting position against the rough bark of the thick trunk. She realized she was about to find out just how long she could hold her breath. Terror oozed from every pore in her body.

"Who is it? Who goes there?" he challenged in a low, deadly voice.

Jessie closed her eyes and forced her ragged breath in and out through her nose. It was Jake. The only thing that had saved her from instant detection, she decided, was that he obviously expected whoever had crunched the twig to be walking upright, and not on all fours. Maybe if she was quiet enough, he would think it was an animal that had scurried away.

No such luck. Even now he was moving around the tree trunk; and the scraping noises of cloth on bark told her he too had his back against the tree trunk. She heard him cock his six-shooter; she gulped hard. She had only a few seconds. If she made a sudden movement, he'd probably shoot first and ask questions later. If she stayed where she was, he'd literally trip over her and come up firing. If she attempted to scoot around the tree away from him, he'd hear the same scraping of cloth on bark that she did and start shooting. What if she just popped up and said "Hello, Jake, how's it going?" No, no, no, she couldn't do that either.

While she considered her options, Jake inched ever closer to her. Looking around wildly, hoping for some inspiration, Jessie's darting gaze fell on her canteen. Her heart sank and her throat constricted. One more step and he would step on it! Jessie's arm snaked out and grabbed the leather thong strap on it and yanked—just as Jake placed his booted foot on the canteen itself.

The still night air was shattered by Jake's startled yell as he lost his balance and was suspended in air for a second before he hit the ground with teeth-rattling finality. His bone-jarring thud on the ground caused his gun to go off when his elbow hit hard dirt. The bullet careened crazily off the various tree trunks before coming to rest harmlessly somewhere in the undergrowth.

Jessie knew she should have been running away as fast as she could, but all she could do as long as that bullet was hunting a target was stay balled up in her squatting position with her arms covering her head. Then it was too late. Jake might be lying there in momentary shock, but not the rest of the men! They were this minute tearing through the wooded area, loudly cocking six-shooters and rifles and calling out Jake's name.

Jessie had the sudden thought that she could use all the confusion and the darkness to maybe get back to the wagon undetected. If she could just scoot away a little bit more from Jake and time her movements to make her getaway while the men were more concerned with seeing if Jake was all right—that stopped her. Was he all right? He'd hit the ground pretty hard and wasn't moving around now at all. Even though her mind screamed out against it, Jessie turned back and crawled over to him. Even intent as she was on Jake's still form, she could not block out the sounds of the men hunting and crashing through the underbrush. They'd be here any second. But she just had to know if . . .

The next thing she heard was her own startled cry as she was suddenly grabbed by her shirt, thrown down on the ground on her back, had a knee placed on her chest and a Colt revolver stuck in her face. Her eyes nearly crossed as she centered on the round, steel muzzle of the six-shooter.

"Don't . . . don't shoot, Jake . . . It's me—Jessie . . . Don't shoot."

Instantly she was hauled up onto her feet. The steel gun muzzle in her face was replaced by Jake's disbelieving eyes. Even though the only light in this tiny clearing was provided by the sharp slivers of moonlight which cut through the tangle of tree branches overhead, Jessie had no trouble seeing the play of emotions on Jake's face. Disbelief was replaced by shock, which gave way to anger. Anger? Rage, maybe. She tried a weak little yes-it's-really-me smile. Nothing. Suddenly the ricocheting bullet seemed a better option than facing Jake.

She was even glad when the other men started charging into the clearing. At least there would be witnesses when he killed her. With them all talking at once and all pointing guns at her, she decided she'd just stand still and concentrate on looking small while Jake assured everyone he was indeed okay and there was no trouble. Now all eyes fell on Jessie. She felt ridiculous with Jake holding onto her shirtfront, her hair tangled, and the accursed canteen dangling from her arm much like a lady's reticule.

One of the men approached her for a better look. It was the driver of the wagon she'd been hiding in. "Why, it's Miss Stuart! Miss Stuart, what are you doing here? Look, everybody, it's Miss Stuart!"

Jessie decided she would push him down hard if he said her name one more time. Now all the men were repeating it in surprise. To her, they sounded like a flock of big, dumb birds—Miss Stuart, Miss Stuart, caw, caw!

Jake's growling voice stopped her insolent thoughts. "Just what the hell do you *think* she's doing here, Patterson?" Exasperation and anger laced Jake's voice. Then he stopped, and a wondering look came over his face. He turned to Jessie. "Yeah, just what the hell *are* you doing here, Jessie?"

Jessie's gaze swept the dozen or so men ranged in front of her in a semicircle. All eyes waited curiously for her answer. She then looked up at Jake. His mouth was set in a grim line and one eyebrow was raised dangerously. Jessie swallowed hard and moistened her dry lips with her tongue. And then she promptly fainted.

Or she pretended to faint. But they didn't know that. As she sighed loudly and went completely limp, sagging toward the ground in a very slow, dramatic sweep, she caught Jake completely offguard. He was so surprised that he forgot to let go of her shirt. So, all he could do was lean further and further forward, taking mincing little steps until Jessie came to a pretty rest on the ground between his legs. Little angry, choking sounds exploded from his throat. It was all Jessie could do to keep her face totally impassive; she wanted so badly to grin triumphantly or poke her tongue out at him.

Her eyes almost flew open, though, when she heard Jake say, "Here, let me slap her face a little to see if I can bring her around." If he dared so much as to . . .

"Oh, no, Mr. Coltrane, Sir, you shouldn't do that." It was Patterson. "Might make her go into shock." He started to gather her limp body in his arms. "Let me take her back to the campfire where we can be sure—"

"If anybody's going to carry her, Patterson, it will be me. You got that?" Jake cut in.

There was a silent moment when Jessie feared she would be in the middle of a tug-of-war as two sets of arms held her about a foot off the ground.

One set of arms let go of her—like she was a hot potato. "Yes, Sir," came Patterson's surprised reply.

Jessie felt Jake's strong arms under her shoulders and knees as he stood up with her. Even though she was supposed to be mad at him and through with him, she still found herself wishing she could put her arms around his neck and her cheek against his broad chest as he carried her through the trees to the campfire. But she forced herself to stay limp and "unconscious" as the rest of the men either followed

Jake or went ahead clearing branches out of the way for him.

Once at the campsite, she felt herself being lowered to the ground. When Jake leaned over her as he knelt to lay her down, she breathed in his deeply male scent and knew in her heart she could find him blindfolded just by that tantalizing smell. But all her tingly, delicious feelings abruptly ended when he plopped her a little harder than she thought necessary onto something only a bit softer than the hard ground she'd been expecting.

"Ouch!" she cried out, her eyes flying open. Her bottom lip jutted out in consternation. "You didn't have to drop me, you know." Uh-oh. She bit at her bottom lip.

Her vision was full of Jake's face directly over hers, not three inches away. The light from the campfire showed his disbelieving features. But he was grinning—well, you could call it a grin, she supposed. "Aha! I didn't think you'd passed out," he crowed triumphantly. He gripped her shoulders and pulled her to a sitting position in front of him. He was squatting, rocking back on his heels beside the bedroll on which she sat. "All right, let's hear it. What are you doing here?"

Jessie rapidly blinked her eyes several times and looked around her, as if trying to get her bearings. "Where . . . where am I?" she asked in her best weak, little voice, putting a shaking hand to her forehead.

"Oh, for crying out loud, knock it off, Jessie. I'm not buying it."

That did it. He was treating her like a child—well, okay, she was acting like one. But that didn't give him the right . . .

"Okay, Mr. Coltrane, I'll tell you exactly what I'm doing here." She was up on her knees now and stabbing angrily at Jake with one finger, poking him in the chest as she spoke. The louder her voice got, the more the other men kept disappearing from around the campfire. "You want to know what I'm doing here? I'll tell you what I'm doing here."

"I'm waiting," he cut in, his forearms resting on his thighs as he remained squatted beside her.

Jessie looked into his blue eyes; they were dancing and sparkling. But she was sure that was because they reflected the wavering light of the fire.

"I'll tell you what I'm doing here," she began again. "Nobody accuses my father of gunrunning and then just rides off. Nobody says he can take away my land and then just rides off. Nobody, do you hear me? My father would never have anything to do with the likes of Hayes. Never! And I'm going to prove it! You can hog-tie me and send me back home if you want, but I'll just ride out again on my own. I'm going to find that Vasquez and confront him and get the truth out of him. My father is dead and can't defend himself, but, by gosh, I'm alive and I can! And you can't stop me!" Jessie had to stop herself to take a breath.

She quit poking Jake's hard, unyielding chest and put her hands to her heaving bosom. Her face felt hot, and burning tears stung her eyes, making Jake look watery and not real. Little hiccupping sounds came out of her when she tried to inhale. But she'd be darned if she would cry in front of him; her bottom lip poked out defiantly, and she raised her chin to a stubborn tilt.

She watched Jake watching her, her look daring him to say she couldn't do this. He put a hand to his mouth and rubbed his fingers back and forth over his lips, like he was thinking and trying to decide something. Then, he took a deep breath and blew it out with a loud, resigned whoosh. When he stood up, Jessie scrambled to her feet. She didn't want to look any smaller to him than she already did. She even mimicked his stance, her legs apart and her hands on her hips. She wanted him to know she was as determined to stay as he was to send her home. But then he surprised her.

"All right, Jessie. You can stay."

She couldn't believe her ears! He was giving in! Her face lit up and she started to reach for him, but his next words stopped her cold.

"But not for the reasons you think! I'm forced to allow you to go with us. And, believe me, I don't like it—not one bit. This mission is as dangerous as hell. We could all be killed. I need every man I've got, so I can't spare the men to take you back home, and I can't send you alone for that distance. Dammit, Jessie! What a position you've put me in. I just knew the broken wheel was only the beginning," he finished, hands and eyes raised to the heavens, as if to say "Will you look at what I have to deal with down here, Lord?"

Later, when the camp had quieted for the night, Jessie opened her eyes. She was tired, but she couldn't sleep. She was in her own bedroll, which Jake had retrieved from the wagon for her after she'd told him how she'd hidden from all of them. She was lying in a ball on her side with her hands together and under her cheek. If she reached out she could touch Jake's face. But she didn't dare. He really was asleep; she'd been listening to his even breathing for about an hour, she guessed.

To her mind immediately came the image of her with his head in her lap and stroking his unconscious face that first night in her cabin. A tender smile found its way to her lips, but she quickly squelched it. She was supposed to hate him. He could take everything away from her. A small tear slipped out of her eye and ran off her face onto her hands. She didn't even try to brush it away. He had already taken everything away from her, and she didn't mean her homestead.

Jake knew that the rising heat in him had nothing to do with the unrelenting sun. Spurring Blaze into a canter, he rode to the head of his two-wagon train. He told himself he wanted to check on that broken wheel they'd fixed last night. But he knew in his heart that was an excuse to get away from the sight of Jessie sitting so close beside Coy Patterson on the buckboard of the second wagon in the procession. It wasn't so much her sitting beside the young lieutenant that was making him crazy, he knew, but it was the oh-so-cheerful patter of their laughing conversation that made him want to take a whip to them.

Only fools and children could be cheerful under the present circumstances, Jake decided. And, looking back to the second wagon, he knew he had one of each with him. He couldn't decide if he was just jealous—but no, he dismissed that immediately—or if he was feeling the weight of his responsibilities and resented Jessie and Coy's carefree attitude. Somehow it seemed to mock the gravity of this mission. The Santa Fe Trail alone was enough to kill you, he thought, without the added problems of a broken wheel, a female stowaway, a load of U. S.

Government guns to protect, and Mexican revolutionaries awaiting you at the end of a long ride.

Jake knew what his problem was, and he finally admitted it. When he was on assignment, he had to keep a tight rein on his emotions, much like he had to keep a tight rein on the spirited stallion he rode. And now here was Jessie, for crying out loud. He couldn't control his thoughts, emotions, or his own damned body when she was around. Last night had been torture having her so close, and once again, so far away. He'd ached to feel her kiss, and to put his hands on her—all over her. He wanted—blast her! he railed. He'd had to call on all his powers of concentration to be able to get any sleep last night. And then his dreams had been of her. Damn! He did not need this complication.

Or all the other men vying for her attention. Jake snorted—hardened old war veterans, indeed. If they weren't still clucking in concern for her after her fainting spell last night, they were running over each other to help her, to smile at her, to talk to her, to make sure she had enough to eat, to see that she was comfortable. It was disgusting, Jake thought, his mouth set in a grim line. If all her smiling cheerfulness and big brown eyes didn't have these men at each other's throats by day's end, he would be surprised.

Jake shifted uncomfortably in his saddle as he rode beside the lead wagon with his eyes trained on the repaired wheel, looking for any signs of new breakage. Thankfully, there were none. But the wheel was not really his main concern; it was just an excuse not to be near Jessie. She'd been very aloof this morning and ever since. Jake supposed he didn't blame her; after all, he had yelled at her a lot last night, and had even insisted she sleep right next to him—so he could keep an eye on her, like a prisoner, she'd yelled right back.

Jake had to smile at that. Here she was, the guilty culprit, caught red-handed being where she had no business, and she'd turned it all around on him. All of a sudden, Jake was the bad guy. No one had said as much, but he knew that the sidewise glances from the men and their avoidance of him today stemmed from their taking Jessie's side. They felt sorry for her, poor little thing. All alone like she was, feeling she had to go herself to clear her daddy's name. Jake rolled his eyes. His plan had always included clearing her father's name. His gut instinct told him Mr. Stuart was an unwitting participant in all this. After all, what would have been his motive for involvement? He had a thriving homestead and business with the wagon trains. He didn't need dirty money from gunrunning.

Doggone it, Jake railed, that was what made him snap at anyone who came close to him today. Why hadn't she trusted him to clear her father? There, it was out. Did she think he'd just callously accept her father's guilt on the word of Vasquez or MacKenzie without getting proof? That he'd just coldly ride in with the Army and throw her off her land? He wasn't hurt by her obvious lack of trust in him; no, it wasn't that. It just made him mad as hell, that's all.

His anger fueling the heat-induced sweat on his brow, Jake untied the bandanna from around his throat and wiped at his face. Then, thinking to put the red cloth in his shirt pocket, he unbuttoned it. But before he could stuff his bandanna in, his fingers came into contact with the two rings he'd stuck in this pocket two nights ago. The sudden rush of memories from two days past—he and Jessie under the trees, her beautiful, demanding body under him, then her angry silence, and her tossing the wedding band on the ground and stomping off—did nothing at all to relieve his anger and frustration. He'd never told another woman that he loved her—and then to have it thrown in his face in more than one way was too much for him. Jake crammed his bandanna in the pocket over the rings. A scowl sat on his face for the remainder of the day.

Chapter Fourteen

Jessie was just as steadfast and as determined in her own private mission as she'd ever been. But the glamor and excitement she'd always attached to a trip on the Santa Fe Trail and the envy with which she'd always watched the wagons leaving her homestead was gone. Endless days of plodding ahead wore one into another. Gone was the easy chatting and bantering she'd enjoyed with the men at first. Gone was her spirit of adventure. Gone was the open prairie with its waving fields of wildflowers, its grazing herds of buffalo, its bright blue sky set against the vivid green of the tallgrass.

The small procession was now into the more mountainous stretch of the trail that led to Santa Fe. Jessie was so trail-weary, she no longer thought the city existed. She felt Santa Fe was a mirage that kept floating further and further away from them, that wavered tantalizingly in their imaginations but wasn't really there. She would always, for the rest of her life, bump along, sweaty and dirty, on this hard buckboard seat. Even Coy's shy flirtations were beginning to set her teeth on edge.

And Jake. Well, she decided that what they had between them now was an unspoken truce. He was no longer angry with her, but he was not himself with her, either. Jessie sighed, how could he be with twelve other men around? Still, she thought, clenching her hands on the hard wooden seat under her to steady herself as Coy guided the wagon up a steep incline, it wouldn't have killed him to find a minute or two for them to be alone. Just one look, a touch, maybe a kiss.

Jessie shook her head to clear away the vibrant images of that afternoon under the trees in her meadow. How long ago had that been? At least a lifetime she concluded. And she admitted that she would not have been content with just a kiss. She knew what it would lead to. And she felt so guilty for her lustful feelings for Jake; they seemed like a mockery of her father's memory. That she would desire her dead father's accuser was too much for Jessie's loyalties. She set her mouth in a grim, determined line.

Okay, how about a bath? Could she just please have a bath—and wash her hair? She felt downright gamey. Their late-evening stops and early-morning departures had left no time for bathing at the few watering places they'd camped at. At best she'd only been able to wash off the top layer of dirt and grime. Jake had expressly forbidden her to bathe. When she'd railed against this order, he'd firmly taken her arm and led her away from the

239

rest of the men. In angry, punctuated words he'd told her in no uncertain terms how the sight of one naked, sweet-smelling woman could turn these decent men into a pack of jackals like Hayes' gang. They had only so much self-control.

And then he'd very curtly reminded her that she hadn't been invited on this trip and that she was a definite burden. He'd left her standing there to contemplate that and had stomped back to the campfire. That was the first and only time he'd touched her on this whole trip. But Jessie had seen his smoldering eyes, the heavy-lidded expression she caught on his face when he didn't think she was watching. But, and this scared her, she'd seen it too on some of the other men's faces. They'd been nothing but kind and respectful so far, but still Jessie did nothing to make them remember she was a woman.

Well, they might forget she was a woman, dressed as she was just like them in pants, shirt, boots, and a hat, but there was no way she could forget it. With a sinking dread that kept her from enjoying the fresh mountain beauty around her, Jessie knew the monthly curse was fast approaching. There was no mistaking her very tender breasts and the heavy feeling in her belly. She even attributed her quick vexation and even quicker tears to her time of the month.

Vexation and tears both came into her eyes now as she tried desperately to figure out just how she was going to handle the flow when it came. Explain those needs to twelve—no, thirteen—men on a secret mission for the U. S. government, Jessie silently challenged herself. She could just hear them now. We have to stop for what? Women!

She was jolted out of her thoughts not by the continued lurching and rolling of the wagon's wheels, but by the stopping of the wagon's wheels. Looking all around her for the reasons for this unexpected break, she could see nothing out of the ordinary. She looked to Coy, who merely shrugged his shoulders and pointed to Jake, who was approaching them on Blaze. All they could do was wait for his explanation. Jessie looked past him to see the men dismounting. This was definitely strange.

"What's going on, Jake?" Coy asked almost before Jake had reined Blaze to a stop.

Jake's blue eyes raked across Jessie's face before he turned his attention to Coy. Jessie felt her stomach flutter, and chided herself—just one look, that's all it takes?

"A hunting party," was all he answered. "Pull up behind Cockburn in the other wagon."

"A hunting party?" Coy repeated, his voice breaking. "You mean Indians?"

Jake gave him a look that could only be called contemptuous. "No, lieutenant, I don't. Just pull up and you'll find out."

Without even a glance at Jessie, he trotted Blaze back up to the knot of men in front of the lead wagon. Jessie watched his broad back as he rode off. She knew how those smooth muscles felt under her hands. She knew how to make them ripple with just one touch . . .

She looked over quickly at Coy, and then sighed in relief. For a second there, she thought she'd spoken her thoughts out loud. But no, Coy was not looking at her as if she'd sprouted horns. But she did recognize the slightly troubled look on his face as

241

he flicked the reins and made git-up noises to the horses.

Jessie hadn't sat here with Coy day after day and not learned anything about him. She knew that he was quite smitten with her. So she was careful not to lead him on in any way. That would be using him. She really did like him, but not like he wanted her to. And she also knew that what gave him the troubled look was his deepest wish to somehow gain Jake Coltrane's respect. And so far, Jessie thought, Jake was either ignoring or hadn't even noticed Coy's many efforts and overtures to be important on this trip, to do his part and even more. Jessie thought this was cruel of Jake. What would it cost him to be nice to Coy? Why was he so abrupt and impatient with him?

While Jessie sat there thinking, Coy brought the wagon into position behind the lead wagon, as ordered, jumped down, ran around the back of the wagon, and was even now standing on the ground with his hands upraised to help her down. Feeling warm toward him, she stood and smiled and started to climb down, much as if she were on a ladder, knowing his hands would encircle her waist momentarily and guide her safely and gently down from behind. He'd done it a hundred times already.

So she wasn't prepared for the strong, large hands which suddenly encompassed her waist and swung her giddily around and down to the ground. Her strangled squawk and shouted, "Coy Patterson!" died on her lips when she found herself facing, not Coy, but Jake. His hands were still on her waist. And she was surprised to see her hands resting on his muscled chest. She could feel the hair under his shirt. She swallowed hard.

"Surprised?" he asked, blue eyes looking like the skies of a hot, summer storm. "Or disappointed?"

Jessie didn't know what to say at first. Her widened eyes caught a glimpse of Coy standing very awkwardly just behind and to the side of Jake. When she looked at him, he pressed his lips together and walked away. Jessie had to wonder what in her face had made him look that way. She turned her attention back to the man in whose arms she was.

"Jake Coltrane," she scolded in a low voice, "you let go of me this instant. The men—"

"—will be gone in just a few minutes. I'm sending them out on a hunting party for fresh meat. We can use it. And you and I are staying here. Look around you, Jessie; what do you see?"

Confusion made her crease her forehead and bring her brows down, but she did as she was told. She gasped when she saw the natural beauty around her. How could she have missed the mountain stream pouring over a high outcropping of rocks in a sparkling cascade to form a deep, inviting pool not more than several yards from where she stood with Jake's arms around her? Well, that explained it, she chided herself. Whenever Jake was this close she noticed nothing else. Her eyes eagerly swept the wooded clearing that framed the gurgling water. The damp rocks to either side of the waterfall gave rise to the first of the mountains this small train would have to pass through on the way to Santa Fe.

Jessie turned excited, laughing eyes on Jake. She just could not be mad at him and hate him right now like she was supposed to. Childlike anticipation made her voice and her feet dance as she breathlessly asked, "Oh, Jake, can I really? Can I really bathe and swim right here? Will it be okay?" She looked meaningfully at the men still milling about what would be their campsite tonight.

The deep rumble of a chuckle, which Jessie felt under her hands on his chest, brought her attention back to him. "Of course it will be okay. They'll all be gone in a minute or so. It'll just be you and me."

In her excitement, Jessie wasn't sure if his voice had actually softened and deepened with his last words, or if she was imagining it. But it didn't matter! She was going to get all this dirt and grime off her and wash her hair and swim and get out of these hot men's clothes and . . .

Then she remembered she'd have to be naked to do all those things. Naked. And alone with Jake. Suddenly she felt very shy and looked from Jake's face down to a button at about the middle of his chest.

When he cupped her chin with a hand to bring her eyes back to his, she didn't resist, but she really didn't want to look at him right now, either. She knew the rising heat flushing up her neck and face would reveal her thoughts.

"Don't worry, little Jessie," he teased her. "I'll behave—but only for as long as you want me to."

"Oh, you!" Jessie swatted at his chest and laughed, trying to push him away.

When he tightened his hold momentarily, looked very deeply and very seriously into her eyes, but didn't say anything, Jessie sobered and relaxed in his arms. Something unspoken passed between them, something that Jessie felt all the way to her toes. The hairs on her arms raised, and she gave an involuntary shiver that had nothing to do with fear.

Jake was the first to break the spell. He chuckled softly, winked at her, and let her go. She watched him walk off toward the men who were just now remounting their horses in preparation for hunting. Jessie knew she was staring quite boldly at Jake's backside, but she didn't care. It really was a nice one. She instantly sucked in air, shocked at her own thoughts, and turned away from the sight he made. She put a hand to her mouth to cover the brazen grin she couldn't suppress. She really was awful, she decided.

Jessie stayed by the wagon while Jake gave last-minute orders to the men. She saw a lot of pointing and head nodding, and heard laughter and high-spirited cheerfulness from the men. She wasn't the only one who needed a break from the monotony of the trail. She knew they'd swim and bathe and splash once they returned from the hunt. Just thinking about the fresh meat they would bring back made her mouth water. Oh, this was going to be a great afternoon!

If Jessie thought that Jake would come over to her by the second wagon once the men rode off, she was wrong. Instead, she watched him curiously as he headed for one of the packs lying in a neat stack by the pack horses. She saw him open it and rummage through, pulling out a few things. He looked up at her and waved an arm, indicating for her to come to him; when she started toward him, anticipation quickening her steps, he stood up and grinned back at her.

Once she'd reached him, she saw what he'd retrieved from the heavy pack—soap and a towel.

Cheryl Anne Porter

He offered them to her, saying "Here, use these. They're pretty rough and not sweet-smelling, being Army issue, but I think they'll do."

Jessie thought they were the most beautiful things she'd ever seen. She almost snatched them out of his hands without so much as a thank-you, and took off at a trot for the water. She didn't even think to ask Jake what he would be doing while she bathed. But, after all, he'd said he would behave; so probably he was going to finish setting up the camp or something, and give her time to herself.

In only a few minutes, following a flurry of undressing, Jessie found herself floating languorously in the softly undulating waters of the pool. This was heaven, she sighed, as she gently broke the water's surface with her easy strokes to take her back to the shore where the soap was. She quickly looked around before she came out of the water to pick up the rough soap off the towel. No one. She stood and walked out of the water, feeling the heavy drag of it against her hips and then legs. It felt so . . . sensual, somehow, like a caress. Lost in her private thoughts, she stood there for a moment or two with her arms upraised to the sun and her head thrown back, letting the now friendly warmth wash over her dripping body. She felt like some ancient priestess paying homage to the sun-god. Then, laughing at her own dramatics, she jumped back into the water to wash.

Playful now, she turned first one way and then the other with her arms outstretched in the water, creating a swirling eddy around her. She then dove and resurfaced, spouting the water out of her mouth like she'd done as a child in Missouri. Settling down some and with a contented smile ever on her face, she began to apply the soap vigorously to her body.

When she came to her breasts, though, she winced at the first swipe of the hard soap over them. They were so sore. But she dismissed this thought immediately and continued on down to her belly. She knew her time was near—her belly was so pouchy and tender. She made a face and then started lathering her hair.

With her head underwater to rinse the soap out, she didn't hear the splash of someone entering the water with her. But when she came up and opened her eyes, blinking several times and wiping at them to clear away the water, she let out an involuntary yelp of shock and surprise. There was Jake's face—right in front of hers! An impudent grin lit up his tanned features, making him look almost boyish.

"You!" she sputtered, treading the water to stay afloat. "What are—! When—!"

Then, as his hands underwater encircled her waist and pulled her to him, she squawked, "Jake Coltrane! You promised to behave!" She tried to push away from him by pulling herself backward as she braced her hands against his chest. But her hands and Jake's chest were too slippery; her hands shot out toward his arms, their force smacking her breasts directly against the wet hair of his chest. Her chin hit his shoulder, stunning her momentarily.

"Now that's more like it," he teased.

Jessie immediately pulled back again, meaning to berate him soundly. But her eyes were caught instead by his male beauty. Locks of his wet hair fell onto his forehead; their dripping blackness played off the bright blue of his eyes, as blue as the water. Jessie knew she could drown more easily in his eyes than she could in this water.

Her anger vanished. She slowly and with great concentration on every detail of his shoulders, upper chest, neck, and face, all she could see above the water, ran her hands over him, finally bringing them to rest on his broad, tanned shoulders. She then lowered her eyes to the healed wound on his left shoulder. No more bandages covered it. Without thinking, she lowered her lips to place a tender kiss on his scar. When she brought her brown eyes back up to Jake's, the boyishness and the humor were gone. There was a tension and a heaviness in his face now. This look had a name: desire.

Jessie forgot to paddle her feet to stay afloat, but it didn't matter. Jake was standing on the rocky bottom of the pool and his arms were completely around her, molding her to his hard-muscled length. "Jessie," he breathed, and began a trail of kisses that started at her jaw, went down the side of her neck, and continued to her breasts as he raised her up in his arms to reach them.

She gulped heavily and then breathed shallowly as he took one already hard nipple into his mouth. Jessie threw her head back, bracing her hands against his shoulders. The little cries that escaped her urged Jake on more surely than words. Shifting her weight slightly, he then took the other dusky-rose peak in his mouth, swirling his tongue ever so slowly around it. Jessie's desire-numbed mind registered that her breasts were so much more sensitive and heavy-feeling than they'd been the first time Jake had done this, but that was as far as the thought got.

"God, Jessie," Jake said raggedly between delicious kisses on her shoulders, "I've stayed away from you as long as I can bear. I need you. I love

248

you." He placed a biting kiss between her shoulder and neck.

Chills ran over Jessie; she entangled her hands in his wet hair and pulled his head back so she could see into his eyes. Seeing what she wanted, she lowered her head to kiss his warm, firm, slightly parted lips. His darting tongue did not have to force her lips apart; they parted willingly, allowing him entry and even dominance. Jessie let her tongue fence tentatively with his to see what effect this would have. A low growl escaped him, and he was the one to break the kiss to take a deep, dragging breath. Jessie could feel his rapid heartbeat and his muscles working in his belly to help him breathe, but it wasn't these which told her boldly of his desire. Her thigh accidently brushed against his hardness, and he reacted almost violently, sucking in even more air and pulling her even closer to him.

"If we don't get out of this damned water, we'll both drown," he ground out, grabbing Jessie's wet, warm, slippery body up in his arms and turning to head for the shore.

As he carried her, taking one careful step at a time, fighting both the slippery rocks under his feet and the heavy pulling of the water against their bodies, Jessie had one arm around his back, the other one on his chest, and a cheek against the solid wall of his chest. When she realized her lips were right next to one of his nipples, she wondered if his were as sensitive as hers. She used her tongue, just as he'd done, to swirl around the brown circle partially covered by the coarse yet soft hairs of his chest.

She had her answer in a flash. A convulsive reflex bent Jake forward; a groaning growl escaped him and he nearly dropped her. "Dammit, Jessie," he breathed, but he didn't sound angry at all. Jessie grabbed onto him more tightly and grinned to herself, placing her cheek against his chest once more. She felt proud that she could do that to him, too.

When Jake put her down to stand on her feet once they were on the grassy shore, Jessie surprised him, and herself, by putting a restraining hand on his arm as he reached for the towel he'd given her earlier. She knew he meant to lay her down on it, but she didn't want to yet. Their first time had been hurried, almost angry, and it had overwhelmed them. This time she wanted to explore his body, as he had hers back then in the meadow; she wanted to run her hands over his sleek, perfectly proportioned contours.

And she did. His being wet only added to her pleasure; he felt warm and firm and . . . what else? Words were inadequate. She wanted just to feel. She saw the smiling wonder in Jake's face when she chanced a look up at him as they faced each other. She made him keep his hands off her for as long as she could, but gave in to his stroking caresses when he grabbed her hand and kissed her fingers.

Then, with his hands cupping her buttocks, he pulled her against his hips. It was Jessie's turn to catch her breath. With her arms around his waist, she very gently and slowly moved her hips from side to side across his throbbing shaft. It felt so good to her, but he was the one who made the strangled cry and grabbed handfuls of Jessie's dripping hair.

"Enough," he almost begged. Jessie now allowed herself to be lowered onto the towel he very quickly spread out for her. She pulled him to her, wanting to feel his weight on her. She got her wish as he lowered himself into the cradle of her hips; she accommodated him by bending her knees and wrapping her legs around his. She loved the contrast of his male body to hers, of his largeness to her smallness, of his rigid muscles to her firm softness. She couldn't stop herself from whispering, "I love you, Jake. I always will."

At her words, he instantly raised his dark, glistening head from the hollow of her neck and looked with hooded, deep blue eyes into hers. "I hope so," he whispered, his lips touching hers as he talked. Jessie let her tongue escape from the cavern of her mouth to run sweetly over Jake's lips. He groaned and tensed, pushing himself against her hips. Jessie voiced her readiness by raising her hips to meet him and cupping his firm buttocks in her hands.

"Oh, Jessie, I want to do so much more, but I can't wait any longer."

His words brought the flood of moistness to her budding desire, the moistness it needed to grow and become the fully mature and bursting flower she knew it could be. "Oh, Jake, now," she groaned. She could hardly wait to feel him ensheathed in her. He'd said it wouldn't hurt after the first time, but right now she wouldn't have cared if it did. She needed him, and that was all there was to it: married or not, enemy or not. Those things didn't matter right now. Just Jake. Only he mattered.

As he began to enter her, Jessie gripped his shoulders. She raised her head and shoulders to place nipping kisses across his shoulder. As he slid smoothly into her, deeper and deeper, Jessie gasped and her toes curled. She put her head back down on the towel and closed her eyes. Then she reveled

251

in the feel of him completely inside her. She was whole again, for only the second time in her life. She was whole.

Realizing Jake must be waiting for some sign from her, Jessie pulled his full weight onto her and instinctively tightened her legs around his hips. She gave a little thrust or two of her own and called his name softly, begging him by her actions and whispered words of love and desire, to take her and make her his, to mold them into one being, complete only when they held each other and soared to the highest peak of their desire.

Jake's strong, rhythmic movements sent thrills of pleasure through Jessie's rippling body. She met him thrust for thrust, increasing her own desire— and his as he called her name over and over. The tension in her coiled and rippled, again and again, until she was gasping for release.

Then the tingling dryness at the back of her throat, the undulating contractions of her already heavy womb, and the weakness in her thighs began. She wanted the rippling sensations to last forever, to carry her to the stars she could see behind her closed eyes, to make her always one with Jake. With one last tremendous thrust, Jake held himself rigidly over Jessie. She brought her hands to rest on his upper arms; she felt the straining muscles of this magnificent male over her. And then he too cascaded over the sensual abyss with Jessie and began the floating descent back to the grassy shore where they'd left their physical bodies.

He lowered his water-wet, love-moistened torso onto hers. Jessie welcomed his tangy dampness. Her hands moved to stroke his back, his arms, his head. She couldn't get enough of him, even though he was still in her. If she could meld her body to his permanently, she didn't feel she would be close enough.

As these and other thoughts, more rational ones, came to her, even as Jake was returning her caresses, Jessie felt not only his weight, but the weight of their separate realities. She wished the thought away, even tossing her head to the side to shake it off.

Jake raised his head and pulled his weight off her as much as possible without separating them. His questioning look was one of tender concern. "Are you all right? Did I hurt you?" he asked, stroking her cheek with a damp tendril of her own hair that he had wrapped around his finger.

By way of an answer, Jessie gave him a little smile and a slight shake of her head. No, he hadn't hurt her physically. But was she all right and unhurt? Not in her heart and mind. She no longer cared that she made love to him without the benefit of being married; her talk of being a fallen woman seemed silly now. She knew she loved Jake, would always love him, so giving herself to him was nothing to be ashamed of. If only the physical aspects of making love were all she had to consider! But making love, to Jessie, was so much more. It was commitment, and Jake had not mentioned anymore marrying her for real; Jessie didn't feel she could very well ask him. After all, she could say she'd forced him into the first ceremony. And his job—it was so dangerous. Could she live with him placing his life in jeopardy every day?

But most of all, what if her father really had been involved with Hayes? A small shudder went through Jessie. Then Jake would be right and it was his job to report it to the government. She could lose everything. She wasn't sure she could forgive him for even suspecting her father, much less if he had a hand in stripping her of everything she owned. A single tear escaped Jessie's eye and ran down the side of her face to disappear in her hair. No, loving Jake did not mean they could make a life together.

"Hey, little Jessie, what's this tear for?" Jake asked tenderly, brushing at its trail with his finger. "Am I good enough to bring tears to your eyes?"

His comical, leering grin and teasing manner lightened Jessie's mood and thoughts. She cuffed at him playfully and told him, "Get off me, you big ox!"

Jake promptly withdrew from her, quickly jumped up, and grabbing one end of the towel, jerked it upward, rolling Jessie very unceremoniously off onto the grass. With a laughing shriek, she jumped up and gave chase as Jake, with a loud war whoop, jumped naked into the water, bearing the towel over his head as a banner. As she dove in after him, Jessie had a last serious thought that she would just be thankful for this time they had together on the trail, but after that, when they went their separate ways, she would have to be content with her memories.

Chapter Fifteen

"Whoopee! There it is! Yippee! Santa Fe—just ahead!" Cockburn yelled, excitedly waving his hat in the air as he stood in his slow-moving wagon; the tangle of reins in his hands undulated up and down in the air like dancing snakes. The horses under his control, excited by his yelling and the whipping reins, surged forward, sending Cockburn back onto his rough wood seat with a thud.

Jake laughed along with the other men who rode with him by the lead wagon. Cockburn's yelling and antics sent all their horses, including the well-mannered Blaze, into a sideways dance, much as if they too were catching the infectious high spirits that the sight of Santa Fe gave their riders. Jake looked back to the second wagon and saw Jessie standing up on the buckboard seat, clutching the front canvas-covered wood rib of the wagon and craning her neck from side to side trying to glimpse the welcome sight.

Jake nudged Blaze's sides and turned him back to the second wagon. When he pulled abreast of this wagon, Coy asked excitedly, "Are we really there, Jake? Do you think Vasquez will be waiting there, or will we have to go all the way into Mexico?"

Jake saw Jessie's open, happy face close as surely as a book at the young lieutenant's words. She lowered her head and sat down quietly on the buckboard seat. She wouldn't look at him. Jake silently damned Coy for bringing up the sore subject of Vasquez and everything he stood for in Jake and Jessie's uncertain relationship. His face took on the highly irritated look that Coy was so used to from him. Jake couldn't help the slightly sarcastic tone of his voice, either. This kid could get them all killed in Santa Fe just by saying the wrong word to the right person. "Yes, Lieutenant, we're really there. And we'll find out soon enough if Vasquez is waiting. In the meantime, I expect you to keep a closed mouth about him and this cargo. You could get us all killed."

Jake abruptly turned Blaze's head and rode to the front of the first wagon to lead them down the gently sloping plain into the dusty, adobe town of Santa Fe. He refused to feel guilt over the whipped-puppy face of Coy Patterson. That damned kid, as Jake always thought of him, had a loose tongue that needed to be curbed. This was no game. Tension arose in Jake to compete with the excitement he couldn't squelch at finally being here after weeks of dried food, scarce water, Indian sightings, the mens' squabbles as tempers flared in the heat, a broken wagon wheel, and last but certainly not least, a most distracting stowaway.

Jake snapped at his own thoughts and cut them off abruptly when one small voice tried to tell him that the real reason he didn't like the lieutenant was because Patterson liked Jessie and hung onto her until Jake wanted to throttle him. And either Jessie didn't realize the young man's feelings were more than mere friendship, or she did, but did nothing to discourage Coy. The tightening in his jaw and the narrowing of his eyes were almost involuntary when he thought of the many times he'd heard and seen Jessie and Coy sitting together, laughing together, acting young and silly and innocent, all the things Jake couldn't do, for over three weeks on this long ride.

Jake forced all this from his mind as he concentrated on what lay ahead. He'd discussed the plan so many times with the men while they were on the trail that they all should know it by heart. They were to mingle in the town—Jake could hardly keep them from it after the deprivations of the trail—but not draw any undue attention to themselves. They were to report anything of relevance they heard to Jake. They would all use their real names (aliases for thirteen men would be too confusing for them to remember) and pass word quietly in the many saloons, or cantinas, and at the many fandangos, the lively dances held virtually every evening in the small but bustling trade city, regarding the nature of their cargo.

Jake had no doubt that word of the guns would reach the right ears. If Vasquez or his emissaries were there, they would come to Jake. The mens' stories about killing off Hayes and his gang for this double shipment of guns would not go unreported. That kind of information could earn a poor but dishonest man some big money. Jake had told the men not to say exactly where the wagons of guns were, because the last thing he needed was to have every lowlife trying to steal the guns for themselves. The wagons would be well-guarded just on the outskirts of the town. They would draw no notice because Santa Fe was teeming with wagons, as always.

As they entered the town, with studied casualness, Jake rode Blaze slowly through the throngs of people, wagons, oxen, barking dogs, horsemen, running children, and hawkers of all sorts of goods. He kept looking back over his shoulder to make sure that his small party did not get separated in this melee of noise and color. As the traders scurried about in a frenzy of selling, not one of them seemed to notice the scorching, late-summer sun overhead or the choking dust churned up by the thousands of feet, both human and animal, running to and fro in the small central plaza.

But Jake noticed both the heat and the dust, as he ran a finger around the bandanna which encircled his neck. He was sick to death of them, just as were all the men. They'd been baked and choked for nearly a month now. Jake knew that the baths, clean clothes, decent meals, drinks, and dances were just what they all needed. Somehow in his mind he hadn't included Jessie in that thought.

Jake became aware of his name being called and turned his head to Curly Burnett, the balding, wiry little sergeant who rode next to him, just in time to see him spit a stream of tobacco juice onto the ground, narrowly missing a stray dog. "Dang,

Ah missed 'im," he snorted. His Southern drawl brought a smile to Jake's face; the fact that they'd fought on opposite sides in the recently ended Civil War had not stood in the way of their developing an easy friendship. Jake had a lot of respect for Curly's experience and good sense. He was a man of few words, but he could cut right to the heart of a matter in a sentence or two. Jake looked questioningly at Curly, waiting for him to speak again.

Curly moved his chaw around in his cheek, finally saying, "Jist real casual-like, Jake, look over there to the left. What do you think?"

Jake did as Curly said. Several rough-looking Mexican men, armed to the teeth, lounged in front of one of the larger cantinas. Jake realized that they were trying as hard as he was not to look like they were watching and waiting. Takes one to know one, Jake snorted.

Jake turned back to the sergeant. "I think you're right, Curly. I'm sure glad they're here, and we don't have to deal with Vasquez and his men in the comfort of Vasquez's compound in Mexico."

Curly spit again, this time hitting the boot of a man passing by. Curses followed them as they kept their horses at a slow walk. "Ah think Ah'll be needin' me a drink from over there real soon."

"I think I'll join you," Jake replied, noticing that two or three of the Mexican men straightened up when Jake's men and wagons rolled directly by the cantina, watched them pass, and then went hurriedly inside. Jake smiled to himself grimly. These men had seen enough wooden crates of U. S. Army guns to recognize them when they saw them.

* * *

Jessie could not get her eyes full. In her excitement she grabbed onto Coy's arm and smiled brightly at him. She saw him widen his eyes and turn a little red. "Oh, Coy," she gushed, "just look at all this! Isn't this exciting? Have you ever seen anything like this before in your life?"

Coy's chest swelled a little bit. "No, I don't believe I have. I mean, we have big cities and all back in Pennsylvania, but they don't look anything like this."

Jessie caught the slightly condescending tone of his voice, but decided to let it pass. She was too excited to argue with him for the one hundredth time over how much better he said everything was back East. She playfully cuffed at his arm, "Oh, Coy, for ever more. Just look around you! So much going on, so many people. The people coming back from Santa Fe who stop at my homestead would tell me how exciting all this is, but I just couldn't imagine it. And now I'm seeing it all for myself!"

"If you like," Coy said shyly, shifting his eyes from Jessie's face to the horses he commanded, and back again, "I can escort you later around the town and maybe to one of the fandangos."

Jessie almost responded instantly with an excited yes, but then bit back her reply, looking toward Jake's back as he rode abreast of the lead wagon. She didn't want to add to the mounting tension between these two. She knew that any attention she gave Coy, no matter how innocent, only inflamed the tension between the two men. Lately Coy had taken to reminding Jake that he, not Jake, was the ranking officer on this mission, and that he, not Jake, would give the orders to the men. Jessie decided that Coy had given up on earning Jake's respect, and was now demanding it through his rank. Also, she had the guilty suspicion that Coy was doing this to impress her and to infuriate Jake. The tension around the campfires of the past week had been almost unbearable as everyone waited for Jake to tear Coy limb from limb. But he never did. He just calmly reminded the lieutenant that Colonel Carson had placed Coy and the other men under his command. And that was the end of it.

Luckily, Coy was too busy with the horses as they weaved their way through the plaza to notice the length of time that had passed without him getting an answer to his proposition. When he got a chance, he turned again to Jessie. "Well, what do you say?"

"We'll just have to see, Coy," she hedged. "We just don't know yet what arrangements Jake will make, who'll be on guard duty, things like that. Let's just see what happens."

"You know I should be the one doing those things, don't you? After all, I am—"

"—the ranking officer here," Jessie finished for him with a sigh. "Coy, please don't start that. You know it gets you nowhere with Jake or the other men. It makes you sound like a whiny, petulant child."

Jessie was instantly sorry for the harsh words she'd just spoken when she saw their effect on Coy's face. His blond, boyish features closed, and he lowered his brows. Without saying another word, he turned his face from her, giving his full attention to his team of horses.

Jessie heaved a sigh and turned her attention to the passing parade all around her. She really did like Coy, like she would a brother, but sometimes he was just too immature. Jessie sat up at that thought and looked at Coy. He was several years older than her! What made her so mature all of a sudden? Then she shrank back on her side of the buckboard seat. Problems, worries, experiences, to name a few—all of them to do with Jake. And her latest worry was her missed flow. She should have had it three weeks ago. Jessie put a shaking hand to her forehead; the nausea was returning. The bright swirl of activity, noise, and color around her paled slightly.

Jessie gingerly lowered herself into the wooden tub full of warm, soapy water. She sat there for a moment, with her back to the door, looking around the private room Jake had secured for her in this small, but clean and comfortable, adobe hotel. The high, four-poster bed, obviously brought in by a past wagon train, commanded the center of the room. The beautiful Indian design on the spread which covered the thick mattress had instantly caught Jessie's eye when Jake had escorted her to the hotel earlier this afternoon. She'd immediately run to the bed and smoothed her hand over the coverlet. She'd then run to the armoire and thrown it open; of course it was empty. But in her exuberance she hadn't cared. Next, she'd run her hand over the rich, dark wood of a lady's dresser with a small mirror attached and a chair in front of it. She declined to look into it yet, afraid of what she'd see after a month or so on the trail.

She'd then run to the open window set in the thick adobe wall to look out again on the busy scene outside. She'd whirled around in delight to see two men struggling to get this very tub through the door. Jake had finally helped them turn it on its side and

roll it into the room. She'd clapped her hands excitedly and waited impatiently as a young Mexican girl
made repeated trips with buckets of warm water.
She'd then brought Jessie two thick towels and a
bar of lavender-scented soap.

And then Jake had excused himself, telling her
to enjoy her much-needed bath—his comment had
earned him the sight of her tongue poked out at
him—and that he would return later. She was to
wait for him. As if she had a choice, she smiled as
she ran the soap over first one deeply tanned arm
and then the other. If she went out now she would
have to go naked. She definitely was not putting on
that shirt and those pants and boots. Ugh! She was
forever cured of wanting to wear men's britches,
she decided. She longed for a soft, pretty dress, or
anything feminine and lovely.

But where—or how—was she going to get those
things? She hadn't brought any money along. Something else she hadn't remembered in her haste to
come on this trip to clear her father's name and
reputation. Jessie tried to turn her mind from this
depressing thought by concentrating on the sensual
feel of the hard soap against her wet body. It felt so
good to her tender breasts.

That did it. Jessie abruptly sat up and brought
her hand with the soap down into the water with a
plop. "Good evening, Jake, how are you? Oh, me?
Why, I'm pregnant, thank you," she said out loud in
a very self-deprecating tone to the otherwise empty
room. There. It was out. She'd said it out loud.
That made it seem more real somehow. As if her
swollen, tender breasts, dizziness, and bouts with
nausea hadn't made it obvious. Hadn't she seen her
mother like this several times—only to miscarry a

few months later each time? Jessie was the first and only child her mother had carried successfully.

Jessie placed a protective hand on her still-flat belly; she hoped she didn't have her mother's problems. As unplanned as this pregnancy was, she already loved it—him—her. This was her baby. No matter what happened between her and Jake, she would always have his child. She hoped it had its father's blue eyes.

Jessie leaned back again in the tub and scrubbed herself vigorously as if she could wash away her troubling thoughts. She bent her knees and slid forward in the tub, submerging her head to wet her hair. She then rubbed the soap all through the length of her hair, working up a rich lather. Then, squinting and blinking from the soap which wandered down into her eyes, Jessie looked around her. Just how in the world was she going to rinse this soap out of her hair? The tub was full of suds, but seeing no help for it, Jessie flipped her thick mane of dark curls forward over her head, pulled herself up into a kneeling position, and bent forward, using her hands to swish the water through her hair.

Without warning, warm, clean water cascaded over her head into the tub. She opened her mouth in surprise, but the sudden feel of an extra set of hands running through her wet, tangled hair shocked the sound out of her. All she could do was grab onto the sides of the tub with both hands as her head was lowered unceremoniously into the water for a thorough rinsing. She came up gasping for air, ready for a fight. Quickly she pushed the sodden mass of her hair apart with her hands to make a decent peephole. Sure enough, there was the leering face of one Jake Coltrane.

"Do we need to rinse it again?" he very impudently asked. And then he jumped back as a soapy wave came at him. He was too slow, as evidenced by his dripping denim pants. "Uh-oh," was all he said as he looked down at himself.

Jessie was frozen in her kneeling position in the tub with her hands parting her hair. Her bottom lip poked out dangerously. But she sucked it in when she saw him very smilingly peel off his wet pants. "Don't you dare, Jake Coltrane!" she threatened. But he kept undressing. Jessie made her peephole through her hair a little bigger. "You stop that right now, or I'll—"

"You'll what?" Jake teased. He flung his boots to the side and took off his shirt. All that remained were his wet drawers—and they did nothing to hide his intentions.

"I'll . . . I don't know!" she finished lamely.

"Oooh, now I'm scared," Jake continued maddenly, now standing before her completely naked, his hands on his slim waist, one knee bent.

Jessie caught her breath. She itched to put her hands on his tall, perfectly formed, muscular body. She wanted to trail her fingers through the black hair on his chest all the way down his belly to where it bushed out again, and—oh, my God. She knew she was staring boldly at his erect shaft, but she couldn't stop herself. All she saw now were muscular legs walking toward her. She gasped and looked up at Jake's grinning face as he stood right beside the tub.

"May I?" he asked most politely. But he was already stepping into the tub and lowering himself into the cooling water. His added weight sent sheets of water over the rim of the tub to splash unnoticed on the floor. Keeping his eyes on Jessie, who finally had the presence of mind to fling her hair back over her head, he began running his hands all along the bottom of the tub, searching for the soap.

But then his hands came into contact with Jessie's calf and he stopped abruptly. Jessie's eyes widened. Jake laughed. "Those big, brown eyes of yours make you look like a little frightened fawn about to run away. Are you?"

Jessie closed her eyes and couldn't answer, because his hands had forgotten the soap and were running up the outside of her thighs, her hips, her waist, and now her breasts. She parted her lips, but it wasn't to speak. She took little gulping breaths and allowed herself to be pulled into his arms for a long, mesmerizing kiss.

When the kiss ended, Jessie looked accusingly at Jake's face. "You've been drinking."

"Yep, just a friendly one or two with Curly at a cantina," he said, but with his eyes on her breasts.

Jake then scooted forward in the tub and adjusted her legs until she straddled his lap. Suddenly the water didn't seem cool to Jessie. It was hot. Burning hot, as she sat with her arms and legs around Jake. She took the initiative and drew his mouth to hers, needing to feel his tongue in her mouth. She made little rocking motions with her hips as she kissed him deeply, matching the movement of her tongue to her hips.

Jake gave a low growl in his throat and tore his lips away to lift her slightly as he trailed biting kisses down her neck and chest. Then he caught his prize—a rosy-brown nipple. The swirling motion of his tongue brought Jessie the rippling motion in her belly that she loved. A dreamy smile lit her face as

Jake finally lowered her again onto his lap.

Jessie's eyes flew open to look into Jake's direct, deep blue gaze. He too was breathing shallowly and rapidly as he helped her fit herself over him. Then, with a forward thrust of his hips as she settled herself on him, Jessie felt her body accepting him, felt herself ensheathe him completely and more fully than she'd ever thought possible. Her arms went instantly around his neck as she sought even more closeness with him. He locked his arms around her back and helped her with the instinctive thrustings she could not stop. Harder and harder, faster and faster she rode; little gasping sounds of her efforts escaped her as she dug her nails into Jake's shoulders.

Jake laid his forehead against her shoulder as their endeavors brought them the release they sought. The great shuddering quakes that ripped through Jessie convulsed around Jake inside her. Now his nails gripped her back and he held her tightly molded to him as he gave small groans in time with his pulsating throbs. Jessie made a guttural, instinctive sound as she enjoyed both her satiation and his.

How long they stayed limply in each other's arms, Jessie couldn't say. But their breathing had long since returned to normal, and the water was definitely very cool. She stirred in Jake's arms, pulling herself back to look into his eyes and brush a lock of blue-black hair off his forehead. For the first time she noticed that he was clean-shaven and his hair had been trimmed neatly.

He smiled lazily and kissed the tip of her nose. With an "upsy-daisy" he lifted her off him by holding her under her arms. Jessie felt his pat on her bottom as she stepped out of the tub onto the soaked wooden floor. Trying to swat his hands away, she almost slipped.

With a chuckle directed at her, Jake once again resumed his earlier search for the soap. Coming up with it, he began to whistle and to wash himself cheerily. Jessie sat on the bed, wrapped in one towel, and using the other one to dry her hair. She watched Jake in the tub; the tender, melting feeling in her heart caught her off-guard. She was suddenly afraid she was going to cry. She wanted so much to tell him how much she loved him and that she was carrying their child, but the words wouldn't come.

Right then, Jake looked over at her and caught her watching him. He hesitated only a second before he very lightly said, "Oh, that's good. I get the cold, dirty water after you've used me to satisfy your lustful ways, and now I get a cold, wet towel to dry myself off."

Jessie felt the heat of a blush on her face. Her own desire and her body's need for him still embarrassed her. She looked down a second and then came up with what she thought was a pretty good retort. "Well, it just can't be helped—the towel I mean," she rushed to say, seeing his quirked eyebrow. "Not my lust—" A strangled sound came out of her. She tried again. "You can use this towel"—holding up the one with which she was drying her hair—"because I have to wear this other one. I have no clean clothes."

"Yes you do," Jake replied smoothly, his arms resting on the wooden rim of the tub. "Over there on the dresser." He inclined his head in that direction, a great, big grin on his face.

Jessie looked at him blankly for a second or two, and then jumped up and ran to the dresser, clutching at the towel around her body to keep it from falling to the floor. There were two packages on the dresser. Reasoning that Jake must have put them there when he'd sneaked into the room earlier to surprise her in the tub, Jessie grabbed them up and padded back to the bed to sit on it cross-legged with her treasures.

"You look like a little kid at Christmas," Jake teased from the tub.

Jessie's only answer was to throw the other towel at him, which he caught deftly in the air as he stood up to dry himself off. Jessie tore her eyes from his naked body, knowing that if she kept staring at him, she'd never know what he'd bought her! Eagerly she tore into the small package first. She gasped her delight at the shining silver brush and comb set that spilled into her lap with her last tug at the brown paper. So caught up was she with these, easily the prettiest things she'd ever seen, that she didn't at first notice the ornate silver and turquoise necklace lying draped over her crossed ankles.

Jake was standing beside her now, the towel wrapped around his waist and tucked in snugly at his hip. "Well, here, what's this?" he intoned, picking the necklace up to bring it to Jessie's attention.

She gasped loudly and grabbed at it greedily, clutching it to her bosom. "Oh, Jake, it's so beautiful! I don't know what to say!" She turned shining eyes to him.

It was Jake's turn to look away, a slight redness showing under his tan. He brushed aside his obvious emotion by saying gruffly, "Well, if you can let go of it long enough and hold your hair up, I'll put it on you."

Jessie jumped up onto her knees on the bed to comply, turning her back to him and holding up the thick mane of her still-damp, black-brown hair with one hand. She held out the necklace in her other hand. But her towel caught under her knee; instantly she was naked as it was stripped off her. She screeched and looked over her shoulder in shock at Jake.

He immediately backed away from her, waving his hands out in front of him. "Oh no. Not again. Please don't make me! I don't think I can again so soon!"

A screaming giggle escaped Jessie as she quickly grabbed the errant towel up and wrapped it around her. "Oh shut up," she tossed at Jake, along with one of the bed pillows. "Now put the necklace on me! Hurry!" She held it out again.

"Hurry? Why? Where do you think you're going?" he teased as he stepped back up behind her, and placed the silver and turquoise work of art around her neck, his large fingers lingering over the tiny clasp.

The necklace on, Jessie let down her hair and pushed the brush and comb to the side so she could get to the big package. As she ripped into it, she very matter-of-factly told him, "You're taking me out on the town. I want to eat; I want to see the sights; I want to dance; I want to—"

"Oh? I wish you'd told me all this earlier. Then I wouldn't have made a date with a pretty senorita that I—"

Jessie rounded on him with the other pillow and sent it hurling harmlessly past him to land with a thump across the room. Jake laughed and surrendered, catching her wrists with his hands and pulling her to him until she quit wriggling. "Okay, okay. I give up," he laughed, peppering her face with kisses; petulantly she pushed away from him and went back to her package. "I think you're worse than a kid!" Jake said, shaking his head and thoroughly enjoying her delight.

The package finally open, Jessie breathed out her intense awe at the sight before her. With tender reverence she held up a peasant blouse of a purplish-blue silk shot with spun gold; heavy stripes of the gold entwined with the pinkish-purple satin ribbons adorning both puffed sleeves. The loose boat-neck would very daringly show off her bosom, she knew, but there was a purple satin ribbon running the circumference of the rounded neck which she could draw up in front as modestly as she wished. Crushing this confection to her bosom, she closed her eyes to squeeze the tears back. She felt Jake's hand on her shoulder, tenderly caressing it.

She opened her eyes and looked up at him. He cupped her face in his hands and used his thumbs to wipe stray tears from her lashes. She caught one of his hands and placed a small kiss in his palm. Jake withdrew his hand and took one step back from her. Jessie could not interpret the look on his face; it wasn't anger, shock, surprise. It was something very unguarded, very tender.

She smiled shyly at him and turned back to her opened package. She next drew out the long, full skirt which matched the blouse. The waist of the skirt was the spun gold material; from there, the skirt alternated with ever wider horizontal stripes of the purplish-blue silk and the spun gold material, woven through with purple and pink satin ribbon into an intricate pattern. The skirt almost seemed to change colors as Jessie stood up on the bed, holding it to her, looking down at it, and turning slowly from side to side.

She turned shining but shy eyes on Jake. "I love them, Jake. They're beautiful." She wanted to say the same things about him, but knew she couldn't. Not now anyway.

For the first time, Jessie saw Jake look awkward and maybe even shy. He took his eyes off her standing there on the bed wrapped in a towel and holding the skirt to her, and took the wrapping paper off the bed. "There's more in here," he said, digging through it. Pantalets, a chemise, petticoats, and even a pair of soft leather sandals with long leather ties were held up alternately by him for her inspection. He then made a very businesslike show of gathering all the wrappings off the bed and tossing them aside. Recovering from his boyish awkwardness, he suddenly reached over and snatched Jessie's towel off her; she shrieked and brought the skirt up to cover her nakedness. "Now get dressed if we're going out on the town!"

Chapter Sixteen

With rising excitement and anticipation, Jessie watched the swirling dancers on the crowded, open-air wooden dance floor in front of her. She clapped her hands delightedly in time with the cheerful tune the mariachi band was playing. Jake's arm snugly around her waist made her feel safe and protected amid the hundreds of people who thronged Santa Fe's central plaza. The night had been chased away by the score of brightly lit lanterns that swayed and danced in the light wind to their own rhythm as they hung suspended overhead.

The tightening of Jake's hand at her waist, pulling her even closer to him as other would-be dancers crowded around, brought Jessie's eyes up to meet his. They were so warm and blue that Jessie could not maintain contact for long. She felt like he was the sun—if she looked directly at him for a long time, she would be blinded by his brilliance.

And he was so brilliantly handsome tonight in his own new clothes—black, close-fitting trousers that hugged his muscular thighs and widened at the hem to accommodate boots; a snow-white, loose-fitting shirt opened at the throat; and, over the shirt, a black, shiny leather vest with hand-tooled designs adorning the pockets. His black Stetson hat, the high-crowned, wide-brimmed popular hat just now making its way west, given to him by Bertha, and his ever-present gunbelt completed his appearance.

Jessie smiled to herself that this devastatingly good-looking man was with her. She had seen all the women, young and old, staring openly at him as they walked by. But she wasn't jealous; no, she felt sympathy for them. Because she knew how they felt—her own knees still shook weakly when he turned his deep blue eyes on her. But they would never know how it felt to be in his arms; now that got her jealousy up. Her chin came up, and she narrowed her eyes, just thinking about some other woman . . .

"Whoa! What or who put that look on your face?" Jake teased her. His even, white teeth brightened his smile.

With a guilty flush, Jessie swatted at his arm playfully and answered his smile with one of her own. And then she lied, "I was just wondering when this song will ever be over so we can dance the next one! I can't keep my feet still much longer!"

"Patience, my love, patience," Jake intoned, patting her head as if she were a child.

Jessie's smile froze; she turned—almost lurched—to face the dancers again. He'd said "my love." Even if he was just teasing, he'd still said "my love." A warm little area of her heart began to believe that just maybe there was a chance for them after this Santa Fe trip. A sudden chill on her skin in the warm night air reminded her of the dangers ahead for her and for Jake, both together and separately.

Before her dismal thoughts could dampen her enthusiasm for Santa Fe and the rich, celebratory atmosphere which permeated the very air, the band ended the tune and waited for the present set of dancers to clear the floor, making way for the next set.

"And away we go!" Jake laughingly called out as he swung her out onto the dance floor, her silk and gold skirt creating its own vibrant pageant of color and motion. His black and white attire, at once so stark and yet so appealing, provided the perfect frame for Jessie's own brilliant color as she abandoned her heart to Jake and her feet to the music. Nothing existed but his hands at her waist and her hands on his shoulders as he twirled her around, executing the lively steps of a fandango.

Jessie had never felt so beautiful. She knew the color was high in her cheeks and her hair, brushed earlier by Jake to a lustrous brown curling cascade with black and red highlights, was held back over one ear by the pink flowers he'd bought her as they strolled through town and placed in her hair himself. "There, now you're perfect," he'd said. But Jessie knew that the clothes and flowers were not what made her feel so beautiful; it was the love she bore for this darkly handsome, virile man in whose arms she was even now dizzily swirling. And whose child she was even now nurturing in her womb.

Yes, Jake would always be a part of her, whether he was with her or not. She turned shining eyes on him and favored him with her most brilliant smile. He leered very archly and comically back at her, pretending he was going to take a bite out of her neck. A giddy giggle escaped her as he spun her into the thick of the dancers.

Jake came suddenly awake in the deepest part of the night. Every nerve sat on edge as he carefully raised his head and reached very slowly and very quietly for his gun on the nightstand beside the huge four-poster bed. Something had awakened him, that was for sure. He blinked a few times, but his eyes readily adapted to his surroundings, lit as they were by the bright moonlight filtering through the open window across the room. His glittering eyes did a slow sweep of the room; nothing was amiss.

He briefly looked over at Jessie, who was lying against him, her head on his shoulder, one leg and one arm thrown over him. Her hair tickled his arm as he worked to free himself without disturbing her deep, even breathing. The corners of his mouth turned up the slightest bit; he knew she was exhausted from too much food, too much excitement, too much dancing, and too much love-making.

Instantly to his mind came her shocked face when he announced that he too was sleeping in this bed while they were here, and then her shyly crawling in next to him and staying so maidenly on her own side until he'd let out a bear growl and grabbed her to him. And there she'd stayed. He shook his head— after all their lovemaking, she was still so damned little-girl shy about some things. He kept forgetting just how young and innocent she really was. But she was so passionate at the same time . . . how could he remember?

With a sigh, Jake laid his head down again on the huge, soft pillow. Maybe it was nothing at all. But then there it was again—a soft, hissing sound right outside the first-floor window across the room. The window opened onto a side street behind this hacienda-style hotel. That was why Jake had deliberately chosen this room. There were two avenues of escape. One was the door, and the other was the window wide enough for him and Jessie to crawl through if the need arose. Then he heard his name being called softly. Jake was out of bed and padding naked to the window in one swift movement. His gun was raised and ready.

"Hssst, Jake!"

Jake relaxed and lowered his gun. That was Curly Burnett's voice. Jake stayed to the side of the window and answered in a loud whisper. "Right here, Curly. What you got?"

"Ah heard some tawlk at a cantina jist a few minutes ago. Seems there's a Seen-yore Vasquez ridin' in about daylight," he said in his slow, Southern drawl.

Jake risked a peek out the window and saw Curly leaning against the adobe building, one knee bent and his booted foot resting against the wall. He was slowly rolling a cigarette and looking all around as he spoke softly. To any chance passersby he would look merely like a lounging cowboy just not ready to go to bed yet. The shadows of night and his hat pulled low over his face masked his alert, darting eyes taking in his surroundings and anyone walking by. Jake smiled. Curly was good—damned good.

"So Vasquez will be here soon," Jake repeated softly, rubbing his hand over his jaw. Out of the corner of his eye, he caught the sudden flare of the match Curly struck. Then he smelled the smoke. "What else did you hear?"

There was a pause while Curly shifted positions and took a puff of his cigarette. Jake jumped when the soft voice outside spoke again. "Ah heard he likes to travel in heavy company. Brings all his caballeros with him. Has a high old time too while he's here. Spends a lot of money, it seems. Folks around here like him for that."

"I just imagine they do," Jake said thoughtfully. He added up Curly's news. It hadn't taken long at all for Vasquez's men to get word to him that the guns were here, thinking back to the men who'd been outside the cantina when Jake's wagon train came into town. He must be staying close by—probably with rich sympathizers to his revolutionary dreams. Jake wondered what Vasquez thought about the news that it wasn't Hayes delivering the guns. He knew this would make Vasquez very cautious. With good reason, Jake thought grimly. Then, to Curly again, "Anything else?"

"Yeah. You got a light? My cigarette just went out."

Jake heard the bemused consternation in Curly's voice. A low chuckle escaped him. "No, I don't, man. Besides, you need to cut back on your smoking."

"Yeah," came the drawled reply as Curly straightened up and pretended to stretch nonchalantly. "Ah sure wouldn't want to do anything to endanger my health."

A strangled laugh on the other side of the window met his words. "Point taken," Jake answered. "I'll see you at the wagons at sunup. Have all the men assembled. And tell Lieutenant Patterson those are my orders."

"Will do," was all Jake heard before he caught the sound of Curly's retreating footsteps.

Jake shook his head and smiled as he climbed back into bed, careful not to disturb Jessie. As he settled in beside her, she turned restlessly on her side, facing away from him. Jake lay on his back with his arm thrown over his eyes. He really didn't think he'd get much more sleep tonight with his head full of the day to come.

On her side of the bed, Jessie lay with her eyes open. She'd been awake since Jake had gotten up a few minutes ago. His taut, muscled body had shone in the moonlight as he stood to the side of the window and talked to one of his men outside. She berated herself for being so taken with his body that she hadn't listened to his words. Something was up. She just knew it. Even though she had not been able to catch most of Jake's words, she had caught the last part about him going to the wagons and the men being ready. Vasquez must be coming. She would be ready, too.

Jessie was wide awake but pretending deep sleep early the next morning when Jake leaned over her with a chuckle, smoothed her hair from her face, and placed a warm kiss on her temple. She became a little nervous that he might realize she was really awake when he stood by the bed for a few more minutes after kissing her. But she relaxed her tense hold on the sheet covering her when she heard his footsteps retreat across the room, open the door, and leave. Instantly Jessie was on her feet on her side of the bed closest to the window.

She had to get dressed quickly if she hoped to follow Jake to know just where the meeting with Vasquez would take place. Instantly she rejected the beautiful, shining skirt and blouse that Jake had given her yesterday. She would attract too much attention in the daylight dressed like that. She looked wildly around the room for her hated pants, shirt, hat, and boots. She had no choice; they were her only other clothes. But where were they? She distinctly remembered tossing them into the corner by the dressing table yesterday afternoon before her bath, but they weren't there now!

"Looking for these?" came a lazy drawl from over by the door behind her.

Jessie froze in shock, then whirled around instantly, momentarily forgetting her nakedness. "You! I thought you left," she accused, her eyes narrowed. She chose to ignore the guilty flush which she could feel creeping up her face.

"And I thought you were asleep," Jake countered. A smile tugged at his lips, but he managed to suppress it.

Jessie advanced on him, unaware of the jiggling, bouncing picture of female voluptuousness she made. "Give me my clothes," she said in a low, threatening voice, her fists at her sides.

"Why?" Jake said in a husky voice. "I much prefer you like this." His appreciative, smoldering eyes raked her up and down. Still, he kept Jessie's clothes flung over one arm and his arms crossed in front of him as he lounged against the door.

His roving eyes struck Jessie with the force of a blow as she looked down at herself. She grabbed for the top sheet on the bed and wrapped it around her. Her fevered efforts to cover herself only brought loud chuckling from Jake.

"See? You don't need these at all," Jake said, holding her pants and shirt up. "You can just wear that sheet. It's most becoming, my dear."

"Jake Coltrane, you better give me those clothes now, or I'll . . . I'll—"

"You'll what, Jessie? I can't wait to hear this." He very maddeningly quirked a mocking eyebrow at her.

"I'll just wear this sheet; that's what. Or I'll wear my new skirt and blouse. Or I'll wear my underwear. I really don't care what I wear, but I am going, too."

That straightened him up. He flung her clothes into the bottom of the armoire as he advanced on her, all seriousness now. "And just where in the hell do you think you're going?"

Jessie pulled herself up to her full, petite height and straightened the sheet around her. Her chin came up defiantly, but she quaked inside when she had to look directly up into Jake's eyes. He was mad; there was no mistaking the deep, almost black blueness of his eyes. Jessie forced herself to keep eye contact, though. She'd come too far to be denied her meeting with Vasquez to try to clear the Stuart name. Nobody else would do it.

"I asked you a question," Jake said levelly. "Just where do you think you're going?"

"I'm going with you, and you know it," she yelled right into his face. Her chest heaved with her emotion, and to her chagrin, she felt a wave of dizziness and nausea begin to sweep over her. Oh, God, not now, she prayed. Swallowing convulsively, she continued, "I have to see Vasquez—you know I do! I have to hear him myself say that my father was or was not involved! Nobody accuses my father—" Her voice trailed off as her legs turned to water; with a hand to her brow, she sagged against the wood frame of the bed.

Jake was instantly at her side, a solicitous hand on her elbow and one on her back. "Jessie, what is it? Are you sick?" Then, a sudden thought struck him; he stiffened and turned her loose. "If this is another one of your tricks—that's exactly what it is! Well, it won't work, Jessie. You're staying here, and that's final." He raged around the room gathering up every stitch of clothing Jessie had. "There's no way in hell I'm going to let you meet with Vasquez. The man's a killer. We might all be dead by this afternoon. You're staying here, do you hear me? I won't have you placing your life in any more danger!" He was now over by the door, with his hand on the latch. "I couldn't live if anything happened to you." With that he flung himself out the door and slammed it closed from the outside.

Jessie ran to the washbasin on a wooden stand and vomited. She then slid, sheet and all, to the floor, drawing her knees up to her chest; her stomach lurched and heaved threateningly. She put her damp forehead to her knees, and stayed that way until the sickness passed a few minutes later. Feeling better, she stretched her legs out in front of her.

Now what was she going to do, she thought hopelessly, looking around the room. Now she really had nothing to wear. "Damn him," she said out loud, emphasizing her words by hitting her fist on her rounded thigh. Then his words came back to her. He'd said he couldn't live if anything happened to her. Jessie opened her eyes in wonderment as she thought about this. But then, with a scowl, she dismissed his words, telling herself he just didn't want another death on his conscience. That was all he meant, she was sure of it. She swallowed the lump forming in her throat.

A timid knocking at the door brought her head around. Maybe he'd come back!

"Senora? Are you awake? It is me, the maid," the petite, fully dressed, unsuspecting, dark-eyed, dark-haired, young, female maid called out.

Even better, Jessie thought.

She lurched to her feet, secured her sheet about her, pasted an innocent smile on her face, and opened the door. "Come in," Jessie said smilingly, sizing the girl up as she walked past her into the room, her arms full of clean sheets and towels.

Jessie closed the door behind her unsuspecting prey.

In less than fifteen minutes, a petite, fully dressed, dark-eyed, dark-haired, young female left the room she'd entered to clean and hurried down the open breezeway of the hotel, her arms full of soiled sheets and towels, past the central courtyard with its flowing fountain and rock-and-cactus garden, past all the other rooms, and turned two sharp lefts to put herself on the side street which would bring her to Santa Fe's central plaza.

Once on the side street, she tossed her load to the ground, caught her hands to her throat, and steadied her breathing. She then smoothed her hands over the woven cotton brown skirt and white peasant blouse. Raising her skirt just a bit, she wiggled her toes, grinning at the leather sandals which encased her feet.

Then, with her chin held high and with resolute steps, she started up the narrow street, really more of an alley, toward the crowded market plaza. The only time her steps faltered was when she passed under an open hotel room window and heard muffled cries from within. With a gulp and a grimace, she hurried even more.

Jake sat in a rough wood chair which he balanced on its two back legs on the cantina's veranda; his long legs were stretched out in front of him, crossed at the ankles, and his booted feet rested on the hitching rail. He rolled a wooden toothpick around in his mouth with his tongue as, with studied casualness, he observed the milling throngs of buyers and sellers in the dusty central plaza. With his thumb, he moved the brim of his Stetson up, pushing the hat further back on his head. The sun had been up only a few hours, but already the frenzy of activity was in full swing as business was conducted from the back of wagons, from established stores, from the wooden walkways in front of every building, and from crude booths set up seemingly overnight.

Jake was surrounded by his men, all in equally casual poses, his supposed gang of gunrunners. Every one of them was as tense as a virgin bride on her wedding night, Jake mused, but to their credit, they were doing a pretty convincing job of appearing relaxed. Except Patterson, Jake grunted; he'd been sick twice already. Make that three times, Jake corrected himself, seeing the young, blond Lieutenant bolt for the side alley.

"Ah shore hope Seen-yore Vasquez contacts us before that young man heaves his toenails," Curly remarked dryly, not even looking up from the cigarette he was rolling.

Several of the men chuckled and shook their heads, but still they kept their keen eyes trained on the plaza, watching for anything out of the ordinary. So far—nothing. But they all knew it would happen. The word was Vasquez was coming with all his pistoleros, his gunmen. He needed these guns. The transaction would take place, no doubt about it. It was what happened after that, that had everyone edgy. According to what Jake had heard Hayes say when he'd been riding with him, and had passed on to these men, this double shipment would complete Vasquez's arsenal, and he would want no witnesses to how he'd acquired case after case of Colt revolvers meant for U. S. Army outposts. But they also knew Jake's plan and had confidence in it. And so, they waited.

Several lovely, young senoritas sashayed with swaying hips down the street in front of the cantina. Some of the men called out appreciatively; the girls responded with giggles and hurried footsteps as their elderly duennas hustled them on, giving stern looks to the rowdy men on the veranda.

Jake chuckled, taking in the full Mexican flavor of this American city. Making New Mexico a U. S. Territory had cost his father his life eighteen years ago. But Jake held no resentment for the war or the people who had left his young mother a widow. His father had died fighting for a cause he believed in—and now here was Jake trying to offset another conflict between Mexico and America. The irony struck him as his eyes took in the adobe buildings, the huge Catholic church at the other end of the plaza, and the dark-skinned, hardworking people who lived simple, honest, productive lives. Jake was determined that he would see that those lives were not disrupted by the corrupt dreams of one power-hungry landowner.

Jake had the thought that these relatively new citizens of the United States were a good-looking people, too. Take this little senorita walking across the plaza now—the one in a white peasant blouse and brown skirt. Her steps were slow and hesitating as she appeared to be looking for someone. Jake tried to imagine what her life was like. He wondered if she was poor and had to work—judging by her simple clothes, she probably did have a job to help support her family. Jake fancied that she was probably looking for a younger brother or sister, or maybe her mamacita, but probably her lover. Jake smiled. A girl who moved like she did, and had a slender yet lush figure like that and long, almost black, curly hair would definitely have a lover. He couldn't see her eyes, but he'd just bet they were big and brown, like Jessie's, and could melt a man's heart and harden his . . .

Wait just a damned minute! Jake was on his feet in an instant. There was something awfully familiar about that girl. Everyone on the veranda came to instant alertness when Jake bolted out of his chair, sending it crashing against the cantina wall. He was leaning his hands against the hitching rail and craning his neck this way and that trying to get a better look at her as she wove her way through the crowd. He kept telling himself there was no way that girl could be Jessie! He'd left her with nothing but a sheet to wear. Still, he kept craning his neck and cursing softly, turning his eyes first this way and then that way. He'd lost sight of her, dammit. He hit his fist against the wood rail, jerked around to retrieve his chair, and saw all his men staring at him questioningly.

"It's nothing," he barked, righting the chair and flinging himself into it. He stared straight ahead without seeing anything as the men resettled themselves. He'd choke her, if she didn't get herself killed first, Jake swore. He'd better find her naked and in that room tonight, just like he'd left her. She never did anything he told her to do, the little headstrong, fire-breathing, stubborn, spoiled, independent . . . woman he loved, Jake finished lamely. He ran his hand over his mouth to smooth away the telltale signs of laughter that twitched at his lips.

What in the world was he going to do with her after this? He sighed. Take her on undercover assignments all over the country? Could he settle down in one place and lead a normal life, like all these people? He knew he'd certainly never even thought of that until he met Jessie. He fingered the two wedding bands in his shirt pocket. He kept them with him at all times. Was he going to marry her all over again and settle down? Could he? Would she even have him—especially if he did find out that her father was somehow involved in this gunrunning?

For the first time in his career, Jake considered not reporting something he knew he should. Jessie would be destroyed—emotionally and financially—if her father had been involved with Hayes or Vasquez. And, if he had been, and Jake knew it, but didn't report it, then what would that do to him? Jake tented his fingers in front of his mouth and sighed deeply. Could he destroy everything he'd worked for all his life to save the woman he loved the anguish and heartache of being thrown off her land because

287

Cheryl Anne Porter

of a crooked parent, one who was already dead and would not suffer the consequences of his acts? Why should Jessie be made to suffer? Jake hoped against hope that Stuart had not been involved.

Especially when he had the sudden vision of Jessie's lush, naked body under him. Despite himself, Jake shifted uneasily in his chair. Thinking of her always did this to him, he grimaced. Scenes of Jessie filled his mind and heart. Jessie naked in her meadow, giving herself so readily to him that first time; Jessie hurling her ring at him when she was angry; Jessie pretending to faint when he caught her that first day on the trail; Jessie's head thrown back, her lips parted in passion as she thrust her petite, lush body against his in that wooden tub; Jessie, scared but brave, in that dark tunnel.

Jessie, terrified and confused, but marrying him nonetheless to protect him, a man she thought was an outlaw; Jessie in that mountain pool, at once a child spewing a fountain of water out of her mouth and then in the next instant a woman writhing under him on that towel, giving totally of herself as his hands and mouth had roamed over her perfect body—from her soft, thick mane of black-brown wavy hair; from her liquid brown eyes with their long, long dark lashes; to her high cheekbones; her sensuous, pouting lips, and down the slender column of her neck to at once capture her rosy-brown nipple, so stiff and proud; to her narrow waist he could easily span with both hands; her concave little belly with its so-sensitive navel and to the dark triangle of curly hair at the vee of her thighs—and her legs . . . those rounded, firm thighs and her shapely . . .

Jake was brought back to the present by a hand hitting his shoulder, trying to get his attention.

He jerked his head up to see Curly standing by him and nodding toward the street. Jake riveted his eyes on the street scene in front of him. At first glance, nothing seemed out of the ordinary. But then he saw what had alerted Curly and the rest of his men. Four heavily armed, swaggering, mean-looking Mexicanos had separated themselves from the milling crowd and were even now making their very deliberate way toward the cantina where Jake and his men waited.

Jessie feigned interest in the colorful array of hair ribbons and ornaments in a makeshift booth in the central plaza. She willed her hands not to shake as she examined an elaborate hair comb inlaid with silver and turquoise. She was sure Jake had recognized her, even dressed as she was and even at this distance from the cantina where he sat with his men. She'd just about given up hope of catching sight of him or any of his men as she'd slowly worked her way through the loud throng until she'd chanced to look over to the cantina they'd passed by yesterday when they arrived in Santa Fe. It stood out in her mind because of the fierce-looking Mexican men who'd stared so hard at them at the time. When Jake had jumped up from his chair just now, she had lost herself immediately in the crowd.

After a moment, Jessie put the hair comb down and turned away from the booth. Using the milling crowds of people as a natural cover, she worked her way into a better position and glanced furtively at the cantina's veranda. Her breath caught in her throat; she anxiously shifted to see better as people walked or pushed past her, intent on their own errands. She could catch the unfolding scene on the veranda only in snatches when the crowds parted.

Frustrated, she practically ran to an adobe dry goods store closer to the cantina. She knew Jake was intent on the four Mexicans in front of him in the dusty street and was not looking for her anymore. She flattened herself against the sun-warmed side of the small store; from here, with her back against the rough wall, but hidden in the shadows cast by the sun's angle into this narrow alley, she could see and hear what was happening.

A calculating grin broke over the ruddy face of a large man standing next to the elegantly dressed, aristocratic, darkly handsome, Mexican man on the second-story terrace of the most elegant hotel in town, which sat at an angle across the plaza from the cantina. The remains of their sumptuous breakfast still lay on the table behind them.

"Bueno, mi amigo, what do you think? Is that the girl?" Don Diego Vasquez asked, pulling absently at one end of his thin, black moustache, and narrowing his eyes.

"I'm almost certain it is," Sergeant MacKenzie answered in a low, sly voice, turning only briefly to look at Vasquez before turning his gaze back to the plaza and to the alley and resting his hands again on the black wrought-iron railing of the terrace.

"There is only one way to find out for sure then, is there not?" Vasquez said, already turning to two swarthy men who stood guard, one on either side of the glass and wood double doors which opened onto the terrace.

Just like his four men in the plaza, these also were armed to the teeth. In rapid Spanish, he issued brief orders to them, pointing in the direction of the dry goods store. The two pistoleros nodded, answered "Si, Jefe," and went through the double doors into the hotel room. In another moment, Vasquez and MacKenzie heard the slamming of the room's outer door.

Neither one spoke as they watched the two swarthy guards moving purposefully toward the small adobe store. The crowds of people seemed to part for them, wanting no trouble from the two Mexicans armed with Colt revolvers and long rifles. They disappeared briefly into the alley and then reappeared with a young girl in a white peasant blouse and a brown skirt between them, resisting as much as was possible their big hands gripping her arms tightly and a Colt surreptitiously stuck in her ribs. The Mexicans had done this before. No one in the plaza even noticed the three.

"Well, sergeant, we will know in a moment if indeed she is the marshal's woman," Vasquez said in flawless English, with only the slightest trace of a Spanish accent. "If she is, she may prove to be a useful pawn. If she is not, she may prove to be useful in bed, no? Either way, we will kill her along with the rest of the Americans once our business is done."

Don Diego Vasquez clapped the big, ruddy sergeant on the back and the two shared an evil, oily laugh.

Chapter Seventeen

Nervous tension filled the thirteen men readying themselves to deliver the two wagons of guns to Vasquez at a private villa on the outskirts of Santa Fe. Maybe on the long ride from Camp Nichols there had been times when they had put this moment out of their minds as they played poker around the campfire or swam in that mountain pool, and had maybe even pretended the danger wasn't real. But no more. The moment had arrived. Some, maybe all, would not make it back to Santa Fe this afternoon. That knowledge quieted their words, but not their hammering hearts.

"All right, men, listen up," Jake called out, breaking into their private thoughts. "This is it." He slowly scanned the determined faces of the men ranged in front of him. At his back were the two gun-laden wagons he was asking these men to possibly give their lives for. "You know what we're up against. And you know what the odds are. And you know why it's important to our country that we're successful. Our orders are to deliver these guns, get the money, and get the hell out. I know that sounds simple enough, but you saw at the cantina a small sample of the army Vasquez has assembled. They're nothing more than cutthroat mercenaries for sale to the highest bidder, who happens right now to be Vasquez."

Jake paused for a moment to let that sink in. Then, he continued. "It's not our job to arrest Vasquez or to kill him and his men. Our President simply wants the facts and the proof to turn over to the Mexican government and let them handle it. That sounds fine in theory, but I'm here to tell you that if shooting starts, everyone is a target, including Vasquez. Now hopefully that won't happen because I expect to see each and every one of you back here with me this afternoon."

Nervous, laughing murmurs of agreement ran through the men as they turned to each other and made a show of bravado by clapping their neighbor on the back or poking him in the ribs or brandishing their guns in the air. Only Lieutenant Patterson remained pale and quiet. When the men turned their attention back to Jake, he handed out assignments.

"Lieutenant Patterson," he began.

When the young man did not respond, Curly poked him in the ribs, got his startled attention, and pointed toward Jake.

"Lieutenant, I am leaving you and Private Dinkins here with the firing pins. You will surrender them to no one but me. Is that understood?"

"Yes—" Coy Patterson croaked nervously as his voice broke. He immediately blushed a deep red when the men chuckled; he cleared his throat and said resolutely, "Yes, Sir. I understand. The Private and I will turn the firing pins over to no one but you."

Jake turned a level stare and a grim face on the young man. Dinkins and Patterson were the two youngest and most inexperienced solders he'd brought with him. He didn't want to risk their lives, or his own and the rest of the men's, if those two did something stupid at the villa, like get scared and start firing. Jake just didn't see how they could mess up sitting under a tree here with their horses until he and the rest of his men rode back here with one of Vasquez's lieutenants for the pins. That was Jake's ace in the hole, his insurance for their safety: without the firing pins, the guns wouldn't work. If Vasquez killed Jake and his men, he wouldn't know where the pins were. Simple, but effective.

Jake now turned his attention back to the remaining ten men. "Questions?" No one spoke; some shook their heads no. "Mount up," Jake ordered, swinging onto Blaze's back. Blaze felt the tension in the air and wanted to prance and plunge forward. Jake swiftly brought the huge roan under control, and with a wave of his hand, set the small train on its course for the villa of Roberto Suarez, Vasquez's suspected co-conspirator.

Jake knew the villa to be an isolated stronghold, a perfect setting for a massacre without drawing any attention from Santa Fe authorities, who were reluctant to interfere with Suarez at any rate. But he hadn't been able to persuade Vasquez's henchmen at the cantina to agree to a more neutral location for this transaction. They were already spooked and suspicious because it wasn't Hayes they were dealing with. Jake hadn't pushed the point of another location out of fear of Vasquez's calling off the deal altogether; that would have put Jake back at square one with still no proof and would have made this a wasted trip. Jake took a deep breath, saying a silent prayer for their safety.

About an hour after Jake, the men, and the two wagons left the small campsite set up the day before just beyond the last adobe dwelling on the south side of Santa Fe, another larger procession paraded past the amazed eyes of Lieutenant Coy Patterson and Private John Dinkins.

The two fresh-faced young men sat on the sandy ground under a tall but scrubby tree, the big, heavy sacks of firing pins protected between them. This was an important job, and they intended to do it correctly. Hearing the sounds of approaching horsemen coming out of Santa Fe, they shaded their eyes and turned their heads to the left.

When the two dozen or so Mexican men rode by them at a thundering pace, churning up choking dust, Coy and John were glad they were sitting about twenty yards away from the road, enough distance to keep them out of the notice of the pistoleros. They exchanged glances and smug grins when the men rode south and disappeared around the bend in the road that would eventually take them to the Suarez villa. Fat lot of good those new guns were going to do those mercenaries without the firing pins that they had right here.

Their attention was immediately drawn back toward Santa Fe by the sounds of even more horsemen. This group was traveling at a slower pace and the caballeros, the horsemen, were riding protectively around an elegant, open black carriage which held three passengers, two men— and a young dark-haired woman in a white blouse. But it wasn't her beauty or her clothes which drew the young men's attention—it was the gag covering her mouth.

This procession too rode by without a second glance at the two young men sitting so innocently under a tree far off to their right. But those two young men did double-takes, their widened eyes and gaping mouths following the carriage until it went around the bend. They jumped to their feet and both spoke at once.

"Lieutenant, you better pinch me to see if I'm dreaming, but I'll be a scalded cat if that wasn't Sergeant MacKenzie in that carriage."

"Did you see who that girl was, Private? That was Jessie! Jessie Stuart!"

They rounded on each other in shocked surprise.

"Jessie?! *Our* Jessie?" Private Dinkins blurted stupidly.

"Sergeant MacKenzie? *Our* Sergeant MacKenzie?!" Lieutenant Patterson repeated just as stupidly.

And then, together, "Oh no," as they both turned to watch the dust settle on the now empty road.

"You got to do something, Lieutenant," the young, redhaired, freckle-faced private said, shaking his head as they retook their seats under the tree. "We got to warn them."

Coy had been afraid that Dinkins would say that. He took a silent moment to curse his rich parents for ever having gotten him this commission. Now look at the mess he was in out here in the wilderness. A life in the military had sounded wonderful, what with getting to wear the colorful uniform and sashaying amongst the young ladies at the parties in the completely civilized and settled large towns back east. He'd never bargained for this.

He stopped his hand in midair when he became aware that he had been repeatedly picking up a handful of sandy dirt and tossing it back onto the ground while he thought, a decidedly childish thing for a lieutenant to be doing. He turned his eyes to Dinkins. The private was obviously waiting for his brilliant plan . . . very well, then, the young lieutenant thought, squaring his shoulders. He would seize the day.

"Very well, then, Private," he began, making his voice as dignified and mature as possible when one was sitting cross-legged in the sand with one's underling. "Since Marshal Coltrane put me in charge of these firing pins, I'll stay here with them, and you can ride for the villa—"

"What, Coy?" John Dinkins cried, forgetting military protocol which had been relaxed on this long trip due to the nature of the mission. "You're crazy if you think I'm going to go waltzing into that nest of hornets by myself!"

"Listen here, John Dinkins, I'm the ranking officer here and I'm ordering you to—"

"Order all you want, Coy, but I ain't going by myself. My mama didn't raise no fool." He crossed his arms and stared straight ahead stubbornly.

Coy thought up all sorts of military punishment he could mete out to John for his disobeying a direct order, including shooting him, but then he also remembered something else that he'd learned at the academy—a good officer never orders his men to do something he's not willing to do himself, especially if it's dangerous. And he definitely was not willing to go to that villa by himself, either—and it definitely was dangerous.

"All right," he began again, trying to muster as much dignity and authority as he could while changing his mind and his orders. "We'll both go to the villa." He waited for a reaction from John. When he saw the private turn his eyes over to him, Coy knew he had his attention and his tacit agreement to this plan. He continued confidently, "We'll just have to see what the layout is when we get there and then do what we can to warn Jake. Agreed?"

John relaxed his stiff posture and turned to Coy. "What about the firing pins?"

Coy looked at him for a long, silent moment. Must he do everything? Then his face brightened. "We'll bury them right here under this tree, so we'll still have that hold on Mr. Vasquez. Even if his men capture us, they won't kill us because we're the only ones who know where the pins are buried."

It was John's turn to think for a long, silent moment. "But then they could kill Mr. Coltrane and the rest because they wouldn't need them anymore—just us. And they could torture us, Coy, until we tell them where the pins are. And then they'd kill us, too."

Coy reached his limit. "Well, dammit, John, just what do *you* think we should do? You got a better idea?" Coy actually hoped he did, because that torture business did not sound like anything he wanted to undergo.

John doodled in the sand for a few seconds before he raised his head to reply. "Well, we could take the pins with us and ride to the villa and warn Mr. Coltrane somehow before Vasquez gets there with Miss Jessie and Sergeant MacKenzie. You know how Mr. Coltrane is about Miss Jessie; no telling what he'll do when he learns Vasquez has her. We got to quit sitting here like two nervous schoolgirls and do something, Coy."

Yes, Coy thought, he knew all too well how Mr. Coltrane felt about Miss Jessie. But he knew how he felt about her, too. This was his chance to be a hero in her eyes and maybe she would then return his feelings. His mind made up, he squared his shoulders, turned to John sitting beside him in the sand, and mimicking Jake's commanding tone, said, "Get the pins and mount up. We're riding for the villa."

Well, she'd gotten her wish. Here she was at the villa with Vasquez. And she was utterly sick about it. Jessie hadn't known what to think when she'd been abducted and made to sit beside Vasquez in the open carriage. But she'd become even more confused and concerned, when, a few miles away from this villa, she'd been untied and ungagged. Jessie shuddered again when she recalled that oily Vasquez's arm around her, holding her tightly against him, and the gun in his other hand, which he held to her ribs. Otherwise, she would have been fighting him and trying to get away.

Being killed trying to escape was a preferable choice to Jessie than once again being used as a pawn against Jake. Jessie put one hand to her mouth and her other hand to her stomach. What must Jake think after seeing her ride into this villa's courtyard in the luxury of the black, shiny carriage, sitting beside Vasquez, who had his arm around her?

She would never forget the absolute shock on his face, which had slowly turned to a mask of stone, when Vasquez had so gallantly helped her out of the carriage—the gun in her ribs still hidden from Jake's view—and had swept her right past him in the hot, dusty courtyard and into the cool, spacious foyer of the villa.

Jessie plopped hopelessly down onto an intricately carved, dark-wood chest which sat under a high window in the very large, very rich bedroom to which she had been escorted and locked in. She tortured herself trying to figure out what Jake must be thinking. Jake probably thought what he was supposed to think: That she, just like her father, was involved with Vasquez. And that she had double-crossed Jake and his men. And that she had probably informed Vasquez of just who Jake and his men really were. He was thinking that she had made fools out of all of them. How he must hate her.

Jessie distractedly ran her fingers over the carved top of the chest and stared blankly across the room as she tried to bring some order to her chaotic thoughts and churning emotions. When she thought about all her actions since she'd met Jake, her determination to come along on this trip, and his suspicions about her father's involvement with Vasquez, Jessie had to be honest and admit that it did look like she was guilty.

She covered her face with her hands, thinking of the feel of his hands on her body, of his body joined with hers, of his laughing blue eyes, of his thick, black hair, of the way he held her last night when they danced at the fandango, of his tenderness with her—and of his child in her womb. New determination took hold of her. She raised her head. No, she couldn't let it end this way—not with Jake thinking the worst about her. She had to find a way out of this room; she had to find Jake.

She quickly stood up on the chest she'd been sitting on and peered out the window. It wasn't barred and it was big enough for her to squeeze through, but standing on her tiptoes and craning her neck, she could see that the window set in the thick adobe walls was also a long way from the ground below. She swallowed hard. This was no time for cowardice. This window was her only hope and it was perfect because it looked out over the open desert outside the hacienda's compound and not the courtyard.

She jerked around quickly when she heard the guard outside her door—the same swarthy, sweating, leering gunman who'd abducted her in Santa Fe—cough and shift his position. She held her breath, but let it out when she didn't hear the scraping of the key in the lock. He'd already unlocked and opened the door twice to ask her if she was sure she didn't want him to join her in the bed. She knew he was just doing that to scare her, because she'd heard Vasquez tell him that nothing was to happen to her until he, Vasquez, called for her to be sent to him. But Jessie did not intend to be here then—she refused to be paraded again in front of Jake.

Jessie slowly scanned the room, looking not at the beautiful dark-wood furniture and the rich wall hangings and bed coverings as objects deserving her admiration, but looking at them as objects she could use to aid in her escape. Finally, her eyes rested on the bed. She went quickly and quietly to the bed and pulled off the light cream-colored

crocheted coverlet, the two sheets, and the pillowcases. She couldn't risk her lecherous guard hearing
her tear the sheets to make a long, knotted rope, so
she would just have to tie them together and pray
they were long enough. And if they weren't—then
she'd just have to let go and drop the rest of the
way. She didn't want to hurt her baby by doing
that, but she knew in her heart that she and her
baby didn't stand a chance if she stayed in this
room. And she had to know what was happening
to Jake.

Jessie worked with one eye on the locked door
and with shaking fingers, almost numb with fear
of being caught. But finally she had a long, knotted rope. She'd pulled each knot as tight as she
could; she hoped they held. Taking a deep breath
to steady her nerves, she looked around the room
for something to anchor her rope, something heavy.
No, she couldn't use the bed—it was too far away
from the window and would use up too much of
her rope. The other furniture was either too light
to hold her weight or too heavy for her to push
over to the window. Frustrated, she sat down on
the heavy chest under the window and drummed
her fingers on its carved top. Suddenly she jumped
up and whirled around as if something had pinched
her. What a ninny, she scolded herself—she'd been
sitting on the solution to her problem! Stifling a
cry of victory, Jessie quickly looped one end of her
makeshift rope through the large metal loop on the
front of the chest that accommodated a lock under
normal circumstances.

But these were definitely not normal circumstances. She tied a thick, double knot and pulled
on it, bracing her foot against the chest to see if it

would hold. It did. Looking skyward, she breathed a thank-you.

She climbed onto the chest and pulled herself up by her arms to look outside. Nothing but sand, cactus, and tumbleweed. In her restricted line of vision through the narrow window, she didn't see any guards. She reassured her hammering heart that there probably weren't any men outside the villa's grounds, because all the action was inside the courtyard. It tortured her not knowing what Jake was going through. And she tried not to think about what she was going to do once she was out of this room and on the ground. She didn't have the slightest idea yet, but she had faith that a plan would present itself to her.

With a gulp and a prayer, she tossed the rope out the window, eyeing it to see how far the end of it was from the ground. She lowered her feet back to the top of the chest, grimaced, and bit her lip. A long way from the ground. But it was too late now to back out. She had to get to Jake. Reaching down between her legs to the hem of her brown skirt, she grabbed the back hem and brought it up between her legs and tucked it in at the waistband. There. She had pants—sort of.

She once again hoisted herself up by her arms until her upper body rested on the adobe sill. A wave of nausea washed over her as she hung halfway out the window. The ground looked so far away. Forget the ground and climb down, Jessie, she admonished herself. Now!—while there's no one out there. Gathering her courage, she levered her body until she was in a scrunched-up, sideways, sitting position on the sill. She had to get her feet out the window first—after all, she wasn't a lizard that could climb down headfirst. With great straining effort, she was finally able to swing her feet and legs over to the outside of the window, without dislodging herself from her perch.

When she'd recovered from that effort, she took hold of the tied sheets and turned her body until she faced into the room and was resting on her stomach on the sill. The hard pressure on her swollen womb was extremely uncomfortable, so she quickly slid her body down against the outside wall, bracing her sandaled feet against the warm adobe so as not to slide too fast. Very carefully, she slowly descended, inch by terror-filled inch. She felt the rushing and ringing in her ears, the pounding of her heart, and the slipping of her sweaty palms. She had such a firm hold on her bottom lip with her teeth that she was sure the slightly metallic taste in her mouth was her own blood.

She moved past the first big knot which tied the first and second sheets together. The pillowcases were looped and knotted through the metal ring on the chest and even now supported her weight and life. Only this sheet and the coverlet to go, she thought, and then the big drop. What if she broke her ankle when she dropped? No, stop, she begged her overactive, sadistic imagination. Think good thoughts. Almost there. Here's the coverlet. Okay, Jessie, get ready. Another few feet and then you're going to let go. She bit down harder on her bottom lip as she slowly climbed down the length of the crocheted coverlet, knowing she would run out of material any second now.

She didn't have time to scream when no less than four hands snaked out, seemingly from nowhere, and snatched her right off her rope. Blinded by panic, hands all over her, one over her mouth, she tried to fight back, even with tears stinging her eyes and her arms locked at her sides by her captors. She kicked back only to feel her bare leg hit warm flesh—horseflesh, judging by the grunt and the pivoting and plunging of the offended animal. Finally, some words of her captors' penetrated her shocked mind, and she became still, listening. Could it be?

"Shh, Jessie. Don't! It's me—Coy. And John. John Dinkins. Calm down now. We're not going to hurt you. It's okay."

"Miss Jessie, it's us—me and Coy. We're here to help you. Shhh!"

Jessie slumped in relief. Coy and John eased their hold on her. She turned in their arms and hugged them both to her. "Oh, thank God," she breathed. She pulled back and looked down to see herself perched across both their horses, which stood side by side. She turned questioning eyes from Coy to John, and then back again.

Coy was the first to answer her, keeping his voice conspiratorially low. "We couldn't believe it when we came around the corner there and saw you dangling here like a spider. We just moved our horses under you, and stood up in our stirrups and grabbed onto you when you came to the end of your rope."

And that was just how Jessie felt—like she'd been at the end of her rope. She hugged Coy again gratefully.

"If I can, Miss Jessie," John asked shyly, having the legs and feet end of her draped in front of him on his horse, "can I ask you something?"

The other end of her, perched in front of Coy on his horse, answered, "You sure can, John."

"Just what was you going to do if we hadn't been there to catch you? Was you going to just drop that far to the ground? You coulda broke your ankle or something."

"My thoughts exactly, but I didn't have another choice, John. I have to get to Jake. Right now." She felt Coy stiffen; she turned her eyes back to him and saw his lips pressed together and his jaw clenched. "Coy, please. You don't understand. Jake thinks I'm in on the gunrunning with Vasquez and MacKenzie."

"Yeah," John broke in, drawing Coy's and Jessie's eyes to him, "me and Coy seen you gagged and sittin' in that carriage with Vasquez earlier. We was sitting by the road when you rode by, but you didn't see us. But why would Mr. Coltrane think you was in cahoots with them gunrunners? It don't make no sense. He loves you."

Coy really stiffened now; but so did Jessie. She didn't even know that, so how could John? Of course, Jake told her he loved her when he was making love to her. But so had she told him then. But not any other time. They both knew they would not be together when this trip was over. Jake was not giving up anything for her, not his job, his way of life. He loved her now, but not enough to change. At least he'd never said it that way. So how could John know that Jake loved her? Had she missed something that was obvious to John, a bystander really? She stared openmouthed at his smiling, innocent face.

Abruptly, Coy pulled his horse away from John's, taking Jessie with him. Perched sideways, she clutched at him reflexively, putting her arms around his neck so she didn't fall off. Coy tightened his hold on her—a little too tightly and a little too possessively for Jessie's comfort. She started to protest, but Coy cut her off with his words.

"Come on," Coy ordered John. "We've got to move before someone sees us." He turned his horse and nudged him toward the hills immediately behind the villa's enclosed compound.

"Imagine my immense surprise, Mr. Coltrane, when I discovered yesterday in Santa Fe that Mr. Hayes would not be delivering my . . . ah, supplies . . . but that you were. I did not know what to think." Don Diego Vasquez gave an airy wave of his hand as he perched on one hip on Roberto Suarez's elegant desk. "So," he shrugged his narrow shoulders, "I must apologize to you for the hundred or so armed men who greeted your small party here at Villa de Suarez. You are obviously a man of your word, and I now know that all my silly precautions were not necessary. I beg your forgiveness."

A thin cheroot clamped between his teeth, Jake slouched in the upholstered leather chair which faced Suarez's desk, content to let Vasquez ramble on for the moment. It gave him time to assess his increasingly precarious position with the two men facing him. He slowly swirled the smooth, expensive whiskey in the crystal glass in his hand. Let them play the polite hosts. Jake knew he'd been separated from his men and escorted in here, as much a hostage as Jessie was, until Vasquez's men determined that everything was in order with the guns. Jake knew what they would find; it was only a matter of time until the fireworks started. He was doubly glad now that the firing pins were safely in Santa Fe with Patterson and Dinkins. He would use that leverage to free Jessie, too. If even one hair on her beautiful head was harmed . . .

Jake tried hard to let out his held breath as if he were totally bored, while acknowledging, with a slight nod of his head, Vasquez's so-called apology, a veiled threat in itself to remind Jake of just how outnumbered he really was. And why hadn't Vasquez even mentioned Jessie? Jake's gut had tightened when Vasquez's carriage had stopped in the courtyard, carrying him and Jessie. He'd known then that the lovely young girl in the plaza this morning had indeed been Jessie. Just who had she been looking for? Him? Or Vasquez? And where the hell had she gotten those clothes?

Only iron control had kept him from spurring Blaze and grabbing her out of Vasquez's clutches when he made such a suave show of handing her out of the carriage and escorting her into the villa. The oily bastard had looked directly into Jake's eyes and smiled. Jake's first thought had been that Jessie had betrayed him, that she, just like her father, was involved with Vasquez and had been playing the spy for him. If that was true, then they were all dead. But Jake had almost instantly discarded that wrenching thought—she wasn't capable of such artifice, such cunning. She was spirited and honest, warm and loving. And stubborn and determined, he thought wryly, but not downright diabolical.

He'd also discarded the notion of her involvement with Vasquez when Curly, bless him, had moved his horse closer to Jake's and said, "Easy now, Jake. The young lady has a gun in her ribs." If that was supposed to make him feel better, it hadn't. Relieved for himself and terrified for her, maybe, but not better.

So Jake had to assume now that Vasquez was using Jessie as his insurance for a smooth delivery with no tricks on Jake's part. Apparently Senor Vasquez did not like surprises, like finding out that Hayes and all his men were dead, including two of his own trusted henchmen. Wait until he finds out about the firing pins, Jake grunted, thinking of the men even now unloading crate after crate of useless, pinless revolvers.

Jake was not surprised at all that Vasquez knew that Jessie was with him. After all, Vasquez's men had been in Santa Fe last night; they could have easily seen him and Jessie at the fandango or strolling through the various stores and booths in the plaza. But how had they known that Jessie was more to him than someone he might have picked up in town for a night of fun? His blood ran cold as he realized that someone in his own camp had to be on Vasquez's payroll. That was the only explanation, because no one in Santa Fe, outside of his own men, even knew about Jessie, what she meant to him, and what a valuable pawn she was.

Vasquez's monologue and Jake's dire thoughts were both interrupted by the sudden entrance into the richly appointed, spacious office of a decidedly upset, large, swarthy pistolero. He motioned for Vasquez and Suarez to come over by the door; once they did, he spoke in low, rapid Spanish to the two, but he kept cutting his eyes over to Jake. Whatever he was telling them was upsetting them, Jake noted with satisfaction, thinking of the firing pins. Vasquez was rigid with anger, while Suarez practically staggered back to his chair, slumped into it, and held his head in his hands.

This game of cat and mouse required steel nerves, Jake reflected calmly as, through his cigar's aromatic blue smoke, he speculatively eyed his sweating host, Roberto Suarez, a tall, silver-haired, Spanish aristocrat. And this man was not a good player. Then he startled Jake out of his relaxed posture for the briefest second when he raised his silver head and turned panicked, pleading eyes on him. To cover his surprise, Jake put the whiskey down on a small table beside his chair and took the cigar out of his mouth. What was Suarez trying to convey? And why in the hell was he involved with the likes of Vasquez?

According to Jake's information gleaned from locals yesterday in the cantina, Mr. Suarez had a reputation for fairness and honesty. It just didn't make sense. And he was an American citizen, thanks to the Mexican War. What would he gain if Vasquez's coup attempt was successful? It occurred to Jake that Mr. Suarez could be an unwilling participant; he certainly looked uncomfortable, and he did not appear to have a strong liking for the thin, conniving man who was now angrily dismissing the pistolero. Mr. Suarez just might prove to be an unexpected ally.

Jake filed that thought away and then turned his piercing, steel-blue gaze back on his real adversary, Don Diego Vasquez, as he stalked back to the desk. Gone was the polite facade of civility; Jake had the distinct impression that he was now seeing the real Vasquez, the deadly, coiled rattlesnake, ready to strike. Jake steeled himself for the attack, but very calmly reached over to put the cheroot in the ashtray next to his whiskey. He wanted both hands free.

"No doubt, Mr. Coltrane, you saw that I was favored earlier by the lovely presence of your . . . ah, woman? . . . in my carriage. Her nearness and, shall we say, warmth made the long, dusty ride from Santa Fe so much more pleasurable for me. So engrossed was I with her many physical charms and her enlightening conversation that regrettably the ride was over before I was finished with her."

Jake fought hard against the rising fury in his chest and the sinking feeling in the pit of his stomach. Vasquez had just confirmed for him that someone had to have told Vasquez about Jessie. And that someone had to have made the trip from Camp Nichols. There was no other explanation. Jake swallowed hard, but very smoothly said, "Well, I'm glad you enjoyed her. I always do. But I never have to put a gun to her ribs to get her to share her charms with me."

Bull's eye. Vasquez stiffened and made fists out of his hands at his side. Jake's own hands, folded so sedately in front of him as he rested his elbows on the chair's wings, itched to choke the life out of this son of a bitch, but he didn't dare appear to be too concerned with what happened to Jessie. His cavalier attitude toward her just might save her life by lessening her value as a pawn.

Then Vasquez surprised Jake by laughing out loud as if at a joke—one that was not on him. Jake felt a cold chill on his skin. Shaking his head and chuckling to himself, Vasquez patted a miserable Suarez on the shoulder, moved to the office door, opened it, and motioned for an unseen person or persons in the hall to enter the room.

For some reason, Jake felt the need to stand, to be ready for what was going to happen. He had the distinct sense of foreboding that something was desperately wrong. And he was right.

As Vasquez escorted the newcomer into the room, Jake felt like he'd been kicked in the gut by an enraged bull. He now had the answer to all his questions.

Clearly enjoying himself, Vasquez triumphantly said, "Marshal Coltrane, you will forgive my sense of dramatics. I must apologize yet again to you for keeping this one last surprise from you until now. You see, he too enjoyed your wife's company in my carriage. But, alas, he wanted to surprise you, so he hid himself outside the villa's gate until you came inside. Marshal, please say hello to Sergeant MacKenzie."

Chapter Eighteen

Her back to the rough adobe wall, her sandals full of gritty sand, her long hair clinging damply to her face and neck, and the hot sun glaring in her eyes, Jessie willed herself not to think about her physical discomforts. Or about Coy's revolver stuck in the waistband of her skirt. He had a rifle also, so she'd cajoled and wheedled him, trying to get him to give her his handgun.

He'd wanted to make a manly show of protecting her, but she'd cured him of that chivalrous notion by finally just yanking the gun out of his hand and telling him that she too was coming along and she too needed a gun. There was no way she was going to sit on the big hill behind the villa like Coy wanted her to do, until everything was over. With her armed with his gun, Coy hadn't wanted to argue anymore with her, seeing her determination.

She'd come too far to be denied her audience with Vasquez, Jessie thought now, and she loved Jake too much to let him think for one minute longer than was necessary that she had betrayed him. Even if she and Jake both died today, she would know the truth about her father and Jake would know the truth about her and about how much she loved him. She would make sure of both things. Somehow.

Willing her thoughts back to the present danger, Jessie put her left foot out to the side and felt the reassuring weight of the bags of firing pins resting safely beside her on the ground. She'd kept her head turned to the right, looking over at Coy and John on the other side of this partially opened, tall, double-width window set low in the thick wall. Coy and John had gotten into position by slinking on their bellies under the low sill from her side and then standing up on the other side of the window, with their backs against the adobe wall just like her.

As she awaited Coy's silent signal that would send them bursting into the office that the window served, Jessie heard the male voices inside without really listening to their words. She couldn't hear them anyway over her heart hammering with what she and Coy and John were getting ready to do. The entire mission had come down to the three youngest and most inexperienced members of Jake's troop.

While Coy worked to screw up his courage and give the signal, Jessie chanced a peek through the window. Her stomach and heart fought for a place in her throat. Jake was the only one facing her; he was effectively pinned in this office by Vasquez, an older, silver-haired man, and now Mackenzie and two pistoleros, one of whom was her former guard. She grimaced; he'd be in a foul mood about now.

She knew he wouldn't have moved from her door if he still thought she was inside that bedroom.

When Vasquez shifted his position to stand behind the silver-haired man and put his hands on the man's shoulders, Jessie got a clear view of Jake. He was so wonderful, she thought proudly, even if he had left her naked in that room. She knew he'd done it to protect her from her own stubborn impulses, but lucky for him she hadn't stayed there. Jessie loved how he was taller than the other men in the tension-charged room. She loved how his powerful, broad shoulders dominated the other men. She loved how his muscular, long legs held him so erect and proud. She loved how his strong, tanned hands, hands that were so tender and loving when on her body, were even now showing his total lack of fear by calmly resting with his thumbs hooked in his gunbelt. She loved how a stray lock of his coal-black hair had fallen onto his forehead. He looked so . . . sexy and so dangerous. Mainly because of his curly-lashed, steel-blue eyes, which even now in the face of death . . .

. . . popped wide open and round when he looked directly into her face. Jessie jerked back to the protection of the adobe wall. At the same instant she heard Jake cough and clear his throat to cover his shock. She looked over at Coy and John—they looked like Jake had just now. She caught her breath and held it, terrified to make a noise. She prayed that her curiosity had not caused Jake to give them away. Jessie let her breath out only when no one from inside the office came over to the window to investigate. They were still safe and still had the element of surprise—if they went in now. Jessie frowned at Coy and jerked her head irritatedly at the window. "Let's go," she mouthed.

She saw Coy swallow the huge lump in his throat and then use his sleeve to wipe the sweaty fear from his brow. He took several deep breaths, but just when Jessie was sure she was going to turn his own gun on him out of frustration, he looked over at her and nodded decisively. Jessie held his gaze for an eternal second; she then pulled the gun out of her waistband and held it up at the ready, like she'd seen Jake do in her cabin when Hayes had come to the door. She smiled briefly at Coy and returned his nod. This was it.

Coy pressed his lips together into a semblance of a smile, saluted her by touching his fingers to his brow, and then set himself into motion. He silently turned his body fully into the open window, pushing cautiously on the double panes to open them further as he stepped over the low sill and into the carpeted room. John stepped in immediately afterwards and turned to give Jessie a hand. When they were all three standing inside, side by side, legs apart, guns trained on the room's occupants, Coy made their presence known. And Jessie was proud of him, too; only a trace of the tremendous fear he must be feeling could be heard in his cracking voice, which boomed loudly and in a high pitch in the otherwise tensely quiet room, spinning its occupants around, but stunning them into inaction.

Pulling himself up to his full height and poking his chest out, Coy bellowed, "Halt in the name of the law of the United States of America and of the U. S. Army. I am Lieutenant Coy Patterson of the U. S. Army, out of Camp Nichols, under the command of Colonel Kit Carson, and these"—indicating Jessie and John with a swing of his rifle—"are my men." He stopped for the briefest of seconds at his

316

own words, looked at Jessie out of the corner of his eye, and went on. "Put down your weapons. You're all under arrest—except you, Mr. Coltrane, of course—for the federal crime of stealing U. S. Army shipments of guns and selling them to this Mexican national, Mr. Vasquez, so he can overthrow his government, a crime of treason, punishable by death under the authority of his own president. And for many other crimes, too . . . I'm sure . . . which Mr. Coltrane can tell you about."

Even though Coy finished lamely and in a lowered voice, his loud and unceasing tirade had a mesmerizing effect on the occupants of the room. The silver-haired man, Roberto Suarez, to whom Jessie had been introduced when she'd been dragged in earlier by Vasquez, was the first to recover. "Madre de Dios," he breathed, moving his eyes from one to the other of the young trio. But still no one moved. Not even to put their guns down.

Jessie's palm began to sweat and itch; the gun in her hand felt like the lead weight that it was. She wet her suddenly dry lips with her tongue and looked at Jake as if to say, "What now?" The gun in her hand faltered the least bit when Jake turned a white grin on her and saluted her by touching his fingers to his hat. Then, he took over.

"Yes, I can add some more crimes, but not so eloquently as my young friend here, to the list, Vasquez. Would you care to hear them?" Jake's commanding but slightly taunting voice had the effect of spinning the five men back around to face him—and his six-shooter in his hand.

Jessie couldn't believe it. She'd never even seen his hand move to his holster. But she could see that the pistoleros had their guns on Jake. Without

Cheryl Anne Porter

a thought to her own safety, she moved quickly across the room, followed by Coy and John when they realized her intentions, to place the cold barrel of her Colt into the back of the nearest man, who just happened to have been her leering guard. "Don't even think it," she hissed into his back.

Coy and John did likewise with the other pistolero and MacKenzie, cocking their guns in their prisoners' backs for emphasis. Jessie felt a twinge of satisfaction as the armed men stiffened and lowered their guns from Jake. But that wasn't enough. "Drop them," she told them in a deadly serious voice. When they didn't drop their guns to the floor, but looked instead to Vasquez for orders, Jessie exploded. "I said to drop them. And I mean now. Vasquez is no longer in charge here."

Jake added in a slow drawl, one which usually preceded his using his Colt revolver, "You better do as the lady says, gentlemen. She's not very good with that gun. She gets nervous and it tends to go off—and she doesn't care who she hits."

With all eyes on the pistoleros and MacKenzie as they hastily dropped their weapons and moved to the opposite wall under Coy's and John's guard, and Jessie moved into the protective circle of Jake's outstretched arm, Suarez's sudden, desperate cry broke the tense spell in the room. In a fear-choked voice, he cried out, "No, Don Diego! No more killing!"

Roberto Suarez grabbed for Vasquez's arm, but he was too late. A growling yell escaped Vasquez as he pushed the older man out of his way, reached into his inside coat pocket, and pulled out a derringer, aiming it directly at Jessie. In one swift motion, Jake hauled Jessie behind him and fired. But he wasn't the only one; several guns went off at once, spinning their target completely around and crashing him into the bookshelves behind him before he landed in a broken, bloody heap on the carpeted floor.

Jake, Coy, John, and Roberto Suarez all looked at each other over their smoking guns. Coy and John looked ill. Jessie, who was still clinging to Jake's back as he kept a protective arm behind him and around her, heard John whisper to Coy, "I ain't never killed no man before, Coy."

Coy answered, "And you can't really be sure you did just now, John, what with all the guns firing like that. You could have missed him."

"Yeah, I could've, Coy. I could've."

The two young men then grimly turned their attention back to their prisoners. But Jessie's attention, like Jake's, was focused on Suarez, whose face was ashen and whose heretofore hidden gun fell to the carpet from his nerveless fingers. He moved to Vasquez's body, knelt down, and cradled the fallen man's head in his lap. Jessie watched him as she moved out from behind Jake, but still in the circle of his arms, and turned a frowning, questioning face up to him. He squeezed her tightly and placed a kiss on the top of her head, but kept his eyes on Suarez, who now had tears streaming down his face. "I don't know why, Jessie. Only he can tell us why," Jake breathed into her hair.

Just then, Jessie jumped and clutched more tightly at Jake as the door to the office burst open, spilling several pistoleros and Curly and his men into the room, all with guns drawn and waving around the room as each man took in the scene before him.

The pistoleros cried out "Jefe" and moved over to where Suarez still knelt; they clustered around their fallen chief. Curly and his men all moved to Jake and Jessie.

"Don't ask me why we're all still alive, Jake. The only thing Ah know is those men outside never pulled a gun on us, not even when the shootin' started in here. They just looked at us and never changed expression. That's when Ah decided you maybe could use us in here. But, Ah cain't tell if the party's over, or if it's just begun," Curly drawled, taking in the room's occupants.

Then his eyes fell on MacKenzie, and narrowed. "Afternoon, Sergeant MacKenzie. Fancy meetin' you here. I expect the next party you attend will be a neck party," he said levelly, referring to the hanging penalty for treason.

MacKenzie seemed to shrink back into the thick adobe wall behind him as several of the men with Curly moved to relieve Coy of his guard duty, clapped young John Dinkins heartily on the back, and turned their guns and censorious eyes on their former sergeant.

Coy moved quickly to Jake. "Mr. Coltrane, I don't think this is over by a long shot. We're still outnumbered and surrounded." Even though his face and voice reflected his nervousness, his hands very steadily clutched his rifle in front of him.

Jake smiled down at Jessie and then looked at Coy. For the first time since he'd known him, Jake turned a sincere smile on the young lieutenant and called him by his first name. "I'm not so sure, Coy. Look." A nod of his head indicated the aristocratic, silver-haired gentleman being very tenderly helped to his feet by the pistoleros. Jessie followed his gaze, too.

As the older man struggled to regain his composure, he spoke in Spanish to the man nearest him and sent him toward the door which lead out of the office and then out of the villa. But the cocking of several guns by Jake's men stopped the man in his tracks. He turned back to Roberto Suarez.

"Please," Mr. Suarez pleaded, but with dignity and great sadness in his voice, "let him go. I told him to tell the men outside to put their guns down. It is over."

Jake played a hunch. "You're their boss, aren't you? Not Vasquez. That's why they call you jefe—chief."

Suarez pulled himself up to his full aristocratic height. "This is so. And the man I helped kill just now"—he turned slightly to look at the crumpled heap which was Vasquez—"is . . . was my son-in-law."

Jessie gasped and put a hand to her mouth. She felt Jake stiffen, too, but he did reholster his gun and nodded to indicate that Suarez's messenger could depart. Seeing that Jake seemed to trust this man, the other men in the room loyal to him relaxed their stances some too, but not their guard on MacKenzie and the two pistoleros. Jake turned to them. "Let them go—except MacKenzie. Lieutenant Patterson has already placed him under arrest, so tie him up in a wagon. I'll talk further with Mr. Suarez."

Suarez also dismissed most of his men and had them carry out Vasquez's body. He then moved to slump into his desk chair; he put his hands over his face and then very tiredly rubbed his hands through his hair. When he spoke, his voice was low and broken. "When we are done here, Mr. Coltrane, I must go to my daughter in Mexico and tell her of this terrible tragedy."

Before he answered, Jake also retook his seat in the chair in front of the desk. He guided Jessie to sit in the other chair facing the desk. Curly and Coy moved to stand behind Jake's and Jessie's chairs. "I understand, Mr. Suarez . . . And I'm truly sorry for—what we had to do. It was never my intention to kill him. But first, I am afraid you will have to answer some questions. There is still the matter of the guns."

Suarez turned bleak, dark eyes on Jake and nodded; then his gaze traveled to Jessie. "I am very happy that you are unharmed, my dear. I must apologize for my son-in-law's behavior toward you. And I must tell you that your spirit reminds me of my own daughter before she . . . I know your father must be very proud of you."

Her father. Tears sprang to Jessie's eyes and she looked down. She felt Jake take her hand which rested on the chair arm and squeeze it reassuringly. In a tear-soaked voice, Jessie replied, "Thank you for your kind words, Mr. Suarez. But there's something I have to know. You spoke of my father. My father is dead, but you are right—he was proud of me, as I always was of him. Mr. Suarez, my father was Cole Stuart, of Stuart's Homestead on the Cimarron Cutoff. Did you know him, or ever hear Vas—your son-in-law speak of him?" Seeing his frowning hesitance, Jessie implored, "Please, Mr. Suarez, this is very important."

"I know it is, my young one, or you would not ask. I am trying to recall just what it is I have heard Don Diego say." A few agonizing minutes passed as no one spoke in an effort not to interrupt Mr. Suarez's thoughts. Then, he made them all jump when he smacked his hand down on his desk and said, "Ah-ha, I have it. Mr. Stuart. Of course."

Jessie felt her gut tighten. What if she could not live with the truth? She swallowed hard, forcing the bile back down. Jake's hand tightened even more over hers; she covered his with her other hand, silently telling him that she had to know. She also knew that Jake, as part of his job, had to know, too.

"Just a moment, Mr. Suarez, if you please." Jake surprised them all with his interruption. Jessie sharply turned her head to look at him. She saw warm, blue eyes; sympathetic, understanding, blue eyes looking back at her. "Jessie, it doesn't matter. Not anymore. We don't need to know the answer to this. It's over. Even if your father was involved, I'm not going to include that in my—"

"But no, Mr. Coltrane," Mr. Suarez cut in. "Mr. Stuart was not involved. I remember hearing Don Diego say more than once about how that awful Mr. Hayes and the big sergeant outside—what is his name, MacKenzie?—would meet there, using all the confusion of the big wagon trains to cover their dealings. He would laugh about how her father knew nothing of what was happening on his own property." He then turned back to Jessie. "I am truly sorry, my child, about your father. I pray that Don Diego had nothing to do with his death."

"No," Jessie managed to gulp out between the tears clogging her throat. "No, he didn't . . . and, thank you, Mr. Suarez." Pulling her hands out of Jake's, she slumped in relief in her chair and put her head back, closing her eyes. But then a sudden thought snapped her head forward; she turned an amazed expression on Jake, taking in his handsome, chiseled profile as he began questioning Roberto Suarez.

When Mr. Suarez had interrupted Jake a moment ago, Jake had been getting ready to tell her that he wouldn't report her father's involvement if that had been found to be the case. Jessie felt a loving knot contrict her heart; his decision to withhold information like that must have cost him dearly. But he would have done it for her. Suddenly, Jessie knew that she would not have allowed him to do that, not to report her father's involvement. She would not have been able to live with herself if she knew that Jake had to live with the knowledge that he had betrayed his oath to his country and to his badge. Not for a piece of land out in the middle of nowhere that meant something only to her.

So this is what love is, she thought. Caring more about him than herself. Putting his happiness ahead of hers. Just like he had been willing to do for her. And his sacrifice would have been much greater than hers, she knew that now. The tears came unbidden to her eyes and her chin trembled as she continued to stare at the man she loved, the same man who loved her. As she let her eyes travel over every loving inch of his face, she forced herself to listen to Mr. Suarez's answers to Jake's blunt but necessary questions.

"If you will allow me, Mr. Coltrane, I believe I can clear this all up for you." When Jake nodded, Mr. Suarez ran his hands through his hair, took a deep breath and began. "As I told you, Don Diego is my son-in-law. My daughter, Marisa, my only child, is virtually a prisoner in their villa in Mexico. This is how Don Diego assured himself of my cooperation. He would kill her if I did not help him.

"All the men here are, as you guessed, my men. They did not fire on you because they were under my orders not to do so. Don Diego did not know that, of course. I knew that he planned to kill every one of you here today. I could not live with that, or with his plans to take over Mexico. He was a madman. And then I saw this beautiful girl here"—indicating Jessie with a sweep of his hand—"in his clutches. God forgive me, but I snapped. No more bloodshed. No more innocent lives lost, Mr. Coltrane. No more," he finished, laying his head down on his folded arms on his desk.

His shoulders shook with each shuddering sob. Jessie's tears flowed in earnest by the end of the old gentleman's speech. She looked over at Jake, and saw his throat working convulsively. From behind her chair, she heard sniffing and throats being cleared gruffly. She squeezed Jake's hand briefly, and then went to the older, broken man who had killed his own son-in-law to save her. As she stood beside his chair, she let him hold her and rest his head against her bosom as she held him in return and comforted him.

Jake got up, went to the bar behind the desk, and poured a goodly amount of a liquor into a glass. He then put it on the desk in front of Roberto Suarez. "Here," he said huskily, "I think this will help."

The silver-haired man pulled himself away from Jessie, took out his white linen handkerchief, wiped at his eyes and his nose, and reached for the drink. "Thank you," he said softly. "I apologize for my breakdown. It is very childish of me."

"Not at all," Jake said, as he returned to his seat. "Very human, I would say, given everything you've been through. But I am afraid I do have one more question."

"Please," Suarez said, taking another sip of the amber liquid, "ask it. I wish to have this over with. My daughter will need me."

Jake cleared his throat and shifted his position in his chair. Jessie, now back in her chair, tensed inside, knowing what was coming. Mr. Suarez's freedom depended on his answer; and Jessie desperately wanted him to be free, to be able to live free of the insane threats and acts of his deranged son-in-law. She wanted his daughter to have her father and to find a real love, one like she had in Jake.

Jake let out his breath. "Mr. Suarez, just what was the nature of your involvement in this gunrunning business, willing or not? My superiors will say that you could have contacted them for help if you were being blackmailed."

"To do so, Mr. Coltrane, would have been to risk my daughter's death. You see, she does not know she is a prisoner and that her husband has been using her as a pawn. She believes herself to be very loved and well protected. But in reality, Don Diego's men at his villa in Mexico have orders to kill her if he does not show up at the appointed time with the guns. This is how he ensured my cooperation and my silence. He knew that I, her father, would never disillusion her and hurt her by telling her the truth. And, sad to say, I am not sure she would have believed me. She loves her husband. My beautiful Marisa has always been very sheltered and very innocent. When I think that I married her to a man like Don Diego—" His face hardened and his hands clenched in front of him.

Jake cut in. "I am almost done, Mr. Suarez. Please bear with me. Again, what was the nature of your involvement in this operation?"

"My home has been a stopping-over point, a place for Mr. Hayes to turn over the guns to Don Diego. I was no more involved than Mr. Stuart. I kept no guns from those shipments, and I received no money. The Colts my men use were bought legitimately from the wagon trains. And I will open my books to you to prove that I have not lied.

"Mr. Coltrane, I could not seek help from the law. The only law out here is at Fort Union, a long, hard, mountainous journey from here. And I knew that the Army sergeant was involved. I had no way of knowing if others in the Army were also involved. You understand my position." He opened his hands in a gesture of supplication.

"Yes, I suppose I do, Mr. Suarez. I was in the same position of not knowing who to trust in the Army only a few weeks ago." Jake then clapped his hands on his denim-covered thighs and stood, signaling that the interview was over. He put a hand out to the elegant gentleman on the other side of the desk.

"What does this mean, Mr. Coltrane?" the older man asked as he put his hand in Jake's and shook it.

Jessie bit her lip and tightened her grip on the chair's arms. She wanted so desperately for this father to be reunited with his daughter. His shouldering of the nightmarish burden of his daughter's fate and her innocence, even before his own honor and his own life, had touched Jessie's heart. She knew her own father would have done the same thing. But, she also knew that whatever Jake had decided, they would all have to live with it. This was his job, and she would not, could not, interfere. The law came before feelings and emotions.

Jake gave a little laugh as he shook Mr. Suarez's hand. "It means, Sir, that you are free to go. I believe you to be a man of honor. I don't need to see your books. I believe you to be as much of an innocent pawn as your daughter has been. Our government does not seek to prosecute innocent citizens. As you have said, there has already been too much death and too much bloodshed. We have the guns, and all the men responsible are dead. Case closed."

When Jessie let out her held breath very audibly and said "Thank God," Jake turned a bemused expression and a crooked grin on her. He arched an eyebrow at her before turning his attention back to Mr. Suarez.

The silver-haired aristocrat now pumped Jake's hand in earnest, covering Jake's large hand with both of his own. "I thank you, Mr. Coltrane, from the bottom of my heart. The nightmare is truly over." He then withdrew his hands, pulled himself up to his full height, and bowed slightly from the waist. "If you will forgive me for being a poor host, I must leave now with my men and free my daughter. Time is very important."

"I wish there was some way we could help you there, Mr. Suarez. But I'm afraid that explaining the presence of U. S. troops in Mexico involved in a gun battle with Mexican citizens would be very difficult."

For the first time, Roberto Suarez laughed. Jessie liked the sound. She was glad he could still laugh. She began to believe that he could indeed bring his daughter through the pain and disillusionment she was about to suffer.

Jessie stood when the older man bowed slightly to her and then to Jake. Silently she and Jake watched him stride purposefully from the room. His voice came to them from the hall as he barked orders in rapid Spanish. His silent, watchful men now came to life, bustling here and there throughout the hacienda and the courtyard.

Feeling Jake's eyes on her, Jessie looked up into his face. A warm smile of love was just lighting up her face when his words doused the tender flame.

"So, Jessie, do you want to tell me where you got those clothes?"

Chapter Nineteen

Jake was afraid he would be taken for a lunatic by his men if he didn't quit laughing out loud when everyone else around him on the trail ride home was silent. His last guffawing outburst had startled Blaze into one of his sideways prances, nearly unseating his rider. But Jake couldn't help himself. The ridiculous irony of the whole situation was just too much. This was one report he definitely did not want to write.

How could he still maintain his dignity, much less his reputation as a tough, hardbitten undercover agent, after reporting that a girl in stolen clothes and two men, who were essentially boys, had rescued the entire mission? Those stolen clothes—another shout of laughter escaped Jake. Would he ever forget the sight of the frightened, naked maid in his and Jessie's room when they got back to the hotel?

Even the reproving look he'd thrown Jessie when he'd opened the door to their room had not brought that stubborn chin down one inch. And the poor maid—once he'd untied her since she wouldn't let Jessie near her—she'd crossed herself several times and fled out into the courtyard, oblivious of her own nakedness.

This was just great! Jake had never known before now that he was so capable of laughing at himself. It was that or cry. And he was about to do that if he didn't quit laughing. The rumblings of renewed laughter threatened from deep in his chest to erupt again. Determinedly, he clamped his teeth and lips together. He would not laugh at the sight of Jessie, tiny, beautiful Jessie, holding that gun on her huge, ugly guard. Or at Coy and John, not much bigger than their rifles, voices cracking, ordering those hired killers and MacKenzie to drop their guns. What a speech Coy had given! That did it— huge guffaws bent Jake over the pommel of his saddle and low onto Blaze's neck.

Blaze too had had enough. The other men riding just behind Jake had to rein in sharply or sidestep their horses to avoid running into Blaze when he stopped short, laid his ears back, flared his nostrils, and threatened to buck if his master did not straighten up.

"Okay, boy, whoa now, easy," Jake soothed while patting the great, curved neck of his mount. "It's all over now; easy, big fella." Jake furtively looked around him. There were the sidelong glances of his men again. He knew that his laughing made them even more uncomfortable than it did Blaze, for they felt somewhat sheepish about being "rescued" the way they had been, too, by Jessie, Coy, and John, the last three any one of them would have thought capable of such daring deeds.

That was it! Jake straightened up even more in his saddle. It wasn't ridiculous at all. Those three had been downright brave, even heroic. And he would put that in his report. Jake turned in his saddle to look at them; they still rode together, Coy driving the wagon, Jessie sitting beside him, and John on his horse next to them. To his surprise, Jake found he was no longer jealous of Coy's shy attentions to Jessie. He was mature enough to realize that she did not return Coy's feelings and thought of him only as a friend. This time, the smile he turned on them was one of respect and pride. Then, with a sudden need to be near Jessie, he turned Blaze's head and urged him back at a trot to the wagon in which Jessie rode.

Jessie's heart soared when she saw Jake ride toward her wagon. She hoped against hope that he would rein in and stay close by for a while. Several times before on this weeks-long, bumping, rattling trip home, she'd thought he was coming to her, but he had ridden by with only a nod in her direction, intending to check on the much longer wagon train he had control of now, what with the confiscated cases of Colts in the wagons behind hers.

But this time he did rein in. Jessie could not hide her radiant smile, even though she knew she should because of all the laughing he'd done at her, Coy and John since they'd left Mr. Suarez's villa. He'd hurt Jessie's pride by acting as if the life-threatening chances she'd taken to save him and his men were laughable and of no consequence. Still, she looked down shyly when he winked at her. He then began talking to Coy about the Army and the wagon train.

But Jessie didn't mind; she took this opportunity to do her favorite thing—watch him when he wasn't aware of her doing so. She could never get enough of looking at his strong, handsome face, but she couldn't keep her gaze there long before it began to wander down the hard, muscled, delicious length of his body. Not surprised at all, Jessie felt the stirrings of her body, the stirrings deep in her belly, that always began and warmed her outward from there when she thought of Jake. She fought to keep from leaping from her wagon seat onto him and taking him right there on the ground. Finally shocked at her own brazenness, she put her hands to her warm cheeks and swallowed hard. What was she going to do when he was no longer around? When he rode off for that last time once she was home? She knew she should begin now to harden her heart and her thoughts against that awful day.

But she knew she couldn't. Not while he was so near. So near? He might as well be on the moon. She hated having to sleep so close to him, and yet so chastely, on this trail ride. She hated never being alone with him. She hated having to watch him from afar and not being able to tell him how much she loved him and how much she appreciated his intended sacrifice if her father had been found to be guilty. She hated the whole mess of this slower trip home, what with all the additional wagons. If he was going to leave her, then she wanted it over with quickly. Yet, she had so much she wanted to say, but even more she wanted to do to him and with him, that she was afraid she would burst.

But not the baby. She would not tell him about the baby. A home, a wife, and a baby were not his life. He'd made that painfully clear from the start. He rode alone, lived alone, and worked alone. She'd been a burden to him since she'd run out of her barn behind him so many weeks ago. The baby was hers. She could raise it alone; no, she wouldn't have to—Bertha would help. So, there was no reason for him ever to know. She would rather have died than have him give up the life he so obviously loved to settle down with her and farm and ranch, something he would hate. Jessie did not want him to end up hating and resenting her. She'd rather part with him still loving her. Memories of her sham wedding assailed her thoughts. Jessie quickly squelched the scalding tears which threatened in her eyes. Yes, the baby was her part of him to keep. Her only part.

Putting a hand to the slight bulge of her belly, she thought, was it really only weeks ago? She looked around her while Jake made small talk with Coy and John. Autumn was definitely here. The leaves on the few trees out here were changing to brilliant reds and oranges, and some even already littered the ground they rode over. And even though it was still warm enough during the days, the nights were cool. A sudden chill passed over Jessie; she came abruptly back to the present by Jake calling her name.

"Jessie? I've been talking to you. What are you thinking about so hard?"

Jessie gave a startled jump and masked the sad, guilty look she feared was on her face. The bemused grin she saw on Jake's beloved face when she turned toward him brought her out of her blue thoughts and mood. Just one look; that's all it took, she thought. What was she going to do without him?

But aloud, she said, "The weather. I was thinking about the weather. All the leaves are changing, and it's getting cold at night. I was just wondering how Bertha's doing, what with all the animals and the harvest and—"

"You really love that place, don't you?" Jake cut in.

Jessie turned her eyes over to him sharply. She couldn't read the note in his voice. He hadn't sounded mad or hurt or anything—more like he was sad, but not sad. Oh, she just didn't know. But what she did know was that her answer was of vital importance to him. She sensed that much.

"Yes. Yes, I do," she replied hesitatingly, biting her lower lip. "But not as much as I love—" She caught herself before she said "you." She looked down at her fingers she had twisted in her denim britches. She was acutely aware of the silence surrounding her. Coy and John were uncustomarily quiet.

The next thing she felt was the horses pulling the wagon coming to a halt. She looked up to see Jake leaning over from his saddle and hauling back on their reins; Coy was doing the same thing, as if an unspoken order had passed between the two men. Jessie looked blankly at John, but he merely shrugged his shoulders and dropped his horse back to a slow walk.

"Come here, Jessie," Jake said quietly.

"What?" Jessie asked, not understanding.

"Stand up and lean over to me. I'll help you. I want you to ride in front of me on Blaze for a while. I'm sure you're tired of that hard wagon seat."

Jessie, feeling suddenly very young and very tired, did as she was told. Reaching out to him from the height of the wagon seat seemed the most natural thing in the world to her; she knew he would catch her and hold her, and never let her fall to the hård reality of the unforgiving ground. She wished her love could hold him as tightly as her arms did now while she settled herself in front of him on Blaze's familiar warmth.

"Where are we going?" Jessie asked, looking around her as Jake nudged Blaze into a canter and rode out at an angle to the wagons.

"Nowhere, really," came Jake's almost wistful reply. Jessie couldn't shake the feeling that he was speaking of their relationship. Then, after a few silent moments and as Jake eased Blaze into a walk, he spoke again. "You know we'll be back at your homestead in a few days."

Your homestead. Not home. Jessie could not help the sigh that escaped her. "Yes, I know."

"Will you be glad?"

Jessie turned to look briefly into his face, but his eyes were straight ahead, and his jaw was set. "I don't know. I suppose so," she answered noncommittally, feeling for what he was trying to tell her—or not tell her.

"You suppose so? I thought that place meant everything to you. You even risked your life to go to Santa Fe to try to keep it. And now you only suppose so?"

The hard edge under his teasing words was not lost on Jessie. She took in a deep breath and thought for a moment. She knew what she wanted to say, but she was so afraid of baring her heart only to have it broken if he didn't feel the same way. She also knew that her words could drive an even bigger wedge between them if they were unwelcome to him. But then she decided that she didn't care. She was enough of a woman now—almost a mother, for heaven's sake—to speak her heart and mind and the devil take the consequences. At least he would know—and she would know.

"No, I guess I more than 'suppose'," she began. "I will be happy to get home. That's what the homestead is to me, Jake—my home. Don't you have a home you long to go to? You've never told me where your home is. Or anything about your family."

His arms tightened around her, but out of tension, not affection. "No, I don't really have a home, if by that you mean a place where my heart longs to be. My father was killed in the Mexican War when I was a boy. My mother was left wealthy and well provided for; she still lives in Virginia. I visit her, of course, and I love her, but she has her own life and I have mine."

"Well, where do you go, where do you stay when you're between assignments?"

"Here and there. I have friends and relatives, you know." A deep chuckle sounded in his chest.

"That sounds awfully lonely, Jake. Don't you ever want a sense of permanence, a sense of belonging somewhere, to someone?" Jessie held her breath while she waited for his reply.

"Yeah, maybe someday."

Jessie turned her head away from him and squeezed her eyes shut tightly to keep in the tears. Maybe someday. She slumped against his hard, warm chest and rested her hand on his arm. She would just have to be content to have him for now. So lost was she in her own misery that she didn't feel him rest his chin on top of her head and draw her even closer to him.

That evening, around the campfire, Jessie watched every move Jake made. He was all pantherlike grace;

even his eyes gleamed catlike in the light of the low fire. More than once he had caught and held her gaze. Jessie did not know what he was thinking, but she did know her own thoughts. She was determined to get him alone and have him at least one more time before their life together was over. The pulsating tightness low in her belly told her that tonight was the night.

Lying on top of her bedroll and watching the settling-down scene before her, she didn't know how she was going to accomplish getting Jake alone with her, what with all the men being so spread out all over the place, and all the wagons, horses, and mules. Wouldn't they ever go to sleep? She only hoped she didn't fall asleep before they did. She seemed to need so much more rest now. But at least the sickness had stopped. She'd been so afraid it would give her away to Jake, but he seemed totally unaware of her condition. And why wouldn't he be? He hadn't seen her naked in weeks, since Santa Fe, to see her swollen breasts and her little belly. She wasn't worried about those things giving her away now, either. The night would keep her secret.

With a start, Jessie looked around the campfire. Jake was nowhere to be seen. She sat up on one elbow and braced herself against the wagonwheel behind her head. Where could he be? Had he gone as far away from her as he could to sleep? Dejectedly, Jessie slumped back against the hard, wood wheel. But instantly she propped herself up on her elbow again. What was that noise? Like a "hssst." There it was again. She looked around, imagining wildcats, snakes, Indians . . .

"Hssst, Jessie. Behind you. It's me . . . Jake. Quietly get up and come around back of the wagon."

The hair on the back of her neck raised. His voice and his nearness did that . . . not the cool night air. Assuming an air of nonchalance, Jessie silently got up, brushed herself off, and started to move around to the other side of the wagon. She saw a few of the men glance her way, but she knew they were so used to her frequent trips out of sight to relieve herself that they wouldn't think anything about this one.

Once on the dark side of the wagon, away from the light of the campfire, Jessie almost gasped when Jake's arms shot out of the darkness and grabbed her to him. The picture of him doing the same thing in her root cellar flashed through her head, but was instantly gone when his kiss drove all rational thought from her mind.

His hunger was as great as hers; he was almost fierce and frightening in his intensity. He couldn't seem to get enough of her. Jessie felt she was being permanently welded to his body. He had a hand clutched tightly in the back of her shirt and one in her hair. He sent kisses over her eyes, her cheeks, her jaw, down her neck, into the vee of her open shirt. . . .

The gasp which escaped her finally made an impression on Jake; he broke his hold on her, grabbed her by her arms, and held her away from him to look into her eyes. Jessie couldn't breathe. She didn't want to—he was her air and he was now held away from her.

Without a word, Jake scooped her up in his arms. Jessie held onto him tightly, her arms wrapped around his neck. She could feel the strong, rapid beating of his heart against her side and breast. She closed her eyes and drank in the sensation of being in his arms again. His purposeful striding quickly covered the ground; Jessie opened her eyes and raised her head from his shoulder only when he stopped walking. She found herself staring into the back of a wagon a ways from the campfire. She turned her face up to Jake, silently questioning him.

"Earlier you said the nights were cold. I cleared out some of the supplies in this wagon and made you a bed. I want you to be safe and warm." His husky voice sent a tremor through her; touched by his concern for her, she placed a small kiss on his neck.

She felt the shudder that went through him at her kiss. She had almost forgotten the power she had over this strong man. When he lifted her up toward the lowered gate of the wagon, Jessie tumbled out of his arms and into the wagon. Jake followed her closely; he then tightly closed the opening in the canvas cover to give them privacy. But the canvas at the other end of the wagon, up by the driver's seat, was left open, allowing in the bright, white moonlight to frame this, their stolen night of loving.

When he turned back toward her, Jessie went into his arms with no prodding. She could not believe that her thoughts had been his thoughts—he wanted to be alone with her, too. Since this would probably be the last time she would ever hold him this intimately, she was glad it was not out in the open on the hard ground, on a bedroll. She wanted this time to be special, to be memorable. Another night, another wagon flashed through her memory. But that time she had been in a wedding dress and wore a wedding band. This time she had so much more than that—she had his child growing in her. And she had tonight.

No longer content to just hold him as tightly as he held her, Jessie reached up, shyly now, and began to unbutton and open his shirt. Her kisses on his bare, muscled chest trailed after her fingers. In no time, Jake caught his breath and stopped her fingers and lips. But too late. Jessie had already felt the ridging of his abdominal muscles at her touch.

If he was going to leave her, he would take with him the burning memory of this night, she determined. He might still covet the solitary life of a marshal, of undercover work as an outlaw, but she was going to do her best to see that this outlaw knew what real undercover work was. Under those bed covers, for sure. She intended to haunt his dreams from this night forward, no matter where this outlaw, this outlaw from love, roamed.

Jessie reached up and brought Jake's head down to hers; she molded her lips to his in a kiss which held all the longings of her heart. She allowed his tongue entrance into the small cavern of her mouth; she let her tongue duel in a loving battle with his. She breathed with him, for him, because of him.

A ragged growl escaped his mouth and echoed through Jessie. He broke the kiss, lifted her once more into his arms and laid her gently on the narrow, makeshift bed. But Jessie thought it was a majestic bed, a marvelous bed. Because Jake was in it with her, pressing her down into the coverings. With his weight on her, she felt whole again. She even hated that he had to hold himself off her by bracing his elbows to either side of her head to keep from crushing her. She wanted the pain of his embrace. She needed it.

"Oh, Jake," she breathed, "I want all of you. Don't hold anything back from me. I need you. I love you."

She felt him tense for the briefest second; she looked deeply into his dark blue, almost black, impassioned eyes.

"God, Jessie, don't ever quit loving me. I couldn't stand it. No one has ever loved me like this before." He buried his face in the soft hollow between her neck and shoulder.

The tears she'd been holding back all day tumbled out of her eyes and into her hair. She wanted to use her body to wash away all the pain and loneliness he didn't talk about, but she knew he felt. She loved the little boy in him as much as she loved the tough, quiet man he had become. He needed her softness and her tenderness. She knew that. She let her hands roam over the broad expanse of his back, and then up into his thick, black, wavy hair. She couldn't get enough of the feel of him. "Please, Jake, don't make me wait. I can't stand it," she begged.

Jake responded by pulling himself up off her and bringing her with him to a sitting position. He very lovingly began undressing her, and Jessie returned the gesture. She tried to move her hands as slowly over his body as his were going over hers, but she couldn't still her desire. Before she knew it, they were both naked. Clothes were flung everywhere around the wagon. Jessie couldn't help herself; a very girlish giggle escaped her. Jake grinned back at her, his white, even teeth flashing in the moonlight.

But then he turned instantly serious, very intent, as his eyes roved over her naked form, backlit by the moon behind her. He made no move to touch her as she knelt there on her knees in the bed he'd made for her. Jessie found she had to look away, out of a sudden shyness. What was he thinking? Did her body please him?

As if he'd read her thoughts, he said, with a slow, wondering shake of his head, "You are the most beautiful woman I have ever seen, Jessie Stuart Coltrane. There's not anything about you that I don't love. I could lose myself in your hair"—his hand reached out to stroke a heavy tress which had fallen over her shoulder—"when the moonlight makes it look like a halo like now. And your skin"—he stroked her cheek with his fingers and let his hand trail to wherever on her body he was concentrating—"it's so soft, so sweet." But then his hand came into contact with her breast, heavy and blue-veined from her pregnancy.

He cupped the firm warmness in his large hand and stroked the ever-so-sensitive nipple. Jessie closed her eyes and swayed with the sensation. The rippling in her belly radiated out to her breast in a searing jangle of living nerves. "And your tiny waist," Jake continued in his reverent, whispering voice, letting both hands now smooth the outline of her, as if he were memorizing every inch of her. "But, God, your hips, Jessie; that sweet little bottom of yours! I can't get enough of touching your legs, of touching you. Come to me, Jessie. I need you."

Jessie opened her eyes, instantly aware of the god-like appearance of the bronzed man in front of her. Before she was crushed to him, she had an instant impression of male muscled angles, of broad shoulders, of a rigid chest covered in fine dark, curly hair, of a narrowed waist, of an erect, proud shaft, of powerful, rounded thighs that . . .

Jessie caught her breath in her throat as her soft female form was melded to the hard steel of Jake's male body. With her arms under his and around his back, she lay back on the sheet. Jake instantly began

343

his hungry, demanding inventory of the body he had just been lauding. To look was not enough anymore. He must feel. Jessie knew this, because she felt the same way, too. Her mouth and her hands sought the same sensations and the same reactions as his did. She kissed his mouth, his face, his neck, his chest; she sucked at his nipples, blazed biting little kisses down his chest, just as he did hers.

This was a frenzied giving, a tender, violent passion that raged between them and threatened to consume them. Jessie was more than ready when Jake positioned himself between her legs. She breathed, "yes, Jake, yes" as he lifted her hips and began to enter her. He seemed as mesmerized by this act as he had been by her beauty a few moments ago. He held himself away from her and watched himself disappear into her until their bodies met and their two souls fused. Now joined, now one, Jessie pulled Jake to her and wrapped her slim legs around him. She desperately needed his driving thrusts to quench the raging fire in her, the fire she had no right to feel, the outlaw love that she sought to express with her body. Her raking fingernails stroked up and down his back with every thrust he made into her; Jessie matched his pace, striving for the tempest that would take her out of herself and make her one with this man.

When the wild storm that raged in their bodies and in their hearts reached its peak of swirling sensations, Jessie clutched Jake to her even more closely. Her body pulled him into her even more deeply. Then, a purely animal moan escaped from the back of Jessie's throat and mingled with the cry torn from Jake as he thrust once more into her and held himself rigid over her, every muscle tensed, as she allowed him to pulse all his loneliness, all his pain, all his love into her.

When Jake finally lowered himself onto her, he nearly slid off her, so covered were they both in the thin patina of sweat. Jessie shared a small, intimate laugh with him over this, and then allowed him to withdraw from her and roll onto his side, facing her.

Jessie held her arms out to him, and he pulled her roughly into his embrace, also entwining his muscled legs with her slim, rounded ones. Jessie let out a deep sigh of contentment and lay against him, her head resting on the junction of his shoulder and arm, reluctant to say or do anything that would break the magic spell. For now it was enough to just lie there and take in the very male essence of him each time she breathed. This was probably her last time to hold him like this, and she wanted to make the most of it.

But then, despite her best effort to stay awake and to savor the feel of him, she felt herself begin to nod off. She was going to sleep in his embrace, with his chin resting on her head, with his heart beating under her hand on his chest. She opened her eyes briefly when he made a sudden movement; but it wasn't to leave her. He was pulling the covers up around them, wrapping them in their own cocoon.

After that, Jessie remembered nothing else of the night, for she slept deeply and soundly, wrapped in Jake's loving embrace.

Chapter Twenty

"Bertha! Bertha! It's me—Jessie! Whoopee!" Jessie cried out joyfully at her first glimpse of her homestead in the distance. It didn't matter to her that Bertha couldn't hear her—or even see her yet; she still stood up, perched precariously on the driver's seat, with only one hand clutching the canvas-covered wagon frame, and waved her hat over her head. Her yelling and whooping startled the horses in the wagon traces, and they shied for a few steps. With a strangled curse, Coy fought with their reins and tried at the same time to hold onto Jessie's pant leg to steady her.

"Jessie, if you don't sit down, you're going to cause me to turn this wagon over and get us both hurt. And I'm sure not going to be the one to tell Jake you're somewhere under this load of guns. Now sit down. Bertha won't be able to hear you for another half hour," Coy fussed, while tugging her down into a sitting position. His newfound maturity weighed very heavily on him, and he now took himself very seriously.

But Jessie didn't. She poked her tongue out at him and cuffed his arm playfully. "Oh, Coy, isn't this exciting?" she breathed, ignoring his scolding of her. "I can't wait to see Bertha! And all my animals! And my home! And my—"

"Here comes Jake now. I'll bet he means to ride you into your yard himself with you up on that stallion of his," Coy laughed, now caught up in her infectious high spirits.

Jessie turned her head sharply to see Jake indeed reining a barebacked Blaze to a walk beside the wagon. He had his hands full with the prancing roan, who fought to get the bit into his teeth. Jake's white grin split his tanned, handsome face as he called out to Jessie, "I don't think you're the only one who's excited to see home. I think Blaze wants to get there in a hurry, too! Come on, Jessie, hop on. I'll take you back home in the same way I stole you away."

He didn't have to ask her twice. Jessie loved the romance of riding once again on Blaze's warm, strong, bare back, of riding at a tearing pace into the courtyard for what her mother would have called a grand entrance. Coy was just bringing his horses to a stop when Jessie made the small leap which landed her on Blaze's broad back. Jake's strong hand had a hold on her arm, helping to steady her until she was safely positioned in front of him and astraddle Blaze.

With a loud, happy whoop, Jake smacked his hat against Blaze's heaving flank. And away they went with a great bunching and flexing of equine muscles, with a flash of Jessie's long, black, blowing hair, with flying hooves and swirling dust devils as their companions. Two happy, carefree, young lovers in a blaze of passion, thundering across the level stretch of prairie.

Until they stopped, sweating and panting with Blaze, in the courtyard alive with people and animals. The adventure was over. Reality met them in the form of a running, grinning, hopping Bertha. Her straw hat flew off and her gray hair blew in wisps around her red-apple cheeks, as she forced her short, chubby legs to cover the ground so she could hold Jessie once more in her arms.

And Jessie was already running toward her, arms outstretched. Blaze had barely been reined to a bone-jarring halt before Jessie's feet had hit the ground.

"Child, child, child! Where have you been for so long? I've just been a-whuppin' you day and night for worrying me so! You coulda been dead for all I knowed! And not a word from you or anyone else to tell me otherwise!" Bertha hugged, scolded, held Jessie away from her, crushed her to her, held her back again, smoothed her hair, grabbed her to her again, and fussed some more.

Jessie had no choice but to submit to Bertha's fussing ministrations. She was still young enough to need motherly attention, and she would not have denied Bertha this chance for anything in the world. She laughed happy, hiccupping, wet, tearful answers to Bertha's one thousand questions about whether or not she was really here and really all right. Finally reassured that her young 'un was indeed okay, Bertha then turned her sharp, gray eyes and pursed lips on the man she deemed the culprit in all this—Jake Coltrane.

Jake had the good sense to straighten up on Blaze's back from the carefree, slouching position he had assumed as he'd grinningly watched Jessie and Bertha's reunion. His face took on a grim, serious look as Bertha turned toward him and walked over to him. His eyes cut from her to Jessie, who strode alongside Bertha, propelled by Bertha's protective arm around her shoulders. Jessie began to get nervous. Would these two never get along? At least for once before Jake left? The painful lurch in her heart at that thought tripped her feet momentarily. Bertha gripped her shoulders even more tightly.

When the two women stood by Blaze's side, Jake chose to speak first. "Bertha," was all he said by way of greeting, but he did have the manners to touch his fingers to the brim of his hat and nod his head.

Bertha instantly let go of Jessie, tugged at Jake's pant leg, and hollered, "Bertha my behind, young man. Git yourself down here! I need to hug on you some, too. And then I'll beat the tar out of you for dragging this child off to heaven-knows-where!" A big grin and raised arms reached up to Jake. Jessie almost clapped her hands together in glee; she knew Jake needed a "welcome home" as much as she did.

With a roll of his blue eyes and a shake of his head, Jake threw a long leg over Blaze's back and fluidly slid to the ground. He wrapped his arms around Bertha in a bear hug, which she returned, and pounded him on the back to boot. Then, with one arm around Jake's waist, and her other one around Jessie's waist, she marched them both to the cabin. The Inquisition was about to begin in earnest.

"You ain't told Jake yet that he's a-goin' to be a daddy, now have you?"

Jessie almost choked on the cornbread she was stuffing down for supper, along with fresh milk, pinto beans, pork, and fresh greens. She took a big, gulping drink of milk before she answered. "How . . . how did you know?" Even to her own ears, her voice sounded small and guilty.

"Well, tarnation, child, ain't I got eyes? Men ain't got eyes like us women. I seen you when you had your bath this afternoon. Not so much in your belly yet, but in your breasts. They tell a story, you know."

Jessie absentmindedly pushed back a heavy, dark tress of her now-dry hair and stared at her food. Her bath had felt wonderful, and it had taken her mind off Jake's leaving her so abruptly to ride to Camp Nichols to report in with the soldiers to Colonel Kit Carson. He hadn't said when he'd be back. Or if he would. He'd just ridden out. Earlier, her heart had soared when he'd said Blaze smelled home, too. She'd thought that maybe Jake—but no, no sense torturing herself. She raised tear-filled eyes to Bertha across the table from her.

"No, I haven't. The time was just never right." She found herself looking down at her clenched hands in her lap. For once she was in a dress, a soft, dark-blue muslin with tiny flowers embroidered on it. Her shame was not lessened by the overly tight bodice filled with her swollen breasts or the narrow waist of the dress that now pinched. "He never said he . . . and I just couldn't—"

"Look at me, child," came Bertha's soft voice. Jessie raised her eyes. To her relief, she saw compassion and love etched there, not condemnation and reproval. "Jake loves you. He don't have to say it for it to be so. Of course, a girl likes to hear it ever' so often, but that's how some men are." Bertha stifled the grumbling note in her voice and once again talked to Jessie soothingly, but firmly. "Either way, he has a right to know. He's the daddy. A young'un needs a daddy. This baby ain't just yours: it's Jake's, too."

"But what if he doesn't want us, Bertha? I couldn't stand it if he turned away from us both! He loves his life as a marshal. He's never said he wants to quit it and settle down. Farming out here would kill him. He's not cut out for it—"

"Now how in the sam hill do you know what he's cut out to do? I'll bet you've never even asked him what's in his heart. You didn't see him a-tear out of my wagon after you when that Hayes fella sent his thugs to steal you outta my wagon. And didn't he stand right up and marry you in front of all those people on that wagon train? He didn't have to do that, either, you know. He coulda lit out right then. But he didn't. He already cared too much."

"Bertha, we're not really married. He used his undercover name—Josiah Tucker. And that man doesn't exist. I'm pregnant and unmarried! And I'm glad my parents aren't alive to see me like this. This would surely have killed them."

"Oh, pish! Now you listen here to me, young lady." Bertha was now leaning across the table toward Jessie, pointing her finger at her as she rested her elbow on the table. "When that young man comes back—don't you set in on me; he's a-comin' back as sure as I'm a-sittin' here—when that young man comes back, you're a-goin' to run straight into his arms, tell him you love him, and tell him he's a-goin' to be a daddy. Then he can make up his own mind about what he wants to do with his life. You hear me?"

Jessie pursed her lips together and swallowed her retort. Even though her eyes blazed her anger at being talked to like this, she had to admit that Bertha's words and certainty about Jake were heartening. She wanted so much to believe. She released her breath and relaxed her stiff spine. She was too tired to fight. Her hands went up to cover her face; when she brought them down, she smiled weakly at her friend and guardian. "Oh, Bertha, you're right. As usual. He deserves to know the truth. I owe my—our baby that much. If—when he comes back, I'll tell him."

Bertha got up with a satisfied smack of her palm to the tabletop, turned towards the now-repaired window that Hayes had shot out about three months ago, pulled back the new curtain, looked out and around the yard outside, and turned back to Jessie. "Well, I'm glad you feel that way, my pretty Jessie. It looks like you're a-goin' to get your chance—and real soon!" A big grin lit up her open, lined face.

"What?!" Jessie half-rose from her chair, but then sank back down onto it. She felt like she'd been hit in her stomach. What was Bertha saying? She gripped the table's edge, her knuckles white. She could barely get her next words out past her constricted throat. "What do you mean I'll get my chance?"

"Why don't you just get yourself up and come take a look?" She was almost hooting with laughter and excitement now as she continued to hold the curtain back.

Jessie jumped up, knocking over her chair in the process. Sometimes Bertha could be so maddening! She brushed past the older woman and held the curtain back herself as she peered out on the sunset scene before her. There was too much going on in the courtyard for her to be able to register it all at once. Her eyes darted from one scene to another, looking, looking for the one man she wanted to see, but couldn't find.

When in the world—? She turned abruptly on Bertha, but had to look for her, too. She was no longer by the window, but had seated herself in her chair at the table and was wearing the biggest cat-that-got-the-mouse grin Jessie had ever seen. "When—? What—?" she stuttered, turning from the window to Bertha and back again about four or five times before she could utter coherent words. "Bertha, what in the world is going on out there?! The place is decorated like for a party or something! And . . . and there's people everywhere! But no wag-on trains! Just real people! And women, too!"

"I know all that, child! We got neighbors now over at the Camp. Colonel Carson said it was safe now for womenfolk, and he allowed his men to send for their women. Now about them decorations and such: Why in the world do you think that I kept you in all afternoon, what with that long bath and your longer nap? And our even longer talkin'? There was things to be done outside that weren't none of your never-mind—'til now, that is."

Jessie advanced on her laughing, smug friend. With her head cocked to one side and her hands on her slim hips, Jessie blustered, "Bertha Jacobson of

Lexington, Missouri, if you don't tell me this instant what in the world—"

The sudden knocking on the door forced Jessie's attention—and Bertha's—there. Jessie quickly cut her eyes back to Bertha, only to have her shrug noncommittally. That did it! Jessie's temper burst, and she took it out on the door. She ripped the latch up and pulled sharply on the heavy door. She thought she knew exactly who was on the other side of that door, and lordy was he ever going to hear about it . . .

"Evening, ma'am. I'm Colonel Kit Carson, Commanding Officer of Camp Nichols. And this is Captain Abe Steadman, our Reverend. We're about ready out here for the wedding; that is, if you are."

"If I am?" Jessie repeated dumbly, looking from one tall, distinguished gentleman in dress uniform to the other.

All of a sudden, the colonel looked decidedly uncomfortable as he shifted his eyes from the chaplain to Jessie and then to Bertha behind her. "Uh, yes, ma'am. You. The bride."

"The bride? Me?" Jessie felt like she'd been ripped out of a dream only to find that it was real. And why were people talking to her from the other end of a tunnel? She hated tunnels. Especially this one that was getting so dark and now there were stars in it. This couldn't be happening . . .

The colonel, the chaplain, and Bertha all made a grab for Jessie as she fainted dead away. And they each got an awkward hold on her before she completely reached the ground. The colonel finally prevailed; he took her in his arms and laid her on her bed. "She didn't know anything about this wedding, did she? This one is a complete surprise, right?"

Bertha, hands on her ample hips, almost laughed at the colonel's unusually high voice and the disbelieving look on his face. With a chuckle and without answering him, she turned her attention to the chaplain, who was ineffectually waving his handkerchief over Jessie's pale face. It was his turn to be shocked when Bertha remarked in an offhand manner, "Oh, don't worry none about her. She didn't know about the first weddin', either. If that shock didn't kill her, this one won't."

"The first wedding? What first wedding? How many weddings do they need?" the chaplain asked.

But Bertha didn't have time for questions now. She shooed them out, politely but firmly, when she heard moaning sounds from the bed. "Now if you gentlemen will excuse me, I have to get the bride ready."

About thirty minutes later, Jessie found herself seated in front of the vanity mirror attached to her mother's dainty dresser. Bertha stood behind her trying valiantly to tame Jessie's wild, curling mass of black hair. The more she pulled it up and tried to twist it into an elegant chignon, the more it rebelled and escaped Bertha's work-roughened hands. Jessie knew that she would be giggling at poor Bertha's well-intentioned efforts and red, puffing face if she weren't in almost tearful pain from Bertha's less-than-tender efforts with her unruly hair to make her "look like a lady" for her wedding.

That thought sent yet another thrill through her. She was getting married to Jake; it was true. And he must want this too, or otherwise why would everyone from the Camp be out there now decorating the barn, setting up tables for food, and tuning up a band? This was almost too much to be believed.

But, after all, here she was in her mother's ivory-lace wedding dress. She lovingly fingered the soft fabric. When in the world had Bertha pulled this dress out of the trunk? Jessie knew that her mother would have been so proud to see her married in this dress. A small sniff escaped her, and she wiped at her eyes.

To keep from crying over what could not be helped, she turned her thoughts back to Jake. She wished he could have found time to come talk to her in private, to tell her the things she needed to hear before this ceremony, to tell her he loved her and would be happy here. But then a sudden thought constricted her throat and made her physically jump in her seat. She heard Bertha's tsk-tsking and gentle scolding to hold still, but she really wasn't aware of her. What if he wanted her to leave here and go back East to live with his mother while he went gallivanting off on some new mission? She couldn't stand that—not seeing him every day, not feeling his wonderful, warm, muscled body. Why, she may as well not be married to him at all, if that was the way it was going to be! Jessie jerked her head reflexively at the horror of this new train of thought, causing her hair to run through Bertha's weary fingers like so much ebony water.

"Well, that does it for me!" Bertha thundered, making an awful face. "The Good Lord Himself couldn't fool with your hair, child, and not get mad enough to raise a big storm! I ain't never seen the like! You'll just have to wear it down your back. I give up!" She threw her hands up in the air in surrender.

Jessie turned on the small settee and stretched

her hands out to Bertha. A bubbling laugh lit up her face. "Oh, Bertha, you dear, I appreciate what you tried to do. Really—"

The knock on the door stopped Jessie in mid-sentence. As she arose and headed over to answer it, she told Bertha, "Now don't you fuss with me anymore. You just get yourself ready. I'll be fine with my hair down." She was now opening the door as she looked back at Bertha and continued to speak. "Really, I will. You'll see. Jake loves me with my—"

"—clothes off," Jake finished for her from the open doorway. His white grin and deep blue eyes sparkled.

The startled yelp that escaped Jessie could not be caught by her hand which flew to her mouth to cover it. Her embarrassment at his words was not lessened any by Bertha's loud guffawing and knee slapping.

"Jake Coltrane, I can't believe you said that! I was talking about my hair!"

"You're not going to take it off too, are you? I don't think I could stand a bald wife. Naked, yes. But not bald!"

Despite herself, Jessie fairly exploded into laughter, along with Bertha and Jake. The man was insufferable! A bald wife, indeed. She'd show him! She reached out to slap playfully at his arm, but her wrist was caught in a viselike grip, and she found herself being hauled up against a hard, warm, broad chest covered by fine, black broadcloth and a snowy-white dress shirt. She even welcomed his crushing hug; she could never be close enough to him.

Over her head, Jake said, "Uh, Bertha, do you suppose I could have a few minutes alone with my wife?"

"I'm not your wife yet," Jessie reminded him gently, her words somewhat muffled against his chest.

"Yes, you are. And you know it. You've been my wife since you found me in your root cellar. At least, I've belonged to you since then."

When he looked down at her with his piercing dark-blue eyes and wonderful grin which dimpled his tanned cheeks, Jessie knew she was going to melt. A great, big, ivory-lace and satin puddle right here in front of him. She'd have to go down the aisle carried in a bucket.

"Why, now that you mention it, Jake, I do believe I'm supposed to be checking on the goin's-on outside. If you two will just excuse me, I'll just squeeze by you here, and—" Bertha's voice trailed off as she shinnied between the wooden doorjamb and the clenched, oblivious young couple, and made her escape out into the brightly lit yard.

When they were alone, Jake bent his dark head to capture Jessie's lips in a hungry, sweet, demanding, gentle, thorough kiss. Suddenly Jessie knew she would not melt. She was too rigid with the shooting desire his nearness, his touch, sent through her. Every fiber of her being either tingled, tightened or teased. She whimpered under his onslaught and tightened her hold on him. But then he pulled away. Jessie made a small sound of protest.

"Wait, my love. We'll have the rest of our lives together," Jake soothed, holding her away from him and then caressing her passion-heated cheek with his fingers. "I have to ask you something."

"What?" Jessie asked numbly, her breath coming raggedly.

"Will you marry me?"

"I already did," Jessie answered from the depths

of her desire-induced stupor.

This brought a deep, rumbling chuckle out from Jake's chest. "So you did, little one, so you did. But will you again, Jessie Stuart Coltrane?"

"I like that," Jessie answered, coming out of her fog to really look hard at him. She loved him so much, she was afraid the spell, or her heart, would burst. But he was still here, and he was asking her to marry him.

"Like what?" he asked very indulgently, his hands now on her upper arms as he bent his head to look down at her.

"What you called me. Jessie Stuart Coltrane. It has a nice ring to it, don't you think?"

"That's not the first time I've called you that, Jessie. Remember the night on the trail home in the wagon? I called you Jessie Stuart Coltrane then. You already were my wife then . . . in my heart. Where it counts. And speaking of rings—" He pulled out the rings that the stranger had given them on the occasion of their first wedding, the same ones Jessie remembered throwing to the ground that day in the meadow under the tree the first time they . . .

"Oh, Jake," she breathed, clasping her hands in front of her breasts, I can't believe that you still have those! I was so mean and nasty that day. I—"

"Shhh." He put a finger to her lips. "It's all over now. It doesn't matter." Then he straightened up and folded his arms over his broad chest and stood with his legs apart. "And now, wife of mine, don't you have something to tell me?"

"I love you, and I'll marry you again?" Jessie asked, screwing up her face into a little pixie mask.

"No, that's not it. Well, yes it is. But that's not what I meant. You know what I'm talking about."

He now tapped a booted foot on the cabin floor and tried to look really stern.

Jessie thought for a desperate few seconds. And then it came to her. "Oh, I know. I'll leave here and follow you wherever you go?"

That got a reaction from him. His arms flew to his side and he took one step closer to her. "What? Leave here? Our home? Not in a million years! I've already resigned my job, and I have great plans for this place what with all my salary I've saved, and the trust my father left me, and—oh, nice try. You almost got me off the subject. Out with it, young lady, we have guests waiting."

Jessie bit at her lip and wrung her hands. She looked around the cabin seeking inspiration. But nothing. "Jake, I don't know what you mean! I swear! Help me!"

Heaving a huge sigh, Jake once more took hold of her arms and bent over to look in her eyes. "Jessie, you're supposed to tell me about our baby you're carrying."

Jessie's throat closed, her eyes bulged, her palms became sweaty, and her knees shook. How did he—? "Did Bertha tell you?"

"No, Bertha didn't tell me. You did. Now don't look so surprised and confused. You didn't say anything, but I could tell. I have eyes, Jessie. And I lived with you for three months on the trail. I saw you sick. I saw you eat enough for three men—I was hoping we'd have enough jerky to satisfy you. I've never seen anybody enjoy beef jerky like that. And your body, Jessie. Your beautiful body. It's changed some, and I love it." His hand moved to caress her belly.

Jessie turned liquid-brown eyes on her husband.

"Why didn't you say something?"

"Why didn't you?"

Jessie looked down, and then back up at him. She hated the little hurt she saw in the depths of his dark-fringed eyes. "I . . . I didn't know how. I mean, what if you didn't want us? You never said you'd stay. And I wouldn't make you. I want you to be happy. I love you—and if that meant letting you go, I—"

She was crushed to him before she could say another word. She was sure she felt a wetness seeping into her hair from where his face was buried.

"Oh, God, Jessie, I love you. I haven't said it enough. I want you. I haven't said that enough, either. I need you. I will always love you and want you and need you. And all our babies. I will always stay, Jessie. I will never leave you. You are my home—only you. I don't need to run away anymore, like an outlaw. I need to be here with you, and our son."

"Daughter," Jessie corrected.

"What?" he asked, raising his face, wet from his emotions. "Daughter? How do you know?"

"I just know," Jessie said, smiling and turning away to get her veil.

"You don't know. You're just guessing." Jake helped her adjust it on her head until they were both satisfied with its angle.

"I'm not guessing. I'm the mother after all. And I say we're having a daughter."

"A son. Okay, a son and a daughter. Aha—got you there. Twins run in my family, didn't I tell you?" Jake pulled her arm through his and handed her the ring she would give him in the wedding ceremony a few minutes from now. If he noticed at all the stunned look on Jessie's face, he chose not to comment on it. "In fact, I myself have a twin brother—Josh Coltrane. Surely I've mentioned him. Well, you'll meet him soon enough."

"Twins? Oh no. How am I going to keep up with twins?" Jessie groaned as she adjusted the long train of her trailing gown as they swept out of the cabin and headed for the barn. She was trying desperately to be as matter-of-fact about all this as he was. But her heart was soaring that he was finally opening up to her and revealing his private self.

"By twins, do you mean me and my brother, or the ones you're carrying?"

"Both," Jessie answered, pinching his arm playfully.

"Well, I was thinking about that, too. I was thinking we'll need to really enlarge the cabin. You know, make it more like a ranch house, more like my family's estate in Virginia. What do you think? And cattle. We'll need to invest in a herd. This land is great for cattle. I'll show you how it's done where I come from." Then, looking down at the perplexed but somewhat challenging look on Jessie's face, he added, "We're going there on our honeymoon trip. That is, if you agree. I think you'll love it. I know, I know, my love, I must get into the habit of discussing these decisions with you. I have a feeling that if I don't, my life will be as full of trouble as a tornado." That dispensed with, he went on with his narrative, the most Jessie had ever heard him say at one time. She delighted in the sound of his cheerful voice. "Now, back to our plans for this place. Of course, Bertha will need her own room, and we'll need guest rooms—for when my mother and brother visit. You and I will need some privacy, too. And all the babies will need rooms—"

"All the babies? Jake, good heavens, just how many babies do you think we're going to have? You're awful!"

"I never said I wasn't, my love. After all, I am an outlaw."

Their retreating figures were suddenly bathed in the light coming from the many festive lamps inside the barn. The young couple turned to each other before they stepped inside for their second wedding. But they had been seen by their many guests, all of whom became hushed by the cheerful whisper working its way through the crowd that the wedding was indeed about to take place. People poked one another, pointed, and necks craned to see the wedding couple.

Then everyone heard the young bride say, "Yes, you are an outlaw. My outlaw. Jessie's outlaw. And I love you."

LOVE SPELL

THE MAGIC OF ROMANCE
PAST, PRESENT, AND FUTURE....

Dorchester Publishing Co., Inc., the leader in romantic fiction, is pleased to unveil its newest line—Love Spell. Every month, beginning in August 1993, Love Spell will publish one book in each of four categories:

1) *Timeswept Romance*—Modern-day heroines travel to the past to find the men who fulfill their hearts' desires.

2) *Futuristic Romance*—Love on distant worlds where passion is the lifeblood of every man and woman.

3) *Historical Romance*—Full of desire, adventure and intrigue, these stories will thrill readers everywhere.

4) *Contemporary Romance*—With novels by Lori Copeland, Heather Graham, and Jayne Ann Krentz, Love Spell's line of contemporary romance is first-rate.

Exploding with soaring passion and fiery sensuality, Love Spell romances are destined to take you to dazzling new heights of ecstasy.

COMING IN JANUARY!
TIMESWEPT ROMANCE

TIME OF THE ROSE
By Bonita Clifton

When the silver-haired cowboy brings Madison Calloway to his run-down ranch, she thinks for sure he is senile. Certain he'll bring harm to himself, Madison follows the man into a thunderstorm and back to the wild days of his youth in the Old West.

The dread of all his enemies and the desire of all the ladies, Colton Chase does not stand a chance against the spunky beauty who has tracked him through time. And after one passion-drenched night, Colt is ready to surrender his heart to the most tempting spitfire anywhere in time.

_51922-4 $4.99 US/$5.99 CAN

A FUTURISTIC ROMANCE

AWAKENINGS
By Saranne Dawson

Fearless and bold, Justan rules his domain with an iron hand, but nothing short of the Dammai's magic will bring his warring people peace. He claims he needs Rozlynd—a bewitching beauty and the last of the Dammai—for her sorcery alone, yet inside him stirs an unexpected yearning to savor the temptress's charms, to sample her sweet innocence. And as her silken spell ensnares him, Justan battles to vanquish a power whose like he has never encountered—the power of Rozlynd's love.

_51921-6 $4.99 US/$5.99 CAN